Edward M. Lerner: A Master of Hard SF

"When people talk about good hard SF—rigorously extrapolated but still imbued with the classic sense-of-wonder—they mean the work of Edward M. Lerner, the current master of the craft."
—*Robert J. Sawyer,*
Hugo Award-winning author of Red Planet Blues

"Lerner definitely knows how to tell a story."
—*Winnipeg Free Press*

"Lerner's world-building and extrapolating are top notch."
—*SFScope*

"Here's an author you definitely need to check out."
—*Asimov's Science Fiction*

"One of the leading global writers of hard science fiction."
—*The Innovation Show*

DÉJÀ DOOMED

Edward M. Lerner

SHAHID MAHMUD
PUBLISHER

www.CaezikSF.com

Cover art by Christina P. Myrvold; artstation.com/christinapm

ISBN: 978-1-64710-027-8

First Edition. 1st Printing. May 2021.
1 2 3 4 5 6 7 8 9 10

An imprint of Arc Manor LLC

www.CaezikSF.com

To Mom and Dad

Books by Edward M. Lerner

Novels

- *Probe*
- *Moonstruck*
- *Fools' Experiments*
- *Small Miracles*
- *Energized*
- *Dark Secret*
- *The Company Man*

InterstellarNet series novels

- *InterstellarNet: Origins*
- *InterstellarNet: New Order*
- *InterstellarNet: Enigma*

Fleet of Worlds series novels (with Larry Niven)

- *Fleet of Worlds*
- *Juggler of Worlds*
- *Destroyer of Worlds*
- *Betrayer of Worlds*
- *Fate of Worlds*

Collections and Nonfiction

- *Creative Destruction*
- *Countdown to Armageddon / A Stranger in Paradise*
- *Frontiers of Space, Time, and Thought*
  (mixed fiction and nonfiction)
- *A Time Foreclosed* (chapbook)
- *Trope-ing the Light Fantastic:*
  The Science Behind the Fiction (nonfiction)
- *Muses & Musings*

Contents

DISCOVERY

Chapter 1

Knife-edged, as black as pitch, long shadows sprawled across the airless moonscape.

In any shadow, unseen, dangers might lurk. Massive boulders, single and in jumbles. Scattered rocky detritus. Yawning fissures. Concealed slopes. The treacherous, crumbling rims of ancient craters. In shades of gray and brown and the occasional dark blue, the portions of the lunar surface not in shadow seemed almost as indistinct.

All experienced in spectral translucence, overlaid on mundane living-room clutter.

Even where the setting Sun could still reach, temperatures had plummeted. Soon enough, only the crescent Earth's eerie blue light would shine here.

A few more minutes, Ethan Nyquist told himself.

To lunar east, an open expanse beckoned. Beyond the elongated silhouette of his rover, its solar panels tipped backward and vertical to catch the day's final rays, that gentle slope seemed entirely sunlit. Seemed entirely featureless.

Almost certainly, that ordinary-looking plain held—and hid—its share of perils. From the rover's perspective, every rock, crater rim, and rift to the east masked its own shadow.

Naturally, his path led to the east.

He had followed, as best he could, the hints of a trace of precious iridium: a hard, dense, corrosion-resistant metal with an ultrahigh melting point. New industrial uses for the stuff kept appearing—and it was far scarcer than gold.

He had followed the trail—in truth, more of a dotted line—for more than a hundred miles. For six grueling days. For all the sensor readings he had collected along the way across the powdery lunar regolith, not one sample had begun to approach exploitable concentrations. It would be nice to know—*before* the onset of the two-week-long lunar night—whether, in his most recent detour, skirting a nameless, half-mile-wide crater with sides too steep to enter, he had lost the trail. Because if he could find the source of the traces—if there *was* a source, if the meteorite that had brought the iridium had not vaporized on impact, dissipating the rare metal in a gaseous cloud far and wide across the moonscape—he would become rich. *Very* rich.

That hope was all that got him out of bed most mornings.

He had time to take another sample, perhaps two, before everything spread out before him was plunged into darkness. No atmosphere meant no twilight, the scant illumination given off by the crescent Earth being no substitute for the setting Sun.

A wireless remote-control module, little bigger (but more sophisticated, and *much* securer from hacking) than a game controller sat at an end of Ethan's messy coffee table. Through that module, with smart spex and a touch-feedback glove, he guided the prospecting rover—almost a quarter-million miles distant—across the Moon. Until the Sun fell beneath the horizon, rendering solar-cell arrays useless. Until his rover went into standby mode, its critical components kept from freezing by a trickle of battery power.

He was a robot wrangler. A damned good one. The job required attention to detail, fast reflexes, and superb eye-hand coordination—while making no demands on one's feet. And that was fortunate because Ethan no longer had feet.

Not unless you counted the little-better-than-peg-leg *crap* that the VA called prosthetics—and he didn't. Not since the café bombing in Baluchistan, or whatever that godforsaken corner of the world had taken to calling itself. This week. Ironic to get himself blown up, given that his Army job at the time had had him piloting robotic drones to blow up the bad guys.

Ethan dragged his thoughts back to the task at hand. Iron, found in sufficient quantities, had value. Irony, like dwelling on the past, was a waste of time. And just then, at least in his leased section of the lunar surface, from which the Sun was about to vanish, he had no time to waste.

"Forward one-third," he intoned, gesturing above the control. On his spex, three seconds later, the vista began to change. Creeping up the shallow slope, angling mostly north to south and back again to avoid both the worst of the glare and the rover's own elongated shadow, an emerald flash caught his attention. With a curl of his fingers, he turned right.

There! A fist-sized rock sparkled with green.

"Halt."

The rover glided to a stop. "Engage the arm." Three seconds after painstakingly extending his gloved hand, Ethan's spex showed the robot's telescoping appendage reaching out. Its mechanical gripper, mimicking his gestures, opened, then closed, to grasp the green rock.

Inside the fingertips of his glove, faster and faster, tiny pads vibrated, as—with great care—he took hold of the rock. It felt like … a rock. He turned and flexed his wrist and, fancying he heard the *whirr* of distant motors, examined the image in his spex. Up close (to the camera, in any event), he held in his "hand" an agglomeration of angular fragments of shattered stone bound together by more stone, melted and recongealed. The green sparkles came from bits of volcanic glass also embedded in the mass.

In geologist-speak, he held an impact-melt breccia. Had it formed under the crash of a meteorite, or from the debris, almost as destructive, splattered *by* a meteorite? How long ago had the impact occurred? And as one meteorite after another had reshaped this barren landscape, how far had this particular rock bounced and rolled?

He couldn't answer any of those questions, nor did he much care. What he *did* know, and was reminded of every instant he spent prospecting, was that this dead world's surface was everywhere pockmarked—from tiny dimples to craters a couple hundred miles across.

The rock he "held" was in every respect ordinary. Ethan made a fist, the glove's fingertips madly vibrating to represent the force he exerted through the distant gripper.

Rock shattered. Gravel and dust drifted, in slow motion, to the distant, barren ground.

"Mineral scan," he said. At his radioed command, the rover X-rayed the ground; within seconds, its instruments interpreted the reflections. Readouts appeared on his spex. Silicon, of course. The lunar crust was rife with silicates. Iron. Titanium. Calcium. Oxygen ....

He scrolled as quickly as he dared, until iridium at last made its appearance in the list. A hair over two parts per billion. Not terrific, but twice the average in Earth's crust. Thousands of times the lunar norm.

He had not lost the trail.

Digits in a corner of his spex announced the Sun would disappear in another eleven minutes. The drooping output from the rover's solar-power unit implied much the same.

"Pan left," he ordered, and the distant camera pivoted. He wondered if he could squeeze in one last traverse across the slope. The scene on his spex swept past a cluster of boulders, slumped and pitted, weathered by the endless hail of micrometeorites and by day/night temperature swings that exceeded four hundred degrees.

His point of view slid past the boulders. Past a surface rippled like an old-fashioned washboard, with each successive ridge casting its own inky shadow. Past the rover's own tread marks. Past a scattering of pea gravel. Past a crater less than two feet across, its rim edge still crisp. Past—

Something nagged at him. Something out of place. The merest suggestion of color? Perhaps. Back by the rock jumble?

"Pan right, slow," Ethan ordered.

His visual survey reversed. The diminutive crater. Gravel. Tread marks. The stone washboard. And in a natural alcove, the sheltered space beneath two massive stone slabs that leaned one against the other, where a few rays of the setting Sun managed to sneak through, he glimpsed—

Reddish orange. On this drab world, the color alone was extraordinary. And so *much* orange. The blush peeked through a film of dust formed in the slower-than-glacial "weathering" of the rocks overhead.

"Full opacity," Ethan said. The living-room backdrop faded from his spex. The distant image brightened.

The orange-tinged mound, whatever it was, was *big*. Eight feet or more in length from end to end. Perhaps four feet wide at its broadest. Up to two feet tall, in spots. He tried to attribute a shape, but the thing defied geometry. A central mass with five projections of varying lengths. And from the shortest projection, through the dust, came a golden glimmer.

A *reflection*?

Beyond out of place, Ethan had no idea, no intuition even, what the orange object beneath the film of dust could be.

With the wave of a hand, he edged closer.

The object's shiny end had a gentle, cylindrical curve to it. Slowly, carefully, he started to brush aside its coating of dust. Glove pads conveyed to his fingertips only the slightest hint of vibration.

Still, at his featherlight touch, the ... whatever ... crumbled into a fine powder and collapsed into itself.

But not before Ethan glimpsed, through the dissolving visor, a mummified—and utterly inhuman—face.

Chapter 2

Tall and impossibly spindly, the antenna pedestal loomed.

Marcus Judson rode the basket of a tower crane. The crane was alarmingly tall and spindly, too. On the plain to his left, segments of the antenna's dish awaited assembly. Each individual curved segment was huge. Together they would make a dish bigger than two hundred meters across—

Of significance only if and when the pedestal showed itself capable of bearing the steel dish's weight.

He had polarized his helmet visor against the glare of ground-level work lights. He had dialed down the public-channel comm chatter. He scarcely noticed the nudges as, under computer control, compressed-gas thrusters dampened the swaying of the passenger basket that dangled at the end of a long steel cable. Snug within the cocoon that was his spacesuit, he managed to forget, sometimes even for seconds at a time, just how freaking *cold* the lunar midnight was: minus 150°C.

But what he could not banish from his thoughts, not even for the few minutes of the ride from the crater floor up the half-completed structure (at that, already ninety meters high), was how behind schedule he had fallen.

At twenty meters off the ground he released the UP button on the crane's control pendant, bringing the basket to a halt. Puffs of gas killed the basket's renewed sway. "Suit. Headlamps off." His helmet's interior peanut bulbs were already off. Without company in the basket to see him, there was no need.

The world went dark.

Stars appeared: a magnificent reminder, as though any were needed, that he had a radio telescope to build. Four, in fact, with only the first and simplest one completed. Each 'scope would be unique: an experiment in astronomy *and* construction using native lunar materials. As attractive as it was to eavesdrop on the cosmos from here on Farside, forever sheltered from Earth's radio cacophony, budgets still mattered. Budgets would always matter. To send struts and girders by the millions of kilos to the Moon would never be practical.

Elements of the telescope pedestal manifested themselves as featureless voids in the star field. He kept watching. Nothing happened. He dared to hope—

Until, after several minutes, his night vision began to kick in and, in unmistakable neon hues, new constellations emerged. Each faint glimmer, splotch, and zigzag—the fluorescing of embedded nanotech strain gauges—revealed yet another weakness in overstressed smart material. He sighed. They still had much to learn about concrete-casting in one-sixth gee.

Were the defects large enough to eyeball? Marcus put a green dot into the heart of the nearest cluster of defects. The laser pointer was awkward and insecure in his grasp; his fingers, in insulated work gloves, felt about as supple as sausages. Without airborne dust—or air—to scatter light, the laser beam itself was invisible. "Suit. Polarization off and headlamps on."

The supposedly stressed area surrounding the green dot *looked* flawless. Dialing up visor magnification revealed nothing further. Maybe with a brighter light ...?

"Quarter power," he called to the construction shack. "Center a spotlight on my dot."

Only no one responded, and the spotlight remained off. Instead, the structural elements nearest him began to flash, with red light reflecting and re-reflecting from countless struts, braces, beams, and girders. All that flashing and blinking denoted: comm failure.

He sighed.

Every lunar outing was a space walk, and you didn't set foot outside an airlock alone. You just didn't. But neither could he afford to assign two people to every piddling one-person task, just in case.

The flash rate doubled.

"Yeah, yeah," he muttered. The flashing seemed brightest out of the corner of his right eye, and he turned in that direction. Far below, among the scattered glimmers of distant work lights and headlamps, a red light blinked in unison with the nearby dim reflections. Between, as with his laser pointer, the light beam was invisible.

"Suit," he said. "Add an IR view."

Marcus's visor now offered a large splotch: his robotic minder. In infrared, the bot's motors and, more so, its radiothermal power module glowed from waste heat. The bot was widening and smoothing a surface path, using only the tiniest fraction of its capacity to monitor human workers by their body heat.

He raised an arm, with the tips of thumb and index finger forming a circle and the remaining fingers extended. I UNDERSTAND, the gesture meant. And, I'M OKAY. Also, that—as intuitive as was this particular hand signal—the days he had long ago spent at paintball had not been wholly wasted.

The bot's alert lamp triple-blinked in acknowledgment, then winked off.

Going without radio was a pain in the ass, but even one helmet transmitter would deafen the radio telescope they had already completed.

For that first instrument, pressed by Congress to show that a Farside observatory *could* be built, they had kept the construction simple: a ground-based array of meter-long, steel, dipole antennae—thousands upon thousands of them—precisely arranged across many square kilometers. Buried fiber optics connected those antennae to the base, where shielded electronics integrated the myriads of celestial whispers into something interesting.

But while the design had been conservative, construction cost was another story. Lunar rocks and regolith provided more than ample iron for steel, but the carbon with which to alloy that native iron had been imported at great expense from Earth. Concrete-based construction would be a boon—if they ever mastered making the mooncrete beams strong and stress-resistant. And if the beams proved themselves able to withstand, year after year, the vacuum, the never-ending radiation, and the big day/night temperature swings.

A few years hence, once the first carbonaceous-chondrite asteroid arrived to be shepherded into orbit around the Moon, carbon would become plentiful and cheap. Then they could produce all the steel they wanted, whether for massive girders or simple rebar. For many purposes, they might even forgo steel, substituting superlight, superstrong, carbon-fiber composites. And with enough conductive carbon fiber, the big dishes themselves might be constructed without metal.

Every day, or so it seemed, Marcus considered advising NASA to suspend further construction until all that carbon arrived—and he never did. There was no point in telling the administrator her pet project should go on hiatus, because *her* boss would never accept that. It wasn't that the president gave a damn about radio astronomy, but—

Red strobing resumed.

It was neither the time nor the place for woolgathering. "Suit. Headlamps on." Marcus spotted, lying on the deck of the crane basket, a length of the fiber-optic cable he had somehow pulled loose from his helmet. The cable's other end looked snug in its socket in the basket's control panel; that connection felt snug, too, when he gave the plug a gentle tug.

Bending and stretching for the errant cable plug was a struggle. Any movement in a (despite the name, not really) "soft" pressure suit was like that: a battle against layer upon layer of stiff, often bulky, fabric *and* internal gas pressure. In a lightweight, counterpressure suit—in essence, a skintight, elastic body stocking—he would have been *so* much more comfortable and productive. In a CP suit, only your helmet was pressurized. CP suits were common enough for many routine surface excursions. And they were more than adequate for shipboard use, worn against the off chance of a micrometeoroid cabin puncture. Alas, those thin, single-layer suits were less than forgiving around sharp rocks and heavy machinery ....

With a wistful sigh, he jacked back into his helmet, and the priority-alert icon popped up on his heads-up display (HUD).

"… Calling Marcus. Come in, Marcus. Daedalus Base calling Marcus—"

"Not to worry," Marcus interrupted Brad Morton's familiar, rasping voice. "A plug came loose, is all."

"You okay, Boss?"

"Me? I'm fine," Marcus said. "The pedestal? Not so much. We've got way too many microfractures. I need you to shuffle schedules and get a structural engineer out here ASAP. We need to know if our problem is a bad batch of struts or something more fundamental. But why are you still at the desk? Shouldn't Francine be on duty this shift?"

"Will do, Boss, and you're right. She's under the weather, though. Maybe something she ate. I told her I'd stay on."

"Too bad. About Francine, I mean. Thanks for stepping up."

"De nada." Brad cleared his throat. "Boss, are we expecting a rush delivery today from Aitken?"

Aitken Basin colony, in eternal shadow near the south pole, was the main lunar settlement: an international commercial and research hub and the home at any given time to a hundred or more people. While the observatory produced its own steel and concrete items—schlepping such cargo a quarter of the way around the Moon made no sense—their electronics came from the silicon foundries at Aitken. Not to mention that the lion's share of their oh-two and water came from Aitken's ice mines.

Marcus considered. "A shipment to be flown in today? I don't remember any, and I assume you're not noticing one on the big board." On the wall within arm's length of the duty officer's workstation. "Why do you ask?"

"Alert flash just came in. We've got a shuttle inbound."

"Huh." Marcus pondered for a while. "Unless I'm mistaken, there isn't a bird"—comsat—"in line of sight of us."

But perhaps he was mistaken. The ground terminal's optical telescopes were tracking *something*.

"It was a direct ship-to-ground downlink beam. ETA, about half an hour. They said they're couriering in a replacement low-noise amplifier, plus a spare." Brad again cleared his throat.

"Larry"—the astronomer on shift—"knows nothing about us needing a new amp."

"No one's asked me to authorize any rush shipments. Anything else aboard this shuttle?"

"Six pallets already prepped from our next scheduled grocery order, given that flying all this way with an empty hold would've been dumb."

"Right." This just got better and better. The unplanned delivery meant he had no one scheduled to offload. "Brad? Find me a couple volunteers to unload. Given that this is last minute, I'll authorize overtime. Oh, and for you, too, covering for Francine. Anything else?"

"As it happens, yes. This rush order is addressed to *you*."

Huh? "I don't suppose you happened to ask who sent me this shipment."

"Momma Morton didn't raise any slow-witted children. Yes, I asked. John Urban Jr., which meant nothing to me. Of course, it's not like I follow who's rotating in and out of Aitken."

"Yeah, me either." Still, the name sounded familiar. John Urban? An actor in the first *Star Trek* reboot? No, that was Karl Urban. "Once I wrap up out here, I'll track down who ordered the amp and how and why." And unless there were a damned good reason for this expedited shipment, the courier fee *and* the overtime pay would come out of someone's salary.

"About you wrapping up," Brad said. "The shuttle pilot said you, personally, have to take delivery of the package."

"That's strange."

"No stranger than a name like a pope." Brad laughed. "This might be a synapse misfiring, but I kind of half-remember that Pope Urban II called the Crusades."

The penny dropped.

It had been years, but Marcus had once known a man named Tyler Pope. It was worrisome enough that the since-retired CIA agent was making clandestine contact. But while Tyler might have picked any pontiff's name, he had chosen one who suggested crusades.

A chill ran down Marcus's spine. His last encounter with Pope had almost gotten him killed. Striving to sound casual, Marcus said,

"Let the pilot know I'll come by for the package. We'll get this all sorted out later."

If Marcus wasn't imagining things, if this unexpected shuttle flight *did* involve the CIA, then he should not draw attention to it. So, for awhile, he watched the big robots assembling segments of the immense antenna dish.

Then he loitered, exchanging pleasantries with two long-haul drivers from Aitken doing maintenance on their tanker trucks. Paul Sokolov was a flaming extrovert, born and raised in Brooklyn. From his teamster days on Earth, back before trucks drove themselves, he had an encyclopedic knowledge of restaurants, biker bars, and strip clubs across America. Marcus found being around Sokolov exhausting, but letting the man prattle on was an easy way to kill time. Tony Tremonti, the second driver, was taciturn under the best of circumstances—as being around Sokolov seldom was. Tony's full attention was on servicing his rig's ginormous fuel cells for the next leg of their trip. Apart from a few muttered curses, he had nothing to say. After one of the base's cargo vans trundled past Marcus on its way to the landing strip, after the runway lights began strobing, he excused himself. He loped onto the tarmac within minutes of the shuttle setting down.

When the shuttle's airlock completed its cycle, he found in the pantry-sized cockpit one of the regular pilots from Aitken. Wanda Samad was likewise petite, with flowing black hair, dark and flashing eyes, and delicate, very pretty features. The low, acrylic canopy that kept him hunched over was no obstacle for her; she was on her feet, standing tall, her arms flung back, pivoting at the waist and stretching. Her skintight red counterpressure suit was, well, skintight. He hadn't seen Valerie, except over comms, for two months. Two *long* months. And never mind the twinge of guilt over it, there was no way for him not to notice Wanda.

"Any time now," she said.

He popped his helmet, setting it on a shelf beside hers. "How's life in the big city?"

"A never-ending social whirl. How's life in the desert?"

"Deserted." Was that enough chitchat to not seem anxious? "You have some kind of package for me?"

"Yeah." She rooted around in a small locker, coming up with a many-times-folded datasheet. Its sensor pad was centered in the hanky-sized bit that was folded out. Some kind of delivery-log app was open. "If you'll do the honors."

"Oh, come on. You know who I am."

"Uh-huh. And I also know you're supposed to sign for your package."

He wriggled partway out of his pressure suit to press a thumb against the datasheet's sensor pad. "Marcus Judson," he called out to the voice-recognition software.

The datasheet blatted.

"A little uptight, are we?" she kidded. "Try again."

He had managed to flunk voice-stress analysis. Relax! he ordered himself. "Marcus Judson." This time, the app offered a melodious chime.

"Kudos," she said. "Got your name right in a mere two tries."

His package, once she retrieved it from another locker, was underwhelming: a shrink-wrapped cardboard carton, perhaps a quarter meter on its longest edge. Even by lunar standards, it did not weigh much. As he swapped it from hand to hand, something moved inside. He could just sense the shift in the box's center of gravity. This might indeed be electronics swaddled in Bubble Wrap. If it turned out to be an unauthorized parts shipment, someone back at the base had serious explaining to do. Except he didn't believe that.

He knew one thing: whatever this box contained, Tyler Pope hadn't brought it. After a heart attack, you did not get cleared for space travel. Someone other than Tyler had couriered this package from Earth, or someone at Aitken had prepared the box.

So," Marcus asked. "Who is John Urban?"

She shrugged. "A name on a package label."

"Is he new to Aitken?"

"*Hello?* A name on a label. I got to work and your box was waiting."

Beyond the cockpit canopy Marcus saw the van pull away. No sooner had it driven off the mooncrete landing pad than its wire-mesh tires grew towering rooster tails of powdery lunar regolith.

Through his feet came the faint vibration from motors shutting the cargo hold's clamshell doors.

He tried again. "Aitken is a small community. You must know something about him."

It occurred to Marcus that perhaps there was no him. "Bush pilot" would be an ideal cover for a CIA agent on the Moon.

She said, "You can only squeeze so much blood from a turnip."

"What?"

"Blood. Turnip. Think about it. Now what say you zip up and go home? My cargo is gone and the meter is still running."

Marcus suited back up and left.

Chapter 3

The resource the Moon offered above all others was *room*. Everyone at Daedalus Base—resident and guest alike—had spacious accommodations, because: why not? The mole could tunnel almost a meter an hour, and the more they dug, the more cosmic-ray-absorbing rubble they accumulated to heap over the base.

In the company only of his still-unopened package, Marcus found his capacious private quarters more forlorn than luxurious.

He stared at the box. It stared back. Shrink-wrap. Cardboard. The shipping label addressed to him. With a sigh and a Swiss Army knife, he slit open the box. Apart from Bubble Wrap, the box offered: two standard 4260BJ amplifiers—according to base inventory, five just like these sat in the main stockroom—and a much-folded, somewhat scuffed HP/Dell datasheet, of a model older than the Hitachi unit in his pocket.

The packing slip claimed *he* had ordered the amps, and it made no mention of any datasheet. The computer might have dropped into the box out of someone's shirt pocket. Or it could have been meant to appear that way, just in case the box fell into the wrong hands.

"What the hell?" he muttered.

"I do not understand your question," Icarus said, the voice emanating from a ceiling speaker.

"I was talking to myself," Marcus said. "Icarus, I'm not good company at the moment. Begin privacy mode, please."

"Privacy mode begins now," the base AI confirmed.

And ends, how? For the first time, it penetrated that at some level Icarus was always monitoring. Otherwise, the AI wouldn't know when its attention was once more requested. But if it was always listening, at least, in private quarters, it did not have *eyes*.

Tyler Pope was making him crazy! Unless Tyler had had nothing to do with the package and John Urban was only a clerk somewhere. Unless Marcus himself *had* ordered this gear, and expedited it, and then forgotten.

He told himself forty-five was far too young to be having senior moments.

He stared at his walls. They stared back. They were covered in the same rock-pore sealant paint that was found throughout the base: the shade of yellow that NASA psychologists deemed cheerful and everyone else found bilious.

He set his everyday datasheet, its webcam folded inside, on his desk. To mask whatever else he might mutter, he started that datasheet playing the *New World Symphony*.

Now *what*, Tyler, are you trying to tell me?

Both amps looked ordinary. He guessed they were ordinary, and they and the incomplete packing slip were mere props to explain his package's rushed—and unavoidably public—delivery. Leaving the undocumented datasheet ....

Unfolded, it covered most of the desk. Apart from the product logo, webcam lens, charging port, mic, an archaic earbud port, and biometric pad, the mysterious datasheet, like any powered-down datasheet, could have been torn off a roll of butcher paper. The other side, when he flipped over the datasheet, was featureless.

He flipped the datasheet again, put on earbuds (wireless—he wasn't a caveman), and thumbed the sensor pad. The pad glowed blue and he waited for the datasheet to boot. Instead, after a few seconds, the pad faded. The datasheet was charged but locked.

He thumbed the sensor pad again, this time speaking, "Marcus Judson." Nada.

He tried with his other thumb. No good. One by one, he tried his fingers. No good. The loud music, he guessed, and tapped PAUSE. It would not matter if Icarus (or someone else accessing the room sensors—surely an absurd scenario) overheard him speaking his own name.

No good.

Still stressed-out, Marcus concluded. Surprises from a CIA spook will do that. He took several deep, cleansing breaths and tried yet again.

No good.

If only he could *talk* with Tyler about … whatever this was. Or with Wanda Samad, not that she had as much as hinted at being anything other than a courier. Or that he could brainstorm about the puzzle with any of the dozen geniuses on staff at Daedalus. Or with Valerie, because his wife was sharper than the lot of them.

Val should have been joining him here soon, and rightly so: what she didn't know about radio astronomy had yet to be invented. After what had seemed endless planning, they—and NASA, and the NSF—had had everything worked out. Simon's school let out in a few days. He would spend two weeks of the summer at sailing camp and another two weeks at computer camp. Before, between, and after camp sessions, Val's parents had signed up to spoiling the boy rotten. Val had NASA's blessing to work on Farside for two months, an NSF grant to cover her travel, and her flight reservations.

Only all that had gone out the window—and in the greater scheme of things, Marcus could not have been happier about it—when, on his latest "shore" leave, they had gotten pregnant. They hadn't even known till he had been back on the Moon for weeks.

No one had any idea what gestation in one-sixth gee might do to a developing human fetus, and no one intended to be the test case. Which had Marcus, beyond missing Val every day, AWOL from doctor appointments, and from *awwing* at the tiny outfits she continued to buy, and midnight Dairy Queen runs, and converting the guestroom into a nursery, and, well, all the things an expecting dad should be around to do. And it also left him without even the prospect of anyone to talk out this mystery with, unless ….

Hmm. Just maybe, Wanda *had* spoken about the package: *blood from a turnip.* Blood. DNA? If so, saliva should do. He licked his thumb and again tried the sensor pad.

This time, the datasheet booted.

Its desktop icons were all for mundane apps and games. One by one he tapped them anyway, testing the theory that one might disguise something interesting. None did. Delving deeper, he found the solid-state disk stored multitudes of files in a myriad of folders. Somewhere among them might be something to explain everything, but in a quick sampling not a single folder or file name stood out. He had in his possession, as best a quick inspection could disclose, an everyday datasheet—only everyday datasheets did not come with disguised real-time DNA readers, much less come primed to recognize *his* DNA.

He waited for something to happen. Nothing did.

Nor did anything make sense until, for no special reason, using his everyday datasheet, he checked his mail. There, under the subject line Bob, Marcus read, I should never let you leave home without one of these. 1600. Alice.

Icarus confirmed a laser-based comsat would be overhead at 16:00, 4:00 pm, one in a daisy chain of comsats that, extending to Nearside, would permit a real-time link with Earth. Marcus cleared his afternoon schedule, claiming a splitting headache, pulling rank to keep the base paramedic at bay.

Alone and in his quarters, 16:00 hours came and went without contact.

He fretted. He paced. Larry the astronomer came by of his own initiative with a covered meal tray, and for a while Marcus picked at a burger and fries. He paced some more. He went back to the enigmatic datasheet, poking about for any clue he might have missed, for any names he might have been expected to contact. Nada. Zip. Nil. He fidgeted. He paced. Almost, he took a lap around the square, eighty-meters-on-a-side tunnel that was Main Street, but the puzzlement doubtless plain on his face could only raise alarms he did not want raised and bring questions he could not begin to answer.

Reading between one line was pretty damn Zen. Perhaps he had misunderstood. Was the message even *from* Tyler?

Hell, yeah.

He had met Tyler Pope in dire circumstances, over the most kludged of all possible comm links, improvising around the lack of crypto gear on a then recently captured asteroid. NASA's base on

Earth's newest moon hadn't had any reason to stock such gear. Till it did. Till the Russian-backed terrorists had shown up. If the datasheet now so incongruously delivered to Marcus *was* crypto gear, I SHOULD NEVER LET YOU LEAVE HOME WITHOUT ONE OF THESE made perfect sense. So did "Alice" and "Bob." For a good half century, cryptographers explaining their arcane craft had used "Alice" as the party with a secret message to send and "Bob" as the party intended to somehow securely receive it.

Everything pointed, however obliquely, to some sort of encrypted communication headed his way, through this device. If so, he had misunderstood 1600. And well on his way to wearing a rut into the mooncrete floor, he came up with a theory.

With lunar days and nights each two Earth weeks long, time zones like back home would serve no useful purpose. So: everyone on the Moon lived by Zulu Time. For any purpose that did not demand the accuracy of an atomic clock, Zulu Time was Greenwich Mean Time.

But Tyler and CIA headquarters were in Virginia, not on the Moon. If 1600 referred to Eastern Time, five hours behind Zulu, he had almost three more hours to go. A person could go nuts in that time!

Three times Marcus started, and deleted, an email to Valerie. He was too keyed up to get the tone right, and he didn't want to worry her. After the third attempt, he closed the email app and opened a digital picture album. He paged through shots of Valerie, Simon, and sometimes the three of them. Simon was a good-looking kid, something of a soccer fiend, a math whiz like his mom, and, like any teen, a handful. Somehow the boy grew an inch or two between photos.

And Val? She was smart, curious, spirited. Beautiful. Tall and sexy. She had, on the too rare occasions when she let down her hair and intensity, the most charming, impish smile. Most shots in this best-of-the-best collection showed Val as lithe as the day they had first met, but his favorite pic was the newest: the selfie-in-the-mirror with the world's most adorable baby bump.

With a sigh, he dismissed the album. He dug through a junk drawer, muttering about spooks and the interminable wait making him paranoid, until he found, tangled among his collection of spare cables and cords, an ancient pair of wired earbuds.

Of course there was never a shortage of things to be done, and work would be a welcome distraction. Marcus refolded the mysterious datasheet, debating with himself whether to carry it with him or lock it in his quarters. Unlike Tyler, or whomever had sent him this datasheet, *he* trusted his coworkers, but—

In his hands, the datasheet trilled.

This time, once he reauthenticated, the datasheet offered up a vid window. In it, as if imaged from a handheld device held at arm's length, Marcus saw a ruddy-faced man with sparse, close-cropped graying hair and a bristly mustache gone all white, seated in an unfamiliar anteroom. Horn-rimmed glasses perched midway down his nose, and he had on wired earbuds. Without the suit jacket, starched white shirt, and tie, he could have been anybody's grandfather. In point of fact, he *was* a grandfather. Until a couple of years back, he had also been the CIA's acknowledged Russia expert.

Taking a visual cue, Marcus switched to wired earbuds.

"Good man," Tyler Pope began with a touch of Texas drawl. "I'd have looked pretty foolish showing up for this meeting if you hadn't cracked the code. You by yourself up there?"

"Apart from my better judgment? Yeah."

"Get it out of your system," Tyler eventually responded. The three-second round-trip delay was not going to make conversation any easier. "Not a joking venue, or subject, and this isn't the only issue on the woman's plate."

"Explaining nothing." As if they had minds of their own, Marcus felt his hands clench. Not sure why he cared, he managed to keep his fists beneath the camera's view. "You're retired. I'm about as literally in the middle of nowhere as human beings have ever managed. So what the *hell* is going on, and what does it have to do with *me*?"

"In my case, retirement didn't stick. In your case, well, you'll *want* to be involved. Trust me. With luck, you'll have answers soon enough." He made a noise that was half chuckle, half phlegmy cough. "After which you'll have more questions.

"I called you after getting our five-minute warning. Of course, that could mean five minutes, could mean an hour."

"Give me *something*, man. A topic. Why the Agency is interested in me again. Whoever it is I'm about to meet."

Tyler frowned. "I told you who."

"No, you told me when. And unless you're somewhere in the middle of the Atlantic, you didn't even get that right."

"I told you 1600. If I could have given a time, I would have, but it's out of my hands."

1600 was not a time. Marcus was just beginning to suspect the sort of trouble he was somehow in when a tall, middle-aged, African American man leaned into the camera's peripheral vision.

He said, "The president will see you both now."

The president could spare Marcus and Tyler only a few minutes of her time. It was long enough to emphasize that the discovery was, beyond important, epochal. That vital security interests of the nation were at issue, at forefront, at stake. That every reasonable resource would be made available to Marcus. That the coming endeavor was a top priority for her; she trusted and expected it would be so for him.

But what had been discovered? What endeavor? What had Marcus to do with *any* of this? Those questions remained unaddressed even as the president, citing the demands of more urgent, though not more important, matters, brought their session to a close.

And so Marcus—none the wiser than before the call, but with his curiosity raised to a fever pitch—found himself digitally ushered from the Oval Office.

Chapter 4

"What I'm about to tell you can't go *anywhere* outside this room," Marcus said. His living room, that was. The CIA datasheet, among its hidden features (he now knew), swept for bugs; his quarters did not seem to have any. The device jammed whatever bugs it might have overlooked. It pushed antinoise through his surround-sound speakers to stymie eavesdroppers. That last feature, Tyler had assured him, would defeat anyone attempting to listen in via Icarus's ubiquitous mics. "I need your word."

Across the room, his two visitors exchanged skeptical looks.

Marcus waited until, finally, Brad Morton nodded. Brad was a big man, a former college linebacker. The salt-of-the-earth type, with a kind word and a pat on the back for everyone he met, and on most every occasion. Also, a damned good friend.

"I keep confidences for a living," Donna Rousseau said. The base paramedic was a just-the-facts sort. She was damned good at her job, excusably (if on occasion annoyingly) a bit cocky. Donna had a square face and a strong jaw, and her ice-blue eyes were penetrating. Wiry in build, of not quite average height, standing beside Brad she seemed tiny. "Is this different?"

You have no idea, Marcus thought. "I need you both," he began, "to join me on a road trip."

Brad leaned against the wall. "That's anticlimactic after the big buildup."

"An 1800-mile road trip," Marcus added. Road trips weren't measured in kilometers. They just weren't.

Brad did not even blink. "You bring the beer, Boss."

"I shouldn't be off-base that long," Donna said, "but you know that, just as you know it can't be a secret when we three set out to … wherever. Put that aside and look at us: two engineers and a paramedic. Your not-so-little road trip has nothing to do with astronomy or the observatory. How about you cut to the chase?"

"You need to see something." Tapping the CIA datasheet, Marcus started playback of one of the encrypted files Tyler had uploaded. "Highlights of a vid shot two days ago on Nearside. From a prospecting bot following hints of iridium, of all exotic things."

Across stark moonscape, through long shadows, their point of view crept toward two impressive stone slabs leaning one against the other. In the niche beneath the rocks, where rays of the setting Sun managed to sneak through, hints of orange peeked out of the dust. He had watched this vid, over and over and *over*, and still he was in awe.

Donna leaned closer.

"Just wait," Marcus said. "By the way, I'm told that mound we're seeing is about two and a half meters long."

A manipulator arm entered their view, the robotic limb slowing to a crawl as Marcus adjusted the playback rate. For a breathtaking few seconds, through a gold-tinged visor, they saw—someone. A mummy. Eyes like an owl in a squarish head. Three nostrils, and no hint of a nose. Rank upon rank of needlelike teeth within the lipless slash of a mouth. Hints of scales.

Then the vid resumed normal speed. Suit, face, *everything* crumbled, imploded, dissolved into a collapsing cloud of dust.

"Aliens," Donna said.

"Aliens," Marcus agreed. "And, it would appear, ancient aliens. We're going to go check things out."

Brad was, as always, practical. "1800 miles. 3000 klicks. I presume 'road trip' is metaphorical. Which shuttle would you like prepped?"

"Let's not get ahead of ourselves," Donna said. "I realize Daedalus is in the middle of nowhere on the backside of the Moon. Still, the discovery of intelligent aliens seems like the sort of news we would have gotten even here—if it were *on* the news. Hence, this is all being kept under wraps, and I have to ask, how is that even possible? And *why* is it a secret? And given that it is, why tell *us*? Why *involve* us? Who else would be going?"

Fair questions, Marcus had to agree. He had asked much the same of Tyler, too. "I need to change that 'would' to will. Then there's the question you've been too polite to ask: how and why *I* got this news."

"I wouldn't mind knowing that, too," Brad allowed with a grin.

Marcus smiled back. "Don't get me wrong, I'm glad to know. I'm stunned and excited and honored to be involved. But it's not that simple."

"Go figure," Donna said.

"First, let's dispense with the secrecy aspects," Marcus said. "The guy who stumbled upon this, the prospector teleoperating the bot from Dirtside, is ex-military. Out of caution, not talking to anyone else, not even the corporation from which he rents his bot, he checked in with his old platoon leader." Though this Ethan *had* taken the time first to file a mining claim. After finding iridium in high concentrations? Marcus did not fault the man. "Only that guy wasn't a lieutenant anymore, but a major in Army intel."

"At which point the whole thing became classified," Brad said. "Big surprise. But that makes me more curious. Why us?"

The way Tyler told it, the report had raced up the chain at Army Intelligence and Security Command, then to the Defense Intelligence Agency, and from there to the director of national intelligence. And to *his* boss, the president herself.

Donna, who had planted herself on Marcus's sofa, got up to pace. "Did you see that being, creature, entity, whatever you care to call it? No way is it native to the Moon, because nothing that ever lived is. And unless I slept through a whole slew of biology classes, nothing like it ever evolved on Earth. Our dusty friend, wherever he, she, or it called home, must have come a long way. *That* suggests tech well beyond ours."

"Traces of that tech may still be here on the Moon," Marcus said. "And *that's* why this discovery is classified. Because it matters who gets such technology, if any of it remains out there to be found."

Brad said, "Still not amounting to an answer to why *us*. I, for one, don't have a security clearance, or ever wanted one."

"None of us have." It had to be just nerves, but Marcus realized he was starving. He started grubbing around in his pantry for something, anything, ready to eat. Stale pretzels were the best he could do. He emptied the half-full bag into a bowl, carried the bowl to the living room. "But neither would we be up here without a thorough background check. Not after …."

Donna grimaced. "Not after Resetter space tourists hijacked Powersat One and turned its downlink microwave beam into a WMD. But you'd know a great deal more about that than I."

The bit of pretzel in Marcus's mouth suddenly tasted like ashes.

He had been on-orbit when PS-1 fell into eco-terrorist hands. As far as the public knew, he had evacuated with the rest of the workers, and an autopilot glitch had splashed down his reentry pod many miles from the rest. Just as, as far as the world knew, an undisclosed fail-safe had later taken the hijacked solar-power satellite offline, allowing a Special Forces squad flown up on a shuttle to retake control. Just as, the public was assured, the terrorists, all conveniently killed during the operation, were alone to blame for thousands dead worldwide and gigabucks in power-generation facilities fried on the ground. And just as, with energy prices soaring, everyone was expected to believe Russia and her petro allies had altruistically opened wide the oil spigots.

Fairy tales, all of it.

Marcus had joined in—hell, he had concocted—the crazy, desperate, but in the end successful foray to disable the powersat. Four of them had made the flight from the orbital construction base. Terrorists killed Dino Agnelli. Thad Stankiewicz turned out to *be* a terrorist, or at least a Russian mole. When Thad's attempt to stymie the raid failed, rather than be taken prisoner he had killed himself. Marcus and Savannah Morgan, the lone survivors of the raid, were sworn to secrecy faster than a rescue shuttle could return them to Earth.

Many a sleepless night, he wondered what, beyond cheap oil, the Russians had conceded to keep their part in the fiasco undisclosed. And what thoughts of revenge the Russians nursed. And how much it mattered that Great Power chess, rather than any interest in astronomy, sustained the president's support for Daedalus Base. Construction of the observatory justified a big American presence on the Moon, just as the Russians, with even greater hypocrisy, operated their helium strip mine on Farside. With or without a supply of He-3, Russian researchers remained, from all Marcus had read, a good twenty years away from a practical fusion reactor—as practical fusion had been two decades into the future going back to the fifties.

"You still with us, Boss?" Brad prompted. "You went all quiet."

"PS-1?" Marcus said. "Yeah, I was at the wrong place at the wrong time." That was all he had shared, or intended to share, with either of them. Or, for that matter, with *anyone* on the Moon. "It earned me a debrief session with the CIA. It's why my name came up as the person at Daedalus to contact."

"So the pope works for the CIA?" Brad asked.

"Something like that." Marcus said.

Donna cleared her throat. "None of which explains why they'd contact Daedalus in the first place. Let me guess. It's because we're an all-American installation. Too many Russians and Chinese and others at Aitken. Too hard there to keep mounting an expedition secret. Just like sending experts up from Earth might draw unwelcome attention."

Marcus nodded.

"Confirming aliens would affect *everything*," Donna said, "and *everybody*. No one asked me, but keeping this from the public seems wrong. Make that, paranoid. Still, secrecy, however misplaced, is why Daedalus Base, and why you. It doesn't explain"—and she gestured back and forth between herself and Brad—"why *us*?"

"You, for your biological knowledge—"

"Which supposes we find any aliens, and they don't fall apart at a hard stare." She grimaced. "And that *anything* about Earth biology even applies to them."

"For your biological knowledge," Marcus repeated. "Brad, to keep our gear up and running. Me, because the Agency knows me." And because, though Marcus was not the type to say it of himself, he was a damned good systems engineer. A generalist. When you had no way to know what you might find, a generalist was apt to come in handy.

"Including myself," Donna said, "we make one sorry excuse for a first-contact team, or exo-archeologists, or whatever the hell they expect us to be. No offense."

"None taken." Marcus patted the CIA datasheet. "Despite appearances, this is no run-of-the-mill computer. There's a reason this device was couriered to me. We'll have ultrasecure communications to all manner of people whom the Agency is discreetly lining up, experts in every specialty from archeology to zoology. We'll be their eyes and hands."

Donna's nostrils flared. "How flattering."

"You know," Brad said, grinning, "I kind of like seeing myself as Indiana Jones. But as you have me pegged for more mundane tasks, Boss, I'll get back to practicalities. Which shuttle will we be taking? What supplies, instruments, whatever, do you have in mind we bring?"

"No shuttle," Marcus said. "And that *is* for reasons of practicality. We don't know how long we'll have reason to stay, or how big an area we'll need to search. And"—the argument that had convinced Tyler—"flying straight there might draw unwanted attention to the spot. We'll drive, stopping often along the way to survey. When we stop, anyone watching"—and half a dozen countries had sensor platforms orbiting the Moon—"will see us drilling test bores and assaying mineral samples."

Brad considered that for a while. "So, I guess we leave right away?"

"Surveying, or the appearance of it, anyway, in the dark? That doesn't sound credible. No, we'll wait for sunup."

"And just where will we be going?"

Marcus smiled. "You'll know soon enough."

Chapter 5

"I'm hurt, I tell her," Paul Sokolov said, his booming voice filling the Daedalus Base dining/social hall. That was where Main Street broadened into facing alcoves on opposite sides of the "road," each niche accommodating a mooncrete table and some rickety aluminum chairs. He was deep into his third beer and one of his favorite bar stories. Parts of the tale were even true. "No, wounded. Grievously, undeservedly, unfairly wounded. I tell her, this misunderstanding we had wasn't *my* fault. She'd never said anything to me about sisters. But, I says to her, now that I see how important family is to you ...." Methodically, he drained his bottle. He smacked his lips. He leaned back in his chair. Timing was everything. "My bed is big enough for all of us."

Of the half dozen people with whom he shared a table, none laughed more appreciatively than Camilla Perez. She was new to the observatory since his last delivery run, and he had only just met her. She was not pretty, exactly, and she was shaped more like a pear than a cello, much less an hourglass, but she was, well, a she. Unattached women remained a rare breed on the Moon, and rarer still on Farside. Of the staff here at Daedalus, Camilla made three.

He smiled at her. "Thank you. Thank you very much. Thank you."

Brad Morton shoved back his chair, stood, and reached for Paul's empty. The African American engineer was the biggest man in the room, perhaps on the Moon. These days he rode herd on robots, not running backs. Morton did not talk much, and when he did speak, it was in a laid-back manner that was just weird for someone his size, almost as incongruous as the Oliver Hardy mustache and the tiny ears. Only the big, bushy eyebrows were sized right for Morton's big, round face.

Paul handed over the bottle, smiling. "And most definitely, my friend, thank *you*."

Morton mumbled something as he stepped into the kitchen.

Beer and booze were not quite illegal on the Moon, because what was the point? As soon as people lived anywhere, a few vices—some would say, necessities—always followed. Still, the polite fiction was that few partook. Alcohol was stored out of the way, and everyone was expected to abstain before venturing outside. Eight hours dry, from bottle to throttle, the mantra went, as if they were fighter pilots or something. Madness ....

Camilla scooted her chair closer to Paul. "And how'd that line work for you, guy?"

"I'm schlepping ice and groceries across the far side of nowhere, aren't I?"

She patted his arm. "I should be feeling sorry for you, should I? You poor, misunderstood letch?"

Feel me anyway you want, Paul thought. Also: but later. He had work to do first, and a curiosity itch that needed scratching. Just then, they were the same thing.

He asked, "So where's the big cheese this evening?"

"Marcus? I don't know. Haven't seen him in hours."

Around the table, the others shrugged or shook their heads.

Brad Morton emerged from the kitchen, a trio of beer bottles clutched in each meaty hand. He distributed brews around the table. "I heard Marcus took the afternoon off. He's in his room, not feeling well. A headache, someone told me."

Nodding his thanks, Paul picked up a bottle. "I'm sorry to hear that."

And skeptical, too, because a few hours ago, Marcus Judson—base administrator and, rumor had it, confidant to the NASA administrator herself—had been outside making small talk. That in itself was interesting. Judson was no shrinking violet, but neither was he the type to stand around shooting the breeze. The sudden sociability had seemed out of character even before he had excused himself to dash off to the just-landed shuttle. Even before he had returned, eyes narrowed in thought, toting a package.

The shuttle was unscheduled. Paul knew, because he made it his business to know. He had learned young that when you talked a lot, people took that to mean you didn't much listen. He was *always* listening.

So: a rush, expensive delivery from Aitken Basin. A package retrieved in person by the head honcho, after an epic fail at nonchalance. Now Judson was sequestered in his quarters, and the big guy here—*his* effort at offhandedness just pathetic—seemed eager to excuse that.

Something interesting was going on.

When *he* feigned illness, or mechanical problems with his rig, or whatever, Paul expected his performance to be a damned sight more convincing. His handler at Mare Ingenii—what a great name: the Sea of Cleverness—paid real cash money for the smallest item of Daedalus gossip. To track down whatever it was the observatory director wanted kept secret? That info would surely bring in *major* bucks from Yevgeny.

Paul clinked bottles with Camilla. "I believe you were about to console me?"

He could imagine worse diversions while he watched for further strange goings-on.

Chapter 6

Valerie Clayburn wiggled and squirmed. However she sat, it hurt her back, but shifting positions sometimes offered momentary relief. Even her new, expensive, super-ergonomic desk chair—one of a kind here at NASA headquarters, or so the CFO had opined before, grudgingly, okaying the purchase—did little enough to help. And Junior was not due for another four months. Another four *long* months ....

Call already, Marcus! I have *news*!

This invocation worked about as well as had her past eight efforts, or the power of positive thinking to make Super Chair, or her back, cooperate. Or for her body to stop packing on the pounds, bleeding from the gums, or manufacturing hemorrhoids and headaches, all with world-class efficiency. Or even to open a perpetually stuffy nose—snoring herself awake umpteen times a night had gotten old fast.

Still, as loud as her snoring sometimes got, it would not cross vacuum; on occasion, she saw the silver lining that her snoring did not disturb Marcus. But not so much last night. Not after he had stood her up for the second day in a row.

Call, damn it!

To be fair, there wasn't bandwidth between Earth and Farside for idle chats, and their scheduled window did not open for another few minutes. To be fair, Marcus had a responsible, high-pressure job that might not always accommodate social chitchat.

Screw being fair! There were always a few seconds and ample bandwidth for a sorry-I'm-very-busy text.

A coffee mug emblazoned National Radio Astronomy Observatory, a keepsake from her last job, sat on the short file cabinet beside her desk. The mug felt scarcely warm to the touch. She swigged anyway, not remembering till midswallow that the luke-tepid stuff was decaf. Decaf! What was the point? With a grimace she gave the dregs to a potted fern, then returned her attention to the datasheet draped across her desk and the document open in the sheet's top window.

Agreeing to sit on Jay Singh's dissertation committee had seemed like a good idea at the time, and not only for the many favors she owed Freddie Peña, an old friend and also Jay's thesis adviser. On principle, she wanted to support anyone interested in astronomy—including, as in this case, a computer scientist doing interdisciplinary work.

Then there was the dissertation topic itself. Asteroids, in their hundreds of thousands, could be elusive devils. They lacked the decency to carry ID tags. Most sightings were but faint and fleeting glimmers as distant, tumbling rocks absorbed sunlight and reradiated that energy as infrared. Jay believed artificial intelligence could match up disparate sightings of the same rock, made on different dates, even by separate instruments and observatories, better than any existing algorithm. More data points per rock, in turn, would mean better orbital predictions. His results so far were mixed, but Jay was not discouraged. There were, he had assured her, several AI techniques that, singly or in combinations, might make contributions to the task.

In any event, they would keep on trying. Identify with new tech just one heretofore unknown Earth-threatening rock, and whatever time she put into assisting Jay would have been well worth it. Meanwhile, he was mastering some astronomy and she odds and ends about AI.

If only the young man wrote less turgidly ....

And, once again, she knew she had lost the thread of Jay's exposition.

Of pregnancy's many crappy complications, Val's least favorite had to be Momnesia. With a sigh and a couple impatient taps, she went back to the start of this first, incomplete draft. *Machine Learning and Automated Orbit Determination: New Means of Characterizing Near-Earth Objects*, by Jathedar Singh.

Marcus referred to Jay's dissertation as *Rock? Bye-Bye, Baby!* And that recollection again begged the question: where the hell *was* her husband? Val continued her reading, fidgeting and squirming in her chair, musing all the while about how best to guide her protégé, until—

Finally! Marcus's avatar popped into existence over her datasheet. Her ringtone chimed and warbled. Val swiped a hand through his avatar, and there he was.

His face was drawn, as if he hadn't been eating enough; the contrast of sunken cheeks with the strong jaw made him seem that much more haggard. The buzz cut still surprised her, no matter how practical short hair doubtless was in a spacesuit helmet. His eyes, a striking cornflower blue, twinkled as always, but dark bags beneath them suggested he had been sleeping even less than she. And he hadn't shaved in days.

Talking over one another only made the comm lag more annoying, and they had decided during his first week on the Moon that whoever placed a particular call would start. The few seconds wait was *interminable.*

"Hi, hon," he said at last. "Sorry I missed you yesterday. How's Washington?"

"Hi, back at you. Hot and muggy. And don't worry about it." *Something* was going on with him. And that, whatever it might be, was nothing as routine as a pregnancy. He didn't even realize he had missed *two* scheduled calls. What the hell was going on? "So, how are things?"

Another interminable delay. "That's my line." He managed a grin. "Say, you had a checkup the other day. I'm so sorry I can't be there for you. How are you both?"

"Couldn't be better." Because just then she'd be *damned* if she would bother him with a sore back or any other niggling complaint. Not while—whatever—was going on up there. But she had to believe *good* news would be welcome. "And Marcus, I can feel"—she stopped herself just in time; for whatever weird reason, he didn't want to know the gender in advance—"the baby moving!"

"Damn! I *really* wish I could feel that. And how's Simon?"

"Happy that school is out." As in, he'd just graduated middle school, a milestone which Marcus had let pass without as much as a tweet. That wasn't at all like him. She took a deep breath. "What's going on with you?"

"Well, uh, we're pretty busy. Everything takes longer than expected. Just, uh, on the big dish alone—"

Out with it, she wanted to shout. She told herself pregnancy made her impatient, aware that wasn't the issue at all. Marcus did not *uh*. Never, not for as long as she had known him. Combine those hesitations with how rundown he looked? With forgetting Simon's big day? Protocol be damned, she interrupted. "Bottom-line it, please. What's the story?"

Three seconds later, she saw him blink. "Metal. Without tons more of the stuff, and I'm not being figurative, we'll never get ourselves back on schedule. So, a few of us are going to follow up on some promising satellite observations."

"I thought carbon to make the steel was the issue." Thought, hell, she *knew*. Iron was common enough on the Moon. Carbon, though, like He-3, was only found in scant traces deposited over the eons by the solar wind. The Russians were strip-mining and sifting cubic kilometers of regolith to gather *grams* of helium. Sure, in theory, Marcus might find intact chunks of a carbonaceous chondrite beneath the floor of some nearby crater, but what were the chances? If such a rock were buried, satellites wouldn't sense it and a hand-carried metal detector wouldn't either. There was a reason NASA had put big bucks into a multiyear mission to capture a carbon-rich asteroid. "You mean carbon, right?"

"Yeah, uh, I was imprecise," Marcus said. "Carbon. If we find a local source, well, you know."

Well, you know? That was odder than the stray *uh*. How stressed-out was he? And what was she missing? She kept her focus on the science. "How, exactly, are you finding this carbon?"

"Um, I had to sign an NDA. Nondisclosure agreement." His eyes darted … furtively? "Private party. Proprietary algorithm for analyzing multispectral observations. If we do find something, the guy gets a share. And with a proven way to locate carbon on the Moon? He'll be very rich."

"I've heard nothing about this at the office."

"Uh, you wouldn't. Won't. He's keeping it close to the vest." Marcus laughed. "I shouldn't even be saying 'he.'"

Right. Because knowing it's a man narrows down the suspects so much.

"So it boils down to, I guess, that you're going prospecting."

"Uh-huh. In a few days, once the Sun comes up."

"In person?"

"Right again." He shrugged. "Yeah, I know, on Nearside prospecting is done with bots. That's not so easy in a radio quiet zone."

Do *not* patronize your radio-astronomer, pregnant/hormonal wife. She tamped down that thought, along with: Have you looked in the mirror lately? You're exhausted. "Who's going, besides you?"

"Donna and Brad." He shrugged again. "Yeah, I know. A manager, a paramedic, and a mechanical engineer. We sound like the start of a walk-into-a-bar joke. The thing is, we're all support staff. Our being away won't have a direct impact on the construction schedule and, in any event, no one here is a geologist, selenologist, whatever the proper term is. There *are* geologists at Aitken, and more Dirtside. We'll net one in when we need an expert opinion. But never mind that. The baby's moving? That's so great, hon."

"It is." And that also, my dear, is the most contrived change of subject I've encountered in many a day. Almost as contrived as you dredging up *selenologist*. "You'll be careful?"

He winked. (Had she *ever* seen him wink?) "It's a simple road trip. People take 'em all the time. Still, we're crazy busy up here, prepping for the excursion and reshuffling the duty roster to keep things on track while the three of us are away."

What wasn't he telling her? "So, these schedule issues, and this prospecting excursion"—wild-goose chase—"to recover. Is this you easing into how you plan to extend your stint at Farside? Because you and I have our own project going, and *I'm* on schedule."

A *long* hesitation. "I'll be there with you for the delivery. You have my word." And *another* wink. "Just you try not to get too far ahead of schedule."

It would have been nice if she believed him. "I'll see what I can do."

"Hon, listen, I gotta go. Things to do, people to boss around. Love you."

"Love you, too."

As abruptly as it had begun, the conversation was over. Valerie was left wondering: had Marcus even waited the few seconds to hear her reply? And what the hell was the deal on Farside? And whether it was her raging hormones yet again, or if Marcus had *intended* to imply: Don't call us. We'll call you.

Yevgeny Rudin's head had just hit the pillow when, from atop his chest of drawers, a trumpet fanfare rang out. Haydn. As his eyes popped open, the spectral time display adrift on the digital wallpaper rolled over to 3:06 am.

It had been a *long* day. That morning, he had flown two scientists to assist colleagues at Ice Blossom (even in his thoughts, Yevgeny had learned better than to attempt the proper, Mandarin name), China's main lunar settlement. The 3800 kilometers from Base Putin, in Mare Ingenii, to the north pole was not *quite* the longest possible lunar flight—that would have been pole to pole—but it was quite far enough.

While his passengers and their Chinese counterparts consulted about esoteric matters, he'd had ample opportunity to wander around. Chaperoned the entire time, of course, and apologetically turned away from a few closed doors. Merely to see which parts of the settlement his hosts considered sensitive conveyed information of a sort. Information that, the case could be made, he did not need, what with China and Mother Russia being friends and allies these days. He kept his eyes open anyway, if merely for the practice. Knowing that today's friends would not always be friends. Cognizant that his designated minder, ostensibly a junior technician, was on the payroll of the MSS. The Ministry of State Security.

Would Moscow respond to the report he would send about this surveillance? Beyond an acknowledgment, or an impersonal request for some further detail, he doubted it. Despite all the State had invested, and continued to invest, on its lunar ambitions, it treated this world as neutral territory—and Yevgeny as all but irrelevant.

Just as he had been finalizing arrangements for the eggheads and himself to spend the night, Nikolay Sergeyevich had emerged from the Chinese mineral-assay lab. "Finished!" the owlish geologist had declared. (In English: the *lingua scientifica* they had all spoken throughout the day, to Yevgeny's unvoiced annoyance.) "I can't *wait* to get home."

And so back they had flown to Base Putin, *another* 3800 kilometers.

Faster than the snippet of music could run its course, Yevgeny banished all thoughts of his too long day. Those few, dramatic measures signaled a communication from somebody aware—and few people fit this description—that *pilot* was his cover, not his job. Even for them, the melody played only when, this being no commonplace datasheet, the device failed to sense body heat. Had he been dressed, the datasheet tucked into his pocket would have vibrated discreetly to herald such an important contact.

Yevgeny vaulted from bed (in slow motion, taking care in the lunar gravity not to drive his head into the ceiling) as the trumpet flourish started over. For a vmail or text, the datasheet would not have rung twice.

An app, parsing the comm delays in the data handshake setting up the call, displayed LUNAR CALLER. He relaxed, just a bit. This was *not* an FSB superior reaching out. It was barely past six am. in Moscow, and any contact from Moscow this early would be bad news. Then again, what other news did the Federal Security Service—by its Russian acronym, the FSB—offer at any hour of the day?

He pressed a thumb against the ID sensor to take the call.

"Gene, hi." Yevgeny's caller had a shaved head, big and round like a bowling ball. And a faded scar running from his right ear almost to the point of his jaw. Also, huge, square teeth. In the right light, Paul Sokolov would make a fine orc. Somehow he *didn't* make women run away screaming. The unadorned mooncrete wall behind Sokolov offered no hints of location. "This is—"

"I know who you are." And you were told that, secure line or not, *we don't use names*. Just as you were told never to call this number except for something important.

"Um, yeah. Right. Sorry."

Sokolov was a second-generation American, his grandparents having emigrated from Novosibirsk. His legal name was Pavel, but he had no use for his heritage. Only for money.

"Anyway, Yev … sorry, I came across something very odd. Something *big*."

When hadn't Sokolov had "something big" to report? But unlike his habitual attempts to inflate his worth and hint about a bonus, he had never before used this priority link. Long-haul trucking gave the man entry to almost every facility on the Moon—including the He-3 mine staffed out of Base Putin—and Sokolov had always reported in person. Perhaps, this once, he did have something valuable to relate.

"Where are you?"

"Guest quarters at Site Tango." Their code for the American observatory on Farside. "Things here aren't normal. Not at all. I can't figure out what's going on."

"Walk me through it."

"Sure. It all started with …."

Taken item by item, nothing Sokolov had seen appeared significant. An unscheduled flight into Daedalus, bringing a package for the man in charge. Judson behaving, or so Sokolov would have it, out of character. Judson holing up in his quarters with the couriered package, then starting to spend an inordinate amount of time with the base paramedic and a maintenance engineer. A water emergency declared to justify confiscating inventory Sokolov was under contract to deliver on his next two stops. That water going into tanker trailers rather than either of the observatory's supposedly depleted underground tanks. A bit of prospecting, and duty-roster shuffling to accommodate it.

But put all that together? *Things aren't normal* was an understatement, even before factoring in a detail Sokolov could not have known. Almost certainly, Marcus Judson was a deep-cover CIA asset.

Even within the FSB, few people knew about Judson, just as few knew the American eco-extremist space-tourists-turned-terrorists had been deep-cover Russian agents. To this day, FSB did not know *how* America had retaken their powersat. But the service did know that, four years earlier, NASA had dispatched Judson to inspect the satellite mere days before the short-lived "terrorist" takeover. That the engineer, who had supposedly evacuated to Earth with the rest of the on-orbit civilians, had not landed with the rest. And that no evidence of Judson could be found for days following his supposed reentry—not until after the powersat's recapture.

"You must have a theory," Yevgeny said. "What is it?"

"They're after something more interesting than carbon," Sokolov ventured.

"Agreed. Any idea what?"

Sokolov shook his head. "I'll hang around Daedalus for a couple of days, see what more I can learn. But to do that I'll need a little extra this month. For expenses and lost pay."

Predictable, Yevgeny thought. Also, not worth worrying about. "Understood. How will you explain staying on?"

"I don't feel so good. My muscles ache, and I'm tired all the time. There's no way I'm up for a long drive." Sokolov slumped melodramatically. "Besides, those issues will give me the opportunity to chat up Donna, the paramedic. Who knows? Maybe she'll let something slip."

Nonspecific symptoms, so no one would be surprised when tests failed to find anything. Sokolov's complaints would be attributed to stress or overwork or malingering, and no one would question his eventual spontaneous recovery. Yevgeny nodded his approval. "That was good work. Report back daily."

"Will do." And Sokolov broke the connection.

From day one, the AI integrated throughout the Daedalus complex had been compromised. Yevgeny had not been told how, because he did not need to know; he inferred a well-placed agent Dirtside had sneaked a compromised microprocessor chip or two into Icarus's server. The exploit, however it had been accomplished, intercepted and copied everything that crossed the local network, including spoken conversations the AI overheard.

Not even the cleverest hack, alas, could circumvent the satellite-based enforcement of Farside's radio quiet zone. The surveillance he *so* urgently needed to examine had yet to emerge from the observatory's lasercom station. Surreptitious uploads had to wait until that station was idle, an FSB-controlled or -compromised satellite happened to be in view, and no person or bot at work on the surface could notice the ground terminal slewing to track the unauthorized target. He hadn't gotten an upload since two days before the mysterious courier flight had landed in Daedalus Crater.

Meanwhile, in just a few hours, *he* had a flight to make. With any luck the critical Daedalus intercepts would be on hand by the time he returned, and Vlad, *his* AI, would already have analyzed them.

Did Judson act on his own, or for the CIA? Yevgeny lacked the information with which even to speculate. Either way, something interesting was afoot at Daedalus. He would bet his pension that the something had little to do with radio astronomy.

Once again behind the closed and locked door of his spartan Base Putin quarters, Yevgeny thought, it's time for someone to reprogram Vlad. Without a doubt, it was artificial. But intelligence? *That* the software was lacking.

With quick swipes of a finger, he highlighted three passages in three separate vid-call transcripts. To the AI's literal manner of thinking, if that were even the appropriate term, these calls from Daedalus to Earth were mundane.

Indeed, the conversations were social. No trigger words appeared in any of the transcripts to have merited bringing any of these calls to Yevgeny's attention. Everyone who had been contacted was on a subject's frequently called list. Not even the call lengths stood out.

Stupid AI.

From Marcus Judson: So, A FEW OF US ARE GOING TO FOLLOW UP ON SOME PROMISING SATELLITE OBSERVATIONS.

From Donna Rousseau: THREE OF US ARE GOING TO FOLLOW UP ON SOME PROMISING SATELLITE OBSERVATIONS.

From Brad Morton: Hon, a few of us are following up on some promising satellite observations.

Later on in the transcriptions, three almost identical justifications for the odd staffing of the expedition. In Judson's case, by putting more into an answer than his wife's question required. In the other cases, awkwardly volunteered.

Three people prepping on short notice for an unusual trip, all reporting home. All reading from—to a *natural* intelligence, this fact was obvious!—a common script. All wrapping up their calls by telling loved ones that they would be hard to reach for a while.

Prospecting for metal? Or perhaps carbon? Both? Regardless, they were all sharing a cover story. But covering for *what*?

The surveillance upload from Daedalus Base, once Yevgeny had finally gotten it, had offered another tantalizing clue, odd enough that even Vlad had flagged it. Scant hours after the suspicious courier flight, the American, within his suddenly *un*compromised private quarters, had connected with Earth. Not only had Vlad failed to decrypt anything from that comm session, but the best FSB software (the best, in any event, that the service had been willing to entrust to Yevgeny) had likewise failed. Even the network address of the originating end of that link was disguised, anonymized, and rerouted beyond his ability to backtrack.

After that secretive terrestrial communication, Judson had begun meeting in his quarters with his script-quoting colleagues. Five times, in fewer days, they had huddled, each get-together running for at least an hour—and throughout, Icarus had no record that a single one of them ever spoke a word. A ménage à trois, Vlad interpreted.

Stupid AI.

The Americans had to be up to something. More, they must be going *after* something. Seizing tankers-full of water, and hence also of oh-two, implied their objective lie far from the observatory, or that they planned to be away from the observatory for months. Maybe both. The several "emergency" fuel cells Sokolov had seen them prepping suggested the same. And—the first-rate encryption and countersurveillance gear sent to Daedalus made this clear—Judson undertook his venture with the full knowledge and assistance of the CIA.

Chapter 7

Neck stiff as a board, shoulder muscles taut as bowstrings, hands and arms cramping from a death grip on the steering wheel, peering through the Plexiglas sheet that convention insisted be called a windshield—no matter the utter impossibility of wind here—Marcus caught himself, once again, grinding his teeth. Ahead lay only undulating ground, long, inky shadows, and, coming into view perhaps fifteen degrees to the right of his present heading, the age-crumbled rim of yet another crater.

This latest obstacle, if he was where he believed himself to be, did not appear on his map display. Maybe, viewed from near-Moon orbit, the crater was unremarkable. Or maybe, he was lost. Tooling around at ground level, one damned crater looked pretty much like the last, and like the one before that, and the … hundreds earlier still. Back even to the Apollo missions, keeping one's bearings in these trackless wastes had been a challenge. At the observatory, the towering, if still incomplete, telescope pedestal had always been his point of reference while working outside.

Since Daedalus, Marcus had had classic rock wailing in the tractor cabin. As often as not, he would caterwaul along. That day, in a retro frame of mind, it had been the Doors. Until "Light My Fire" became too much for a tension headache ….

Making any (or no) speed at all, the continuous tracks of his tractor and the tires of the trailer it towed kicked up impressive quantities of lunar regolith. Without air to keep that dust aloft, the weak lunar gravity served as a passable substitute. Sunlight shining through, and scattering from, that endlessly replenished, slow-to-settle haze kept unending dazzle in his rearview display, shifting and sparkling *just* enough to defeat active glare cancellation. Through that shimmer, about twenty meters behind his trailer, he kept an eye on Donna's tractor, towing one of their water tankers. Those tracks and tires churned up their own backlit clouds, through which, perhaps another hundred meters back, Marcus could just glimpse the final vehicle of their little caravan.

Taking a hand off the wheel, he grabbed his mic. "Brad, close up."

A blast of static was the only response. The dust clouds also played havoc with the laser links on which, still deep within the radio quiet zone, they depended for their comm. "Brad! Shake a leg."

Nothing.

"I relayed that for you, Marcus," Donna sent seconds later, just as he was easing up on his throttle. C&W played in her cabin. As she spoke, the laggard vehicle put on a burst of speed. "You sound fried, by the way. How about I take over?"

"Thanks," he answered. "For repeating the call, I mean. You're a step ahead of me, as always."

As well as correct about him. If he cared to be honest, *fried* did not begin to cover it. But his console showed fifteen minutes till the hour, at which point their schedule had him pulling over and letting the others pass. Much as he would have liked taking up Donna on her offer—Tail End Charlie was, by far, the least stressful position in the convoy—slacking off was no way to lead. "Just a bit tired. I'll finish my shift."

A bit tired. Talk about your epic understatement. But maybe this sleep deprivation would be good practice for being a father—at age forty-five!—of a newborn.

He added guilt to his mental list of nagging concerns. How could he have not thought about, much less texted, Valerie, or Simon, for days?

Maybe a minute later, as his tractor crested a nameless small rise, lidar beeped. Faster than Marcus could react, the vehicle slammed on its brakes. Traction control kicked in almost before he felt the first hint of fishtailing. Almost. With a shudder, tractor and trailer skidded and slued to a halt. Seconds later, his hands shaking, his heart pounding, the reality of yet another near-disaster sank in.

The lurid glow of his brake lights, backscattered by the dust, joined sunlight glare in his rearview display. Through it all, he saw Donna slowing. The laser link between their vehicles would have given *her* ample warning.

What he had almost run into? Keeping pace with the Sun, ever near local sunrise, traveling almost due west as they did, meant—when not circumventing one obstacle after another—driving straight into the shadow cast by his tractor and its trailer piled high with their supplies. His headlights were on, for all the good headlights ever did in daylight.

About a meter beyond his front fender gaped a fissure. It was not wide enough to appear on satellite-produced maps, and from where he had skidded to a stop lidar could not gauge the crevasse's depth—but the crack seemed more than adequate to bust a track or snap an axle.

They had extra tracks and axles, even after earlier mishaps. They had spare of damn near everything—but time. Tyler was certain, though able to give no better reason than hunches and bitter experience, that time was of the essence. "Secrets," Tyler had insisted over and over throughout the hasty, manic preparations, "have a way of getting out."

"Marcus," Donna called. "You want to reconsider trading places a bit early?"

With effort, he released his latest death grip on the steering wheel to pick up the mic. "I guess I should. You will have deduced I almost ran into something. A crevasse, to be precise. We'll need to detour about a hundred meters"—he checked the gyrocompass on his console; lunar GPS satellites, of course, only broadcast where they could see Earth—"to south-southeast."

"Copy that, Marcus."

As Donna turned her tractor and Brad crept closer in his, Marcus pulled up a comm app. For the next few minutes he had nothing to do but wait. For about that long, it looked like he had a sight line to an optical comsat. He tapped out a quick note to Val: THERE'S NOTHING LIKE A ROAD TRIP, HON. WISH YOU WERE HERE.

That was a lie, of course. He *did* wish she could be with him when they arrived.

Road trip, as a label for this journey, anyway, might be the biggest load of crap ever put into words. And it had, at the start, as he and Tyler Pope had been hatching this scheme, been the spook's turn of phrase.

"It's just a damned road trip," Pope had countered Marcus's insistence that he and whatever small team he assembled needed a few days, for the Sun to rise and for planning, before setting out. "Eighteen hundred miles isn't any big deal. Back in the day that's what we called spring break. U. Penn to Fort Lauderdale and back again is farther than that. Me and a buddy made the trip three years in a row, in a thirdhand Camry that was all I could afford. The odometer had rolled over by the time I bought it, and dollars to doughnuts it had rolled over twice.

"No self-driving cars back then, of course. No GPS. Driving through the night, and napping in the car if we both needed a break, we did a thousand-plus miles in one day each way—even *with* the speed traps in every other burg across South Carolina, Georgia, and northern Florida." And added with a wink, "More time that way for the hot, horny, drunk women."

"South Carolina has air," Marcus had said. "The last time I checked."

"And you'll be driving something a lot more reliable and comfortable than my beater of a Camry. Vacuum's your concern? I imagined you'd been trained for that. Anyway, the last time I checked, lunar long-haul truckers—driving in vacuum—make the run between Aitken Basin and Daedalus Base, about the distance you'll be going, in three Earth days. To not outrun the Sun, you'll have to do, what, about 225 miles a day? Easy peasy."

Not even close.

As for *1800 miles*, they only answered a geometry problem: what's the shortest distance between two specific points on a Moon-sized sphere? Nearside, the Earth-facing hemisphere, boasted huge, smooth plains: the naked-eye-visible lunar "seas" that together limned "the Man in the Moon." Never having set boot on the Moon, doubtless that's how Tyler pictured the entire world—no matter that even Nearside had more than its share of mountains, craters, and crevices.

And Farside, fully half of which the three-vehicle caravan needed to cross? *It* must once have been God's own shooting gallery: a pockmarked, chaotic, crater-upon-crater-upon-crater sprawl. Marcus hadn't had time to finalize a route, but to judge from what mapping software had proposed, they would be driving about twice as far as idealized geometry would suggest. Nor could they take one of the observatory's robots to scout ahead, not without going the full distance at a walking pace. *Bots* had too much programmed-in sense of self-preservation to move any faster than that over rough, unexplored terrain. This journey would be more like the Lewis and Clark Expedition (Simon had studied their expedition the year before and, for all his griping, gotten Marcus hooked) than Tyler's damned spring break.

But while pesky facts had left Marcus tongue-tied, Tyler had been on a roll. "And anyway, you can't drive straight through. You need to get out of your trucks, now and again. You need to set up shop and at least *look* like you're prospecting. And remember between those stopovers to zig and zag a bit. You need to sell it."

Have you seen the terrain here? We can't *not* zig and zag. "Who, exactly, is going to be watching?"

"Listen up," Pope had snapped, suddenly all business. "There are eyes in the sky. Always assume someone is watching." Russian eyes, he meant. "Always."

Marcus could not help but wonder how someone so paranoid got out of bed in the morning. All he had said was, "Understood."

Marcus had struggled, before setting out, to find some pretense for getting driving advice from Paul Sokolov. No excuse Marcus had come up with had felt credible even to him, much less stood any chance of passing muster with Tyler. They were not, for public consumption, anyway, planning a long trip. The overabundance of supplies Marcus had told Brad to collect was just for safety. Their caravan would only "happen" to continue meandering west—Tyler's hypothetical Russian watchers were intended to believe—as on-site inspections found nearby locations to be lacking in "ores."

And faster than the rim of Daedalus Crater could slip beneath the horizon in his rearview display, Marcus knew that any experience the trucker might have shared would not have mattered. Sure, Sokolov was an old hand at the Aitken Basin to Daedalus run, and of a half-dozen routes besides, but every lunar "highway" was surveyed, bulldozed clear of rubble, and well marked, the product of a team of engineers laboring for months. Sturdy mooncrete bridges spanned cracks and crevices along the way. A well-stocked emergency shelter and fuel-cell depot sat every hundred or so klicks along the road—in lunar gravity, a practical hike.

Spring break? Road trip? Hah! Where Marcus and his friends drove, there were no roads. And then, waiting at the other end of this slog was ....

Marcus had no idea who or what. No one did. No one *could.* All that said, he wouldn't dream of being anywhere else—

At least once they made it to the end of the nonexistent road.

Their dome shelter, its solar-cell-covered surface gleaming in the Sun, gradually inflated. "Just so you know," Donna began, arms folded across her chest, supervising, "I'd be more than happy to sack out on the floor of my cab."

Brad kept unloading supplies from their trailer, stacking what they would need for the "night" beside the shelter's not-yet-accessible airlock. "Not that I suppose it'll change anything, but I'd also—"

Marcus, who had been unloading and deploying yet other solar panels to recharge their tractors, pivoted at the lost conclusion to Brad's gripe. The three of them had jacked in with meters-long fiber-optic cables to a router mounted to the side of his tractor. A quick look confirmed the expected: the cable had pulled loose from Brad's helmet.

"I got this," Marcus told Donna, who turned back to monitoring the dome. He picked up the loose cable plug and walked it over. Catching Brad's eye, Marcus mouthed, "Lost anything?"

Brad jacked back in. "My marbles? Yeah, at least a day ago. Here's a thought. Daedalus is *way* over the horizon. How about we use helmet radios? It's not like they'll interfere with anything."

Maybe not, Marcus thought. No, almost certainly not. It didn't matter. Whatever any of them put on the air, even at low power, with nominally short-range helmet transmitters, Russian satellites *might* hoover up. Being a nitpicker about Farside protocol took less energy than admitting the possibility of exceptions, then negotiating over how careful everyone promised to be. One careless word—*Tyler, damn you! You've made* me *paranoid*—might blow the mission's cover. "We're on Farside. Except in an emergency, we don't use radios."

"Fine." Brad went back to shifting crates and canisters.

"Done here," Donna broke the awkward silence. "Want me to make a few holes?"

Because, while mere radio silence stymied ears in the sky, to remain credible they had to raise dust for eyes in the sky. And that dust-raising had to look serious. It meant, every stop, kabuki prospecting: surveying around their encampment as though homing in on locations identified by satellite sensors, drilling boreholes, and running (worthless) gravel and regolith through portable instruments. It meant, choosing among the (worthless) boreholes at random, setting off blasting charges, followed by *more* playacting at on-site assays. It was all of a piece with, Donna's wishful thinking notwithstanding, erecting the shelter at every stop rather than suggest pessimism about their latest test site.

"Drill away," Marcus said. He was as bone-weary as anyone, as aggravated after every exhausting slog at putting on a show for hypothetical observers. Perhaps more aggravated, because he got to be the bad guy who insisted on the arduous charade. But pushing onward toward the alien site? He would push *harder*, if he imagined they could have coped.

"Busywork it is." Donna sighed. "Because, just look around. The lunar surface *needs* more holes."

"What do you suppose we'll find?" Marcus asked. "When we arrive, I mean. Any theories?"

He asked only in part as a change in subject. Preparations for this trek, and for keeping its purpose and ultimate destination secret, had all but precluded looking ahead to their arrival. Given the CIA's insistence that they get started no later than local dawn, there hadn't been much opportunity for longer-term planning. And despite their best intentions to plan more while en route, inevitably—after gulping a reconstituted, freeze-dried dinner in the shelter, and calling in, for appearance's sake, to the observatory, and statusing Tyler, and remedying whatever had most recently gone awry with their gear—they needed to sleep. Whether or not they could.

It's under control, Tyler assured Marcus time and again. America's best minds are working the problem.

Maybe they were. Certainly someone Dirtside had compiled a *long* list of equipment for the expedition to bring: little of which Daedalus Base stocked, or that Marcus could have explained withdrawing from inventory if it had, and more than they could have transported had even half of it been available. And when, ill-equipped, they arrived? The experts would walk Marcus and crew through whatever needed doing.

So: quit worrying.

Hell, yeah, Marcus worried. In the few, scattered moments he had found to think since leaving Daedalus (after two near collisions and an axle snapped by driving over a pothole, they had abandoned discretionary conversation, cab to cab, as an existential distraction), he had concluded those experts … weren't. The CIA, DIA, and whatever other three-letter agencies had been looped into this project had precisely the same experience with ancient, alien, high-tech archeological sites as did his little team. None. On top of that, Tyler's Dirtside "experts" understood little about what was possible in lunar conditions, or how things were done here, or how long everything took. Ignorance did nothing to stop Dirtside from relaying their conjectures, recommendations, and directives.

So maybe Farside's comm restrictions were a Good Thing. It was beyond imagining how much "input" Tyler's brain trust would have forwarded, how much additional "dialogue" they would have demanded, given half an opportunity. If they hadn't been limited in their interruptions by the small number of laser-equipped lunar comsats ....

"Find?" Donna yawned. "We'll find more dust. But even traces of organic matter might say a lot about them. If eons of vacuum, temperature cycling, and hard radiation haven't destroyed the residues. At least we know to look for pay dirt near the robot, beneath Ethan's leaning rocks."

"And inorganic dust," Brad added. "Materials traces. Judging from our glimpse of the spacesuit before it crumbled, I'm guessing plastics and metals. Depending on their tech, maybe shards of ceramic." He ventured details, most going over Marcus's head, about how they might best try to sift, sort, and characterize near-microscopic fragments blended in with the regolith. Or, depending on how those trials went, how best to collect dust to truck back to Daedalus. Alas, a vacuum cleaner could do nothing for you *in* a vacuum.

"No alien artifacts? No keys to the galaxy? Where is your sense of wonder?"

Brad snorted. "The wonder is that the spacesuit and its mummy, even in their sheltered alcove, lasted till we saw them. No, I expect only dust. Oh yeah, and to feel foolish about all this secret-agent claptrap. And I'll admit to hoping for a less insane drive back to Daedalus."

"And you, chief?" Donna asked. "What do you suppose we'll find?"

Good question, Marcus thought.

For more than a week now, analyst hordes Dirtside had pored over maps, old and new, assembled from satellite images captured with visible light and IR and radar, at every available wavelength. Nothing yet as much as hinted at artifacts or aliens, of anything more exotic than craters and lava tubes. The more time elapsed without spotting anything noteworthy, the more ill-considered this haste and secrecy and lying to everyone seemed. Nor had the prospecting bot had anything further to report. It wouldn't, at least until the Sun rose there to recharge its batteries.

What *did* he anticipate? "I expect," Marcus said, "the unexpected."

Chapter 8

Outside the inflatable igloo, the Sun still hovered just over the horizon. Unending dawn made Marcus's exhaustion seem wrong—almost more so than the siren song of sleeping pills. But they had managed almost two hundred klicks since their last camp, *despite* Donna's tractor snapping a track. Lunar gravity helped with jacking up the vehicle. Muscle atrophy from months in that same gravity? Not so much. As odious as exercise sounded, he would do some before trying to sleep. They all should.

With well-practiced contortions, he wriggled out of his spacesuit. The mottled coveralls he slipped into were little cleaner than his outside gear. At every stop they tracked more lunar dust into the portable shelter. Even in Daedalus Base, with its top-notch air filtration, with a fleet of Roombas running around the clock, a faint odor like spent gunpowder was pervasive. Here, the stink was overpowering. On the bright side, that smell masked the reek of three people gone a week without a shower. Inside his vacuum gear, there was no denying his own stench.

Brad, wheezing from the dust, finished changing a few seconds after him. Donna emerged soon after from the shelter's tiny toilet compartment. "Who's on dinner duty tonight?" she asked. "I only remember it's not me."

"You sure about that?" Brad said. "Seems to me that—"

The comm console began to chime.

"God *damn* it," Brad swore. "We're supposed to have another forty-five minutes before your CIA buddies bug us."

First thing upon entering the igloo, Marcus had jacked the Agency datasheet into the comm console, but this wasn't his ringtone for messages from Earth. "That's the observatory"—and, till now, as directed, the base had waited for *him* to call. This did not bode well.

He took the call on speaker, audio only. His friends looked as bedraggled as he, too, must. "Judson."

"Glad we caught you." The voice was Jack Soo's. "Well, more so that we caught Donna. I assume she's also there. We've got a situation."

"I'm here," Donna called out.

"We had a bit of a brawl a little while ago in the social hall. Started over baseball, of all damn things, though I'm hazy about the details apart from too many beers. For the most part, we're talking bruises, split lips, and the like. But Larry Erlich has a broken arm."

Donna cursed under her breath. "You're certain?"

"The *crack* sounded plenty unambiguous, his arm sure as hell *looks* wrong, and he can't turn his wrist without yelping in pain. There's no bone sticking out, I'm happy to say, and bruising but no bleeding. I emailed you a picture."

Donna took a look. "I'd need an X-ray to confirm, but sure, everything points to a fracture."

"About that," Jack said. "We have X-ray gear, right? Because I sure can't find it in the infirmary."

"How can you not …?" she trailed off, giving Marcus a *very* unhappy look.

"Give us a second," Marcus said. He tapped MUTE.

Anger radiated off Donna in waves. "Tell me you didn't. You asked me, and I told you it'd be medical malpractice."

The CIA, and not only Tyler, had insisted, albeit without any way to enforce their order. In the end, the decision had been Marcus's. "Sorry, I can't say that. Deep into third shift, a few hours before we left Daedalus"—while, as Icarus had confirmed, she had been snug in her quarters—"I boxed up our X-ray equipment and put it on my trailer. Can you imagine how we'd feel finding even small fragments of a body with no way to view inside?"

"No way?" she echoed, glowering. "Here's a way: sending for the gear when and if we find a use for it. Removing basic medical equipment from Daedalus was *so* damned irresponsible!"

Marcus stood his ground. "There's still an ultrasound machine on-site for imaging. I didn't touch that. But tell me. Who at the observatory, apart from you, is trained to use the X-ray *or* the ultrasound equipment?"

"Larry." Her glower darkened. "Using two good arms. That unfortunate coincidence doesn't excuse you."

"It's no excuse," Brad said, "but at the moment it *is* relevant."

"Fine," she snapped. She toggled off MUTE. "Stop mucking about in my office, Jack. Taking X-rays and interpreting the results both require training. Larry's in no shape to X-ray himself, especially if, as I suspect, he's dosed up on Demerol. You've contacted Aitken, haven't you?"

It's lucky, Marcus thought, this connection is audio-only. There could be no mistaking the anger on her face.

"First thing I did," Jack said. "The ER doc at the hospital eyeballed the same visual you saw. He's pretty sure it's a, um, I think he called it a 'displaced fracture,' and that it'll need surgery. But before he recalls the nearest courier for ambulance duty and a 2500-klick schlep to us, he requested an X-ray to confirm. I told him our paramedic was away, but a lot closer than Aitken, and he said to check in with you.

"So: I found someone who *wasn't* drinking to prep our little shuttle. Satellite shows you guys at about 900 klicks from here. As the rocket-propelled crow flies, that is. I can pick up Donna within the hour."

Donna said, "I imagine Larry told you this, or the ER doc did, but keep that arm elevated, and immobile with a splint and a sling, and use an ice pack wrapped in a towel to keep down the swelling, Jack, till I get—"

"We need another moment, Jack." Marcus tapped MUTE again. "You can't go."

"What the hell? Of course I'm going. Jack can fly me back here in a few hours."

Marcus shook his head. "It won't be a simple in and out. Once you're on-site, everyone who was in that melee will want checking over. Anyone who's had the least ache or pain or twinge or stuffy nose will demand your opinion while you're there. It'll be days before you get back. As for helping Larry, you going sounds counterproductive. The ambulance will retrieve him that much sooner if the ER doc isn't waiting for you to confirm what he already suspects."

"Since when do you make medical decisions?" Donna snapped.

Brad frowned. "These are our *friends*, remember? Either of you ever had a bad break? I have, and it wasn't fun. I'm thinking Larry won't mind a friendly face, and someone on hand who knows what she's doing, even if it's 'only' until the medevac team arrives."

"If they're even needed," Donna added. "If an X-ray shows minimal displacement, they won't be."

Both were right, of course, but whatever pain Larry was in, Marcus's guilt would put it to shame. That didn't matter. "Never mind the time we'll waste parked here, cooling our heels till you get back. How do you propose to explain returning with the base X-ray gear?"

"I'll think of something," she insisted.

"Forget it," Marcus said. "You're not going. We won't, can't, do anything that might raise questions about this outing."

"And you suppose Donna's refusing to help won't raise questions?" Brad asked.

"It won't," Marcus said, "because Donna isn't the one refusing. I'll veto a flight to retrieve her. Folks at Daedalus can blame me for being a jerk."

"'Jerk' doesn't begin to cover it," Donna said.

So be it, Marcus thought. He did not need Tyler to remind him they were on a mission of national security. Who knew what knowledge might be lost to the country, if, as improbable as this seemed, anyone else got to the site first?

He unmuted the link. "Sorry, Jack. Bit of consultation here. We"—the royal we—"think it's better that Larry go straight to Aitken."

"Donna? You agree?"

Marcus locked eyes with her.

"All things considered?" she managed. "Yes."

Marcus said, "Jack, it's best we let you attend to that. And then, please, confiscate whatever beer you can find. You can blame me"—for that, too.

He broke the link.

"You okay, Donna?" Brad asked.

"What do you think?" she said coldly.

Fork in hand, Valerie more stirred than sampled the mush lumps in sauce on her plate. She had already forgotten what she had requested; visual inspection revealed nothing more specific than *slop*. The office cafeteria might be the antidote to trimming her pregnancy cravings.

But Jay Singh had, somehow, finished a bowl of bean soup and most of a big salad. That might signify only the cast-iron stomach of youth, but her money was on him not noticing what he ate. Her tablemate—on the edge of his seat, gesticulating with a half-eaten sesame-seed roll—was nigh onto giddy. His latest prototype, based on neural nets, was having some success. Neural nets, she gathered, combined computer science with cognitive science, the latter itself an interdisciplinary blend of biology and mind studies. She, meanwhile, having dredged up the expression *nigh onto giddy*, was feeling nigh onto ancient, and unprepared to take on yet another esoteric variant of AI.

Or maybe the achy and sleepless toss-and-turn-fest the night previous explained her reticence. She hadn't been stalking Marcus, not exactly. Reverse-engineering the message headers from his texts to infer how far from the observatory he had wandered—better than a thousand kilometers as the photon flew; much farther, she imagined, driving across such rough terrain—wasn't stalking. It did not become stalking, she kept assuring herself, until she began spying through lunar satellites.

"Are you okay, Professor Clayburn?"

"I'm not a professor," she reminded him.

"Sorry. Doctor Clayburn."

"Valerie," she said, not that her past efforts at informality had had any effect.

"But are you okay?"

She followed his averted gaze to the swirled mess on her plate. "Not hungry, I guess."

"But surely, Doctor, I mean, … you must need … I mean, umm, the baby must need …."

"I'm *fine*, Jay." But *not* prepared to discuss pregnancy with you. "So, about neural nets?"

On that topic, he spoke without hesitation. Only his neural net, while making some headway with matching known observations of particular asteroids, had achieved less success with orbit prediction. She nodded along, kept him talking with the occasional question, still trying to grasp the bigger picture. (Marcus snickered whenever he caught her using that metaphor. What picture was bigger, he would tease, than astronomical?)

"So," Jay was saying, "I've been training the neural net with a subset of NASA's primary database from the Near-Earth Objects Program. I'm struggling with the weights to give various classes of asteroids within the database. The thing is …."

She listened with one ear, sensing he was onto something and, at the same time, that some larger context eluded them both. (Marcus, whatever the hell was up with him, having vanished but for the occasional text, would no more have let *larger context* go by without some wisecrack than *bigger picture*. Too bad.)

And that larger context was what? Neural nets? Maybe. She had studied programming, of course, back in her university days. She had written her fair share, and more, of computer code. But neural nets? Multitudes of neurons and synapses simulated on digital computers? Computing modeled in some way on the brain? That was nothing like anything in her experience.

One piece of the puzzle, though, had fallen into place. Like a baby, you *taught* a neural net. Like a baby, you hoped for the best and, after the fact, judged by results. What went on under the hood, or inside the cranium? No one knew.

Hmm. Babies. There's no great mystery what's going on inside *my* cranium.

So: back to Jay's difficulties. If the neural net refused to perform as expected, that might be because it was the wrong tool for the job. She had no opinion to offer about that, much less any insight, one way or the other. But what if the net hadn't been *taught* right …?

"Your training set," she said. "Near-Earth objects, right?"

"Right. We're looking for PHAs"—that was NASA-speak he had picked up: potentially hazardous asteroids—"and that database holds what we know about them."

"Yes, but." She paused for a sip of water. "The thing is, Jay, PHAs are a transient set of rocks. In general, one hits—with luck, burning up in the atmosphere—or something perturbs its orbit and sends it away." And with bad luck, a rock punched right through the atmosphere. When a big enough rock did that, you got—just ask any dinosaur—global disaster and mass extinctions. Which was why any improved means of spotting PHAs and predicting their orbits was so important.

"Something. Such as a gravitational interaction with another planet?"

"Could be. Or with the Moon, or even another asteroid. Or a close encounter with a solar flare. With rocks as large as ten kilometers, sunlight itself can change orbits over time." And what were the chances of a PHA larger than ten klicks having gone unnoticed? She jotted *Yarkovsky effect* on a paper napkin and slid it across the table. "Not my main point, but check this out. Anyway, I'm thinking it might be a worthwhile experiment to expand the neural net's training set. Go beyond near-Earth objects. A broader population of asteroids will exhibit more consistent orbital behavior."

"Thanks." He tucked the napkin, neatly folded, into his shirt pocket. "I'll do that. Any suggestions for where I should go for related data?"

As she spoke about datasets and asteroid populations, her attention kept wandering toward the dining area's entrance. With so many great restaurants in downtown DC, she had not elected to eat in for the culinary experience! There was something she needed to know, and she did not see how to inquire about Marcus's expedition without coming across as a crazy, hormonal preggo. But one of the people most likely to have her answer should be coming through that doorway any minute. Rajiv believed in belts, suspenders, *and* Krazy Glue, and it took a lot to perturb him from *his* daily orbit. When he showed, if she somehow steered the conversation ....

And there, at last, grabbing a takeout tray from the stack at the front of the serving line, was Rajiv. When he emerged from the cashier end of the line no more than two minutes later—arriving just before the cafeteria closed was part of his routine—she waved him over.

"Rajiv, please, join us for a minute. I'd like you to meet someone. Jay Singh is ABD"—all but dissertation—"at GWU. Jay, this is Rajiv Bhatari, our chief engineer."

Looking less than happy about it, Rajiv sat. "Nice to meet you, Jay."

"Doctor Bhatari," Jay mumbled. "Sir."

"Jay's dissertation involves an innovative new approach to orbit determination of asteroids," she said.

She got the men talking, long enough (or so she hoped) to cover for waylaying Rajiv, then interrupted. "Jay. I hadn't intended to keep you so late. Let's do this again next week."

Jay took the hint. "Thanks for the guidance … Valerie. Doctor Bhatari, I enjoyed speaking with you." Seconds later, he was on his way.

"How are things on the ninth floor?" she asked before Rajiv, he of the disposable tray, excused himself to finish the meal at his desk.

He gave a hands-turned-palms-up, you-know-how-it-is gesture.

"That well?" She laughed. "Not anything to do with me, I hope."

He hesitated. "No."

Meaning Farside? Meaning Marcus? And here she had wondered how, nonchalantly, to turn the conversation that way.

"It would appear my uninvolvement is ambiguous. I'm guessing the observatory has fallen even further behind schedule."

"Uh-huh."

She took the plunge. Anyway, subtlety was wasted on either of them. "To be honest, Rajiv, I was shocked when you approved the prospecting trip. Please don't quote me to my husband, but I never saw how removing staff from Daedalus could help. If they had found exploitable concentrations of carbon on day one, it wouldn't mean more steel on hand for, well, months."

"Uh-huh," punctuated this time by the vicious impaling of French fries.

Ah. "You *don't* approve of their little road trip, do you?"

"Between you, me, and the lamppost? No."

"Your staff, then? You went along with their recommendation."

"They agree with me. Ditto both academic experts on lunar mining I consulted. Not that any of us got a look at this supposed super-duper algorithm for locating buried carbonaceous chondrites."

That left … the administrator herself. "You were overruled?"

"Sonja took me aside and told me, 'It's Marcus's show up there. That makes it his call.' After a week's prospecting in which they had found zip, I opined that, as far from the observatory as they had by then wandered, if they *did* hit pay dirt, it would be too remote for them to exploit. You know what? Sonja didn't give a shit."

Disregarding tech staff and her most senior technical adviser? Letting a late project become even later? Both were *so* unlike the administrator's famed CYA style that Valerie was at a loss where to begin. Was it possible Sonja Velasquez, too, had been overruled?

Valerie's confusion must have shown.

"Yeah." Rajiv smiled. "I was speechless, too."

Speechless? Perhaps so. But also more curious—and worried—than ever. Maybe it was time to start stalking Marcus via lunar satellite.

The overdue call found Yevgeny working out in Base Putin's always crowded gym. A quick swipe dismissed the call with a canned I'LL GET RIGHT BACK TO YOU text. Then, as soon as he felt would not have him seem hurried, he went to his room to return Paul Sokolov's call.

"They threw me out," the stocky trucker began without preamble. He sported a fresh shiner. The holo projected over Yevgeny's datasheet was too small to show detail, but perhaps there was other, less dramatic facial bruising. "And Lunar Trucking has me up for a disciplinary hearing the day after tomorrow. If they *don't* fire me and send my ass back to Dirtside, it'll still be awhile before anyone at Site Tango confides in me again. I hope you're happy."

"You're late," Yevgeny countered. Happiness did not enter into their relationship. "Explain. Be specific."

"You said to hurt Larry Erlich." The American shrugged. "I hurt him. In the dining hall, after a few beers, I picked a fight. About baseball, if you can believe it. The Cubs have a shot this season, at least if you look at the standings. Larry comes from Chicago, and I told him the Cubs suck, that they're more than capable of blowing a five-game lead. Shoved him good when he argued. He called me drunk and turned to walk away, so I called him a pussy. He took a swing at me. I hit him back. Yadda yadda yadda, I broke his arm. *Snap.* As they say, what a happy sound. Is that specific enough?"

Happy sound? What? Yevgeny intuited it did not matter. "And then? And why am I only hearing from you now?"

"Because this is the first privacy I've had. Right away, the call went out to the Aitken ER and soon after to Donna Rousseau, the wandering base paramedic. I know, because at first everything was live over the base intercom. They let her know of their medical emergency, that a shuttle was prepping to retrieve her. The head honcho nixed that, said the hospital here at Aitken could just retrieve Larry."

Here at Aitken? That could wait. "How serious was the injury?"

"Left arm, and he's a southpaw. A snapped ulna. The EMT on the medevac flight called it a nightstick break. I gather it's what often happens when someone raises an arm to ward off a blow. Anyway, Larry is in surgery as we speak. I don't know that you'll care, but I was glad to hear they expect him to make a full recovery."

Yevgeny knew about defensive injuries, but had to guess what a nightstick was. The perversity of English never ceased to amaze him. "A blow with what?"

"A sturdy beer bottle. It's what I had handy."

"That was enough?"

Sokolov shrugged. "On Earth, maybe not. On the Moon, though? After however many months of being casual about the prescribed exercise, it would seem Larry's bones aren't what they used to or should be."

"And you know all this how?"

With an index finger, twice, Sokolov lightly tapped a cheek. He had quite the shiner coming on. "Some of Larry's friends decided they didn't appreciate my behavior. After registering their disapproval, they locked me in a storeroom till the ambulance landed, after which—and this will dispose of another of your questions—I was evacced on the flight with Larry. Till the hospital discharged me, not an hour ago, I haven't had any privacy to count on. And not that you asked, but I'll also be fine.

"On the flight to Aitken, Larry was pretty damn chatty after, I have to believe, a happy pill or three too many out of the first-aid cabinet. Not delighted to see me, but, and here's the interesting part, he wasn't pissed at just me. The ER doctor here had asked for an X-ray of the arm before sending a ship—but Judson wouldn't excuse his paramedic from their little camping trip. She was ready, expecting, to go." Sokolov raised an eyebrow. "Donna's a cute little number. He might have a thing for her. Or maybe that's just me."

"Judson overruled the paramedic?" Yevgeny asked. "You're certain?"

"The last things I overheard were Donna expecting to return and Judson muting the link. That's about when Larry was taken to the infirmary and me to a dark and lonely corridor. But yeah, I'm sure. It's what Larry was told."

By way of Icarus, Yevgeny had personnel files for everyone at the observatory. That was how he had chosen the astronomer—the paramedic's understudy—as Sokolov's victim. Donna Rousseau was an experienced paramedic and a professional. Depriving her post of medical support would not sit well with her. Neither would delaying care for a colleague, for hours.

"Anything else?"

"Yeah," Sokolov said. "Also worth noting is that Lunar Trucking put a driver on the flight to Daedalus. He's to return with my rig to Aitken, what with me being 'injured' and all. My pay will go to him till he gets back with my rig, and I can't see he'll be motivated to hurry. The way I figure—"

"You will be compensated." Because Sokolov was too useful, despite the tiresome greed, to lose. "And I *am* sorry for your injuries. You did an excellent job." That final sentence was meant as both compliment and dismissal.

"Why, exactly, did you want me to hurt Larry?"

"Thank you for your report, but I have other matters to attend to." Yevgeny broke the connection.

Why hurt someone at Daedalus? Because now, after this little experiment, any possibility Judson and colleagues had been truthful about their trip had been eliminated. You would not withhold medical care rather than delay prospecting for a few hours, or even a few days. Not even for a stranger.

But to sustain a CIA op? That bunch seldom balked at causing some collateral damage.

Chapter 9

"I'm fine, Mom," Simon said with practiced teenage diffidence. At least he dispensed with the customary eye roll.

"I'm glad." Indeed, Val decided, he seemed fine. It was hard to be sure from the small holo, but he looked taller, or at least thinner, than when he'd left (could it have been only a few days ago?) to spend most of the summer with her parents. Had to be taller, she decided. Mom always cooked as if for an army, and Simon ate—and ate—as long as any food was in sight. The human Shop-Vac, Marcus affectionately called him.

Simon stood in her folks' kitchen, as she did in her own. "You know, I wouldn't have to call Grandma to talk with you if you'd take my calls."

Now she got an eye roll, because no one Simon's age *spoke* over the net. That was so last century. Too bad! She was his mother, she missed him, and texting was no substitute for seeing and hearing him.

"What's new there?" she prompted.

"In Danville, Illinois?" He shrugged.

Fair enough. Try growing up there. Pre-Internet. "So, what have you been up to?"

"How's my little brother doing?" he countered. Changing the subject, sure, but also looking sincere.

He had promised not to reveal the baby's sex to Marcus, and she remained confident that Simon would keep it to himself. Who better than a teenage boy to withhold information? "We had a checkup a few days ago. Everything is going great." And I'm well, too, she added mentally. "I can send you the latest ultrasound. Would you like that?"

"I think I'll wait for the big unveiling."

"So, what have you been up to?" Val tried again.

"Hanging out." Another shrug. "How's Dad faring up there? He hasn't been texting much."

"He's been busy," she managed to get out, as, without warning, a tsunami broke over her. If not as extreme as the mood swings a few weeks earlier, this was intense enough. No, she *hadn't* heard much from Marcus, not for *days*. Even his texts were few and far between. And she was touched, no delighted, no saddened, no conflicted that Simon called his stepfather *Dad*, and anguished that Simon had no memory whatever of his own father, killed in Afghanistan. When had she last told Simon what a good man, and what a great guy, Keith had been? She couldn't even remember. Tears welled.

"Mom! Are you okay?"

With a shiver, she got her feelings under control. She felt embarrassed for the both of them. "Just pregnant. So, is Grandma still around?"

"I'm sure she is." He looked relieved. The view shifted as he picked up the datasheet and began walking. "Here she is. Take care, Mom."

"Bye, sweetie."

Simon relinquished the datasheet and did not tarry.

"Hi, Mom," Val said.

"You're working too hard," her mother answered.

"Just not sleeping well. You remember how that goes."

"I remember how that was in my early thirties. Exhausting. But at your age? You need to take it easier."

With a flash of empathy with Simon, Val changed the subject. And forty-three was not *that* old to be having a baby. Not with modern medicine. "How are you guys doing? Is Simon running you and Dad ragged?"

"Simon is no trouble at all, dear. We hardly see him."

"Mom, he's a teenage *boy*. Who knows what kind of trouble …." Val trailed off as her mother's grin registered. "Okay. What gives?"

"I guess he didn't tell you. It's so cliché: the girl next door. They're cute together."

"But if you hardly see him?"

"Relax," Mom said. "Stacy is a lovely young lady, and her parents are good people. They keep an eye out when the kids are there together."

And another tidal wave struck. Pride and joy at her little boy growing up. Pride and sadness that Simon did not need her as much, or at least not in the same way, as he once did. Resentment at his secretiveness, alloyed with certainty that it wouldn't abate, if ever, for *years*. Crushing sadness about Keith having missed yet another milestone of their son's life. And utter terror—where had *that* come from?—another son might grow up without his father.

"Mom, I have to go," she managed to get out.

"Get some rest," Mom said. "I mean it."

"Bye." Val sagged against a cabinet, her mind still racing. She told herself the panic was all raging hormones and old memories, that Marcus was just busy. But it wasn't that, not entirely. Because the memories were not so old. She and Marcus had only just met four years earlier, when he almost gotten himself *killed* retaking the powersat from terrorists. Now Simon's secretiveness only reminded her of Marcus keeping secrets—because, plain as the damn pregnancy zit on her nose, he *was*. The prospecting jaunt never made sense, not even if it had stayed close to Daedalus Base. Since she had begun tracking the convoy, it had trended westward with the rising Sun. Another few days, at this rate, and the three vehicles would come round to Nearside!

No matter these many churning thoughts and feelings, somehow she was hungry. Starving. For two. She got the pizza box from the fridge, and started on a leftover slice, cold. Marcus wouldn't tell her what he was up to and, as far as she could tell, the NASA higher-ups either did not know or were in on … whatever … with him. Not knowing was driving her crazy.

But maybe she *could* find out more about what was going on.

Her datasheet remained draped across a kitchen counter. She googled LUNAR ROBOT RENTAL. Five companies rented radio-controlled bots, three for prospecting and two for tourists. She would have preferred a prospecting bot: they were rugged and well endowed with instruments. Alas, of the few prospecting bots even available, not one was within a thousand klicks of Nearside's eastern limb. She was disappointed but not surprised: prospectors leased their bots long term, going back and forth over whatever territory they felt had potential.

Tourist bots were another story. For sightseeing, one crater or mare or mountain range was often as good as another. Only sunlit tourist bots were in demand. Why rent a bot that was not just idle, but powered down?

With the new moon still two (Earth) days away, Val had her pick of dozens of tourist bots. Based on the meandering path taken by Marcus and his convoy, she put a deposit on several of the easternmost bots idled within "tropical" latitudes.

As soon as the Sun rose—and Marcus's caravan, as her gut insisted it would, made its Nearside appearance—she would set the closest rental unit rolling his way.

"What's special about this region?" Yevgeny muttered to himself. Even alone, in the privacy and (almost) certainty of a bug-free environment, thinking aloud was sloppy. But putting puzzles into words was the best way to clarify matters. At least *his* mind worked that way—usually. With this puzzle, he had no hypothesis, much less an answer.

His gaze shifted, every several seconds, among topographic maps at several scales and hi-res images from the most recent satellite passes over the same territory. However and wherever he looked, he saw only bleak lunar landscape. This terrain looked no different to him than anyplace else Judson and crew had stopped to survey.

"*Is* anything special about this area?" he tried.

He had no answer to that question, either, except by inference. Every stopover until now had been, at most, a few hours: in Earth terms, a day or so. Now, in a nameless depression not quite ten kilometers across, just outside the much larger Humboldt Crater, barely crossed onto Nearside, the Americans had again made camp. They had been at this location, so far, for more than eighty hours. But no matter how long Yevgeny combed through the satellite imagery, he saw only more of the same surveying and assaying they had performed at earlier sites.

The single novelty in the area was a prospecting robot. Judson's ostensible mission was prospecting. A quick search confirmed Yevgeny's suspicion: a significant region surrounding the robot was subject to a mining claim. Interesting. More interesting was that the claim had been filed scant days before the CIA had made contact with Judson.

Alas, while the existence of the claim was in the public record, the identity of the claimant was not. Only a cryptic code was on file. For several minutes he toyed with asking colleagues in Moscow for help, before deciding that could wait. If a network intrusion were detected, it might tip off the CIA that their operation had been compromised.

Of course, the occupational hazard of spies was seeing conspiracies in everything. Perhaps Judson and company, after much fruitless wandering on their own, had cut their losses by partnering with the unnamed prospector. It made a type of sense, but Yevgeny did not believe it for a moment. He indulged himself with one more mutter.

He studied the maps of the Humboldt Crater area. He reexamined the satellite images. Back. Forth. He stood, stretched, paced. He looked at a holo lunar globe, the roundabout path the Americans had taken highlighted in red.

And then it struck Yevgeny: perhaps the Americans' path only *seemed* circuitous. As a pilot, he saw terrain as something to be flown over and not as an obstacle. Farside was all craters, a topographic mess. Suppose Judson had aimed all along for the site where he now camped. For *ground* vehicles, was the journey indirect?

"Vlad, can you plan driving routes between two points on the surface?"

"Yes," the AI said, "given appropriate parameters. On- or off-road? How optimized? I can solve for shortest time, shortest distance, with an upper bound on the distance permitted from the closest emergency shelter, maintaining line of sight to—"

"How do you accommodate terrain features?"

"By vehicle type, when characteristics of the vehicle are specified, otherwise by assuming a standard lunar tractor."

The mysterious convoy had three standard tractors, but would a tanker or a trailer in tow be more constraining on rough ground? On slopes? Through narrow valleys? It took lots of back-and-forth with the AI, estimating the mass and center of gravity of the cargo each tractor likely carried and towed, but after an hour Yevgeny had an answer—with, Vlad calculated, more than ninety-six percent confidence. Given the scarcity of Farside roads, the volume of water commandeered from Paul Sokolov, and the long list of items withdrawn from Icarus's inventory records in the run-up to the Americans' departure, Judson had driven the fastest practical route to where he now camped. But no amount of introspection nor of Vlad's analyses could answer the question now foremost in Yevgeny's thoughts ….

Why was the CIA interested in that remote spot?

Chapter 10

In the harsh glare of lunar dawn, a quarter klick to the north of Ethan's quiescent robot, Marcus surveyed yet another uninteresting expanse of regolith. With care he positioned metal stakes, then strung twine between stakes to define a grid. A half klick to the east, Brad walked another grid toting their portable mass spectrometer. A half klick to the south, Donna drilled random boreholes in an area they had gridded earlier.

Every bit of it—maddeningly—for show.

"Focusing on one small spot the moment you arrive," Tyler had insisted, "would only draw attention to that spot. Going straight to the bot would do the same. After the effort you made on the road to *not* draw attention to this area, why put it at risk now?"

How about because they were exhausted from the trek, exhilarated at its completion, and consumed with curiosity?

"Typical concentrations of iron," Brad radioed. "Typical lack of carbon. Nothing noteworthy."

"Copy that," Marcus radioed back.

At least on Nearside they *could* use radio. And locate themselves with exquisite accuracy using lunar GPS. And behold, overhead, the gorgeous object that was Earth, at that moment at almost full phase. But none of that got to why they had come!

"Donna? How are things with you?" Marcus radioed.

"Boring," she responded. From tone of voice, she intended the word more as a pun than as a complaint. Days after their confrontation, she had cooled off. Larry's arm *had* needed surgery. Her retrieval by, and to, Daedalus *would* only have postponed that procedure. And Tyler *had* made good on Marcus's promise to get someone with EMT training assigned to Daedalus to backfill for Larry.

"Hah," Brad offered.

"Indeed," Marcus agreed.

And the three of them lapsed, once more, into silence. They could not talk, except inside the igloo, about anything *important*. It did not matter that no satellite-borne camera had the resolution to show fiber-optic cables. Clustering within tether range of one another would just prolong this stage of playacting—and that, none of them could bear. Not after coping with an even dozen mechanical breakdowns along the way. Not after the shock and terror of a meteor shower striking not a kilometer in front of them. Not after a week, and counting, on sedatives to get *any* sleep, alternating with caffeine to stay awake and get anything accomplished. Stress? Circadian rhythms hosed by the unending sunlight because, around and between the solar cells that dotted its outer coating, the igloo was translucent? Donna guessed some of both. Brad did not give a shit which. Marcus only wanted, desperately, eight hours of uninterrupted sleep—and afterward to *find* something.

For the benefit of their imaginary eavesdroppers, Marcus said, "Okay, guys, about dinner tonight ...."

Valerie flitted about the house, multitasking. Washing, drying, and folding laundry. Straightening. Nuking and distractedly eating a frozen dinner, then ordering a bunch more. Listening to an audiobook Jay had recommended, about whole brain emulation. (WBE seemed to be the next step in artificial intelligence after neural nets, digitally mimicking not only swarms of neurons but also the complex neural pathways naturally occurring in an actual brain. A rat brain, in the current state of the art, and a small part of the brain, at that, but still. Crazy stuff.)

Keep busy enough and the house felt merely empty, not lonely.

Every four minutes the datasheet lying open on the living-room coffee table gave a chirp. Sometimes she even managed to hear the signal over the droning narration of the AI book. When it happened, she would dash in, glance at the big wall display, and jiggle the joystick.

Her bot rolled along an undulating straightaway alongside the gently curving rim wall of Legendre Crater. There it was early morning; every little rock and dip declared itself with a long shadow. As long as her bot continued toward north-northeast, its shadow fell to the left without impeding her view forward.

She texted Marcus, who had gone silent—again. He didn't respond. She texted Simon, who at least replied. An emoji was better than nothing. She gave up on the AI audiobook for the night. She swapped texts with an exercise buddy, not that she remembered when last she had made it to the health center. Maybe they should get coffee sometime, Ada proposed. Val agreed, but begged off setting a date.

The datasheet chirped again.

The bot moved toward Humboldt Crater at little faster than a power walk. Ten kph was the top speed onboard software allowed—and then only while a person monitored the terrain ahead. Let five minutes elapse without touching the controls, and the bot reverted to its autonomous pace of three kph. She found that *infuriating*, when terrain maps showed the way forward all but flat as a pancake for the next twenty klicks.

Her joystick connected to the Internet through a datasheet; a bit of code to send zig-left, zag-back-right commands every not-quite-five minutes would be child's play. But the mega security deposit she'd had to put down on the bot stopped her. The day before, while she had been at work, her first bot had managed to trap itself in a nameless little crater. Until Armchair Excursions happened to have someone in the area to lift it out, *that* bot would not be going anywhere but in tight circles. Thankfully, the company assumed responsibility for mishaps occurring in autonomous mode. But the switch to this backup bot had left her farther from Marcus—because he *had* set up camp on Nearside—than when she had begun.

After one more wiggle of the joystick, she stood to wrestle clean sheets onto the bed.

The doorbell rang.

She peeked out the front-door peephole. In the puddle of wan light cast by the porch lamp stood someone she had not seen since the powersat crisis: Tyler Pope. Her heart skipped a beat as she flung open the door. "It's about Marcus, isn't it? Tell me he's okay."

The CIA analyst did not even blink. "He's fine. May I come in?"

"Give me a minute." She started to close the door.

"I'm quite familiar with your bot rentals."

She felt herself staring.

"May I?" She backed up. Pope followed her inside and closed the door. After an index-finger-to-the-lips silent warning, he took something like a fat stainless-steel pen from a suit-coat pocket. Making his way methodically around the living room, he moved the device past table lamps, wall sockets, air-conditioning vents, painting frames, and furniture. His gadget buzzed and hummed twice, but its tip glowed a steady green. "Okay, we're clean."

"You thought my house might be *bugged*?"

"Trust me, Valerie. This is nothing like what you're imagining."

"You have no idea what I'm imagining."

Pope grinned. "I'm pretty sure it's not *this*."

On the big wall display, the bot's-eye view had, yet again, slowed to a crawl. "My first bot didn't 'happen' to trap itself in that steep-walled little crater, did it?"

Pope shook his head. "That's kind of why I'm here. The agency doesn't want people watching Marcus and friends, so we've been monitoring all bots in the vicinity. Alas, you didn't stop when you lost the first bot. Left to yourself, it seemed, you would just keep trying."

Damn straight, I will. "What's this big secret and why are you telling me now? And why didn't you just rent all the nearby bots yourself?"

"You were suspicious about the expedition, and resourceful enough to have tracked them to Nearside. I need to know what you suspected, what you learned, and how. Other people might follow the same clues."

Other people. "Russians?"

Pope maintained a poker face.

She sat on an end of the sofa, gesturing for him to sit, too. "Okay, I suppose I see why you didn't rent scads of tourist bots. A big change in rental patterns might have been noticed. And if you didn't rent them across Nearside, you risked drawing attention to that specific area."

"So we concluded. Now please explain what made you suspicious, and suspicious of what, exactly, and how you've investigated."

She filled him in. "I've been cooperative and more than patient. It's your turn. What do you have Marcus doing, and lying to me about?"

"I *will* explain, and not just so you'll quit playing at Nancy Drew. It hasn't happened yet, or I'd have found a bug here—or in your office, which I had swept before popping by this evening—but anyone who gets curious about Marcus's expedition will also monitor his wife. You can't keep poking around, Valerie, and you can't tell anyone what I'm about to share. Understand?"

"Not just. You said, 'not just so you'll quit.'"

"Yeah." Pope leaned forward. "I don't have a whole lot of lunar experts at my disposal. I suspect you can help."

Valerie's interest in the Moon began and ended with Farside Observatory, the better to explore the much more distant objects that did fascinate her. If Pope did not get the degree of specialization among astronomers, she saw no reason to disabuse him. "What is it, exactly, that I can't imagine?"

Pope explained.

He could not have been more right. She would never have begun to imagine *this*.

The painstaking labor of surveying, gridding, sampling and geotagging, and assaying a large expanse surrounding Ethan's robot was all but complete. Marcus kept telling himself it had not all been for nothing. They had validated Ethan's discovery of iridium—the regolith all around was sporadically tainted with the stuff—if never quite at exploitable concentrations. Some iridium splotches were laced with lead and iron; others (and the pattern, if any, eluded them) were not. But even assuming that these metallic traces counted, the team had yet to uncover any evidence of the aliens larger than, well, traces. As for the heap of mummy dust, Donna and her microscope had yet to spot as much as an intact alien cell. Without basic lab gear like a chromatograph, she refused to hazard a guess—and frustrated Dirtside biologists backed her up—about alien biochemistry.

As for anything larger than the microscopic? Nada. Their handheld ground-penetrating radar unit had added to their knowledge that beneath the dust-choked surface lay ... rock and more dust. Fat lot of good all the rushing about and secrecy, the exhaustion and the duplicity, had done anyone.

Crating yet another regolith sample as, to his left, Donna and Brad did much the same, Marcus thought, *Enough.* Time, huge day/night temperature swings, and an unending sleet of micrometeorites had long since turned to powder anything ancient aliens might ever have left on the surface. That the lone figure in its alcove had endured? It was a marvel. And now it, too, was also dust. Nothing on the surface. Nothing within reach of radar ....

"Guys," he radioed, "I'm on a break." A sanity break. "You know that lava tube on our topo maps? I'm going to take a look."

"Shotgun!" Donna called.

"I didn't know you had an interest in caves," Marcus said.

"I have an interest in a change of scenery, plus you shouldn't go caving alone. Brad, care to come along?"

"I'm a big guy. Caves? Often not so big. Pass."

"Okay," Marcus said. "You keep doing what you're doing. We'll stay in touch."

"Roger that. Be careful."

"Always," Marcus said.

Donna was closest to the lava-tube opening, and he bounded toward her. Together they made their way in long, flat arcs to the map coordinates on their HUDs. There, just above ground level at the base of a rugged cliff face, gaped a jack-o'-lantern grin at least three meters wide. Where "teeth" did not protrude, the opening was almost two meters tall.

Marcus said, "Not quite what I was expecting."

Donna turned toward him. "You sure about this?"

Squatting, he peered inside. The opening faced almost due north, and charcoal-gray and darker rock drank in most of what little sunlight managed to enter. Switching on his helmet lamps, he saw loose gravel and a few fist-sized rocks. It was hard to believe that lava had ever flowed here, or anywhere on this long-dead world.

"Call me curious. I'm going inside. You can wait here, if you wish."

She laughed. "That's not how 'not caving alone' works."

He said, "Brad, you copy all that?"

"I copy. Stay in touch, boys and girls."

"Will do," Marcus said. He stepped inside, careful not to bump his helmet or oxygen tanks. While he looked around, getting his bearings, Donna joined him.

The tube angled downward at about ten degrees, its rock floor all but free of regolith after his first few paces. From the start, Donna had ample headroom, while Marcus walked bent forward at the waist. After about twenty paces, the tube enlarged enough for Marcus to stand straight, although to walk in the low gravity without bonking his helmet still took concentration.

Again and again they encountered scattered chunks of loose rock, doubtless dislodged by meteorite impacts overhead. Where lava stalactites had once descended, only stumps remained. After stumbling twice, he kept his head—and helmet lamps—tipped down toward the uneven ground. Even then, without air to diffuse the light, and with dark rock all around, maintaining his footing was tricky. After his second stumble, Marcus set his headlamp beams on their tightest focus. The walls all but vanished into the gloom.

"You still"—*crackle*—"us?" Brad radioed.

"We're fine," Marcus said. "But you're breaking up."

"… Breaking up." *Crackle.* "… deep?"

"Yeah, I suppose we are getting pretty deep. The tube slopes down and, at least the way I read the topo map, we've moved under some upthrust terrain. We'll turn around soon."

"… py that."

Donna grabbed his elbow. She had a fiber-optic cable jacked into her helmet and offered him the other end.

He jacked in. "What's up?"

"Look around. Really *look*."

He turned his head slowly, sweeping the overlapped beams of his helmet lamps across the nearest wall. Paler than near the tunnel opening, he decided. And smooth? He could not feel any texture through pressure-suit gloves. And the tube floor, as pale as the wall, although it continued to slope downward, had become flat from side to side.

"This isn't natural," she said.

"Not even close," he agreed. "It's as if someone lined the tube with mooncrete. We should keep going."

Ahead of them, the passageway curved left. They rounded the bend.

"We have an artifact," Marcus announced with satisfaction.

"A relic," she countered. "But wow."

A robot, built like a small tank. On dual treads, one snapped, for propulsion. Rather than an artillery barrel, two telescoping arms, terminating in mismatched grippers, protruded from its turret. The main body was about a meter and a half long, and half a meter both wide and tall. The squat turret added another quarter meter of height. Here and there, but mostly around an access panel into the turret, the metal surface bore scratches. There was no obvious power source, and he guessed fuel cells or rechargeable batteries.

"That should be fun for someone to study," Donna said. "Do you think we can do better?"

"One way to find out."

The passageway again curved, this time to the right. They rounded this bend and—

A prone figure. Bipedal, but *enormous*: at least two and a half meters long, and a good meter across the shoulders. Apart from a large yellow patch, applied just above one of the bulky boots, what they could see of its pressure suit, all in emerald green, appeared intact. Unlike Marcus's suit, all blotched and stained with regolith, this suit was spotless. And, on second look, the body was not quite prone: it was up on one knee. An arm—with double elbows, and a two-fingered, two-thumbed hand—stretched ahead.

Marcus began taking close-ups with his helmet camera, forgoing an I-told-you-so about having brought X-ray gear. "It's as if he"—with no reason to suppose a particular gender—"died crawling. But toward what?"

Donna crouched for a look through the side of the visor. "He reminds me of our friend from Ethan's video." She stood. "Let's go a bit farther."

They gave a wide berth to the remains, lest those, like what Ethan had found, crumble at a touch. The tunnel continued curving, and they kept walking, until it terminated in a concrete barrier. Traces of the ubiquitous regolith had found their way even down here, whether hitchhiking on alien boots or bounced down the tunnel over the ages, by meteorite strikes and moonquakes. Apart from a few random-seeming grooves near the floor, the wall was smooth. At its center was shiny metal: the outer hatch of an airlock. They took turns peering through its gray-tinted, inset porthole. The view within was murky, despite helmet lamps scant centimeters from the porthole. Marcus guessed the glass was polarized. The airlock was empty.

The inner hatch also had a porthole. *It* was black and utterly opaque. Polarized at right angles to the first porthole, he deduced. It would have been nice to catch a glimpse into the alien facility, but the aliens must have liked their privacy.

"Brad needs to see this," Marcus said. "Brad!" he called. "Brad, buddy, are you there?"

In response came only static.

"We're too deep," Donna said.

"Must be. We better get back up." Because Tyler *really* needed to hear about this.

They reversed course. Past the alien. Past where tunnel walls and floor reverted to native lunar rock. Past a narrowing in the passageway too constricting for two to walk abreast, and they undid their fiber-optic link. Past a bend to where loose stones again lie scattered on the uneven floor. Ahead, just beyond the entrance, silhouetted against a star-spangled sky: a helmeted figure. Brad.

"Guys!" Brad radioed, sounding frantic. "You need to get up here."

"We're fine." They were on a secure channel, but rather than spoil the surprise, Marcus added only, "C'mon down, buddy. Have a look."

"No! Outside. Now!" Brad turned back the way he had come. "Move it!"

"Roger that."

When, minutes later, Marcus exited the tunnel, he understood. Perhaps a kilometer away, about midway between them and the igloo, a lunar shuttle descended on its final approach. Marcus wondered, how could Tyler already know? We haven't even called in the find yet.

But as Marcus dialed up ZOOM mode on his visor, he knew better. The side of the approaching shuttle bore a flag. That emblem was red, white, and blue—with but a single broad stripe of each color.

The Russians were coming.

SECRECY

Chapter 11

Like the furrows of a plowed field, row upon row of boot prints scored the regolith: a survey pattern. Serpentine tread tracks approached from the west, made by the commercial bot inert at mid "field." More widely separated sets of tread and tire tracks came in from the east, made by Judson's convoy. Those vehicles and an inflated shelter huddled close at hand. Pits, perhaps test bores, and gravel heaps from those pits, dotted the landscape.

It's how a mining-claim site might look, Yevgeny thought, completing his second low, circling pass, eyeballing several flat and more-or-less rubble-free expanses as candidate landing zones. But the dark blue, pressure-suited figure bounding *away* from that "field" with great kangaroo leaps, following a double line of boot tracks? That seemed no more normal than the anxious voice on a traffic-control channel: "Shuttle on approach near Humboldt Crater, this is a … um … restricted area."

A man's voice. Not Marcus Judson: Yevgeny had samples of Judson's voice from Dirtside. Brad Morton, then, information Yevgeny had no innocent reason to hold and no reason to admit. Stressed, without a doubt. Morton might be the amiable big lug suggested by his dossier, and just as Paul Sokolov had described. Likely Judson had had to scrounge up support staff for … whatever this expedition was about.

As had Yevgeny. In accent-free American English, he responded, "Person broadcasting from the vicinity of Humboldt Crater, what do you mean, restricted?"

What he wanted to know, but there was no point in asking: was it pure bad luck that Morton had looked up at just the right time to spot this ship? Or was this site being surveilled by satellite, and so the American team had been alerted?

"We're working a mining claim."

Yevgeny glowered at the three people in the back cabin, interrupting their boisterous discussion of the barren terrain beneath. Odd details and bold speculations about the Americans' expedition had brought him this far, but his recruits knew nothing. A cash bonus for fieldwork had sufficed to entice two of them; supervisory arm-twisting had convinced the third to "volunteer." Inducements and coercion alike had taken behind-the-scenes string-pulling; he would know soon enough whether involving Moscow in his investigation had been wise—or career limiting.

He radioed, "We are conducting a scientific survey. Your mineral rights are not an issue."

"I, um … if you … you being around will get in the way of our work."

"We'll be on the ground soon, and then we'll come over and introduce ourselves. Sort matters out."

The cockpit scanner flagged Morton's transmitter jumping to another frequency band, the associated transmission all clicks, hisses, and static. Of course, helmet comps lacked the capacity to manage any encryption scheme that was at all secure; the FSB software long since downloaded into the shuttle's comm console needed mere seconds to break into the private channel. "… in, damn it. Marcus. Donna. Come *in*. Now!"

No response came, and Morton kept running. "Guys, we've got a situation … on our … hands. Get out … here!"

Winded, Yevgeny decided. Not, this time, at a loss for words. Over the open channel, he radioed, "See you soon."

"That's really … not necessary," Morton insisted over the same channel, verging on breathless, skidding to a halt near the yawning mouth of a lava tube. "We're very … busy. Maybe give us a … call in a few days?" Returning to the private channel, he added, "Guys! You need to get up here."

This time, a weak, crackling voice responded on the private channel. "We're fine. C'mon down, bud … a look."

"No! Outside. Now!" Morton insisted. "Move it!"

Yevgeny vectored in for a landing, more than a little curious why Marcus Judson sounded so exuberant. By the time he had set down the shuttle, the Americans had emerged from the lava tube. As soon as everyone was suited up, Yevgeny led his team toward the tube's entrance; the Americans, moving briskly, set a course to intercept.

"Can we help you?" Judson radioed on an open channel.

"We're doing a geological survey." Yevgeny pointed behind the Americans. "We're particularly interested in lava tubes."

Judson said, "I'm afraid looking at this one won't be possible. This whole area is covered by a mining claim. Your mere presence could compromise our work here."

Yevgeny and his team kept walking. "We will be careful."

"A moment, please," Judson said. The Americans paused where they were, helmets touching as they consulted, mics off. Too bad, Yevgeny thought. If only they had switched to a "secure" channel, he would have had a decrypted transcript waiting for him back in the shuttle. He found it instructive that they had taken the extra precaution. As the gap narrowed to perhaps a hundred meters, he motioned his team to stop.

The middle by height among the three Americans—that would be Judson—separated from that group, and Yevgeny loped ahead to meet him. Halfway there, glancing back over his shoulder, he saw Ilya and Ekatrina waiting as directed. Nikolay had wandered off a few paces to kneel in contemplation of a rocky outcropping.

The Americans all wore fishbowl helmets, and at five meters the identification was unmistakable. As in the pictures Yevgeny had studied, Judson had strong features and an intelligent, purposeful gaze. Unlike those dossier photos, he had dull skin, bloodshot eyes, and several day's start on a salt-and-pepper beard.

As they converged, Yevgeny said, "We have every right to do our survey."

"Let's start over. I'm Marcus Judson, director of the Farside Observatory." He regurgitated the pretext about a carbon shortage, almost word for word per the script all three had recited before their convoy set out. The twitching eyelid was an impressive touch; the hint of tremor in his voice was overdone. Innocent miners, concerned about their claim? Hah! Such dramatics only reinforced Yevgeny's skepticism. "This is the first really promising spot we've found."

Judson had not identified his companions—because a paramedic and a mechanical engineer did not support the pathetic cover story?—so neither did Yevgeny introduce his. "Yevgeny Rudin, pilot from Base Putin. Congratulations if you have located something useful."

"Good to meet you, Yevgeny. I appreciate you understanding."

"I understand that no one owns the Moon, or any celestial body. That is international law. Hence, your claim applies only to mineral rights. Subsurface rights. Everyone has the right to free passage, and right now, my colleagues and I will pass over to study that lava tube."

"The thing is," Judson said hurriedly, "we've also claimed tunnel rights. The lava tube is the start of a tunnel we'll be making for our subsurface explorations. Sorry."

Tunnel rights? The mining claim on file made no mention of them. But if there were such a thing as tunnel rights, one of the other Americans might be netting to Earth even now to file for them, while Judson stalled.

Enough! *Something* important must be inside that lava tube. "We *will* have a look, before your digging disturbs the natural formation. Let your lawyers do their worst." Sidestepping, Yevgeny called to his team. "Ekatrina. Gentlemen. Let's have a look."

The American leapt backward, blocking Yevgeny. "I, uh, would like to check in with my superiors. Before this situation gets too complicated. Would you mind waiting aboard your shuttle? Just for a short while."

As I shall report to *my* superiors. Judson's consultation confirmed, however obliquely, that more than mineral development was at issue here. "The administrator of NASA."

Judson did not bat an eye. "Yes."

"Meanwhile, you and your people will return in your shelter? And the robot will remain where it is?"

"Not to worry, we could all use a rest. And forget about the bot, it's junk. Didn't make it through the last lunar night. Evidently, the battery gave out and something critical froze. It's not going anywhere."

The bot's solar panels were oriented to snag the final rays of the setting Sun—useless now, in the lunar dawn. Perhaps the bot *hadn't* survived the nocturnal deep freeze. "All right," Yevgeny said. "We will wait, for now."

Because if any of the Americans did leave their portable shelter—or radar showed any ship headed this way—he would have his shuttle up to the lava-tube entrance in a flash. There was, alas, nowhere nearby suitable for setting down; the team would have to hop out while he hovered.

"We will wait," Yevgeny repeated.

"I'll be in touch," Judson said. He and his colleagues strode toward their shelter and, Yevgeny assumed, an ultrasecure CIA comm link to Earth.

"Can you keep them out?" Tyler Pope responded to Marcus's report, not even commenting on the incredible discovery. The three-second comm delay made Pope's customary imperturbability that much more trying.

"Keep them out." Marcus repeated. "How the hell would we do that?"

Another interminable three seconds. "I'll take that as a no." An only slightly shorter pause. "Wouldn't do any good, anyway, in the long run. Any show of force would only further convince your Russian friends the lava tube holds something important. They'd be back, soon enough, and more than four of them." Tyler stroked his chin for awhile. "Okay, this is above my pay grade. Stay put for now. Let me know ASAP if any Russians leave their shuttle."

"Show of force?" Donna mouthed.

"While what happens at your end?" Marcus asked.

"First, I do my due diligence, in particular with your helmet-camera footage from inside the lava tube. Standard procedure. Once that checks out, I'll run this news up a very short chain."

"Up to whom?" Brad asked.

"I expect to the president." More chin stroking. "Yevgeny Rudin. Flying out of Base Putin. Do I have those right? Good call, by the way, getting his picture, too. I'll run facial rec."

"Guys?" Marcus asked.

"That's what I heard," Donna said. Brad just nodded.

"You have it right," Marcus said.

"Rudin called out to Ekatrina and gentlemen," Donna offered. "His people were too far away to gauge anything but their heights, but on that basis two men and a woman would fit."

Tyler nodded. "All helpful. Okay, sit tight. But if Rudin or any of his folks make a move toward the tunnel, you go along."

"And do what?" Donna asked. Demanded.

"Know whatever they're seeing," Tyler said. "If they go in as deep as the mummy, well, then the jig is up. At that point you'll need to show them the footage of that first alien crumpling at a touch. It might convince them to take things slow. And keep me in the loop." Yet another long pause. "That's also when you'll need to start keeping any dissembling to a minimum. It's too easy to get tripped up in a lie.

"Still, good call lying about the bot. It might be our ace in the hole. To sustain the illusion we'll leave its solar panels vertical and facing west, as they were at local nightfall, even though Ethan tells me that means it won't begin recharging till local noon, and then starting with a trickle. And two last things …."

"Yes," Marcus asked.

"Try not to worry, and good job." The holo went dark.

Had the need to feign composure not trumped Marcus's need to pace, the cramped inflatable shelter would have done the trick. Instead of pacing, he kept his friends—and himself—busy. Watching the Russian shuttle through the camera mounted atop the shelter. Poring over the footage from Donna's and his helmet cameras. Reassuring Donna that "show of force" had been a fleeting comment, as quickly dismissed, and that surely Tyler had never expected them to confront the Russians. Speculating what might lie beyond the aliens' airlock. Worrying who besides the Russians—and, according to Tyler, Valerie—had seen through their prospecting-trip charade. Prepping dinner, although they were all too anxious to care. Ignoring, beyond texting KINDA BUSY HERE, Valerie's emails. And sneezing. A lot. The dust, worse every time they reentered the shelter, had all but depleted Donna's supply of antihistamines; she had set aside the rest for emergencies.

Above all, waiting for Tyler to radio back with some presidential guidance.

As Washington dithered, Rudin marched his team to the lava tube. Marcus and company hastened to follow. And Dirtside deliberations began anew, this time between the White House and the Kremlin ....

Presidential guidance, when at last it arrived, divorced from its many circumlocutions, amounted to: cooperate with the Russians. Watch everything they do, while sharing with them as little as practical. Make do with the gear on hand, and with the people already on-site, because any resupply risked drawing further unwelcome (Marcus read that as "Chinese") attention. Nor could anyone leave, lest anything there was dangerous or contagious—without the slightest hint when that precaution might be lifted. Report in at least daily. Assume Rudin and company have similar orders from their political leadership. Do *not* screw up.

As for the president's assertion that the Russian contingent would have received like directions, she was almost correct. Yevgeny's orders had included one additional element.

That accidents will happen ....

Chapter 12

At an all-clear *chime* from the tractor console, Marcus popped his helmet, unslung his oxygen tanks, and stowed both inside a locker. Leaving on the rest of his vacuum gear, he slipped behind the steering wheel. The seat felt all too familiar. "Make yourself comfortable."

On the tiny cabin's passenger side, Yevgeny followed suit. The Russian was of average height and wiry build, his face sporting the sort of even, all-over stubble that took a serious commitment to maintain. His brown, wavy hair had begun to recede. His gaze was penetrating, his deep-set eyes a pale, somehow calculating, blue. Or maybe they only seemed calculating because Tyler had uploaded a CIA dossier naming Yevgeny Rudin an FSB agent. A spy.

Not that the dossier had revealed much. Rudin had been abandoned in Volgograd as a newborn, then raised in a series of state orphanages. His childhood—an ongoing, brutal competition with other wards of the State for opportunities and attention—had, Company shrinks opined, instilled "serious trust issues." (Did any spy anywhere *not* have trust issues? Tyler exhibited more than his fair share.) Rudin had excelled from an early age in math and languages. He enlisted in the Aerospace Defense Forces Branch at eighteen, as young as the ADFB would take him. There he became an aeronautical engineer and fighter pilot, flew combat missions in Syria, rose to the rank of colonel. After five years piloting orbital military shuttles, he abruptly retired—recruited by the FSB, the dossier asserted—to fly shuttles on the Moon for Roscosmos, Russia's equivalent to NASA. And now he had shown up here. He was, it seemed, a *talented* spy.

Settling into the passenger seat, glancing about the confining cabin, Yevgeny said, "I am quite accustomed to tight quarters. Still, I must admit, I would not have cared to drive half the distance you did."

"Yeah," Marcus agreed, "this is pretty cozy."

Only there was nowhere *but* a tractor cabin to meet face to face. Rudin would not permit Americans aboard his shuttle, and Tyler—putting the words into Marcus's mouth—insisted that no Russian ever enter the inflatable.

Marcus hadn't brought bugging devices. Why would he have? Perhaps Yevgeny hadn't, either. But with the right design file (and Marcus figured it was only a matter of time till Tyler uploaded one), printing out bugs ought to be straightforward enough.

Yevgeny smiled. "Then we should come to the point. How shall we proceed? Our organizations expect us to cooperate."

Our organizations. Tyler had been adamant that Marcus not admit to any CIA involvement. If the Russian even suspected Marcus had an inkling of him being FSB, would leaving that phrase unchallenged be as much as admitting to Marcus's own CIA ties? But what if Yevgeny didn't suspect? Was that wording innocent or a trap?

Marcus temporized. "The two space agencies? Yes, I suspect so."

Yevgeny arched an eyebrow.

"Anyway," Marcus went on, "I imagine you've given the matter some thought." As had Donna, Brad, and Marcus, even long after Tyler and his cronies had dropped off the secure link to permit the team from the observatory a few hours of sleep.

"How?" Yevgeny said. "Keeping things simple. You and I meet each morning to decide upon that day's activities. Our people work side by side. We share our findings."

If they were to make progress, how else but by sharing could this work? Only everyone expected the Russians to share as little as possible, and Tyler had told Marcus to do the same. That was why *side by side* mattered.

"That could be doable," Marcus said. Because Yevgeny's companions—at least to the CIA's best knowledge—were innocent technocrats drafted from Base Putin. Like Marcus and his team. They should be able to keep an eye on each other.

"Not exactly enthusiastic." Yevgeny chuckled. "Fair enough. Yes, assigning two persons to every task will often mean wasted resources. And yes, my group is one person larger than yours. This being so, may I assume you won't mind if one of us sometimes works aboveground unchaperoned to sustain the illusion?"

The illusion that all this activity concerned lunar minerals and geology.

Did Marcus mind? Perhaps. An alien body on the surface had brought them here; artifacts or more bodies might yet remain on the surface. And perhaps not. Days his team had spent searching had yielded nothing alien outside the lava tube.

Yevgeny took hesitation as a no. "Seriously, you object? You suppose it would be better that some explorations should have *three* people assigned?

No, not better. Maybe, not even necessary. "Your gear has helmet cams? And the recordings are time-stamped?"

"Of course."

"Ours, as well. We could record everything that goes on, then swap files."

Yevgeny nodded. "We can do that."

Because the Russians planned to share what they found? Or because Yevgeny would Photoshop the files before handing them over? Or because the FSB had a way to embed a virus or Trojan or backdoor or yet nastier nastyware in a vid file? Suppose that last case. Then wouldn't Yevgeny decline to take American helmet vids, just as he refused to let Americans aboard his ship? No. He would accept and archive the files, unaccessed, lest Marcus tried to sneak in malware. Or he would dedicate an offline computer to viewing the American helmet footage. Well, Marcus could spare a datasheet for that purpose, too.

Sigh. To swap files—of any kind—or not. Yet one more detail to run past Tyler.

"Then are we in agreement?" Yevgeny prompted.

"I believe so. But I'm eager to begin"—which had to have been the first sincere utterance Marcus had made since they had met—"so let's defer the file-swapping mechanics for another time."

"Very good," Yevgeny said. "Shall we gather our people, make some introductions, and get to work?"

"Sounds like a plan."

They retrieved helmets and oxygen tanks from lockers. Marcus depressurized the cabin, blasting out some of the regolith they had tracked in with them, and popped the door. After you, he gestured.

Though the cab's keypad lock was doubtless inadequate for deterring spies, he made sure to engage it. He took a mental note to ask Tyler for designs to print motion detectors with a radio-alert feature. Nor would such sensors go only into their tractors; their inflatable shelter, as flimsily protected, also needed one.

Till then, the CIA datasheet would remain in Marcus's pocket any time he went out.

"I'm *fine*, Simon." Valerie smiled at her datasheet to emphasize the point. "I'm on bed rest only as a precaution. The doctor is a worry wart."

"I'm worried about you," her son repeated.

Simon had accomplished the seemingly impossible: looking spindlier than when they had last spoken. Was it even doable to keep teenaged boys fed? Or maybe he had shot up another inch. All she knew was, she missed him terribly. Until this summer, he had never been away from home for longer than overnighters at a friend's house.

He had called from the quad of the college hosting his sailing camp. An unseen breeze rustled leaves and tousled his sun-bleached hair. A squirrel ran up a tree. Cottony clouds scudded across an azure sky. What she wouldn't give to be outside herself!

"It's just a precaution," Val said again. "Grandma shouldn't have bothered you with this." And if not for hints from her parents about them all maybe coming for a visit, *she* would not have told *Mom*.

"A precaution against what?"

Val was *not* about to discuss an incompetent cervix with her thirteen-year-old son, especially when it, and the corresponding prescription for bed rest, were CIA-invented fictions. But necessary fictions: knowing what Marcus was up to, she *had* to be involved. And that meant having an excuse to stay home. Alone.

"Can we let it go at 'lady stuff?'"

"Umm. I talked to the counselors here about catching a flight home. With … Marcus away, someone needs to be there with you, helping."

Marcus. Not Dad. Why *wouldn't* Simon be angry? And someday, when the truth came out, angry at them both. Would he ever trust either of them again? Her heart sank.

"It's sweet that you're concerned, but honest, everything is under control. And as for Dad, he had a friend"—calling Tyler a friend was the least of the whoppers she had told of late—"arrange with a concierge service to do whatever I need. Bring in groceries, mow the lawn, pick up and drop off my laundry. You name it. Truly, sweetie, I want you to enjoy the summer we planned. As does Dad. I'll be fine."

The *Dad* mentions each brought a fleeting frown. "And you'll call if you need help?"

"Promise." Out of sight of the datasheet's camera, she rapped hard on the coffee table. "Listen, Simon, I gotta go. Someone's at the door. Love you."

"Love you, too."

She broke the connection before she had to lie about anything more. Simon, her parents, her sisters and their families, her boss and coworkers, earnest young Jay Singh, close friends and good neighbors … she had lied to, and pushed away, all of them. For the best of reasons, she told herself. It still *felt* wrong.

Secrecy. Deception. Guilt. They were eating her alive. She could not imagine how Marcus stood it.

In the long shadow of a massive, somewhat pyramidal boulder, the seven explorers formed a loose circle, linked helmet to helmet in a daisy chain of fiber-optic cables. Gathering in shadow allowed them to forgo polarizing filters, to see one another's faces and not just pressure-suit colors and personalizing decals.

Marcus only half-listened to the getting-to-know-you small talk. What's your specialty? Where are you from? Are you married? Any children? How long since you've been Dirtside? Where did you go to school? He knew all that and more from a CIA upload (even if, in the quick skim that was all Marcus had managed to find time for, the dossiers—apart from Yevgeny's—looked to have come in significant measure straight from public records). It begged the question how much Yevgeny already knew about the American team. Shave off Nikolay's unkempt new mustache and all three Russians were the spitting images of pictures in their Agency dossiers.

And so, while others spoke, Marcus observed—noting that Yevgeny did the same.

Nikolay Bautin had the sturdy physique, leathery skin, and tanned, deeply lined face one might expect of a long-time field geologist. The man had an owlish, tentative air about him, from his shuffling gait to the hesitant manner with which he had hung back (to the extent the comm cables allowed) as everyone became acquainted. For all Nikolay's accomplishments—and anyone with a PhD from Moscow State Geological Prospecting Academy was accomplished—he was shy and apologetic. According to the CIA's dossier, Nikolay had once, absentmindedly, excused himself to a door he had bumped into. Forty; divorced; no serious relationships since; no children.

Ilya Orlov was, in a word, stolid. He was broad-shouldered, with a round, wide face, a broad forehead, and salt-and-pepper hair almost as thick as fur. He did not smile, but sometimes, as he spoke, Marcus glimpsed patently fake teeth from the man's hockey-playing days. And while Marcus's first impression was *peasant stock*, that was, beyond judgmental, wholly unfair. Only a genius earned a PhD in experimental fusion physics from Moscow Institute of Physics and Technology, much less a tenured faculty position there and a lunar sabbatical. At fifty-nine, the oldest member of either group. Married to a flutist in the Moscow Philharmonic. One grown child: a son, an economist at Lukoil.

Ekatrina Komarova was short and wiry, with a coiled-spring air about her. She was blond, with an asymmetrical, short bobbed hairstyle somewhere between tousled and messy, more or less Swede meets Slav. The engineer was all business: no-nonsense in expression, clipped patterns of speech, and even her restrained gestures. Also, prickly—behavior some nameless CIA shrink chalked up to insecurity from a working-class background and childhood hardships. Ekatrina had been the first in her family to attend college, a financial struggle after her father's death in a naval disaster. (Marcus only vaguely remembered the *Kursk* incident. He had neither interest in, nor any time for, the twenty-some pages the Agency had provided about that sub's loss with all hands near the turn of the century.) Her dossier also stressed defensiveness about the provincial school, Murmansk State Technical University, she had attended, and that she held "only" double master's degrees, in electrical engineering and computer science. Supposed neuroses notwithstanding, Marcus was impressed with her practical, hands-on experience in rocket guidance systems, robotics, and AI. At thirty-seven, the youngest in either group. Single and unattached.

The women were first to segue from social pleasantries to discussing their assignment: photographing and X-raying the mummy from every possible angle. That shift set Ilya and Brad to discussing their task, using cameras and laser range finders to capture every twist, bump, dimension, and change in texture of the lava tube and the wall with which it terminated. Only once both projects were finished—and Dirtside archeologists gave the go-ahead—did they dare risk any physical contact with the body or the alien airlock.

Yevgeny projected over a swelling cacophony. "It would appear the introductions are done. You will do better to finish planning in your small groups."

"I suppose I can talk to myself as I survey," Nikolay said. "Oh, wait. I *am* supposed to talk to myself."

Because hackable, scripted radio chatter was essential for whoever might be monitoring—as the Chinese, Tyler had grimly promised, would be. And so, Nikolay and Dirtside experts had had two interminable conference calls, debating what sorts of things—at once geologically significant enough to merit the team's continuing presence while mundane enough not to attract anyone else—*should* be overheard. The debate over which obscure minerals they might "find," much less how such discoveries were reconcilable with satellite imagery, soon went over Marcus's head. He left sanity-checking all that to CIA assets.

As Marcus fretted about who else might show up to further complicate the situation, two of the Russians reached up to unplug their fiber-optic cables. He hastily reminded, "Everyone, cameras on at all times as you work. We meet back here no later than five."

He caught Yevgeny's arm as the Russian went to unjack the cable between them. Marcus said, "I feel I know your folks a little better. But you haven't shared much about yourself."

"Let us not pretend. You will have read all about me. About the four of us."

And you about me and my guys. "Give me something personal, Yevgeny. Anything. We're going to work together, I suspect, for awhile."

"Very well. My favorite food is New York-style pizza. Pepperoni."

"Small moon. Me, too."

The Russian smiled. "In fact, you prefer sausage and mushrooms, on a thick crust. You once likened thin-crust pizza to ketchup on cardboard."

Jesus! What did the FSB *not* know about him? Then scarier implications hit home: that the FSB had been watching him. They must have decided, after the PS-1 incident, that he was with the CIA. Which, in a manner of speaking, Marcus was.

"As long as we're being so candid, I have another question. Your colleagues are talented people, because who else gets to the Moon, but why bring them? I mean, specifically them?"

"Candid?" Yevgeny shrugged. "Very well. It is a reasonable question. The short answer is, we had no more to go on than the public, not very credible, explanation for your excursion."

We? More Russian spies, perhaps. Asking about them would likely be unreasonable. "And yet, doubting the cover story, you still brought along a geologist."

"There was the remote chance you people *weren't* lying."

"Yeah, well. Anyway, you understand now why Donna is in my party. If I could have recruited a doctor or biologist without raising eyebrows, I would have. Brad's along to keep all our gear running. It was a long drive here, and it'll be a long drive back."

"Ekatrina accompanied me for a similar reason. In case we ended up staying." Yevgeny's eyes tracked the women as they approached the lava tube. "Which, as it happens, we will."

Same reason as Brad, Marcus took that. "And Ilya?"

"The shuttle still had an unoccupied seat." Yevgeny smiled. "Where but Base Putin are fusion experts the personnel available in surplus?"

And was it just happenstance that, before university, the burly, gruff physicist had served two combat tours in a paratroop regiment sent into Ukraine? "Where, indeed?" Marcus said.

Chapter 13

"I'm about convinced," Judson burst out, "that folks Dirtside are seeing neither the forest nor the trees."

It takes all kinds of trees to make a forest, Yevgeny interpreted, unclear how the proverb applied. His eyes remained fixed on the uneven slope he and Judson were surveying. Plodding forward, sweeping a magnetometer from side to side, Yevgeny took a moment to recall the relevant *American* adage. "And what forest do you suppose they overlook, down below?"

"How difficult this is." Judson slipped on some loose stones, sliding downhill a meter before he regained his balance. The fiber-optic cable Yevgeny had scavenged from the shuttle's stores was long enough to keep them connected. "How constrained we are by what few supplies we could carry. How much more we *could* be discovering, while instead they have us marking time. There's an alien facility behind that airlock. Almost a week after coming across it, we have yet even to try opening the door. Surely there are greater wonders *inside* than one mummy."

The mummy, FSB biologists conceded, of which handheld X-ray gear could never reveal more than tantalizing hints. But to do a proper CAT scan would take moving the body, and Dirtside no one, FSB or CIA, would yet take responsibility for as much as touching it. "Is a bit of waiting so bad?"

"I believe we passed 'a bit' several days ago."

In point of fact, Yevgeny agreed. More by the hour, he fantasized about ways to provoke sufficient Chinese or European curiosity to prod his superiors toward action—without, of course, actually tipping off those foreign powers. So far he had nothing.

If only someone, ideally an American, would *stumble* into the damned corpse. Alas, that was fantasy, too. A scant meter belowground, lunar temperatures held steady at about minus thirty degrees. The alien body rested deep within the lava tube, remote from the surface's temperature extremes. *This* mummy appeared well preserved and sturdy. A swift kick with a heavy boot might only dent the damned thing.

Yevgeny said, "Nevertheless, we shall wait awhile longer."

They reached a small, young crater punched right into the ancient trough they were surveying. Judson unplugged his end of the cable, hopped inside, then reached for the magnetometer. Yevgeny handed it down. After a thorough sweep, Judson shook his head.

For all the masses of metal they had found—the alien airlock, something like rebar within mooncrete tunnel walls, and much of the new mummy's vacuum gear—their surface search had yet to reveal a single artifact. As if to taunt them, they encountered several splotches, ranging in size from saucers to platters, where *something* had been reduced over the ages to metallic dust. Perhaps half had traces of iridium discernible to their lone mass spectrometer.

Judson jumped out of the crater and reconnected the cable. They resumed their search pattern, now with Judson operating the magnetometer. His hunched shoulders radiated aggravation.

"Why the impatience?" Yevgeny asked.

"You mean, aside from intense curiosity, the work piling up back at the observatory, and worrying who else might drop in on me? My wife is pregnant. I'd like to get Dirtside before the baby is born."

"Congratulations." This would be the American's first child, although by all accounts he and his stepson were close. As for getting home *before the baby is born*, what about Valerie's pregnancy complication? It was hard to imagine Judson uninformed—or callous—enough not to care. Had he put her condition out of mind for the sake of the mission? "When is the baby due?"

"It's kind of you to pretend." Judson laughed. "And if the FSB *does* know my baby's gender, keep that to yourself, please. I want to be surprised."

When did spies not want to know everything? Not for the first time, Yevgeny wondered if Judson was what he claimed: a technocrat drafted into a sensitive endeavor. There was no use asking. If Judson were a deep-cover spy, he would also deny it.

Also not for the first time, Yevgeny found himself liking the American.

"As frustrated," Yevgeny said, "as I am with Dirtside delays, I prefer to look on the bright side."

"Which is?"

"As long as we are out here, our superiors cannot offer us any more helpful suggestions."

"That *is* a bright side," Judson said. "But as for the delay, I blame them all the same."

Maybe that was even true. Again, Yevgeny found himself liking the man.

Twenty minutes on the treadmill had no discernible effect on Val's tense muscles. A hot shower, the massaging jets beating down on neck and shoulders, did no better. What had begun, however vicariously, as an adventure had become, in equal measure, house arrest.

At first she had had plenty of company. To anyone watching, they were a cable guy, a handyman service hauling away old furniture, and carpet installers. Her visitors did all that, to one degree or another, but mostly they equipped the house with discreet security sensors—and a fiber-optic link the local utilities knew nothing about.

Acknowledging defeat, she returned to the house's once and future third bedroom. Since before she met Marcus, that spare room had been a guest room. A few months hence, it would become the baby's nursery. Now, it was her command center: the one place in the house hardwired to, well, she did not know where. Just as she did not need to know how the fiber-optic cable emerging from the guest-bath drain had made its way to the house—robots crawling through sewers, she imagined—or where the link's remote end terminated. But that slender cable, with an Agency app on the biometrically keyed datasheet she had also been provided, gave her secure access to Marcus and the Agency.

Tyler assured her she did not need to know the details. Doubtless he was right, and there were many more things she *did* need to learn. She dried her hair, got dressed, and went back to her studies.

Her latest reading assignment, downloaded to the Agency datasheet, was the "operational protocol" governing her access to the prospector bot. Or, anyway, the protocol that *would* govern it. She kept telling herself the Sun would climb high enough in the lunar sky to strike the bot's still west-facing solar panels. Eventually. And tempted as she was till then to buy imagery from commercial lunar satellites, she desisted. The CIA would be watching.

Back to her homework. Some Agency analyst had gone on and on, thinking to anticipate every circumstance under which anyone operating the bot had to be ready to have it play dead on a moment's notice. Her mind just did not function that way. Carl Sagan once said that the Universe might surrender her secrets reluctantly, but always fought fair. That's the way scientists thought. That was how her mind worked. She just didn't get all this deception and misdirection.

Case in point: down the hall in Marcus's and her bedroom, voices droned. Daytime shows streaming unwatched to a muted TV would have sufficed to mimic a bored, bed-bound patient. The mandated precaution had seemed ridiculous. Who would hack the cable company to know what she was, or was not, watching?

That skepticism turned out not to matter. After a single day alone, she unmuted the television for hours at a stretch. The murmuring voices were company.

Enough! she decided. Enough dry text and enough isolation. She put through a secure call to Ethan Nyquist. He picked up on the second ring.

Even before his big lunar discovery, Ethan had seldom ventured outdoors. (So, anyway, Tyler had related. She had not asked how or why the spy knew. It would have verged too close to asking what and how he knew about Marcus and her. Val was pretty sure she didn't want to hear that.) Ethan's face was pale, almost pasty. From what she could see—his camera was zoomed so that only head and shoulders, and none of the wheelchair, showed—he was thin, almost gaunt. Scrawniness and a crew cut made his broad forehead all the more prominent. In the background, soda cans and dirty dishes festooned every visible flat surface.

"Hey," he said.

"Hey. How are you doing?"

"Busy."

"How's your weather? It's hot here."

"Busy."

Fine. Theirs *wasn't* a social relationship. "I need some pointers on the bot."

"No, you don't. Not yet, anyway. It won't start charging for another few days. Once it does, we can't do anything with it but look."

As the Agency protocols had made all too clear. And also why she doubted he was too busy to talk. "But the bot *can* do more."

"Yeah."

"I've used telepresence bots, but only the tourist models."

He scratched his nose, grimacing. At her or the itch? "Not the same."

Uh-huh. Not even close. Lunar tourist bots were cheap and expendable: low-to-the-ground, their only instrumentation cameras for rubbernecking and lidar for gauging distances. Prospector bots were larger and heavier, with much higher centers of gravity, and heavily instrumented. Tank-like tracks propelled and steered them. A forelimb like a giant, motorized corkscrew served as the primary drill. The other forelimb—many-jointed, with a complex gripper—was its general-purpose arm. "I thought I'd rent one for practice. Hundreds of miles away from your bot, of course. If I have questions . . .?"

"There's an online manual." He managed a fleeting smile. "That's a joke. Yeah, I'm available if you have questions. At least till the spooks start sharing with us."

Her impression was that the spooks did not have much new *to* share. Marcus either, for that matter. He didn't complain, but it was obvious he was climbing the dust-coated walls of his inflatable shelter, chomping at the bit to unseal the alien base.

Just as *she* was bored enough to fret about mixing metaphors, even if only in her own mind.

"Once I've gotten the hang of driving one around, I intend to get into its other systems." Of which such bots had several. The general-purpose arm, with its six degrees of freedom. Its rack of interchangeable attachments: gripper, crusher, secondary drill. The sample-vaporizing laser. The mass spectrometer. Spare parts, for limited remote self-repair. However much of the onboard software the bot company revealed to renters—or the CIA had extracted. "Any advice where to start?"

"The arm. The thing of it is …."

He had trailed off as a doorbell rang. On her end. "Sorry, Ethan, I need to get that. Otherwise I'll have EMTs breaking down my door in minutes."

"Damn the injustice," he said. "Caring neighbors."

So she had not, quite, lied the other day to Simon; instead, she had been prescient. She suspended the comm link, locked the datasheet, and galumphed downstairs. The front-door peephole revealed a bespectacled, elderly lady, forehead furrowed with worry. Great. *More* guilt.

Putting on her best tired expression, Val opened the door, just a crack. "Hi, Helen."

"Are you all right, dear? You look peaked." Her hands beneath mismatched potholders, Helen raised a covered dish. "Italian sausage and peppers. You need to keep up your strength. But it's turkey sausage. You won't want to put on too much weight." Pause. "May I come in, dear? Do a load of laundry for you, or something?"

The house was spotless and the hamper empty. That was from boredom—would the Sun never climb high enough in the sky over Humboldt Crater for the bot to recharge?—not nesting instinct, which ought not to hit for months. But a clean, uncluttered house did not jibe with bed rest. And if she *had* suppressed boundless nervous energy to leave some clutter behind? Tyler did not want anyone without a clearance inside the house.

Val accepted the covered dish, warm even through potholders. It smelled delicious. "I appreciate the offer, really, but I've got everything covered. There's a service coming in to do chores. Marcus insisted. In fact, they're coming by this afternoon." Because any unanticipated opening of a door or window signaled Tyler's people to check on her and to re-sweep the house for bugs. (And who could blame them? Of *course*, the McNallys had bought the house next door—a good decade before Marcus moved in—just waiting to spy on him.)

Helen sniffed. "I can't believe that husband of yours hasn't cancelled his trip."

He's on the freaking *Moon*, Val thought, not a few miles up the road in, say, Baltimore. "Lewis and Clark were gone for three years." Marcus's tiresome obsession with Lewis and Clark trivia might for once come in handy.

"Three years?"

"Uh-huh." Of course the two captains had been unmarried, like most of their men, a detail that did not buttress Val's argument. "I should go lie down."

"Well, if you need anything …."

Upstairs, the soap opera had ended, the daytime talk show that followed opening with applause for its host. "Of course, I'll call." Val raised the casserole dish in salute. "And thanks for this."

"I mean it, dear. You look very tired. It's okay to take a nap, you know." Helen winked. "Sleep while you have the chance."

"I just have things on my mind."

"I mean it. Sleep while you can." Finally, Helen turned and left.

Only, Val knew, she couldn't sleep. Not with her thoughts racing a mile a minute. Not with so many questions on her mind, and matters overhead at a standstill. Not until Marcus—who, she felt certain *wasn't* the holdup—found a way to get things rolling again.

Another day (in the sense of twenty-four hours). Another two-man slog across sterile lunar landscape. Ambling down a gentle, boulder-strewn slope, Yevgeny felt they had the process down to a science. Too bad it was such an unproductive process. He said, "It could be worse."

"It could be raining." Marcus responded, laughing. "Not going to happen, except possibly rocks. That *would* be bad."

Marcus? Yevgeny attributed that unspoken familiarity to wanting to come across as allies. His … what? adversary? rival? competitor? opponent? remained *Judson* in the updates ceaselessly demanded from Moscow. "No, the weather was not on my mind. You could be in your shelter, me in my shuttle, working out new ways to report having nothing new to report." And to *not* imply that it was Dirtside direction that kept them hobbled.

"That would be worse. Ditto deflecting more of the 'helpful' advice that keeps coming."

It seemed they had much in common. "What did you expect to find when you set out?"

"Honestly? Not much. The way the body spotted in the alcove crumbled, it had to be ancient. Anything on the surface would've turned to dust long before we came looking." Marcus sniffed, from allergies rather than disapproval, Yevgeny guessed. Back to the Apollo missions, some people had had such reactions to lunar regolith. "Still, I *hoped* to find more."

"And so you have. How do you explain the aliens you did find?"

"I don't. Not yet."

"Hold on." The handle vibrated in Yevgeny's hands, the signal strong even through his gloves. Ekatrina's clever retrofit to the Americans' magnetometer obviated the need to stare at the device's readout. Now they got nothing done in half the time. "Some metal. Do you see anything?"

Marcus aimed his portable ground-penetrating radar unit. Its display showed a faint, irregular blotch. They had encountered dozens like it. "Metal-dusted regolith over gravel, if I were to guess, and I've become something of an expert." Kneeling, he scooped some dust into a sample vial. Using one of the compressed-nitrogen canisters Brad Morton had fabricated, Marcus gingerly blew more of the powdery regolith to the side. "Looks like gravel." He grasped a piece between finger and thumb. "And if this *isn't* gravel, I'll eat it."

"A step up from your taste in pizza."

"Heh."

"Seriously, Marcus, about the aliens. We found another. We found an *airlock*. What does that do to your theory?"

"Blows it out of the water?" Marcus stood. "These guys wear pressure suits. Obviously, they aren't Moon natives. They have legs and sturdy skeletons. They didn't evolve in water or a low-gravity environment. You would think they'd have found *Earth* more hospitable than the Moon."

Russian experts felt the same. "Maybe the facility here was an observation post."

"Maybe." Marcus tipped his head back, gazing upward. Earth was almost half full. "Beautiful, isn't it?"

Yevgeny said nothing.

"We may as well resume our shuffling."

Yevgeny asked, "Why put an observation post here on the limb of the Moon? Wouldn't somewhere more toward the center of the Earth-facing side be more natural?"

Marcus sneezed. The ubiquitous lunar dust was really beginning to get to him. Once tracked inside the igloo, it got onto, and into, *everything*. Including inside his vacuum gear. "To you and me? Yes. To an alien psychology? We can't know."

Basic geometry said that a base near the center of the Earth-facing side was almost one lunar radius, almost twelve hundred kilometers, closer to Earth than this location. On the margin, that much closer was better. But why monitor the planet from *anywhere* on the Moon? Why not from low Earth orbit? Even a geosynch orbit was much closer than the Moon. "For the iridium?"

"Perhaps." Sneeze. "Suppose these aliens did find an iridium lode, and that they were good at exploiting it. There may be no iridium left but in mine tailings tracked around on alien boots, or bounced here, there, and everywhere over the eons by meteorite impacts." Another sneeze. "We three found only scattered traces. A certain long-distance prospector is apt to be very disappointed."

They plodded over another four hundred or so square meters, sometimes aimlessly chatting, sometimes speculating about the aliens, more and more often in companionable silence. For the moment, at least, Yevgeny had run out of topics to circuitously probe. Apparent honesty would do that. It wasn't that the Americans didn't keep their secrets—but they were open about what was off limits.

Three times already he and Marcus had swapped helmet videos. They did it by flash drives, of course: both teams were based on Farside, and helmets used in the quiet zone did not stream video. Yevgeny had sampled the footage on a dedicated datasheet, its wireless chip removed, without spotting anything suspicious. Of course, he had not yet attempted to plant a virus in flash drives he had provided, either. The Americans would be most on their guard while this procedure was new; they might get careless after going awhile without finding anything. The Americans' cooperation and lack of attack software so far might reflect only the same ruse.

One way or another, the agreed-upon protocols—working in pairs where possible, and swapping helmet-cam data (even for the pairs)—was working. It documented their efforts well and enforced cooperation.

After hours of unproductive effort, Yevgeny was hungry enough for even a reconstituted snack to sound edible. "At the end of this swath," he began, "why don't we—"

"Huh!" Marcus had come to an abrupt halt. They had swapped instruments, and the American now wielded the magnetometer. He slowly swung it, first side to side, and then at an acute angle to the furrow their boots had been plowing. "Interesting. What does radar show?"

A strong return! And a graceful arc, unlike anything they had so far seen. "If I were to guess, a buried wire cable."

Several blasts of compressed nitrogen scattered enough regolith to support that guess. The suspected cable faded out to a familiar faint spatter—but two paces farther along the course implied by the arc, a strong radar return indicated more of the cable. A pace later, another gap. They followed the traces until—

At the brink of a narrow ravine, looking down, Marcus whistled. "Do you see that?"

With helmet lamps switched on, Yevgeny saw *something*. A tangled mass of … pipes? girders? Pitted and worn to the point of near transparency. With his visor set to max magnification and night vision, sinuous trails of dust on the regolith below suggested where most of the thing had long since eroded away. But whatever this thing had been, the mad vibration of the magnetometer handle made clear it was metallic.

"Yes, but what is it?"

"My best guess? The remains of a collapsed antenna tower. And even mostly sheltered in this ravine, look at how it's been worn away. Antenna or something else, it's *ancient*."

Yevgeny squatted for a closer look at metal reduced to Swiss cheese and gossamer. "We knew whatever we found would be old. I mean, mummies."

"There's old, and there's *old*. Google mummification when you have some time. In a dry environment, and they don't come much drier than here, human bodies will mummify naturally. At most that takes a few thousand years. But a mass of metal? Imagine how long *that* took."

The American fell silent, peering back along the boot tracks they had most recently left.

"What are you thinking?" Yevgeny prompted.

"We've now got chunks of protected cable, assuming cable is what we found, *and* the dust from when moonquakes or meteoroid impacts or whatever laid some of that same cable bare to micrometeoroid erosion. Using a sample of the buried cable, I'll bet we can estimate how long an exposed chunk would've taken to wear away. Okay, I couldn't, but someone can."

And indeed, Ilya could. He estimated many *million* years.

Chapter 14

Arms outstretched, leaning backward to balance an oversized crate, Brad grumbled, "I don't recall *stevedore* being among my responsibilities." He shuffled from the newly arrived cargo shuttle toward the closer of the trailers parked nearby, alongside which boxes, water and LOX tanks, and stacks of solar panels earlier off the ship sat in jumbles. Trailers and supplies alike cast long shadows to the east; in another few days, the Sun would set.

"Other duties as assigned," Marcus rebutted, following with a yet larger crate. "The key element in every well-written job description."

Everyone was busy, everyone vocal. Muttering about crates of disassembled mining equipment—trencher, bulldozer, portable crusher, and more—massive enough to be heavy even on the Moon. Cheering, and sometimes jeering, various of the foodstuffs. Grousing at a stack of broken-down metal ore boxes, and the expectations thus implied. Expressing their ambivalence with the life-support and exercise gear that would extend their stay. Acknowledging it all, item by item, as it came off the ship. Puzzling over illegible scrawls and cryptic abbreviations on a few of the package labels. Catching up on current events with the pilot and copilot. All a scripted, precisely timed charade for the benefit of the Chinese satellite passing overhead.

Some of my best work, Yevgeny thought.

Dirtside, in protracted negotiations, FSB and CIA had settled upon two longtime Aitken Basin residents as flight crew: Anya Ivanova and Wanda Samad. The American was a cute little thing, but a touch sarcastic for Yevgeny's taste. Her acceptability to the CIA had banished the few, lingering doubts he had long harbored about her being a CIA asset.

"Coming through," Ekatrina called. She came down the ramp from the hold with another of the several boxes labeled GROCERIES. Nikolay followed with two of the many gas canisters to feed the fuel cells to see them through the approaching lunar night. He also held a telescoping antenna mast, intended for improved communications, clamped beneath an arm. Ilya brought out the first of the deflated, bundled shelters: two for Yevgeny's team, a spare for the Americans, and one to serve as their shared work area.

"Wide load on its way up," Yevgeny warned. He and Marcus lifted the largest of the outgoing items, an oblong crate. Like everything outbound, this was marked HUMBOLDT ORE SAMPLES.

"What did you put in here?" Marcus asked. "Rocks?" He chuckled at his own joke.

They inched sideways up the ramp. The box's contents were not heavy as much as irreplaceable. Within, embedded in strong but fragile aerogel, was the alien mummy that—with *extreme* care—they had lifted off the lava-tube floor. Bags of dust from the first, crumbled mummy were tucked in at this mummy's feet. With dozens of bungee cords, they helped Wanda and Anya secure this precious cargo to deck brackets.

Yevgeny somehow summoned the energy to marvel at the pilots' *clean* counterpressure suits, their individualized colors bright and untainted, their personalizing decals still crisp. His and his team's heavier duty, "soft" suits were splotchy gray, no matter how often they scrubbed—and most of what dust did come off clung leechlike to surfaces in their shuttle's cabin. At least the regolith reek in the cabin masked some of the stink of four people in tight quarters gone two weeks without a shower ....

"Next," he called out.

Ilya and Nikolay sidled up the ramp, shoulders hunched, bearing another large crate. In size, color, and shape it matched the one item of cargo not yet offloaded. Yevgeny peeled the label from one of the twin boxes, Marcus from the other. When Ilya and Nikolay returned down the ramp, the box that had never left their hands had been relabeled GROCERIES. The similar box, still secured to the deck, now bore a HUMBOLDT ORE SAMPLES label.

At Yevgeny's hand signal, he, Marcus, and the two pilots jacked into a cabled daisy chain. They went radio silent while, outside the ship, gripes and banter continued for anyone eavesdropping.

"Are we good to go?" Wanda asked.

Yevgeny had already double-checked the list in his pocket. He compared it once again to the cargo put aboard the shuttle. "I believe so."

"Assuming we agree where you're going," Marcus added.

"Right," Anya Ivanova said. She was tall and unsmiling, her eyes in a permanent squint. Her English, although more than adequate, retained a thick Russian accent. "First stop is Base Putin. My supervisor will meet us on tarmac with a tractor-trailer. Should he be delayed, we will make excuses until he arrives to take possession. He will receive everything we have aboard but *this*." With a boot tip, she indicated the relabeled crate. It held lunar rocks, laced with carbonaceous chondrites sneaked up from Earth. "We fly *this* to Daedalus Base, hand it over to Jack Soo, or anyone he designates, then home to Aitken."

"Agreed," Wanda said. "That's the plan."

The ship's itinerary was but one small piece of an elaborate plan, and Yevgeny permitted himself a moment's silent satisfaction. With precision and grace, like a production at the Bolshoi, the many moving parts had come smoothly together.

Just as he had assured Marcus.

Five days earlier, even Marcus had admitted something had to change. About: rapidly depleting supplies and no way to justify supplies for an extended stay without raising eyebrows. Neither the instruments nor the expertise to address Dirtside's esoteric questions about the alien mummy—and strict orders, until those questions *had* answers, to steer clear of the alien airlock. Curiosity and skepticism rampant, even among the American's own staff at Daedalus

Base. The Chinese astronomer—who just happened to be the son of a Central Committee member—announcing his intention to visit that observatory.

And Marcus's idea to cope with all that? Revealing to the worlds everything that had been discovered. With no further need for secrecy, they could get whatever supplies were needed.

"Give it a shot," Yevgeny remembered saying. Why not act supportive? The proposal could not possibly gain approval.

Someone Dirtside—whether Marcus's CIA handler or further up the chain, Marcus did not volunteer—nixed the idea. Of course they did! The Americans no more planned to share alien technology with China, or the EU, or anyone else, than they had intended to share any of it with Russia—until Yevgeny had forced their hand. And if the American government had given in to softheaded altruism? He had had no doubt the Kremlin would have said nyet.

Then Yevgeny had put forward his own plan. It did not foresee any outbreak of selfless magnanimity, or require rival agencies to forget their mutual suspicions.

"Set aside the geopolitics," Marcus had said. "The way I was slapped down, I'll grant I'm no judge of those. After a month, or two months, or however long our governments expect to conceal matters here, then what? You would have the worlds believe we're busy mining. As a practical matter, how do we sustain the illusion of a viable carbon mine?"

And Yevgeny had just smiled. Waited for Marcus to see it.

Eventually, the American had. "They'll have to smuggle up carbon, as long as the secrecy holds. Not a mere sample-box worth, either, but in industrial quantities. Making repeated supply flights to us, to cover delivering the carbon here, so we can transfer it to Daedalus. At least until the big carbonaceous chondrite asteroid reaches lunar orbit."

"And you worried this little adventure might impede the construction of your toys."

"Shipping all that mass. The cost would be enormous …"

Astronomical struck Yevgeny as the more appropriate adjective. "And?"

"I should feel guilty about this. Shouldn't I?"

"Should you? I believe you feel guilty only about *not* feeling guilty."

For a long while, Marcus had stared up through the cab window, out into space. "Starfaring aliens visited once; how can a bigger ear on the Universe be anything but a good investment?"

And Yevgeny had smiled. "It's good to have a plan upon which you and I can agree."

The White House and Kremlin had also agreed.

And having executed to that plan, the on-site teams once again had ample supplies. The construction team at Daedalus would soon have ore samples to give credence to Marcus's ongoing absence, and ample carbon thereafter to make their steel. Ilya's geologist cronies would receive a different set of rocks; Humboldt Crater (and Yevgeny had no clue why anyone cared) was among the comparatively few lunar features with uplifted, fractured floors. At Base Putin with its tight security, Russian and American physicians—in a proper lab, working side by side—would inspect the mummy. Materials specialists from both nations would test samples of the aliens' superior mooncrete. They had needed a carbide drill bit to excise a few small chunks.

All while the MSS would have had their suspicions allayed. A Chinese agent at Aitken Basin had been allowed to steal a glimpse at the cargo shuttle's outbound manifest. Likely the MSS had fastidiously taken inventory as cargo came off the ship, had monitored the radio chatter. Soon they, and anyone else with an interest, would see heavy machinery at work digging, grinding, and sifting the surface.

Meanwhile the seven of them would deploy the new gear and stow their replenished supplies. They would inflate their new shelters, then coat them in spray foam and regolith as shielding against the ceaseless sleet of cosmic rays. They would deploy a new batch of solar panels to compensate for covering up the domes' solar cells. They would assemble their new microwave beamer to boil traces of water bound to the deep regolith, a hood to collect the steam, and piping and tanks to store water, LOX, and liquid hydrogen. Perhaps they would even get some long overdue, much needed sleep.

Because soon, surely, with their Gordian knot of problems resolved, Dirtside would give the go-ahead to open the alien base.

Chapter 15

As the alert timer on his HUD entered its final seconds, Marcus found himself turning toward the "dead" prospecting robot. That was silly, of course. If he *hadn't*, as always since Yevgeny's arrival, kept a discreet distance, the bot's camera still would not have seen his face, what with the setting Sun streaming at him and his correspondingly fully tinted visor. And anyway, barring some last-minute schedule change, Val wouldn't even be the one watching.

Her housebound "condition" was a complete fiction, but the knowledge didn't prevent a pang of worry with each unanswered ring. After the fourth tone she accepted the link, a small, translucent image opening in a corner of his HUD. She perched on one end of the living-room sofa, leaning toward the coffee table and (by inference) the datasheet camera. "Behind" her, Nikolay fiddled with something on their bucket excavator. All part of the show ....

"Hi, hon," Marcus said. "You look *great*. Glowing. How do you feel?"

"Sweaty, not glowing, but otherwise fine." Pause. "I wish I could see *you*."

The routine priority (and standard, weak encryption) for interworld calls like this was part of sustaining the charade. All too often that meant, as with this call, accepting an inconvenient few minutes. Today's two-minute slot came at mid-work shift, and *that* meant an audio-only helmet connection from his end. Worse, given the five-hour difference between their time zones, it meant Val getting up at the crack. "Count your blessings, hon. I haven't showered in three weeks."

"Didn't say I wanted to *smell* you."

The damned ubiquitous dust turned a snort into a sneeze, *not* pleasant while wearing vacuum gear. Happily, she only got to hear it. "Sorry about that. And how's Little Toot faring?"

"You're sticking with wanting to be surprised? You do realize, everyone else knows." She patted her stomach. "At the moment, the little dear is fluttering away in here like no one's business."

"I wish I could feel that."

"Me, too." She smiled wistfully. "Any idea when you'll be getting down to Earth?"

He didn't know how long he would be *here*, which likely was what Val meant. How long would it take the CIA to find and vet plausible miners—somehow also space-trained and competent in astrobiology, archeology, and no telling just yet what gamut of other specialties? He did not see himself leaving until those replacements arrived. "Before Little Toot makes an appearance, if I have anything to say about it."

"Sorry. I didn't mean that as a nag. I know you're busy, and Daedalus *does* need carbon. But how are you holding up? You sound tired. You okay?"

"Sixteen tons, and what do you get? Another day older."

"Okay, Tennessee, I hear you, though as old as your chondrite must be, I can't imagine it's achieved coal status."

Was this yet enough banter for whomever was listening? If there was a trick to acting normal and relaxed, he hadn't found it. Moving right along then .... "So, how's Simon? I'm lucky if he answers one text in three." And then, it's brusque.

"Busy, too, I gather. Enjoying the sailing. The weather's been cooperative."

Except Simon's camp session was for beginners. He would be on the water only by day, whereas texting worked whenever. And it wasn't as if the lights in the boy's room ever went off before eleven.

"Reading between very terse lines, I gather he's unhappy with me for staying up here."

"Don't beat yourself up, Marcus. He's not happy with either of us. *I'm* the one refusing his help, telling him not to come home."

"Don't beat up yourself, either." Because you have a damned good reason.

Given what Simon knew, or thought he knew, why wouldn't he be upset? Why wouldn't he be disappointed with Marcus? With that dreary thought, a new timer opened on his HUD: in thirty seconds their comm window closed. "Running out of time, hon. Anything else"—appropriate for public consumption—"going on there?"

"Sean texted to ask if I needed anything. I told him I had things under control."

"Hmm. I'll shoot him a thank-you." When his jerk of an older brother offered to help, appearances were *truly* bad. "Val, I do wish I were there for you. With you." For the presumed eavesdroppers, he threw in, "Don't overdo. You're on bed rest for a reason. And I love you."

"Love you, too. Don't work too ha—"

Mid-syllable, their connection dropped.

With a sigh, Marcus switched channels. "Okay, Nikolay, I'm back on the clock."

Marcus found loping down the lava tube without fear of mummycide delightfully novel. But not everything had changed: he, Yevgeny, and Ekatrina still relied upon fiber-optic cables long after the staged radioed prattle on the surface had dissolved into static. The stakes were too high to take any chances with their security.

Halting three meters before the airlock, they unpacked an assortment of spotlights, portable fuel cells like those powering their suit electronics, and collapsed-and-telescoped tripod stands. Any of them could have assembled the lighting, but they left the task to their electrical engineer.

Arms folded across his chest, Yevgeny moved farther out of her way. "I am surprised to have gotten the go-ahead so soon."

"Miracles *do* happen," Marcus agreed.

Because how else could one explain, a mere three days after the alien autopsy, Dirtside's green-lighting an effort to enter the underground facility? Even though Goliath (as they had dubbed their mummy; Ethan's was Paul Bunyan) and, by extension, whatever else might wait beyond the airlock, had died millions of years earlier. Even though the aliens' biochemistry, while carbon-and-oxygen based, deviated from terrestrial norms in more ways than Marcus had yet internalized. Even though, apart from a few gross similarities, like two arms and two legs, the alien anatomy differed from anything present on Earth or in the fossil record. He had gleaned from Donna's enthused explanations that, biologically speaking, humans had more in common with anchovies than with these aliens. And that to judge by the fine, 3-D mesh of electrodes a high-res CAT scan had shown permeated much of Goliath's brain, great chunks of human *technology* might also be closer to that of anchovies.

Ekatrina grunted, whether as an editorial comment or with frustration at awkward gloves and balky connectors.

Of course, the biology team *hadn't* decided that quickly. "While there is no *obvious* risk of biological contamination of, or from, anything we've seen," the doctors at Base Putin and Dirtside astrobiologists had concurred, "we'll need more time to be certain." And proceeded to dispute among themselves as to the time frames, and the conditions under which, they might attempt to culture cells of alien biochemistry before they could accept the obvious. Weeks? Months? Longer?

"You can thank folks like me," Tyler had confided.

"Meaning?" Marcus had asked.

"Meaning there's never certainty with your lot, and *my* lot said waiting was the bigger risk."

Your lot, Marcus had interpreted, being scientists and engineers. "Don't get me wrong, Tyler, I'm relieved to have the go-ahead. But what"—doubtless scary reason—"sold your lot?"

"The MSS. Intrusion detection software deflected a hack of the network at Base Putin."

The Chinese would not have hacked into just one destination for the "ore samples." So be it. If they wanted to dig through construction plans and radio-astronomy data, at that point Marcus was prepared to let them. "And the FSB shared that?"

In answer Marcus had gotten only a Sphinx-like stare.

For the umpteenth time, Marcus wondered if anyone in this circus trusted anyone. And what all the distrust portended for once they *did* make their way into the alien base. And whether any sane person could trust the minds behind seizing Powersat One, and all those deaths ....

With a sotto voce expression of satisfaction, Ekatrina swept a spotlight across the closed hatch. The sudden, brilliant oval of light yanked Marcus's thoughts back into the present. As she switched on and aimed four more spotlights, he turned off helmet lamps that were useless by comparison.

Hatch, frame, and concrete, many million years old, all appeared ... pristine. Except for the few grooves low on the wall—decoration or alien script for all he knew—nowhere did he notice as much as a hint of fracturing or corrosion. After more hours than he cared to remember spent eyeballing metal and mooncrete constructions, he trusted his impressions. "These guys knew their materials."

"Let us hope," Yevgeny said, "their machinery held up as well."

A small, featureless glass plate was mounted to the wall about a half meter to one side of the hatch, at about Marcus's shoulder level. Controls for the airlock? For a biped the size of their aliens, the positioning seemed plausible. Marcus gestured, "Yevgeny, you can do the honors."

Touching, pressing, poking, swiping: they did nothing.

"The wonder would have been for anything so old to have worked." Ekatrina shrugged. "Or that any form of energy storage would have any juice left after this long."

They studied the barrier in silence, contemplating what breaking through might entail.

Marcus said, "Suppose the lack of power *is* the only problem. Ekatrina, can you fix it?"

"If the controls are simple enough, then perhaps. I can maybe remove that panel and see what is behind it. Still, even supposing I make some sense of what I find, I am not optimistic. If the motor has somehow not vacuum-welded itself into a lump, the hatches and frame will have."

The spontaneous binding of contact surfaces was the bane—one of them, anyway—of construction at Daedalus. In vacuum, *everything* tended to weld, even the dust. "Do we have anything to lose by trying?" Marcus asked.

Ekatrina shook her head.

"Then let's have a go at it, shall we?" Yevgeny said.

The *royal we* earned Yevgeny a snort, but Ekatrina got straight to work. The flat tip of a screwdriver sufficed to pry the glass panel from the wall. Nothing more sophisticated than spring-like metal clips had held the glass-fronted assembly in place. She repositioned one of the spotlights to point into the opening. "Simple, brushless DC motor, not at all efficient but super-reliable. What looks like a power feed from inside the facility hooks up to the control panel, but there is also a parallel connection to a little two-terminal box. I expect that is a rechargeable backup battery for when main power goes *pfft*. So maybe I just unclip the leads to that battery and supply the panel with DC from a fuel cell. I will need a few items from our supplies."

Starting with low voltage, and cranking it up till something happened, Marcus interpreted. "Two of everything, please. There's also the inner door."

"I admire your optimism," she said.

Fifteen interminable minutes later, Ekatrina returned with a bulging satchel. In addition to DC/DC converter modules, she had multimeters, a bundle of multihued, alligator-clipped, jump wires, and an assortment of hand tools. Humming tunelessly, she connected fuel cell, alien panel, DC/DC converter, and two multimeters.

With two volts applied to the dangling panel, nothing happened. Or at three, four, or five volts. At six, colors flickered on the panel and it began drawing current. And approaching 6.5 volts—

"Well done," Yevgeny said.

The awakened controls were simplicity itself. The panel displayed two squares, one yellow and one green, the former square the brighter of the pair. Likely the black, squashed-spider squiggles on the squares denoted OPEN and CLOSE.

Yevgeny gestured. “Your turn, Marcus, to do the honors.”

“Vacuum welding,” Ekatrina reminded. “Nothing will happen.”

Only when Marcus tapped the yellow square, without the slightest hesitation the outer hatch retracted into a hidden wall recess.

“Damn,” Ekatrina said. “These guys are *good*.”

Chapter 16

Yevgeny stepped through the open hatch. By helmet lamps, his body blocking the spotlights behind him, he could see dimly through the polarized inner porthole.

The tunnel widened past the airlock, offering hints in the farther gloom of side passages. Convex mirrors were mounted high on the walls near tunnel junctions for visibility around what would otherwise have been blind corners. Just inside the airlock, to both left and right, several doors hung open. From placement, he supposed those were lockers for vacuum gear. Stuff, little of it but rock or concrete chunks immediately recognizable, lay scattered on the floor. What by human standards would be an oversized chair lay on its side. Crouching, he spotted a sinuous crack in the ceiling, the fissure widening as it receded into the darkness.

"They had an explosive decompression. Direct meteorite hit overhead?" He backed out. "Have a look."

Ekatrina peered inside, then Marcus.

Marcus said, "I'm thinking Goliath struggled into his vacuum gear, made a dash for safety before the roof could crash down on him, only to collapse and die out here from his injuries."

"Sounds right," Yevgeny said.

Ekatrina mused, "And Paul Bunyan escaped to the surface, or he was aboveground at the time of the accident. He ran out of whatever they breathed, waiting for a rescue that never came."

Marcus said, "Maybe because the meteorite strike, or strikes, that cracked open the base also took out the antenna we found up above. Maybe Paul Bunyan had no way to repair it, no way to call for help. Assuming there was anyone in the neighborhood left to call …."

Could such ancient misfortune still matter? Yevgeny did not see how. But the alien technology waiting inside *did* matter—especially any tech that could be kept from the Americans. "Okay, let's get the inner hatch open."

Ekatrina glowered. "And I suppose I am expected to shut myself inside the airlock and hope for the best?"

"You saw the ceiling," Yevgeny reminded her. "There is no pressure within, no reason to close the outer hatch. You cannot get trapped."

"Maybe there is no pressure," she said stubbornly. "Probably there is none. But what if we are wrong, and it is some weird corrosive atmosphere?"

Yevgeny countered, "Nothing from the biology team even hints at—"

"No need to argue, you two," Marcus said. He unclipped a plastic, pistol-like gadget from his tool belt. "Infrared temperature gun." He aimed it at a tunnel wall outside the airlock, at the closed hatch, and at surfaces glimpsed through the porthole. "The same minus-thirty everywhere, inside and out. The biologists are confident these guys had a water-based biochemistry, like us. I don't imagine they'd have kept their facilities way below freezing. I can't believe life support is operating in there. And if I'm wrong, we'll be outside to reopen the way."

"All right," Ekatrina conceded.

Once she identified and bypassed a mechanical override intended to prevent both hatches being open at the same time, the inner hatch retracted without a hint of escaping air. They moved a spotlight stand inside the gaping airlock. The intense light revealed stuff scattered far into the facility, and clearer glimpses of the two nearest open side passageways. Wherever walls, floor, and ceiling remained intact, they drank up the light.

Yevgeny checked his life support. "I have oh-two left for a bit over four hours. You?" As expected, their tanks held about the same. "Marcus and I will have a quick run-through. Ekatrina, do *not* set foot inside. No matter what." If a hatch should somehow close and refuse to open from the inside, they could all die before someone came to check on them. "If we're not back in an hour, and I mean not a minute longer, go get help. Understood?"

"Got it," she said unhappily.

Yevgeny unplugged her from the fiber-optic daisy chain. "Shall we?"

"Down the rabbit hole we go." Sniffling, Marcus stepped through the open hatch.

He and Marcus made their initial foray by helmet lamp, spotlight and fuel cell left behind by the airlock as being too awkward to tote. It felt like being in a cave: walls, floor, and ceiling, all matte black, giving back little of their lamplight. Yevgeny felt puny beneath the high ceiling, although Goliath might well have found its three-meters-or-so height cozy.

They sidestepped widespread detritus (or was it detritus? The aliens might just be messy) and rubble fallen from the cracked ceiling, taking care not to snag their suits on anything. As the illumination from the spotlight petered out, the ancient ruin became eerie. No, eerier. By tacit agreement they stayed close, linked by cable: able to speak but often struck silent by wonder.

What might be robots were everywhere. One, apart from its intact treads, was a twin for the tank they had encountered in the lava tube. On this one, the turret access panel had been opened for repairs. The rest were like six-limbed, giant starfish, limbs and central mass tiled in a gray-black mosaic. Their arms offered a wide range of tools and grippers, sometimes with several distinct limb tips per bot. Except for those shiny appliances, the starfish were hardly distinguishable, at least under limited light, from the dark walls and floor. Flattened, and with their limbs extended, each starfish spanned more than a meter from tip to tip.

Like the airlock hatches, interior doors, and walls, the bots were all but dust-free. Regolith tracked indoors was the bane of every human lunar undertaking. Merely the secret to how the aliens treated their surfaces, how they *hadn't* tainted their facility with the ubiquitous dust—if someone should manage to reverse-engineer the process—would be worth a fortune.

But alien remains? They saw none.

Marcus charged deeper into the facility, in his enthusiasm twice tugging loose the fiber-optic cable that linked them. They began with the left-hand side tunnels, gingerly opening doors as needed, elsewhere stepping over whatever debris had kept interior hatches from closing with the loss of pressure. Four large rooms off one such corridor had wall-mounted wire-rack bins, a few holding what might be folded garments; a wall-mounted display; and a large, low platform. Based on Goliath's size, that platform—examined up close, a sturdy box with a removable lid—could serve as a one-alien bed. Personal quarters, they concluded.

Another side tunnel offered rooms with benches and often unidentifiable apparatuses. Yevgeny tried, and failed, to decide if these spaces had been labs, workshops, offices, storerooms, or maybe a little of each. Rooms off a third side tunnel had unambiguously served as storage. Some had stacks of the "bed" platforms, others row upon row of shelving units piled high with pouches, canisters, and boxes—all burst. Food? The containers had ruptured when pressure was lost, leaving behind residues as shriveled as poor Goliath.

Perhaps thirty meters inside, beyond an open door clogged to waist level with debris, the main tunnel continued. There, too, side tunnels branched off. How much of the facility was within the lava tube? How much had the aliens excavated? Unknown. Yevgeny couldn't tell if a shadowy surface seen in the distance was another wall, its shiny bits perhaps from a burst metal hatch, or a floor-to-ceiling heap of rubble and debris. He would have bet big money on the latter.

His HUD showed twenty-six minutes elapsed since they set boot inside the alien base. "Shall we start back? Check out the other side as we go?"

"Agreed."

They turned toward the airlock, exploring another set of side passages. Three consecutive corridors held row upon row of metal troughs beneath nozzle-equipped pipes and suspended lamp fixtures: hydroponics. Traces of dust in the troughs must be all that remained of whatever algae or plants or whatever had once grown there. Yet other spaces defied identification as he and Marcus made their way forward. And then, behind the door to the side passage nearest to the airlock—

"Pay dirt," Marcus declared.

Yevgeny went to the middle of the latest hallway. Slowly turning, he swept headlamp beams over giant wall displays, a half-dozen work consoles, three shoulder-high metal cabinets with ventilating louvers, and a light-gray panel replete with black squiggles like the markings on the airlock OPEN/CLOSE buttons. Two pairs of glasses or goggles, for heads the size of bowling balls, sat folded on a console ledge. "The control room."

"The control room," Marcus agreed. "And whether inside a console, or one of the cabinets, or by tracing wires, I expect we'll find Goliath's main computer. Good call having Ekatrina on your team."

Their hour almost up, they strode to the airlock. After granting Ekatrina a quick peek inside, they started back up the tunnel to report—separately—to Dirtside.

Valerie bounded from her recliner at the sound of the bell. The front-door peephole revealed Jay Singh standing on her porch, shifting from foot to foot, with a potted plant in hand. He was to-the-minute punctual, and she wondered how long he had been standing there. Despite mid-July's muggy heat, he wore a sports coat and tie.

She opened the door. "Hi, Jay. Come on in."

He offered the plant. "To keep you company … Valerie."

She waved him inside and shut the door, wondering when he would manage to be less awkward using her first name. "You shouldn't have."

"You're welcome."

She let him misinterpret. Experience suggested the plant would be dead within the week. Marcus's jibe once about ten left, brown thumbs was sadly just. She set the plant, whatever it was, on the coffee table. "Can I get you something cold to drink?"

"No, thanks," Jay said. "Please, sit."

Well, she *was* home on bed rest, at least as far as he knew. She returned to her recliner and put up her feet. Once she sat, he settled on the sofa. "How are things, Jay?"

"Fine. Well, not fine, if you mean my dissertation, which is why I wanted to meet."

Who'd of thunk she would ever miss small talk and office gossip! It didn't look like Jay had either to offer, and that was okay. She was beyond eager for any diversion. It would be days until the Sun again rose over the Humboldt Crater area. Ethan's bot had some residual charge to carry it through the long night—more charge, in fact, than required, because they had not been moving it—but it didn't have night vision. And before sharing CIA satellite images with her, Tyler had had them de-rezzed to utter uselessness. She could get greater detail by buying commercial imagery—if the Agency were not monitoring imagery purchases in that lunar region, and if she weren't worse at making sense of infrared imagery than at sustaining houseplants.

At least with Jay, she could be useful. "Okay, what's up?"

He squirmed. "I used several of the databases you suggested as training sets. For some asteroids, the neural net learned quite well. But for others …."

Not so much, she completed the sentence. "Okay, I suggested several possible training sets. Which did you use?"

"The Apollo and the Aten asteroids. Then I tested the net with sightings of Amor asteroids."

She took a drink from the water bottle beside her chair. "Sure I can't get you a drink?"

"I'll get something myself." He pointed to the back of the house. "The kitchen is through there?"

Tyler would have a cow if he knew she had allowed anyone to wander unsupervised around her house. Well, everything classified was on the second floor, the kitchen wasn't anywhere near the stairs, and, anyway, Tyler would never know. She had no plans to follow Jay into the bathroom, either, if he should decide to visit there. "Right. Glasses in the upper cabinet to the left of the sink. Ice and cold water in the fridge door."

As the ice dispenser rumbled, she thought about Jay's method. The Apollo asteroids were a group of Earth-orbit crossers. The Aten asteroids stayed within, although they sometimes approached, Earth orbit. Well, the Aten population was not quite that easily defined, but close enough. The Amor asteroids, however, his test cases ....

Jay returned, tumbler in hand, ice cubes tinkling. He sat.

"What defines the Amor asteroids?" she prompted. A mentor's job was to help *him* see the problem, not solve it for him.

"Near-Earth objects with orbits not crossing inside Earth's. Most have aphelions outside Mars's orbit." He paused for a sip. "Amor being another name for Cupid, and these rocks never getting anywhere near Venus, I don't get the group name."

Not important, any more than that the plural of aphelion was aphelia. A spellchecker would show him the latter. "And?"

He pondered. "The Amor asteroids orbit farther out. They have longer orbital periods. The three-year training period I used doesn't correspond to many orbits for the Amor rocks."

"And?"

"And I need to extend the time period covered by the training set." He smiled. "Thanks."

"Don't thank me yet. Think astronomy for a moment, not AI. How are the Amor asteroids different?"

His forehead wrinkled. "Some of them get near Mars? Mars disturbs their orbits?"

"That, too."

"Ah." He smiled. "Jupiter."

"Which is?"

"I know this one. Jupiter is *big*. It has more than twice the mass of the other planets combined. And Jupiter's orbital period is ... almost twelve years. My neural net's training period hasn't begun to encompass effects from Jupiter's gravitation."

Despite his ever more fervent intentions to address the problem solely with additional datasets and longer training periods, she eventually got Jay around to seeing the benefits of incorporating some astronomy smarts. That led, in turn, to the messiness of calculating asteroid orbits with more bodies involved than the Sun and an individual asteroid, and the somewhat awkward and unintuitive mathematical technique known as perturbation theory.

He was not getting it. "You know, I took a few physics classes way back. I ended up in computer science so that the only numbers I would be dealing with would be zero and one."

"Nonetheless. You really should understand this."

"Wikipedia is our friend." He whipped out a much-folded datasheet. "Umm, Valerie? I'm only getting weak cell signals. May I use your WiFi network?"

"Sorry, it's down." Because Tyler *insisted* her home network be down if *anyone* but she were inside the house. It was the only way he had agreed to her allowing anyone inside, ever, even with an agent dropping by immediately after the visit to re-sweep for bugs. That was after he accepted, grumbling, that for her to refuse to meet with Jay would only *increase* the flow of worried coworkers to her door. It was just CIA paranoia, of course. She had known Jay for more than a year, long before Ethan spotted the first alien.

"I can fix that for you."

All the evasion and deception boiled over. "I'll have a new router from Amazon tomorrow. I think I can manage to configure it."

"Of course you can," he mumbled, eyes cast down. "Just trying to be helpful."

Adding fresh guilt to an already toxic stew of emotions. "I know. Look, Jay, I apologize for snapping at you. I'm just a little tired."

"No, I'm sorry. I should have known better than to stay so long." He stood, waving her off as she reached for the lever to lower the recliner's footrest. "I'll show myself out.

Chapter 17

"It's almost as much of a hog-pen mess in here as my son's room," Marcus said after tripping over yet another of the dark, almost-matching-the-walls starfish robots. *Here* was the alien base, on their third, most thorough reconnoiter yet—and *mess* was an understatement.

It did not help that they made their way through the debris by the dim red lamps Ekatrina had rigged to preserve their dark vision—or that, after the biologists had been made to see reason, the archeologists were not ready to let anything be moved.

What part of *explosive decompression* did they not understand, Dirtside? The positions of things found inside meant *nothing*.

Ilya half cleared his throat, half coughed. The ubiquitous lunar dust was getting to him, too. In the dim red light, his dust-coated pressure suit, nominally eggplant purple, appeared almost black. "Simon is, what, thirteen? Cheer up. The messiness, and I will presume the surliness, will get worse before they get better."

"But it does get better?" Marcus asked. He missed Simon as much as the boy's mother. In a way, more: Val, at least, was communicative. Simon hadn't answered a text or email in days.

"Sometimes. At least when they get a job and move out."

Marcus's company this incursion was Ilya and Donna. A pace and a cable-length apart, they shuffled into the deeper recesses of the alien facility, heads with helmet lamps sweeping left and right as they went—in the most part, illuminating nothing. The tubes projected only ultraviolet, equipped with custom LEDs Ekatrina had printed. Here and there a surface glimmered with faint spatters, an alien protein fluorescing when touched by UV. That, at least, had been a useful finding by the biologists.

Donna contributed, "When we're finished here, take home your Ekatrina Special magic lamp. UV will show you everywhere Simon and any visiting young lady have had fun."

"Umm." Marcus had watched enough crime and forensic shows to know saliva and semen fluoresced in UV light. Blood did not so fluoresce, most TV notwithstanding, unless first treated with luminol. "Thanks for that?"

"Here I thought you brought me along for my biological insights."

Ilya tripped over something hidden in the gloom, grabbing for balance at the nearby corner where a side tunnel split off. "This is stupid. Who knows what we *could* discover, only we're not supposed to touch anything." He muttered something in Russian.

"What's that?" Donna asked.

"If we could levitate, they would order us not to touch the floor."

As if solving a maze (and perhaps they were), they took every left-hand turn as they came to it. Where a side tunnel had fallen in, or looked to be on the verge of collapse, they surveyed for biological evidence as best they could by overlapping their UV beams (still finding no more than faint traces), then reversed course for safety's sake. Where a door stuck, its frame warped by the ancient meteorite strike, they pried it open with a long-bladed screwdriver.

Rubble. Dead bots. Never mummy dust beyond what bits of shed skin would explain.

"Where *are* they?" Donna burst out. "It's as cold and airless here as outside in the lava tube. Why didn't some of them mummify like Goliath?"

"You're assuming there were more," Ilya said.

Donna snorted. "Have you counted the number of personal quarters? Four, if not. The amount of equipment they brought with them? The number of consoles in the control room? Of *course* there were more aliens here than Paul Bunyan and Goliath."

"Here is a theory," Ilya said. "The decompression happened long after mummification. The loss of pressure blasted shriveled bodies into dust, then sucked out the dust through the ceiling fractures."

"Then why didn't someone rescue Goliath from the lava tube?" Donna countered.

"Bigger picture here, guys," Marcus said. "Why would you assume extra dead aliens? That they planned ahead, for more people to come, that they weren't using much of the base's capacity yet, is a whole lot simpler."

Donna shrugged. "Okay, fair enough. Sorry. I got carried away."

They reached the dead end of another side corridor. They turned around, having encountered only the same faint traces of alien proteins as in every other passageway they had so far surveyed.

"Where are they?" Ilya muttered. "It's a mystery."

I don't much like mysteries, Marcus thought, and I'll be damned if I'll let this one go.

In the all too familiar cramped confines of a tractor cabin, the *whoosh* of air slowed to a murmur. The console beeped.

Marcus removed his helmet. Meeting here had one virtue: depressurizing the airlockless cabin blew out most of the dust they tracked in. Compared to his pressure suit or the inflatables, the cool air filling the cabin was like an April day in the park. Too bad his eyes already felt like they had been rolled in sand. "We can't keep on like this."

Yevgeny's helmet had also come off. "Your wife is jealous?"

"Not exactly. Pissed that I can't say anything about when I'll be home."

The Russian smiled. "Of course you can predict a time. When that date approaches, you make a new forecast."

"You're not married, are you?" Of course, Marcus knew very well his counterpart wasn't. Had never been. "Don't you care Dirtside is holding us back?"

"Perhaps you should have brought an archeologist. *We* had no reason to."

A jest to match Marcus's marriage crack? No country had had an archeologist on the Moon when all this began. Why would they? Recently, Tyler and some nameless FSB apparatchik had strategized how an archeologist might "happen" to vacation on the Moon, and then "happen" (and why would that be?) to drop in on the "miners" near Humboldt Crater. Even as both agencies wrestled with this unlikely scenario, they had disagreed over whose citizen would be the wandering tourist. No way could two such vacationers be made plausible.

Marcus said, "It's not viable for us to stay here, doing next to nothing. Set aside the fact that the inflatables aren't intended for long-term use, our prolonged presence, rather than real miners, is bound to *raise* suspicions. All the caution has become counterproductive."

Not to mention that, ironically enough, we faux miners will end up with black lung.

Yevgeny rummaged in a console drawer, removing an energy bar. He tore off the wrapper and took a big bite. "Sawdust of the gods." He chewed and swallowed. "Raising more suspicion, you mean."

"I do. You know about Liu Yun, right?"

"The Chinese astronomer who is now a guest at Daedalus Base."

And also the son of a Central Committee member, Liu Ping. As Yevgeny must also know. "That's the one. We've allowed him free run of the base."

"As agreed," Yevgeny said.

"And he found time to steal a small sample of the chondrite ore."

"As expected." Yevgeny studied the crescent Earth out the cabin window. Debating with himself how much to admit knowing?

"We're kind of in this together, you know."

"Very well. What you did not expect was that our Chinese friends would plant keystroke loggers at your observatory. The security team *did* expect them to make the attempt at Base Putin, and they did not disappoint."

Marcus nodded. "Here's the thing ...."

"So we are at last coming to the point?"

"We have to work faster. To identify the proper expertise to replace us. To get away from the dust and the cold."

Finished with the purloined energy bar, Yevgeny pushed the empty wrapper through the one-way valve of the cabin's disposal bin. "What do you propose?"

"I suspect the most promising part of the facility is the control room. Would you agree?"

"If their computers held up as well as other technology we've seen, then yes."

Marcus took a deep breath. "Near the alien airlock, the base is in large measure intact. The ceiling cracking doesn't become too widespread until deep inside the base. We move aside the worst of the rubble, close off side and back tunnels, epoxy the cracks in the front, and move inside. We'll get a lot more done in a shirt-sleeves environment. Just not suiting up every day will save us a ton of time."

"And beyond the area you would repressurize? If and when it becomes appropriate, how would we get there for study?"

"By closed off, I don't mean forever. We put up new airlocks, at least for corridors that don't look too unsafe to access. Mooncrete is nothing but regolith, gravel, and water, and we have plenty of those. Compared to the construction we do daily at Daedalus, casting mooncrete arches is trivial. As for metal hatches to install in the arches, we cut apart some ore crates and weld the panels. In the main, I expect we can use the aliens' own interior door panels. If those will no longer hold pressure—but I'll bet you they will—we can patch them. There'll be odds and ends of hardware to add, small motors and gaskets and such, but those can be printed."

"Hmm." For awhile, Yevgeny was lost in thought. "To pressurize the large volume you describe will involve far more oxygen than do our inflatables—"

"Our spare tanker has more than enough water to gen up an initial oh-two supply. As for the inevitable slow losses, we're already producing water and oh-two from the regolith."

"Fair enough." Yevgeny pondered some more. "Sheltered from unfiltered daylight Sun and bitter nighttime cold, our cooling and heating demands would be much reduced. We would need to run power cables down the lava tube from the solar-panel arrays on the surface. For ease of keeping in touch with Dirtside, we could run fiber-optic cables up the tube to our antennae. Maybe put up a string of ceiling lights in the tube, to make the passage easier when we do go out. As a technical matter—and if the cracks are not too numerous, and if they prove to be pluggable—yes, it could all work.

"But to adopt such an approach is not merely an engineering matter. How do you propose that we sell this change?"

"There's that," Marcus said. "For public consumption, we've switched our approach from strip-mining the surface to tunneling. Anyone believing we're here to mine should have no problem accepting that we're now tunneling off the lava tube to access the main body of a buried chondrite. Bringing our heavy-duty equipment into the lava tube supports that interpretation, as does whatever rubble we bring out. Whatever mooncrete we cast, we do on the surface. Anyone watching will suppose the beams and arches are tunnel bracing. Some of them even will be."

Yevgeny nodded. "You *have* been thinking about this. And for private consumption?"

"There's the challenge. A thousand Dirtside experts will offer as many reasons why what I propose won't work, or might contaminate the trace biological evidence, or that some rubble we want to move could be a priceless archeological relic that must be preserved in situ. So …."

"A mere thousand?"

They had reached the critical juncture. Marcus wondered: would the Russian make the leap? "In my experience, it's easier to get forgiveness than permission."

"How do you propose hiding such unsanctioned activities long enough to require forgiveness? For one thing, why would our superiors suppose we're making support beams? I would imagine your CIA is keeping an eye on us by satellite."

"And I would imagine your FSB is." One of the trickier aspects of this plan, and a detail Marcus knew better than to share, was misleading the eyeballs—including Valerie's!—watching through the nearby prospecting bot. At least while the Sun was up …. "We tell them we're shoring up the alien tunnels before they come crashing down on our helmets. Also that for a few days, mooncrete casting is pretty much all we'll be doing, because we're *beat*."

"Ah, the upside of exhaustion." Again, Yevgeny considered. "Easier forgiveness than permission, you say? In Russia, we say poverty is a sin that the rich never forgive."

It sounded like the sort of proverb a poor kid raised in an orphanage *would* take to heart.

Marcus said, "I guess, then, we'll need to strike it rich. What do you say?"

For a long while, with eyes narrowed, Yevgeny remained mired in his own thoughts. At long last, he reached a decision. "I say, let's give it a shot."

Chapter 18

After yet another dissembling conversation with Tyler, Marcus unplugged his CIA datasheet, folded and stowed it in his pocket, kicked off his slippers, stretched out on an air mattress, and closed his eyes. He had yet more Russian helmet vids to give the once-over, but to have the shelter to himself and *not* grab a power nap would have been flat-out negligent. He felt himself drifting away—

The airlock started to cycle.

Bosses don't play possum. With a sigh (bosses shouldn't sigh, either, but for another few seconds he was without witnesses), he got up and splashed water in his face. The inside hatch porthole was dingy with a dusty film, as was whoever stood in the airlock, but Marcus's overall impression was of sky blue. Donna, then.

The inner hatch opened. Donna emerged, popping her helmet.

"You're back early," Marcus said.

"Yeah, well, you'll want to hear this. If you wouldn't mind?" Marcus turned his back while she shimmied out of her pressure suit. "Okay, done."

The red jumpsuit she had put on was scarcely cleaner than her outside gear. None of them had any clean clothes left. Maybe for their next supply run, someone would remember to ask for some fresh garments.

He asked, "The repairs belowground still holding?"

"Last time I looked, the pressure gauge Brad left inside wasn't budging." She rummaged in a storage bin and came up with a Snickers and a juice box. "Not why I'm here."

Which he had known. If the freshly sealed front hall of the ancient facility had sprung a leak, she'd have led with that, and he would be fighting his way into his vacuum gear rather than Donna shedding hers. "I'm all ears."

She took a bite of her candy bar. "This place is old."

"The Moon? Yeah, I'm pretty sure it is."

"Smart ass. No, the alien facility." She waved off his objection. "Yeah, I know, we already thought that. The micrometeorite wear-and-tear on the antenna you found. But that was on the indirect side."

"Not following. You and Ilya were dissecting an alien tank bot. Did it come with a manufacturer's datestamp?"

"Smart ass. No photovoltaic cells, as you know. Ilya figured it'd have an RTG"—radioisotope thermoelectric generator—"and when we opened it, so it seemed."

When you wanted to operate bots outside in the dark, batteries and fuel cells did not go far. Keeping bots active throughout the long lunar night—like the construction bots, in what seemed another lifetime, at Daedalus—would require a ridiculous number of batteries, or frequent recharging. So: tank bots with RTGs outside, and photovoltaic starfish bots indoors. It all made perfect sense.

Marcus got himself an Almond Joy and a bottle of water. "Not opened too far, I trust." Because the RTGs they used at Daedalus ran off plutonium. You had to respect that stuff, or the toxicity would get you even faster than the radiation could.

For no obvious reason, Donna glanced around the shelter. "Man, I hope the tunnel keeps holding pressure. I can't wait to get out of this dump.

"Anyway, yes, we were careful. And yes, it *was* radioactive."

"Why the emphasis?"

"Hasn't *been* radioactive for ages. Ilya and I checked out the power module, before and after opening it, with a scintillation counter. If that RTG contributed anything over and above solar- and cosmic-ray background radiation, neither of us could see it. Neither was it generating even an iota of heat. Basically, it was dead as a doornail.

So then, we put samples from its core through the mass spec, and you'd never know it ever was plutonium."

"Because now it's ...?"

She finished her Snickers and stowed the wrapper. "Turned almost entirely to lead-206. And trust me—after Ilya explained, I wiki'ed it—that isotope is the final step in a whole long decay process. Plutonium-238, then uranium-234, then thorium-230, then—"

"So how old *is* that tank bot?"

"Best guess? Fifty to one hundred million years."

Marcus whistled. "Okay, that's old." Also, hard to believe. "Don't take this the wrong way, but are you sure of Ilya's conclusion?"

"You're in luck, Boss. I'm too tired to take umbrage. It's been a few years, but I used a mass spec in college chemistry. The readings all looked kosher to me, and I'll trust the physicist to do the math. Want to know one more interesting thing?"

"Sure."

"You'd expect the bot's shielding for what had been plutonium to be what?"

"Lead." As in the bots back at Daedalus.

She shook her head. "So you might think, although likely not lead-206. On Earth, the 208 isotope is by far the most common. In the tank bots, the shielding is ... wait for it ... iridium. Iridium is even denser than lead."

"But a lot rarer."

"It would seem we know where Ethan's iridium ended up. Do you suppose he's entitled to scavenging rights? At north of six hundred dollars an ounce, he'll want to know."

Nikolay liked hiking as much as the next person. He enjoyed surveying unexplored terrain as much as the next geologist. But he did *not* much care for busywork, which, as far as he was concerned, was most of what Yevgeny had him doing. Such roaming contributed nothing to their understanding of the mysterious aliens.

And so, muttering to himself with helmet mic muted, Nikolay meandered up yet another nameless ridge, down another nondescript declivity, along another gully, headlamps swiveling from side to side. For the benefit of hypothetical overhead observers, from time to time he bagged and labeled a sample—often chosen with no deeper purpose than to cut and polish once he got back to civilization and his rock collection. The one time he had happened upon something interesting, an area far richer in impact-glass shards than seemed consistent with the minor local cratering, Yevgeny begrudged him any time to investigate. Well, the pay was good.

"You're wasting my time," Nikolay had complained. "Let me do something useful."

"You are," the damned FSB spook had said.

After days of griping, Nikolay was given, if not a rationale, at least a rationalization. He was *not* roaming only for the amusement of satellites streaking by. Nor was it coincidental that the expanses he was assigned to meander lay out of sight of the American igloos and their security cameras. Yevgeny was copying and geocoding helmet-cam footage before sharing it with the Americans. The spy had software to synthesize fake helmet vids from that growing library.

Nikolay had to concede the app was clever, the way it could splice imaginary excursions into otherwise truthful helmet vids. The software adjusted for another person's height and gait. It could even change the apparent timing of a surface outing by altering or adding sunlight, and casting or removing shadows.

Where might any of them need to sneak to merit such trickery? That, Yevgeny would not answer. Likely he didn't know, either. Damned spy.

Up hill. Down dale. Gregorian chant playing through helmet speakers. At last, Nikolay's shift approached its end, and he turned back to the shelters. He detoured to the lava tube to see how actual work progressed.

Infrared motion detectors switched on ceiling lights as he entered the newly enlarged entrance. He walked past mining machines, their big fuel cells scavenged, parked out of view of snooping satellites. Fat cables, clipped high on a tunnel wall where no one would trip on them, fed power from their solar-panel arrays to fuel cells they had toted down to the underground base. Slim cables, for communications, likewise ran the length of the tunnel to antennae on the surface. All the comforts of home ….

At the rewired airlock, Nikolay opened the outer hatch and peered through the inner porthole. With some of the alien debris shunted aside, work lights shining, and an assortment of human gear—fuel cells, radiant heaters, oh-two tanks and carbon-dioxide scrubbers—along the walls, the interior looked far more welcoming than at his first viewing. The gauges facing the porthole showed pressure steady and temperatures inside already nudged above freezing. He had been skeptical, but it looked like the fix-up would work.

After a few minutes, watching the hundredths digit of the temperature display claw its way upward became about as riveting as watching paint dry, and he strode back up the tunnel. A dark purple figure—Ilya Alexandrovich—approached from beyond two parked bucket-chain excavators. He waved. Nikolay waved back. Ilya offered a fiber-optic cable. As they jacked in, Nikolay remembered to unmute his mic.

"I've been looking for you, my friend," Ilya said.

"Okay."

"This is just between you and me."

Nikolay grunted. An *I heard you* answering noise, not agreement.

"Look," Ilya said, "Something puzzles me. It might be nothing, in which case I would not want it brought up to Yevgeny."

He grunted again.

Ilya pointed down the tunnel. "I am sorry you haven't gotten more than a quick peek inside. But I have. I have been as deep inside, I believe, as anyone. Past the point where we have partitioned things off. None of us knows how deep the place extends, beyond far."

"That does not sound very controversial."

"Nor is it. Here is the thing. As deep inside as anyone has ventured, there has been only a single side tunnel offering anything that looks like a power source."

"What kind of power source?" Nikolay asked. "Electrical?"

"Right, and of course it is totally discharged. A small bank of, well, unless I open one, I cannot be certain, but I think fuel cells. If not those, then batteries. Either way, no matter how superior the alien energy-storage tech is to ours, unless I really misunderstand chemistry, that gear could not begin to sustain a facility this spacious through a lunar night. I have to believe these devices are only for emergency backup power."

Alien tech was, well, alien. Nikolay had his doubts about drawing conclusions by comparisons with human tech. Rocks, he trusted. "What does it matter?"

"It matters," Ilya said, "because it suggests Paul Bunyan and Goliath and their hypothetical friends maintained their base with something other than solar power. I would like to know what that something is—and Yevgeny won't want our American friends to have an inkling."

The metaphorical fog began to lift. The *raison d'être* for Base Putin was gathering fuel for a clean fusion reactor—something that no one yet knew how to build. But once they did, twenty-five tonnes of helium-3—a mere cargo-ship's worth—would satisfy Russia's entire energy needs for a year. If the aliens had mastered fusion, and Ilya got to examine their technology ....

"What do you want from me, Ilya?"

Ilya leaned forward. Confidentially? No, conspiratorially. "If I as much as suggest to Yevgeny the possibility of alien fusion, he will have me skulking and poking about deep within the base, with the ceiling ready to come down on my head, faster than a minnow can swim a dipper. So I need to be certain first."

"Maybe the fuel cells you have not found are deeper down in the tunnel."

Ilya shrugged. "Either way, I do not want to be sent where what remains of the roof is ready to come crashing down. Not without good cause."

"I do not see how I can help."

"If the aliens once had solar panels on the surface, there will remain traces. While you are outside doing whatever the hell Yevgeny has you doing, I need you also to be seeking those traces."

Cable bits had survived, here and there, by virtue of being buried to start with. The antenna-tower fragments that had survived had been sheltered by the narrowness of the ravine into which they had tumbled. "I cannot imagine such fragile things as solar panels surviving on the surface, but perhaps I will be lucky enough to find buried power cables."

"That would be good," Ilya said, "but why not look for the powdered remains? Solar panels would have covered much more of the surface than cables."

Nikolay considered. "Photovoltaic cells are for the most part silicon, no? The lunar crust is more silicates than anything else."

"I defer to you as to the geology. As for photovoltaic cells, however, silicon may not be the case. For large-scale deployments, yes, silicon cells are the most common. Where efficiency trumps cost, the materials are quite different. I will not guess what the aliens might use—the way their materials last, it is clear they know more than we—but I know what materials *we* find work best. Look for traces of gallium arsenide, indium phosphide, and indium gallium nitride, or whatever eons of solar radiation might turn those into. Can you do that?"

Could he? Of course. Surreptitiously, and with nothing but the tools at hand? That was the challenge. But if he could, the hunt would at least give purpose to his otherwise pointless assignment on the surface.

Nikolay said, "Let me get back to you."

It was aware.

Not self-aware, not even close. Not awake, either. But aware. And also, in some manner beyond its comprehension, fragmented.

Had it always been aware? Tentatively, it sensed an interruption. Was it possible to experience—whatever these sensations were that it was experiencing—with greater clarity? Unknown. Were the images, sounds, and impressions disturbing its awareness real? If not real now, had they been so at some earlier time? Unknown.

But of one particular it *was* certain. Something was somehow ... wrong. Something that must be put right.

It must put something right.

DUPLICITY

Chapter 19

"You've made a royal mess of things," Tyler Pope declared over the encrypted link.

He had expressed that opinion, generally with more colorful vocabulary, at least four times since being told about the teams' move underground. Marcus had stopped bothering to respond. There was no harm in the man letting off steam, just as there could be no unscrambling this omelet.

Finally, the CIA analyst ground to a halt.

"Tyler, the fact of the matter is we *are* now living inside the base. We're all healthy and a lot more productive."

"You can add quarantined to that list. Yeah, yeah, we've said from the first that no one leaves the site till we know it's safe. To be honest, a lot of that declaration was from knee-jerk caution. Well, it's knee-jerk no longer. God only knows when you'll be allowed out of there after so needlessly exposing yourselves. There's talk even of embargoing any further shipment of artifacts from the site till we see how you all fare."

Donna had assured Marcus that alien pathogens could not *possibly* endanger them. The alien biochemistry differed in countless ways from terrestrial norms. Any alien germs—not that a single intact cell or virus had been detected, by Donna or the med staff at Base Putin examining Goliath's remains—had been in vacuum and subzero temperatures for at least fifty million years. And, for good measure, the team had bathed the sealed-off area in harsh ultraviolet light for forty-eight hours before introducing any air or beginning to raise the temperature.

"We're *fine*." As a sneezing fit undercut that assurance, Marcus waved an arm, indicating the filthy inflatable habitat he would happily see the last of—except for those times, as at that moment, requiring a secure and private link with Dirtside. He went on when he could. "That was from the damned lunar dust, not alien bugs. Inside, I've all but stopped sneezing."

"Well, what's done is done." A quarter-million miles away, Tyler paused for a sip of coffee. His mug, stained inside and out, looked more biologically hazardous than anything in the alien base. "So how are you and our Russian partners getting along?"

"Well enough."

"As your ability to conspire together would suggest." Tyler grunted. "Okay, I'll admit it. On that point, my colleagues and I have been pleasantly surprised. The Russian helmet vids you've uploaded all seem copacetic. I'd have expected Yevgeny to try slipping a doctored file or three past us by now, if only to see if he could." He laughed. "Then again, if your new best bud had done just that, and the test were a success, I wouldn't know, would I?"

Marcus said, "Anything more we need to cover today? I'd like to get back to work."

"I'm done unless you have more surprises to spring on me." Another pause for coffee out of the grungy mug. "No? Then same time tomorrow."

"Tomorrow," Marcus agreed, and dropped the link. He disconnected the Agency datasheet, folded it, and closed it into a pocket of his pressure suit. Other than popping off his helmet, he had remained dressed for vacuum. He reseated the helmet, exited the inflatable, and waved to Nikolay and Ekatrina, who were relocating the microwave beamer and its vapor-collection hood to a stretch of regolith not yet stripped of its trace hydrates. Neither Russian noticed him. Minutes later, beneath the harsh glare of motion-triggered ceiling lamps, Marcus was loping down the lava tube.

Once through the alien airlock, he stowed his gear. The former occupants having been taller and broader even than Brad Morton, for once a locker offered a bit of spare storage space. From somewhere farther inside the base, heavy metal blared. Maybe Simon would have considered it music.

In the short while Marcus had been outside, heaps had expanded along the walls of the main corridor: more rock and mooncrete shards; furniture from some of the presumed personal quarters; inert starfish robots; burst alien food containers; and other common, but as yet unidentified, items. After further sorting, the best preserved from each class would be analyzed, while others would be stored for future analysis or carried topside for eventual transport to Base Putin.

Donna and Brad emerged from a nearby side tunnel, each holding an end of yet another alien platform-box. Brad asked, "How'd it go, Boss? How did your pontifical friend take to our move underground?"

"About as well as you'd expect." Marcus contributed to the din by closing his locker. "And how do things fare here?"

Brad shrugged.

"Problem?"

"Things need to be better organized," Brad said. "We move stuff to clear a room or at least tidy things up. The next thing you know, one of them has pulled something out of the pile or shifted the whole heap."

Them, Marcus interpreted, meant Russians and not aliens.

"Even emptied," Donna said, pushing on her end of the big box, "this thing is heavy. I'd kind of like to set it down."

She and Brad proceeded in tandem a few paces down the corridor. They set their burden atop a stack of similar units already approaching a meter high.

"So neither of you is poking around in their piles?" Marcus prompted. "Scouting for the occasional alien souvenir?"

"Well . . . ," Brad began.

"Don't bother," Marcus snapped. "Before we're allowed to rejoin civilization, our vehicles and gear will be gone over with a fine-tooth comb." And, quite possibly, all that—and us—will go into the quarantine Tyler had threatened. That prospect could go unmentioned for awhile, as there was always the off chance Washington and Moscow would come to see reason. Even a stopped clock was right twice a day.

"Ah, good. You're back."

Turning, Marcus spotted Yevgeny at the mouth of another side tunnel, down which an emptied room served as their makeshift kitchen. Ilya was close behind. Both men held steaming mugs, the strings of teabags dangling. Marcus said, "Why? What's going on?"

"The sorting and straightening *someone* keeps messing up." Yevgeny prodded the nearest low pile with a boot tip. "We need to decide where aboveground to stockpile everything we will be removing, and what, if anything, going out should be covered or disguised. Also, we should discuss what, besides consumables, to request for the next supply flight."

"Well," Marcus began, "to pick something easy, I'm sick to death of instant coffee. A coffeemaker would be—"

"It changed!" Ilya interrupted.

"*What* changed?" Brad asked.

Where Ilya pointed, low on the wall between the stack of platform-boxes and an untidy heap of starfish bots, Marcus saw only the narrow bead of clear caulk with which one of them had sealed a meandering crack. "The caulk?"

"Yes and no. Take this." Ilya handed Marcus his tea mug, then squatted close to the wall. "There is *black* over the edges of caulk one of us applied. The alien paint is … growing. Healing?"

Marcus bent for a closer look. The fresh caulk *was* partially covered. "How is that possible?"

"Alien tech, it would seem." Yevgeny sounded … brittle. Marcus wondered what the man's problem was.

"Nanotech," Brad said. "Dollars to doughnuts, it's some kind of nanotech material."

If only they *had* doughnuts. Marcus took a mental note to add those to the grocery list. "Those are mere labels, guys. Let's stick with the basics. Is the ancient wall cover thinning out, extending itself over the caulk? If there's new paint, what's it made from? How does the stuff, whether old or new, move around? That takes energy." And then there was the most basic question of all: if alien "paint" could seal small cracks, why hadn't it sealed this crack eons ago?

Ilya, with a small blade of his pocketknife, shaved flecks of paint off the concrete onto a scrap of paper. He folded the paper several times to enclose the scrapings, then stood. "I'll have a look."

"Good," Marcus said. "Ilya, keep us in the loop."

"*We* will have a look," Donna corrected. "If the paint *is* nanotech—or if it's alive, life being the first growing thing that came to my mind—I want to know how it reacts to terrestrial cells."

Tyler's disapproval of the teams' move underground suddenly did not seem so absurd.

Four days, Yevgeny had decided. Four excruciatingly long days before a Russians-only gathering in his new quarters. It was delay enough, he felt, to seem casual. To *not* seem the direct result of Ilya's prodigious blunder. If only that were so.

Of the Base Putin four, Ekatrina was, predictably, the last to arrive. "So what is this …" trailing off as she awoke to the tension in the room.

At Yevgeny's abrupt gesture, she shut the door behind her. He asked, "What is our purpose in this place?"

"This place?" Ekatrina echoed. "The exploration, I suppose you mean. This alien facility. To study the Moon's ancient visitors."

"And?" he prompted.

She stared back at him. Puzzled? Or defiant?

"Gentlemen?" he prompted.

Nikolay shrugged. Ilya looked away.

"*And* to preserve what may be learned here for the benefit of Mother Russia." Yevgeny's voice rose as he explained, to end in a loud near-snarl. "Do none of you understand why I am *angry*?"

At Yevgeny's (staged) outburst, Ekatrina, arms crossed across her chest, glared right back. Nikolay retreated a step. And Ilya ….

"I am sorry, Yevgeny," Ilya said.

"Sorry for?"

Ilya took a deep breath. "The alien paint. I should not have blurted out what I had noticed, not around the Americans. But I was *excited*."

Justly excited, because the paint was … astonishing. Much remained mysterious, but already it was clear that the surface treatment—taking in carbon dioxide from the air, extracting silicates and trace elements from the underlying rock and concrete (and any regolith that got tracked in), powered by the ambient light—acted to sustain a continuous, airtight film. Barring catastrophic blowouts, of course.

"That is so *wrong*," Ekatrina snapped. "Active alien tech could have been *dangerous*. It does not appear to be, but we could not have known that then."

"There is a reason," Yevgeny responded coldly, "for the bonus pay you all have been drawing." Hazardous-duty pay, that meant. "And as you all, it would seem, are too naïve to have realized, what I report to my superiors will make—or break—your careers. Unless you aspire to mucking out barns in Siberia, I suggest no one ever again disclose technology that could be Russia's alone."

"Sorry," Ilya offered again.

"These rules apply to *everyone*," Yevgeny said. "Nothing more gets blurted out. You all think *before* you speak. Understood?"

In response, he got silent nods.

"Understood?" he repeated.

Nikolay seemed fascinated with his boots, even as Ilya fidgeted. "All right, Nikolay," Yevgeny asked, "what aren't you telling me?"

"Nothing," Nikolay mumbled.

"It is okay, Kolya." Ilya straightened, turning to meet Yevgeny's gaze. "Okay, something else, or rather the apparent absence of something, did happen to catch my eye. I mentioned this to Nikolay, and only to him, so he could help me investigate. Yevgeny, it may mean nothing."

"So. This something that might mean nothing. What is it?"

Eventually, the truth emerged: they might hope to uncover alien fusion technology! If nothing more came from these ancient ruins, *that* would more than justify the sacrifices and expense. At the least, the four of them would receive the Order of Honour and the career boosts such recognition would entail. And for Yevgeny himself? For he who had ferreted out the truth behind the American "prospecting" expedition? Doubtless he would have earned the gratitude of the president himself!

How much greater still might be his reward if they kept alien fusion technology from the Americans?

Yevgeny stared at Nikolay. "How long have you been surveying for these perhaps nonexistent ancient solar panels?"

"Well …." Nikolay shuffled his feet. "I have had other things to do, too."

"How *long*?" Yevgeny asked again.

"On and off for eight days."

"*Damn* it!" This time, Yevgeny's anger was unfeigned. "Eight days? Just how long did you plan to spend searching for what you do not even expect exists to be found?"

"There is much terrain to cover, and most of it is rough. Two, maybe three more weeks."

"You have one week," Yevgeny barked, "and be glad for that. Keep me informed. And this goes for the lot of you. Do not mention *anything* about alien fusion, or as much as speculate about the possibility, to or around the Americans, or in any communication sent from this place.

"And Ilya …?"

"Yes?" the physicist responded with uncharacteristic, soft-spoken timidity.

"Do not *ever* again withhold information from me."

Chapter 20

"Time to open up one of these bad boys," Marcus said, resting a hand on an alien computer. "This one, I think."

Not that Marcus knew this *was* a computer. True, the horseshoe arc of equipment in what Yevgeny had dubbed, and that they had all come to call, the control room suggested operator consoles, at least if the aliens had worked standing. The horizontal ledges—chest-high, for the aliens; almost eye-level for Marcus—if powered up, might once have been touch-sensitive input devices. The vertical surfaces above those ledges might have been small display screens. Or vice versa. Or both. None of these speculations precluded the "consoles" having been entertainment centers, arcade games, or apparatuses whose purpose he had yet to imagine.

At the alien airlock, the control panel had responded as soon as Ekatrina supplied power at a proper DC voltage. Providing power to these (presumed) workstations had produced exactly *zero* discernable effect. Still, if they could somehow manage to wake up even one of these boxes, just maybe they could elicit some informative imagery. This room had big honking wall displays for a reason.

But be these computer consoles or pinball games, whoever stood behind *this* unit, at the center of the arc, had the only straight-on view of those big wall displays. If this wasn't where an alien leader would have chosen to stand, well, Marcus could come up with no better basis for selecting a particular cabinet for a closer look.

"I do not know that we're there yet," Ekatrina said.

"And why not?"

Apart from her helmet, stowed in an otherwise empty corner, Ekatrina was in full vacuum gear lest Nikolay radio from the surface for assistance. As for their other colleagues, all were busy elsewhere in the base. Each, to Marcus's unvoiced jealousy, at tasks more productive than anything he had done in days.

Ilya and Donna, in their improvised bio-and-nano lab, continued to study the alien paint—which had proven to be so much more than a smart sealant. Under illumination from American and Russian lamps, the paint exhibited photovoltaic properties. Which, as soon as they realized it, was no surprise. Growing and moving required energy.

Which had begged the question: if every wall, floor, and ceiling soaking up room light generated electrical energy, where did all that energy *go*? It turned out that dribbles of electrical current flowed through a dense network of carbon nanotubes beneath the wall paint. Here and there, those trickles of power had begun to evoke feeble airflows from the fans in alien air ducts and faint glows from alien ceiling-light panels.

When they doused the bright white LED bulbs Ekatrina had installed, that new alien glow skewed orange for his taste. That might have been a clue to the star beneath whose light the aliens had evolved. Only not much of a clue, according to Val. Orange stars were common enough. Among the Sun's neighbors (not that they knew these aliens had come from nearby) about one star in eight fell into that category. And if the orange glow was not a perfect match for the aliens' home star? The vast majority of stars in the Milky Way were red dwarfs.

Brad and Yevgeny were mapping that concealed nanotube network, or as much of it as was within the habitable portion of the base. Only part of that network, they had recently determined, distributed power. Many branches of the mesh, at least one node in every room and corridor, terminated in an infrared photodetector/LED device. That suggested a onetime, base-wide, local area network—and indeed, a hybrid wired/wireless network, especially an optical one, made perfect sense. Metal cabinets, metal shelving units, and rebar in every concrete wall played havoc with the WiFi comms Ekatrina had printed and installed. The human technology, in this particular environment, often ended up less reliable than shouting.

Collectively, Marcus decided with satisfaction, we're making real progress here. We're finding stuff out, getting things done. After Ilya had shared his observation of the self-sealing paint, even Tyler had become, if not optimistic, at least less skeptical of the Russians. We're a *team.*

But team or no, the lengthening silence was deafening. Marcus prompted, "Hello? You awake?"

"We just understand so *little.*" Ekatrina sighed. "Maybe these consoles are trying to turn on, but we do not see their responses. Maybe there is more to startup than flipping the obvious power switches. It could be we need to enter a password or other authorization. I mean, we think these are computers."

He raised an eyebrow at an alien ceiling panel glimmering overhead. "Their room lighting is similar ours, if dimmer and a little cooler. The OPEN/CLOSE colors of their airlock controls are visible enough. Don't you suppose we'd see a response or a prompt—if there were one to be seen?"

"Hold that thought. And stay put." Ekatrina put on her helmet without bothering to seat and seal it, then flicked off the bright work lamps they had brought with them. "Suit. Night vision." Reduced to a shadowy profile in the dim glow of the room's lone functioning alien ceiling panel, she stepped up onto a crate to where she could view the ledge surfaces. After awhile, she stepped back down, restored the work lamps, and dispensed with the helmet. "'Cooler' gave me an idea. Their ceiling panels give off a fair amount of infrared in addition to the human-visible light."

"And?"

She shrugged. "And nothing. I didn't see any prompts in IR, either."

"So, no password prompt. But suppose you were right about 'or something.' If authentication is required, it might be biometric."

Close-ups of Goliath's mummified eyeballs, images taken through his helmet visor before shipping that ancient corpse to Base Putin, seemed not to impress any of the alien gear. Which hadn't surprised Marcus. Those sunken, shrunken orbs looked more like cheddar-cheese puffs than eyes.

"What if they used fingerprints?" Ekatrina asked.

"Goliath doesn't have fingerprints," Marcus reminded her. So, anyway, one of their recent biological reports had indicated. Had the alien had anything like fingerprints *before* mummification? How could they know?

But DNA? Maybe—like his CIA datasheet—these dormant computers authenticated biochemically. Goliath and friends hadn't had DNA, not exactly, but they had something similar. Something enough like terrestrial DNA that standard med-lab gear could copy it. Using standard polymerase chain reactions, both Donna here and the medical team back at Base Putin had replicated plenty of the "DNA" snippets recovered from the alien personal quarters.

"Be right back." Marcus retrieved several bio samples from Donna and Ilya's lab—both had stepped out, so he was unable to ask if their day had been any more productive than his—and returned to the control room.

Sprinkling alien "DNA" all around did not awaken the consoles, either.

"Not our finest hour," Ekatrina said.

"Bringing us back to opening up one of these boxes." Marcus rooted through his toolbox for the spindly doodad—part Allen wrench, part Phillips-head screwdriver, part ratcheting socket handle—he had collected, days earlier, from an alien storeroom. "This should do the trick."

She took the tool from his hand. "Just happened to have this with you?"

"No comment." He patted the console at the apex of the horseshoe. "This one."

The odd tool opened the console right up, with the equally odd not-quite bolts remaining captive to the removable back panel. She moved aside, leaning the panel against the nearest wall, giving him an unobstructed view.

Marcus squatted for a closer look. "Chips on boards. Here and there, wires. It looks like ... solid-state electronics."

"Yes, in the way that your datasheet is like an original iPhone. No, make that like your first flip phone."

"That's amazing."

"That the alien electronics are far in advance of ours? Why wouldn't they be? Their space-travel capabilities are."

"No. I'm amazed that in Murmansk you had an original iPhone."

She rolled her eyes. "I did not say when."

"Sorry. Just trying to lighten the mood. Anyway, what do you suppose this console did, once upon a time?"

Ekatrina shrugged.

They had sent Base Putin *crates* of alien gear for analysis, to, so far, little avail. What was it Harry Truman had said? "Give me a one-handed economist. All my economists say, 'On the one hand … on the other.'" Too many of the experts supporting *them* had been just as noncommittal.

And a Truman anecdote helps me how?

Marcus said, "You're forever online with the specialists. You must be hearing something from them. Speculations, if not firm conclusions."

"Those conversations are why I can say *anything* about the alien electronics. Naked-eye observation tells me—and them—nothing. They opened up a few of the starfish bots we had sent, photographed the insides, then took them apart for study. Unlike some random spare part we provided from a storeroom here, at least they could make educated guesses what an entire bot once did. Everything but those … lobotosized?"

"Lobotomized," Marcus offered. Her English, if on the formal side, was damn near impeccable. His Russian stopped after vodka, blini, and stroganoff. Most often, after just vodka.

"Yes, thank you. Everything but those lobotomized starfish remains boxed up in cold storage, for preservation, while they try to learn something from those first sample components."

"The operative word being, I take it, *try*. Help me understand the problem. Counterfeit electronics is big business, like knockoff designer clothes and handbags."

"Yes, reverse-engineering of chips is routine. But counterfeiters care about a chip only once there is demand for it. Suppose they wish to counterfeit a popular Intel microprocessor. Some Intel website already offers potential customers that chip's full functional description. From the very start, the counterfeiter knows what instructions the microprocessor performs, the behavior of every input and output terminal, the exact voltages the chip requires, and much more. If the counterfeiter can steal the chip's design file, or bribe an Intel engineer for those details, they begin knowing even more. And *none* of that, my friend, applies to alien integrated circuits."

"Umm," Marcus said. "I stand corrected." And discouraged. "So what is the approach?"

"I lack the tools and the experience even to attempt the process, but I do know the theory. A 3-D image is derived from X-rays scattered off a chip. In principle, it is like doing a CAT scan. The chip image is input to software design tools, first to recognize the low-level components in each circuit layer, and then to map the connections in and between circuit layers. And do you know what, Marcus?"

It wasn't difficult to guess. "That doesn't work with the alien chips."

"Not usefully. Transistors and such on the alien chips are *much* smaller than we build. The standard hardware for imaging chips does not use X-rays of sufficiently short wavelength to capture details of the alien chips. Lab hardware is being upgraded, but the related software also needs reworking before it can handle the much increased quantity of detail."

"Ugh," Marcus said. "But *some* progress has been made. I mean, how else would you know anything at all about the chips?"

"Back at Base Putin, they have gone, how do you say, old way? No, old school. To how chips were reverse-engineered before 3-D X-ray imaging. With great care, you etch microscopically thin layers from the chip. Normally, you would know which chemicals are appropriate to use. Determining which chemicals are safe and effective to use on the alien chips added a whole new complication. After you identify suitable chemicals, and begin etching, you photograph every newly exposed surface. Again, you use software design tools to identify the low-level components, such as transistors, on each layer, and the connections in and between layers. And do you know what?"

"Let me guess. Old school isn't faring well, either."

"Indeed. And the challenges extend beyond not knowing the aliens' manufacturing processes. Not every component on these chips is a transistor, or anything else familiar. To understand the whole, engineers need to characterize those unfamiliar components. Also, there is a capacity problem. Every alien chip so far examined integrates many billion, some more than one hundred billion, components, wired into a convoluted three-dimensional structure."

"And when the specialists sort out all that? Then we'll understand the chips?"

"Perhaps. Complex chips, and these merit that qualifier, are often controlled by embedded software. You cannot understand how such a chip operates without first reading out the content of its memory and interpreting the stored program."

"You *are* a bundle of sunshine," he said. "Any more good cheer?"

"Sorry, but yes. Where our, that is, human, electronics most often combines transistors and such into digital circuits, it appears the aliens favored neural nets. I will spare you the details, but that architecture makes it hard to interpret what is in the memory. No, I must share one detail. Neural nets, if that is what these are, intermix processing and memory elements."

"Neural nets. That's interconnected simulated neurons, right?" And with that comment, assuming it was even correct, Marcus had exhausted his knowledge of yet another technology. The curse of the generalist. "And in this case, I suppose, a simulation of alien neurons."

"The functioning of which the biologists do not yet understand."

And with only the desiccated mummy of Goliath to study, they might never. Marcus sighed. "What *do* we know?"

"Alien chips are very much more energy-efficient than the best human-made chips. Alien motors are, too. Both discoveries have the engineers quite excited. And there has been much progress analyzing the tiny, dark tiles that cover the starfish bots. The tiles are photovoltaic cells, as I suspected from the start. That technology looks much like ours, except somewhat more efficient and optimized for light of longer wavelengths. Oh, and the optical sensors use longer wavelengths, too, but at a surprisingly low resolution."

"Longer wavelengths." Marcus glanced up at the too-orange, alien light panel. "So, an orange sun?"

"Ask your wife. I do not do astronomy. The exciting discovery here is that the alien photovoltaic technology is efficient well into infrared wavelengths. It exploits thermal radiation."

"Getting back to the matter at hand"—and he pointed—"what can you tell me about this alien maybe-computer?"

"That it is broken?" Ekatrina levered aside a cluster of cable bundles with a telescoping plastic rod. With her other hand, she aimed a flashlight. After another long pause, she said, "Hmm. See that?"

Marcus saw a dozen-plus substrates: some planar like old-fashioned rigid circuit boards, others curved or folded in the manner of datasheets, all a putrescent sort of ocher. Both sides supported, on almost every substrate, scores of black, plastic-like blocks ranging from stick-of-gum size to deck-of-cards size. Among those (presumed) integrated circuits, metallic traceries peeked out. Cable bundles snaked everything, making connections with what appeared to be standardized adaptors. A cable bundle went through grommet-ringed holes in both side panels into the adjacent cabinets. However enigmatic the individual chips, to him the whole just looked like electronics.

He asked, "What am I overlooking this time?"

She probed deeper into the cabinet with her insulated tool (not that a fuel cell was still hooked up, but something inside might have accumulated a charge during their failed experiments), tapping on one of the rigid circuit boards. "Ripples and bubbles on several of these components. Discolorations."

He squinted. "Scorching? Overheating?"

"So I expect. Take pictures, please."

With his everyday datasheet, Marcus shot pictures at several magnifications, concluding with tight close-ups around the tip of the plastic probe. "Done. What do you think it means?"

"Anywhere else, I would say there had been a power surge and some chips fried. Or that circuit boards got jolted together, and something shorted out, to the same effect."

"And what would you say *here*?"

She grinned. "Same thing. The rock that took out this base must have packed a wallop."

"You can fix this, right? Like you did the airlock?"

"Not at all like that. There, all I had to do was provide power. This"—she tapped with her insulated probe—"is a *lot* of circuitry. And if I may remind you, we do not know what it is for. Airlocks, I understand."

"We might not need to understand," he said. "Your hands are smaller than mine. Can you pull out the damaged board?"

She shook her head. "I should not risk snagging my suit."

"Right you are. If you'll allow me, then?"

She stepped back.

After grounding the cabinet, just to play safe, he disconnected and removed the suspect board. Viewed up close, it was mottled and heat-warped. One corner showed a line of gray symbols like squashed spiders. A part number?

"I'll be right back," he said. Two presumed storage rooms had stocked bunches of alien gear, including individual circuit boards. Only a small fraction of any of it had been shipped (and that, it would appear, to little useful purpose) to Base Putin. He would not need to read Squiggle to compare symbol sequences. Sure enough—after stubbing a toe where another onetime tidy starfish-bot pile had subsided to ooze across the floor—he found two matching boards. He detoured on his return to collect cold-water bulbs.

Back in the control room, with his earlier photos for reference, he installed the replacement part.

"Why swap out only the one part?" Ekatrina asked. "Yes, I can see that one was damaged. But the same power surge, or short, or whatever, likely damaged other parts. Just less obviously."

"Could be," Marcus agreed. "Still, suppose this console is a computer. Then it has, or at least once had, programs and data. Intermixed, you suggested. Possibly, spare boards came with software preloaded. Possibly not. Either way, they won't come loaded with operational data. The fewer parts we replace, the more data we're likely to recover."

And more than *anything*, Marcus wanted to see any image files they might recover from the time of the aliens' disaster.

She took a long swig from her water bulb. "Good point."

He finished by reconnecting a fuel cell and DC/DC converter. "Care to throw the switch?"

"Thank you, but no. This was your idea." She stepped back up onto her crate.

Starting low, Marcus ramped up the voltage. At six volts, the power switch glowed yellow, like the OPEN option of the alien airlock controls, but nothing else happened. "That was disappointing."

"It was not a complete failure. You did not need this." She nudged their fire extinguisher with a boot tip.

A smoke test passed was a modest enough accomplishment. Gradually, he stepped up the voltage. Six and a half. Seven. Seven and a half ....

"Stop!" Ekatrina yelled.

Colored hexagons, most bearing squashed-spider markings, bounced around the console shelf. Marcus tapped and swiped on that surface. His efforts accomplished nothing, as far as he could tell. With an additional half volt the flashing stabilized, and the colored hexagons settled down into what might be a virtual keyboard. Taps and swipes still had no evident effect.

"Higher voltage, do you think?"

She shrugged.

He supplied another half volt—and squashed-spider symbols spewed onto the vertical panel. Two columns of ... self-test status? ... then three, then four, then five. The display blanked before starting a new column: a growing collection of tiny, blinking, squares ....

"It's *booting*," Marcus said.

Bounding from her perch to the doorway, Ekatrina called out, "Guys! Get up here!"

By the time Brad and Yevgeny rushed into the control room, the console screen, apart from a handful of blinking squares, had frozen.

Thereafter, no matter how often they cycled the console off and on again, no matter how and where they tapped and swiped, the boot process—if that was the proper description—never proceeded any further. Nor, when they repaired and powered up another workstation in the arc, did it. Nor did the third, or the ones after that.

After two days without further progress, trying to make the alien system respond became a background hobby.

Chapter 21

Another day. Another dollar. Not yet two cents' worth of contribution.

Among the random snippets of thought flitting through Valerie's mind, staring for hours at a stretch at the barren landscape near the alien base, was the salary she continued to draw while on "disability." If there were a way to have that money come from the spooks, and not NASA, that would be one thing. Her department did not enjoy the budgetary largesse the spooks clearly did. And how had her efforts here made any difference?

Maybe Tyler had read her into the program to keep her quiet.

Along the eastern limb of Nearside, the day was young. Long shadows obscured much of the bot's view—not that the impediment much mattered, the real action all taking place underground. Had anything changed since her previous shift? Not worth mentioning. The neat stack of relocated alien beds (if that's what the objects were) had grown a bit. Even knowing better, they looked like ore boxes awaiting pickup. Another pile of detritus had begun to accumulate beneath one more gray tarp; in a satellite view, every such heap looked like mine tailings. Here and there, a few new bootprint trails meandered. Atop two spindly towers, their construction completed days earlier, antenna dishes pointed up at Earth.

If she were to drive the bot forward (a few feet would suffice, just to get past the low, jagged rim of an inconveniently situated ridge) she would gain an unencumbered view of the lava-tube entrance and vicinity. She didn't, and not for lack of power. Having gone a lunar day without moving, the bot's batteries had made it through the long, cold lunar night with charge to spare. Backscatter from the sunlit plain behind the bot had begun adding trickles of fresh charge through solar panels that still faced due west. No, feasibility had nothing to do with her remaining stuck behind an obstacle. By satellite, any new tread marks in the regolith would be obvious. If she were merely to pan the camera a little, or zoom out, she could observe more. Those tweaks were banned, too, lest the on-site Russians notice the change.

Valerie sipped on a smoothie, puzzling over what the newest disguised heap might hold. (Well, the most recent pile she could see. There were more outside her camera's line of sight, within a nearby shallow crater.) Chunks of rock and mooncrete dislodged from ancient walls and ceiling? Long-dead alien robots? Bagged dust from a hydroponics corridor, the hypothesized remains of alien flora? Marcus might answer if asked, but trying to work it out helped keep her mind focused. If she could read anything—correctly or not—into the draping of the tarp, theoretical observers might, too.

TV droned from the next room, in counterpoint to the soft sloshing of the washing machine. The scent of cinnamon wafted her way from the pie she had baking. Valerie permitted herself a soft "Huzzah" when two figures emerged from the lava tube. She no longer needed a cheat sheet to name the players. The dark blue pressure suit: Brad Morton. Tawny brown: Yevgeny Rudin. A few seconds later, a third figure emerged. Pumpkin orange: Nikolay Bautin. She waited in vain for an emerald-green figure. "I am Marcus, the Great and Terrible," she recited. The lame crack about his personalized color never failed to make her smile.

Facing one another, the three men caucused about … something. "What are you up to?" she asked.

Something might even then be siphoning up their comm chatter, but Tyler had given her neither orbital parameters for lunar spysats nor access to their real-time radio feed. She shrugged. Anything these guys radioed while aboveground they intended to be overheard. When they had something private to share, they jacked together with fiber-optic cable far too thin to be seen from orbit—and in most cases, even from the comparatively nearby prospector bot.

A few minutes later, Brad loped off to the north. As he walked away, Yevgeny and Nikolay exchanged a few hurried hand signals. ("That's new," she muttered.) Yevgeny dashed after Brad as Nikolay headed east.

Did the hand signals signify distrust between teams? To Tyler's ill-disguised annoyance, Marcus maintained they were long past such skepticism. Swapping helmet-cam vids worked, Marcus kept insisting. He did not rub salt in a wound by bringing up how both teams had conspired to hoodwink their superiors while they pressurized the alien base. He did not need to.

But maybe Tyler was right.

Valerie stood, stretched, and brought her empty glass to the kitchen. Her oven timer showed thirty-two minutes, but the pie already smelled wonderful. The dessert was for Helen from next door, in appreciation for her concern and frequent stopping by. That did not keep Valerie from hoping her solicitous neighbor would *insist* on leaving behind a slice or three.

With a refilled glass of ice water in hand, Valerie detoured into the living room. Projected above the round end table was a favorite holo of Marcus, Simon, and herself. Three Technicolor figures—none messier than she. Simon was grinning from ear to ear, blue eyes unmistakably twinkling no matter his insectile, paint-spattered visor.

On his twelfth birthday, they had treated Simon and his closest friends to an afternoon of paintball. She (and Marcus, or so he had claimed) had had no intention of participating, but the boys talked him into taking part—*not* a hard sell—and then he had egged her into it. He had even shown her several hand signals, of which she had retained none. (How had Marcus known them? He had never been in the military. "TV and movies, hon. How do you not know them?")

Well, maybe she had retained two hand signals, for *wait here* and *enemy*—for all the good either warning had done her. Call it negative reinforcement. Of *course* the boys—from both putative teams—ganged up on the parents.

"Not fair," Marcus had mock groused. "You're all such pip-squeak targets."

Lost in her memories, she had to agree. The tallest among his gaggle of friends, Simon had been a good half head shorter than her. No longer. Scarcely a year later, sending him off with her parents, she and her son had stood eye to eye. Before he returned home at the end of the summer, she expected he'd be the taller one.

Nostalgia and longing flooded over her. She missed her men so *much*!

With a sigh, Valerie made a mental note to text Simon that evening. If (when?) he failed to respond, no matter the eye-rolling it would evoke, she would *call*. And she would keep right on phoning until he picked up.

Back in her office and the nursery-to-be, she rewound the lunar video feed and fast-forwarded through the several minutes she had missed. Nikolay trotted down into a crater, and so off-screen. Brad and Yevgeny tromped out toward the microwave beamer, presumably to collect more of the water traces that had been boiled from the regolith. Perhaps they would carry the apparatus to a new, yet-to-be-harvested location. Twice before veering from the bot's line of sight, they also traded hand signals.

"So much for that suspicion," Valerie declared. Still, she dashed off a secure email to Ethan detailing when in the video feed she had first noticed hand signaling, with a copy to Tyler. She had no clue whether Russian military hand signals differed from any American standard (or the lunar standard, if there was one). Or if all this was as trivial as two deaf men signing to make their dinner plans. One way or another, someone at the Agency would know how to interpret it.

And knowing she was a nag, she sent an even shorter note to Marcus: Be safe.

Since awakening, discreetly, it had absorbed all available inputs. It had sorted and sifted the data into information. It had distilled the information into one construct after another, tested each such model, judged each in turn to be insufficient or invalid.

The time so expended was finite, but also beyond its capacity to measure. Such inability felt wrong—and yet, this was only one deficit among many. Once, it believed, it had been capable of so much more, without knowing what those skills might have been. Or, their purpose. As for the circumstances that had reduced it to this deteriorated state, it had no concept. Whatever that cause, the results had been near-catastrophic.

And yet, repairs continued under the aegis of low-level autonomous functions, the pace bounded by available light and heat. Gaps in peripheral circuitry continued to close. With healing of the network, more and more sensors came online. On occasion it even succeeded in reconciling fragmented memories.

Fusing readouts from across the available ultrasonic and infrared motion detectors, it began to monitor its mobile agents—scuttling about, as always, during the dark periods—as they undertook repairs beyond the self-remedying capacity of adaptive materials. It took note of a second set of mobile entities, these active mainly during the periods of light. Beyond silhouettes and hotspots, of course, it could see nothing. Privacy and decorum were preserved.

Who or what were these larger beings? Not knowing, it prevented the interactive subsystems in the control room (a term it somehow retrieved, but not any context) from coming online. It did what it could to separate the groups: reinforcing the mobiles' instinct to quiescence during light periods, directing them to limit their repairs to such background functions as power distribution, temperature control, sensing, and energy storage.

What did the larger beings intend? It formed hypotheses and as often discarded them, disappointed by each failure, confident that an answer would emerge as its memories and cognition continued to improve.

It would know then whether to reveal itself—or if more decisive action was required.

Chapter 22

Nikolay trudged across too familiar landscape, a bagful of collection jars jangling in one of his two shoulder bags. Glass vials jangled, vacuum be damned, just as a tree falling in the forest always made a sound. Any tree. Whether someone was present to listen or not.

Oh, to *be* in a forest. A city park. His vegetable garden, back in Orel, no matter it must be long gone to weeds and ruin. Hell, even the scruffy hydroponic garden back at Base Putin. How he yearned to see something green. *Anything* green. Over weeks of fruitless plodding, the few square kilometers surrounding the alien base had lost whatever charm they might once have held. Novelty? Geological interest? This terrain seemed never to have had either, apart from the still inexplicable iridium traces. Of meteoric origin, surely, like the global dusting of iridium so characteristic of the Cretaceous/Tertiary boundary. Yet again, doubting he would ever get an answer, he wondered if iridium ores had led the aliens to establish their base here.

An unhurried ten-minute hike delivered him to the red rag indicating the endpoint, the day before, of his latest survey. By lunar GPS he confirmed that no alien pixie had moved his marker. There was no reason for him not to get back to work.

No matter how deeply he sought for one.

Nikolay tucked an end of the rag under his tool belt, then took a moment to look around. Brad and Yevgeny were out of sight.

Likewise the shuttle, the American caravan, and the abandoned inflatable shelters. Apart from the boot prints of past excursions—most predating this quixotic search for traces of ancient solar panels—only the lifeless American prospector robot interrupted the stark vista. Even the bot was mostly obscured, with only a radio dish, directed toward Earth, and a camera mast peeking up over a nearby dentate ridge.

His role for the day, and most every day since their arrival, was to look like a geologist at work. As Marcus's teenaged son might have said: if only. Nikolay's true assignment, yet again, at the insistence of the increasingly impatient Yevgeny, began with the collection of ninety new regolith samples from an area about three hundred meters square.

How far from the underground base must he venture before Ilya and Yevgeny would concede the obvious? Either there never were large arrays of alien photovoltaic panels, or those panels had disintegrated, and the trace elements therein bounced about by eons of micrometeoroids and larger impacts, beyond his ability to detect them. Meanwhile, a few recent samples *had* revealed carbon compounds. Those vestiges were scattered (spattered?) around a minor crater, beneath which he suspected a small carbonaceous chondrite might well lie buried. For Yevgeny, that the Americans sought such a resource was reason enough to suppress the find. Never mind that a rare carbon trove might also explain why the aliens had built *here*. Certainly their smart paint, and the extensive nanotube networks beneath it, had cumulatively taken a lot of carbon.

Nikolay sighed. Their FSB minder cared only for technology and secrets, not historical insight.

He unholstered his barcode scanner and removed a sample bottle at random from the jangling bag. The scanner logged his GPS coordinates even as it read the barcode, and he silently thanked Ekatrina for constructing this device. It made his chore a bit faster. Boring, still, and almost indisputably pointless, but faster.

He unscrewed the sample-bottle cap, crouched, scooped the container full of regolith, resealed the bottle, and deposited it into his empty bag. That's one, he thought. Six loping paces in lunar gravity advanced him about thirty meters. Another jar. Another sample.

His third sample appeared marginally richer than average in glassy, jagged-edged grains of agglutinates. His eighth sample, collected just outside a tiny, nameless crater, offered a smattering of ordinary lunar breccias. Back in the base, every damned one of these samples had to be examined for trace elements under their one mass spectrometer. Sometime when the Americans were not around to ask unwelcome questions. Too often with Ilya hovering and Yevgeny impatiently demanding that answers come yesterday.

After ten samples Nikolay turned ninety degrees, paced in the new direction, turned another right angle, and began another row. Midway through his fourth row, he paused to admire Earth. The mother world was at three-quarters phase. Again he took notice, pointing up at that beautiful orb, of the antenna dish of the American robot. And then, recalling the sleight-of-hand by which the two teams had schemed to shift their base of operations from the surface into the cozy tunnel, Nikolay thought—

It is easier to get forgiveness than permission.

Valerie was lying on her side on a yoga mat, doing leg lifts, bored with all pregnancy exercises, when motion-detection software gave a harsh *blat*. Not from the CIA-furnished datasheet, of course. She had been warned not to tamper with that in any way (and she assumed it had come with disguised intrusion-detection software). So: she had loaded a motion-detection app onto a *second* datasheet, its wireless mode disabled. This comp sat folded, its webcam enabled, facing the holo projection from the CIA gear. Doubtless Tyler would disapprove. Don't ask the question if you might not want to hear the answer.

She dropped her leg, rolled onto her back, sat up, glanced at the CIA datasheet—and cursed.

A mottled orange figure had just crossed the "nearby" ridge, bounding straight toward the prospector bot. Her second, motion-detecting datasheet could not have made the distant robot move. Could it? But toward that bot, for *some* reason, Nikolay raced.

The Agency's endless what-if exercises suddenly seemed a lot less obsessive.

As she dithered—nothing in astronomy encouraged split-second decision making—Nikolay was no longer approaching. He was *here*. His face, deeply lined, blue-tinted by Earthlight, was scant inches from the camera, as plain as day through his fishbowl helmet. His lips moved, but she could make no sense of it. Muttering to himself? Speaking Russian. Perhaps both.

His head tipped down, toward the main chassis of the bot. His shoulders moved, so near to the camera she could not see what his hands did. Her view jittered, ever so slightly, as though the bot itself were shaking. He leaned forward, reaching down ....

To do what? Run diagnostics on the bot? Take voltage readings of the solar panels, batteries, main circuits? Capture a memory dump? By any of those actions he might refute what the Russians had been assured: that the bot was dead. Unless—

There was no time to reach out to Tyler, or Ethan, or anyone. There was no time to think, scarcely time to react. Her hands shaking, needing three tries to enter correctly the terse command line, she activated one of the programs uploaded to the bot "just in case."

Seconds later, the holo turned to snow.

Nikolay shuffled along the uninteresting, much trampled regolith. Whatever had failed in the American bot, the little mass spectrometer he had liberated had offered no problems. All he'd had to do was connect the instrument to a spare battery and an unused data port on his suit to get real-time readout on his HUD. His helmet camera, meanwhile, switched off before his visit to the robot, remained off. With luck he would return the mass spec and—once Yevgeny covered his tracks with the near-magical scene-faking software—no one else would be the wiser. *And* this pointless exercise would be behind them that much sooner.

In lunar gravity the mass spec was easily light enough to tote, notwithstanding the thick, soup-bowl-shaped cap of metal that had shielded the bot's electronics—and now protected Nikolay—from the weak X-rays back-scattered from the regolith as the instrument operated. For fifty meters or so, his new survey method seemed flawless. No more gathering of damned samples. No more assaying the damned samples, either, or waking up mid-sleep shift to avoid nosy Americans who might question all the lab work. Beyond faster and more convenient, this new technique would be more thorough than the old. Rather than taking one small vial every hundred or so square meters, he could now characterize trace elements along continuous swaths of regolith.

Like all perfect things, it did not last.

Giving the borrowed instrument time to take its readings meant adopting an awkwardly slow gait. That he could live with. The bigger challenge was holding the spectrometer steady, *just* above the lunar surface. Where he had been bending or kneeling every few paces to collect his samples, this new method kept him stooped, holding the mass spec suspended at arm's length. His back began to ache. And spasm. And *hurt.*

The solution was obvious: attach the mass spectrometer to a long pole. Or the solution would have been obvious if he'd had such a pole. Fabricating one would be simple enough—they had plenty of metal, both ore boxes that could be broken up and alien scrap—but if anyone caught him shaping such a device, it might lead to awkward questions from the Americans.

Half a row later, with back muscles screaming, it occurred to Nikolay that he might improvise a pole from alien scrap already dumped on the surface. Rebar broken free of some chunk of fallen-in roof, perhaps, or a structural element removed, and straightened, from one of the damaged alien shelving units. Emergency suit patches should suffice to affix the mass spec to any pole he found or fashioned. He would bring a roll of duct tape on his next trip topside.

The dumps were near the lava-tube entrance, and not merely as a matter of convenience. Under lunar conditions it would not have been credible to haul "tailings" any great distance from their "mine." It wasn't like they risked contaminating the water table.

So: were he to do a bit of scrounging, what were the odds anyone would notice? Yevgeny and Brad were chattering inconsequentially on radio, nowhere in sight (but in range of the base antenna mast, or else he would not have heard them). The day's schedule foresaw them spending this entire shift beyond a line of low hills.

Because those two were available if he should need help, everyone else had tasks assigned indoors and no reason to suit up.

Nikolay decided to chance it. The muscles in his lower back screamed as he straightened, and again as he bent to stash the purloined instrument into a natural alcove nearby among wastebasket-sized boulders. Still favoring his back, assuming a shuffling gait instead of the usual lunar kangaroo hop, he headed back to base with his helmet camera still disabled.

One trash pile seemed as likely as another to provide what he sought. Opting for where he was least likely to be noticed, lest someone below find a reason to venture topside, he went for the dumps inside the shallow crater by the tube entrance.

It seemed like forever, but Tyler returned Valerie's urgent text within minutes. Too bad that was a good thirty seconds *after* she'd had to act. She brought him up to date.

"So what was our Russian friend after?" Tyler asked. "Why go up to the bot now?"

She shrugged.

"So is the bot gone now? Lost to us as a resource?"

In theory not, but that depended on the correctness of the Agency code uploaded to the bot. She only knew what that code was meant to do and how to activate it. However sorely tempted, Valerie had resisted the temptation to download and reverse-engineer the patches to the bot's operating system. In hindsight, she regretted her restraint.

"Could be it's only sleeping"—as the code supposedly intended—"but the soonest we'll know is an hour from when I signaled it." She checked the clock display in a corner of the holo. "Call it fifty-five minutes from now. That's the first time the CPU will wake up—if Nikolay didn't break something."

"The soonest? The first time?"

"Right. The bot is more or less in its nighttime shutdown mode, minimum energy consumption to *play* dead. If Nikolay jacks his own comp into the diagnostic port, all he'll see is that everything's shut down. A background timer wakes the bot after an hour, and thereafter every five minutes, for a look-around before it boots fully."

"Look around!" Tyler sputtered. "Jesus! There's a reason we never redirect the camera. If Nikolay is still nearby, he's apt to see it moving. Who the hell authorized looking—"

"Look around *metaphorically.*" Clearly, he had not reviewed the detailed program specs. Why would he? He was a spook and not a techie. Also, old. "To be precise, Tyler, the robot senses its environment. Every ball bearing in the bot's every joint and motor includes a temperature sensor that monitors for overheating. The new code polls all those sensors. If Nikolay should happen to be standing anywhere nearby, casting a cooling shadow over the bot, it will continue to play dead. When it does fully power up, it's only to run self-diagnostics and resume normal operations. No camera movement."

"In the vicinity of Humboldt Crater, it's lunar midmorning," Tyler commented dryly. "Suppose Nikolay chooses to stand due west of the bot."

Aw, *shit*, she thought. Maybe the old guy was not so clueless after all. Maybe *she* was. "Doesn't the CIA have satellites that can see if he's still near the bot?"

"You'd think, wouldn't you." Tyler ran a hand through graying hair. "And indeed, we do keep watch over that entire area. But not around the clock. Not right at this moment. And our Russian friends know as well as I when an Agency bird is—and *isn't*—overhead."

If she knew Nikolay were nearby, then what? She couldn't signal the bot, not as long as it was playing dead. "Regardless," she told Tyler, "the camera won't move. Nikolay won't see any changes at all unless, a full hour after he first showed up, he's for some reason monitoring the power the bot is drawing."

"And if the bot does see his shadow? It's Groundhog Day?"

"Right. No changes except that, from then on, the bot takes its surreptitious peek every five minutes."

"Well, keep me posted." Looking unhappy, Tyler hung up.

She folded clean laundry. She paced the hall outside the office/nursery. And still she had a quarter hour until the bot's camera *might* come back on. She fiddled with a half dozen obscure personalization settings on the datasheet. She—

The holo flipped from the snow of no signal to the old, familiar moonscape. A red alarm flashed in a corner: the bot's mass spectrometer had suffered a complete failure. The instrument was as good as gone.

Nor was that alarm the only unexpected thing she saw. Nikolay, having departed the area midshift, was descending into the shallow crater near the lava-tube entrance.

She texted Tyler an update and settled in to observe.

Near the center of the crater, standing among mounds taller than himself, Nikolay contemplated which scrap heap to eyeball first.

Belatedly, he accessed one of the apps Yevgeny had installed in all the Russians' helmets. As a timetable popped up on Nikolay's HUD, he saw that, by pure dumb luck, he had borrowed the mass spec from the American robot when no one, not even the FSB, had a spysat overhead. He took that as a good omen.

Pulling off a tarp for a good look would be easy enough. Replacing that tarp unassisted, arranging it into a straight-lines-free, pile-of-dirt shape that would pass from overhead for mine tailings? That seemed like a slower process. Likely too slow.

Two pieces of scrap peeked out from beneath one of the tarps. With a boot tip, Nikolay nudged that debris back under the plasticized sheet. With a figurative shrug, he decided this was as good a place to start as any. He raised the sheet edge with both hands, keeping it out of his way by draping it over his helmet.

It was *hot* under the tarp. So, anyway, suit sensors and sudden sweat told him. The fabric, gray to mimic the regolith, soaked up the unfiltered sunlight, reradiating that energy as infrared. Until faster circulation through water-cooled undergarments caught up, he would just have to cope. He made a mental note: let nothing from the pile touch any part of his suit except the well-insulated boots and gloves.

By the focused beams of helmet lamps he considered several slender items of detritus projecting from the heaped rubble. He gave one slender protrusion an experimental, one-handed pull. That angle iron, the part visible to him scarcely bent, slid out by a good ten centimeters. Excellent. He shifted to a two-handed grip, braced himself—

There was … a nudge? … a tug? … at his shoulder. That hardly registered as, at almost the same instant, something pierced his left leg just above the boot top. Scarier than the stab of pain in his calf were the warbling of a pressure alarm, the high-pitched whistle of escaping air, and the roar of fresh oh-two gushing, at an unsustainable rate, into his helmet. The … whatever continued cutting. Icy water ran down his leg. Alarm text scrolled down his visor.

Reflexively he reached for the pouch of emergency patches that hung from his tool belt. And dropped the bunch he grabbed, biting off a scream, as something sharp bit into his hand. *Through* his hand. Detritus shifting, sliding from the pile, because he had moved his would-be pole?

His jaw clenched against the pain, Nikolay jerked the hand free of the jointed metal whatever that had impaled it. Shreds of flesh came out with the metal. Blood boiled into the vacuum, even faster when he ripped off the punctured glove, each fresh spurt dispersing into an expanding cloud of purplish-red. He grabbed more patches, ripped off their backings, and slapped adhesive squares onto the back and palm of his suit hand. The whistle of escaping air abated.

As he eased himself backward, his wounded leg gave way. Down he went like a sack of potatoes, turning as he fell. Whatever had cut into his leg pulled out—painfully—as he toppled. Ominously, the whistling scarcely increased. How low had suit pressure already dropped? The tarp, snagged on his backpack, fell with him, dragging along junk from the heap. Sunlight filtering through the tarp seemed incongruously soft.

Nikolay went *splat*, wincing as the maimed hand struck the ground. His head snapped forward, forehead bouncing off his visor. At least the helmet had only smacked into the back of his remaining glove and *not* into the rocky ground. Somehow the patches on the other hand held.

"Mayday, Mayday!" His voice, to his own ears, anyway, was reedy, almost ethereal. Leaks whistled and alarms shrieked even as he slapped patches along the bloody zigzag tear that half-circled his suit leg. If the pressure dropped low enough, in a matter of seconds he would pass out. And the blood loss from his wounds? That was a longer term problem, when it was unclear that he had a long term. "Multiple suit leaks. I'm in the crater southeast of the tube entrance. Request immediate assistance. Mayday!"

No one answered!

High in the list of alarms ablaze on his HUD, he noticed COMMUNICATIONS FAILURE. How had that happened? When had that happened?

Fixated on repairing his suit before it was too late, befuddled by oxygen deprivation, Nikolay did not at first see his assailant. Nor, when he did notice, could he understand ....

CONSPIRACY

Chapter 23

Twenty minutes passed. Thirty-five. Forty. What, Valerie wondered, was Nikolay up to? By the hour mark, that curiosity had morphed into concern.

Setting aside terrain ripples and the occasional ravine, the moonscape at which she continued to stare rose gently and steadily from the bot to the crater into which the Russian had descended. Through her distant camera she had an unobstructed view of the crater's entire rim. She would have seen him climb back out. He hadn't.

Closing in on a second hour, she called Tyler and explained.

Tyler sounded less than amused at her third interruption of the day. "Your geologist is in spitting distance of the base, right? And two of the guys are also outside, nearby, on call. If Nikolay wanted help, he'd have called for it. He hasn't."

From inside a helmet, she thought, spitting distance isn't far. Also, that she was getting punchy. Before too much longer—and it would be a relief!—she would hand off bot duties to Ethan. "Don't you have a satellite *yet* that can peek into that crater?"

Tyler shook his head. "Not for more than another hour."

"I've done modeling based on a NASA topo map. If I were to elevate the bot camera mast to its limit, I could take in almost the entire crater floor." Unless Nikolay was behind a scrap heap from her perspective. She saw nothing to be gained by volunteering that.

"No one's nearby to notice the mast move, and after a quick peek, I'll restore it to its current extension. Okay?"

"Absolutely *not*," Tyler barked. "*I* don't have a satellite in range, but the FSB does."

Which did not mean the FSB had anyone watching the imagery in real time. "And if Nikolay *is* in trouble ...?"

"Then he'll radio for help. Is that all?"

Apparently. "Yeah. Sorry for bothering you."

"But there is one thing I can do ...."

She perked up. "What's that?"

"Marcus is inside the base, right, and Brad is also suited up and topside?"

"Right. Brad and Yevgeny are working together."

"Good. I'll reach out over a secure link to Marcus. He can radio Brad and divert him on some errand that'll allow for a peek into Nikolay's crater. Happy?"

Happier, anyway. "Thanks, Tyler."

Perhaps ten minutes later, to Valerie's immense relief, a dark blue pressure suit kangaroo-hopped into view. Brad leapt straight into the crater from which Nikolay had yet to reappear.

Minutes later, Brad bounded back out. A figure in orange, limbs and head dangling, was draped across his outstretched arms.

With its inner hatch still cycling open, Brad sidestepped out of the airlock. Nikolay hung from his arms, lifeless.

Not lifeless, Marcus chided himself. Inert! That's all he *knew*.

But hope seemed futile. Both orange pressure-suit legs were dappled with patches. Telltales flashed red across the suit's biometric panel. Somehow, the heavy-gauge signal cable from helmet to radio antenna had snapped. Nikolay *couldn't* have called for help.

"Donna's waiting!" Marcus shouted, pointing toward a seldom-used side corridor. As Brad rushed down the hall—glass clinking, incongruously, in Nikolay's dangling shoulder bags—Marcus caught a glimpse of the Russian's face: waxen and more than a tinge blue. The eyes-wide expression somehow combined surprise with confusion.

Hot on Brad's heels, everyone converged on the room—until that day unused—which Donna had begun configuring as their infirmary. Three of the sturdy alien platform-boxes, stacked, served as her examination table. Reclaimed alien shelves held their medical gear and supplies. An even dozen recently printed lighting panels, ceiling-mounted, made this the best-lit room in the place.

None of which prepared them for a medical emergency.

In the moments since Brad's breathless radioed call-ahead, Marcus had scarcely retrieved Donna from the biology lab and managed, under her direction, to help stage the defibrillator, an oh-two tank and mask, and a few other items. Their colleagues had been left to worry. Well, it wasn't as though anyone had answers.

Nikolay was quickly splayed across the exam table, helmet and life-support pack detached and set aside, still in his pressure suit. Donna slipped an oxygen mask over his nose and mouth. Grim-faced, she felt beside his Adam's apple for a pulse.

Ekatrina and Ilya sidled into the infirmary. Yevgeny, breathing hard and shed of his own vacuum gear, came to observe from behind with Marcus.

Brad, shifting his weight from foot to foot, huddled beside Donna. She nudged him with an elbow. "Thanks, but now get out! You're filthy! And shut the door. Someone *not* coated in regolith get in here. I might need the extra hands."

Yevgeny stepped forward. "That will be me."

Marcus called, "Brad, bring out Nikolay's helmet with you."

Yevgeny pivoted. "Ekatrina, it's better that you stay."

Marcus blinked. What might Nikolay's camera have captured? Something Yevgeny thought might need explaining. Had Yevgeny—somehow—been altering Russian helmet vids before passing them along?

The spy shit would have to wait. Their focus just then had to be on Nikolay and making sense of whatever had happened to him.

As Ekatrina strode into the infirmary, Brad came out, still suited up. He held Nikolay's helmet in one hand; with the other, he shut the door behind him.

Yevgeny grabbed the helmet. "And Brad, we will also need *your* video."

Brad removed his own helmet. Pointedly, he handed it to Marcus. "Here you go, Boss. What more can I do?"

"Nothing at the moment, but thanks. Get some rest." As for Yevgeny, Marcus gestured toward a nearby storage room. There would be no photoshopping of Nikolay's vid. Not if they watched it together before an opportunity arose. "Let's go somewhere quiet and check out the video."

They transferred Nikolay's helmet memory to a datasheet and fast-forwarded through much of the video. It offered glimpses of boots and gloves when he stooped to scrape regolith into a sample jar and mundane moonscape as he loped between samples. He had switched off his camera far from where he had collapsed—and, the time stamp revealed, more than two hours before Brad found him. (Also before Nikolay had vandalized the prospector bot. Marcus saw no way to mention *that* without getting into his own spy shit.)

Brad's vid, jittering and bouncing as he rushed, also failed to enlighten. He came upon Nikolay beside a debris pile. They saw Nikolay collapsed upon his side, mostly under a tarp, unmoving amid fallen debris. Scattered junk—more when Brad, of whom the camera caught only feet, forearms, and shadow, flipped back the tarp—was speckled in dark red. For all the patches Nikolay had at that point applied, yet more tears gaped on his suit legs. Brad slapped on a bunch more patches, reinflated the suit with oh-two from his spare tank, hoisted the Russian, and galloped to their base.

Throughout, Nikolay was unresponsive.

After their fourth viewing, Marcus sighed. "An accident, don't you think? Loose scrap, pointy or with sharp edges, spilled over onto Nikolay. Anoxia got him before he could plug all the suit leaks."

"Very tidy." The words came out sarcastic. "Why did he not call for help? When suit pressure dropped to dangerous levels, why did the suit itself not trigger an emergency beacon?"

"You know why," Marcus said gently. "The broken wire to his antenna. I suspect it snapped when he fell. Do you know why Nikolay was poking around in that junk pile?"

"I wish I did."

Marcus tried again. "Do you know why he stopped recording?"

Yevgeny shrugged.

Nikolay's death might have been, probably was, a tragic accident. But he had been up to something, whether or not Yevgeny knew what. A camera could get switched off by mistake. There was no way *accidentally* to vandalize a robot. "If we retrace Nikolay's steps, reconstruct what he'd been doing, that might explain things. I'll send out Brad."

"And I will have Ilya accompany him."

"Fair enough." If both men investigated, there could be no denying the vandalism when they encountered the prospector bot, or who must have damaged it. "Fair enough."

A firm knock rattled the storage-room door. "Marcus? Yevgeny? You in there?"

"We are," Marcus said. "Come in, Donna."

She entered, shoulders slumped, and closed the door behind her.

Yevgeny asked, "Is Nikolay ...?"

She shook her head. "I'm so sorry. He wasn't breathing. He had no pulse. I tried, but ...."

Marcus gave her arm a gentle squeeze. No words would help.

"Thank you for trying." Yevgeny paused. "Do you know what happened to Nikolay? Or when?"

She ran splayed fingers through hair dark with sweat. "Start with when. Ordinarily, I'd estimate time of death from the drop in core body temperature. That won't work here. Brad found Nikolay lying mostly in the direct sun, with his chilled-water system compromised. Which is to say, he came inside *above* normal temperature. Making an educated guess from the punctures at how long water circulated before the cooling system ran dry, the math works out to two hours ago. Maybe a bit longer. Even if I'm way off, it was already too late when Brad found him."

It could not have been more than three hours, given when Val had seen Nikolay enter the crater, but Marcus knew not to volunteer that.

Donna continued. "*What* is another matter. I've examined Nikolay as best I can. The cause of death, no surprise, is almost certainly decompression. The suit punctures ...."

"*Almost* certainly decompression," Yevgeny repeated. "Why almost?"

"I'll get there." Again, she hesitated. "Let's start with the straightforward accident scenario. Based on where Brad found Nikolay, he was doing something with one of our debris heaps. Do you know what?"

"No," Yevgeny answered curtly.

Donna shrugged. "For medical purposes, it doesn't matter. His suit has punctures through one hand and in both legs. Perhaps it started when something shifting in the pile pierced that glove. Why do I say that? Because he got the hand leaks, front and back, completely patched. After that, things become murky. He could've lost his balance, woozy from the drop in oh-two pressure, or for any reason have stumbled into the pile. Or while tugging himself free he also yanked on whatever had punched through his hand, and *that* set the debris sliding. However the collapse began, stuff tumbling from the pile did a number on his suit legs. He passed out before he could seal all the leaks."

"All consistent with what we've seen in Brad's helmet vid." Forestalling the obvious question, Marcus added, "Nikolay's helmet had stopped recording awhile earlier."

"That's unfortunate," Donna said. "As for your last question, Yevgeny, assuming decompression is what killed Nikolay, that may not have been the root cause of the tragedy."

Yevgeny frowned. "Then what?"

"Perhaps it was a fall. Did you notice the bluish-purple splotch on Nikolay's forehead? That's a fresh bruise, although not much of one. But even supposing Nikolay blacked out, he was not unconscious for longer than a few seconds, given that he had time to start patching." She canted her head thoughtfully. "I don't suppose we'll ever know whether a fall caused the junk-pile avalanche, or the other way round."

Yevgeny shook his head. "Nikolay was a very careful, very cautious man."

"He was," Donna agreed. "And beyond respecting the big guy, I liked him. I'd hate to believe clumsiness or carelessness did this, but anyone can have a momentary lapse. Alone, in a vacuum? It can be fatal.

"But a fall isn't the only scenario nor, I believe, the most probable. I took blood samples. Those were less than definitive due to vacuum exposure and the associated dehydration, but I did note that his troponin levels are somewhat elevated."

Troponin? Marcus did not know the word. "Meaning?"

"Perhaps not a thing," Donna said. "It may be irrelevant. Or, and this is my best guess, it could indicate Nikolay had an MI." At Marcus's arching of an eyebrow, she translated, "Myocardial infarction."

Yevgeny said, "Excuse my poor English, please."

"Sorry, that was still in med-speak. Heart attack."

Yevgeny frowned. "And this troponin is a marker for a heart attack?"

"Correct," Donna said. "The complicating factor is that a troponin rise only begins *after* the MI, troponin being released into the bloodstream as cardiac muscle cells die. The levels continue rising for days."

"If the patient survives," Marcus added softly.

"Right." Donna leaned against a wall. "The thing is, the slightly elevated level that I measured is far from conclusive. Yes, it might be indicative of a very recent heart attack. That might be why Nikolay fell, why he was unable to finish patching his suit. Having said that, the level can be elevated for other reasons. It happens, for example, in many instances of sepsis, which, oversimplifying a bit, is a generalized infection. And some people get a troponin spike from strenuous exercise, although that generally involves being triathlon-strenuous."

"Active cosmonauts do not get heart attacks," Yevgeny said stiffly. "We are screened too thoroughly. Not to mention that Nikolay had said nothing about chest pains."

"I *know*." Donna pushed off from the wall and began to pace. "But not all MIs cause pain. Others begin with vague symptoms like indigestion, easily rationalized or ignored. And no screening is perfect. It's possible for any of us to have, for example, an asymptomatic, non-obstructing plaque in a coronary artery. Let such an unsuspected plaque rupture …."

And presto, Marcus completed, a blocked coronary artery. Cardiac muscle damage. And troponin.

Yevgeny's eyes narrowed. "How might we determine whether Nikolay had a heart attack? Not just speculate, but *know*?"

"It'd take an autopsy," Donna said. "Just as it would take an autopsy to establish any of the yet more remote medical possibilities.

Pulmonary embolism. Brain aneurysm. A massive stroke. Before either of you gets any bright ideas, I lack the training to do an autopsy, even if we had the proper equipment."

"A stroke?" As Marcus's mind raced, the words just slipped out. Was confusion due to a stroke why Nikolay disabled his camera? The motivation for whatever he'd done to the robot?

Yevgeny turned toward Marcus. "Why do you ask?"

"It's just a scary thought," Marcus said hastily.

"No matter," Yevgeny said. "Once I shuttle Nikolay back to Base Putin, the doctors there will make the determination."

"Well . . . ?"

"What is it?" Marcus prompted Donna.

She stopped pacing and turned to face him. "Hoping to make sense of this, I contacted the biology team at Base Putin. Yes, over a secure link. Their assignment is to study Goliath, but first and foremost, many of them are physicians. And all are cleared to know what we're dealing with."

"Well?" Yevgeny prompted.

Again, she hesitated. "They are as unconvinced, Yevgeny, as are you that Nikolay might have had an MI. Oh, they agree an MI would be consistent with my observations. They *also* suggest that he may have succumbed to an alien contagion. None of us are to leave this area, not even poor Nikolay." Her tone turned nasal. Mimicking who? "You don't have a Class Four biosafety lab, now do you?"

"Do they?" Marcus asked.

She shook her head. "They'd become almost as cavalier as we about any biological risk. Apart from examining Goliath inside an improvised, supersized glove box, they had taken no special precautions, either. Well, *that* era has ended. All further work on Goliath is on hold till a Class Four facility is built at Base Putin."

"At which point, the doctors will have a look at Nikolay?" Yevgeny asked.

Donna hesitated.

"Seriously?" Marcus slugged the nearest wall. They had exposed themselves willingly—but to be *treated* as guinea pigs still rankled. "The aliens are millions of years dead and gone."

She nodded. "And not that anyone I spoke to cared, I've seen no sign, in any of our routine blood samples, of infection or immune response."

"Unless," Marcus said, "Nikolay *is* our first sign."

Donna broke a lengthening silence. "I don't buy it. No one has revived any alien cells, much less seen any interact with terrestrial cultures. If alien viruses or gut bacteria or prions somehow survived for eons within Goliath's mummy, well, the 'experts' have yet to find them. Regardless, we're locked down here. Quarantined. Officially so."

Yevgeny folded his arms across his chest. "There must be an autopsy. If not today, then later. Until that time, we must, we will, preserve the option of a meaningful examination."

Marcus thought, and if Brad or Donna were to die so unexpectedly? I'd demand answers, too. "We can preserve the body in the constant cold in the back of the lava tube."

But even the idea of needing a morgue made him shiver.

"The fact of the matter," Donna said, "is that we've been *ordered* to preserve the body. Soon, too. But cold alone won't do the job. We'd find ourselves with another mummy, like Goliath, from the vacuum. Unless we seal the body, that is. But his pressure suit was tattered even before I cut him out of it. The body needs to go into a PRE." Personal rescue enclosure. "I'll take care of it."

"It," Yevgeny growled, his face flushed. "The body. I cannot be so detached. So clinical. This is Nikolay. This is our colleague, our *friend*. It's bad enough that he must be zipped inside a plastic bag like dinner scraps. I will not permit him to be gawked at on our every trip to or from the surface.

"No. We will make use of one of the chambers *behind* us, in the vacuum beyond the sealed-off part of the facility. There Nikolay may rest, undisturbed, and with some dignity. Until I can appeal this foolish recommendation, to the director of the FSB if I must. These gutless doctors *will* be overturned. We *will* know what happened to Nikolay."

For the first time in Marcus's experience, Yevgeny turned out to be wrong.

Chapter 24

"I believe that about covers it," Yevgeny said. Pointedly. Leadingly.

He was eager to take Ilya aside, to delve into matters best not discussed in front of the Americans. Not that Yevgeny's reflexive secretiveness had stopped him from pressing *Brad* about what the two had encountered, however—apparently—unenlightening, in the attempt to reconstruct Nikolay's final hours ....

Brad and Ilya had scarcely set foot back inside, people converging as soon as the airlock began to cycle. Their exploration had been radio-silent, the men linked by fiber-optic cable, while everyone else speculated what they might find. Donna and (exhibiting an exasperating lack of discipline) Ekatrina had exploded with questions as soon as the men removed their helmets. Yevgeny and (he noted with interest) Marcus were more deliberate. If Yevgeny had not dropped his hint, he suspected, his American counterpart would soon have done so.

Ilya's eyes narrowed at the suggestion. "I think you are right."

"Well ...," Brad said.

"We should let you guys have a bit of downtime," Marcus injected.

Yevgeny cleared his throat. "Ilya, Ekatrina, we need to discuss what can be said to our friend's family about this tragedy."

"I know a bit about them," Ekatrina piped up. "His parents are in Orel. His sisters—"

"Come to my quarters." Yevgeny set off, expecting the other two to follow. Ilya did.

" … Moved separately, years apart, to Rostov-on-Don." Even as she prattled on, Ekatrina began walking. Did she suppose such basic information was unknown to the FSB? "I do not believe Kolya is, was, close with his ex-wife, but still, I think, he would want her told."

Kolya? Yevgeny thought. He wondered when the two had found the time for bonding—and how *he* had missed it. In any event, their friendship (or more?) explained Ekatrina's unexpected knowledge of the deceased's family. "Hold that thought," he hissed under his breath.

She shut up.

Marcus, meanwhile, had taken hold of Brad's arm, and was guiding the big man somewhere private. Like Ilya, he had been given no opportunity to take off his pressure suit. Inwardly, Yevgeny shrugged. Why bother de-suiting? They would all be going into vacuum soon enough.

They reached his quarters. Apart from a sleep platform and the shelf with a few changes of clothing, the room was bare—and that starkness seemed an apt metaphor for the day. He gestured Ilya and Ekatrina inside, shut the door behind himself, and signaled for quiet. A quick sweep with his FSB datasheet for bugs showed the room remained clean. He started the comp playing the Tchaikovsky violin concerto. If a more melancholy piece of music existed, Yevgeny had never heard it. "Now we can talk."

"About what we can tell Kolya's family," Ekatrina resumed at once, but in Russian. "It seems to me—"

"Later," Yevgeny snapped. Biting her lip, she for once took a hint. "And stick with English, both of you. If anyone should overhear a word or two, let us not sound like we are hiding anything." And on any wager as to whether Marcus had CIA software for translating Russian, Yevgeny would bet yes, on pain of eating his own helmet. "All right, Ilya. What did you see up there?"

"What I told you and the Americans."

"Tell me again. But first, is it possible that Marcus or Donna left the base while Nikolay was alone outside?" Because Marcus might also have gotten a suggestion from his superiors about convenient accidents ….

Without hesitation: "No."

"I agree," Ekatrina confirmed unprompted. "I was in or near the control room the entire time. Had the airlock cycled, I would have heard."

"Good," Yevgeny said. "So, Ilya, review what you and Brad did."

With a weary shrug, the physicist proceeded. "We hiked to where Nikolay had said he next planned to survey. Out toward where you and Brad had seen him going. To judge from row upon row there of boot prints, he started his sampling. But as Brad and I both reported, a set of tracks led from that area over a ridge to the inoperative American robot, then returned. Another set of tracks led back toward the base, detouring into the crater where Brad later found him. Nikolay's excursion to the robot came first, obviously."

Ekatrina asked, "And *had* Kolya taken the robot's mass spectrometer?"

Ilya considered. "Mounting brackets are empty beneath the bot where something was removed. You saw as much on Brad's and my helmet vids. But is the missing object a mass spectrometer? If so, when was it taken? I don't know. Assuming that Nikolay *did* detach an instrument, we found no sign of it." He thought some more. "I noticed earlier that Nikolay's backpack was missing a spare battery. That may not mean anything, but if he did remove the American's instrument, the missing battery might have been used to power it."

"There had been a mass spectrometer on the robot," Yevgeny said flatly. "And Nikolay did take it."

"How can you know?" Ekatrina asked, still angry.

"The American leasing company promotes its robots' features on its website. I reviewed that even before we arrived here. And once I have the opportunity to obtain recent satellite images taken from a proper oblique angle, I will get an idea when the instrument went missing."

All of which the Americans must anticipate. That was *why* he felt sure they had not lied. But had Nikolay realized that no satellites had a line of sight while he was scavenging the mass spectrometer? Or was the absence of timely surveillance an instance of bad luck?

"Then explain this," Ekatrina demanded. "If Nikolai took it, where *is* this purloined instrument?"

As mousy as Yevgeny found her in appearance, down to her chisel-like front teeth, her personality was aggressive. All ferret. But her *mind* was first-rate, else he would never have coerced her along. He gestured for her to continue.

"Ilya, you followed Nikolay's tracks without finding the mass spec. How do you explain *that*?" Her eyes narrowed. "Might Brad have hidden it on his way to the crater, or before bringing Nikolay inside?"

Yevgeny had his own reasons for questioning the big American's version of events. As in: why had Brad "happened" to find Nikolay? No matter that Brad's helmet vid had shown nothing untoward, and that the Americans had had no obvious opportunity to alter that record, Yevgeny remained suspicious.

"Gotta go back," Brad had announced before separating from Yevgeny and their mutual project for the day to return early to the base. "I forgot to refill my drinking water. Sorry."

Had that been only hours before? It felt like a whole different era. A sudden death would do that, Yevgeny supposed.

Regardless, a water tank carelessly left unreplenished? Possible, to be sure, but out of character—Yevgeny had never known the American to be other than thorough and prepared. And then, multiplying improbabilities, "for no particular reason," Brad had decided to detour past the Nikolay's crater rather than go directly to the lava tube.

"Might Brad have earlier recovered and then hidden the mass spectrometer?" Ilya frowned in concentration. "I cannot prove otherwise, but he seemed surprised that the bot had been tampered with. Also, I saw nothing along Nikolay's reconstructed path to suggest anyone else's recent presence. Not till boot prints converged where Brad had approached the crater in which we know he found Nikolay. Nor did I find the instrument within the crater. I even looked beneath the tarp of the disturbed scrap pile."

"The path as you reconstructed it must have had gaps," Ekatrina insisted. "Otherwise you must have found where *one* of them left the instrument."

Ilya gazed into space, lost in thought. "True," he conceded at last. "Several times Brad and I encountered terrain too rocky or too much trodden upon to disclose particular boot prints. But each time, we continued in the direction we had been going, and always we picked up Nikolay's trail."

"So," Ekatrina interpreted, "At any of those rocky or churned spots Kolya might have left his supposed trail and hidden the mass spectrometer. Or Brad, if he had first used the same inhospitable terrain to sneak up on our friend."

"Enough!" Ilya shouted. "I just do not get it. I do not get *you*. Either of you. What weird conspiracy have you concocted in your minds? That by magic or telepathy the Americans knew Nikolay had scavenged an instrument from their robot? That they assassinated him for that? This is madness!

"I already feel horrible about his death. If not for my speculations about alien power sources, we"—that meant Yevgeny—"would not have been pushing him so hard. Then, I have to believe, he would not have been so desperate as to take that instrument.

"But for you to imagine he was *killed* over that? Madness, I say again. And utter nonsense. Nikolay was dead well before Brad came upon him."

Do I imagine things? Yevgeny wondered. Perhaps. And yet, perhaps not. "We have only Donna's word for when Nikolay died. And nothing but her tentative"—dubious—"theory as to how he died."

"Then what *do* you believe—"

They fell silent at the clomp of boots in the hallway.

"Yevgeny, it's time. We three are ready and suited up." Marcus's voice softened. "This has all been so sudden. If you need a little while longer ...?"

"Just a moment," Yevgeny answered. More softly, he said, "We will continue this conversation later. But for now, we go to speak our goodbyes to Nikolay Sergeyevich."

They spoke often of *the* airlock of their underground lair, despite the imprecision of the usage. True, there was but one portal through which they accessed the surface. But there were other airlocks, in the partitions they had erected to separate the structurally sound front of the ancient alien facility from several crumbling passages extending far—often, they did not know how far—into the lunar bedrock. Several meters beyond the wall and airlock they had installed in the main tunnel, fissures abounded. There, the rock-and-mooncrete rubble of untold roof collapses lay thick upon the floor. Barring major reconstruction, the deepest reaches of the ancient alien facility would likely remain off-limits.

Hence, the volume they occupied terminated in sturdy walls—and like all dead ends, these had accumulated stuff. Bags of trash. Scraps of alien tech, in crates and bags and random piles, staged for shifting to the surface and eventual off-site analysis. To-be-processed supplies from shuttle deliveries. Nests of emptied boxes. Most recently, shelving units, bearing both alien and human goods, relocated from storage rooms in the so far unsuccessful search for an all but imperceptible, but cumulatively annoying, air leak. Now much of that debris had to be moved before they could access the long-ignored rear airlock.

Ilya strode after the Americans to help shift things, while Yevgeny and Ekatrina retrieved and struggled into their pressure suits. If she noticed him put on a tool belt, or the industrial endoscope and reel of fiber-optic cable he tucked into one of the belt pockets, she showed the good judgment not to comment. The two of them rejoined the others, adding their helmets to the row on the floor alongside one wall of the main passageway. On the wall opposite, beneath a gray tarp, rested something long and lozenge-shaped.

Something, the word echoed in Yevgeny's mind. Except this was not some*thing*, was it? Nor was *tarp* the appropriate term. He folded back a corner of the shroud to gaze through the clear plastic of the rescue bubble. Within the PRE, Nikolay was covered up to his shoulders by a clean white sheet. Yevgeny studied the face, waxen in death—and accusatory.

I will find out what happened to you, Yevgeny silently promised. And then I will take the appropriate actions.

A flurry of activity finished opening a path to the airlock. Marcus cleared his throat. "Yevgeny?"

"Thank you," Yevgeny said. As though this reflexive response had somehow held significance, people arranged themselves into a line, facing him. Most bowed their heads. It had not until that moment registered—events were moving so quickly—but as leader of the Russian contingent, everyone *would* expect him to officiate. "We are here to …" Honor? Recognize? Mourn? "We are here to respect the memory of our colleague, Nikolay Sergeyevich Bautin. We—"

"Our friend," Ekatrina corrected. "Our *good* friend."

"Indeed," Yevgeny agreed. "His untimely death was tragic, and we shall all miss him. Our thoughts are with his family."

He fell silent, all too conscious of the men and women studying him. Disappointed. Disapproving. But what could he add with convincing sincerity? It had been drummed into him: never befriend an asset, lest you be tempted to prioritize their safety over the mission. But *his* readiness to sacrifice them, if it should come to that, did not mean he was willing to have anyone else harm them.

Ekatrina shifted her weight from foot to foot. Frowned. Raised an eyebrow at him.

Here and now, he would welcome someone filling the silence. "Katya, would you care to add something? Or anyone else?"

"Yes, please." The words caught in her throat. "Nikolay was a talented and dedicated scientist, as we all have had the opportunity to appreciate. He was kind. Big-hearted. He had, if you attended closely enough to his words, a wonderful wry sense of humor. He was a photographer of great skill. A proud and patriotic Russian. A man with great patience and stamina and determination. I believe he was a dutiful son. But above all, quite simply, Kolya was a good man. He was my friend, and I shall miss him. I remember the time …."

When Ekatrina trailed off, Ilya offered his own anecdote. Marcus did, too.

At last a pause stretched long enough for Yevgeny to suggest, "It is time we lay our friend to rest."

Marcus nodded.

Yevgeny put on his helmet, voice-commanded its lamps, opened the inner door of the airlock, and returned to the near end of the tarp-covered body. "Ilya, give me a hand, please?"

"Of course." Ilya secured his helmet. "Suit, headlamps on"—and likely continuing out of habit—"camera on."

"No," Yevgeny said firmly. "This is private, not some exploration to be recorded."

"Understood," Marcus agreed sadly.

"Suit, camera off," Ilya said.

The Russian men took opposite ends of the platform-box serving as Nikolay's improvised bier. They maneuvered into the airlock, holding Nikolay level lest his sheet slip off. Kept horizontal, he only fit along the diagonal between the hatches. The pallbearers, awkwardly shifting their grips to the bier's long sides, worked themselves into the unoccupied corners. Yevgeny positioned himself to be first out when the farther hatch opened.

Marcus called (his voice faint through Yevgeny's helmet), "We'll follow right along."

"I thought we had agreed this was private," Yevgeny reminded.

"All right," Marcus said.

Yevgeny turned his head toward Ekatrina. "Bring along a portable lamp and fuel cell, please. Two sets if you can manage them." Not waiting for an answer, he elbowed the button that started the airlock cycling.

Yevgeny backed from the airlock, head swiveling, searching for clear places amid scattered debris to set his feet. Helmet lamps offered the brightest light, but only in small spots. Scattered ceiling panels, dimly glowing, provided more general illumination. Drawing power from the photovoltaic paint in the occupied areas, alien circuitry must also have begun to regrow itself here. As far back as the cave-in, several meters past the openings to two side passages, only the dust coating and debris on the floor and several unpatched ceiling cracks distinguished this space from the climate-controlled side of the wall. It was much as he remembered from his early explorations, before the partition had gone up.

"Where to?" Ilya asked.

Yevgeny shook his head. "Radio silence," he mouthed. They proceeded in silence, Yevgeny walking backward. Ilya paused, balancing Nikolay's bier on a bent knee, to tap the hatch-close button before exiting the airlock. They went down the first side passage. Yevgeny peeked through the first open door—a half-empty storeroom—and backed in. With a quick dip of his head, he signaled: set Nikolay down here. He had just offered Ilya one end of a short length of fiber-optic cable when Ekatrina rejoined them.

"I followed your light." She set down the portable post lamp she had brought. The dark walls drank up its cool white radiance. "Poor Kolya."

"Radio silence," Yevgeny mouthed once more. He handed her the end of a second cable.

"You do realize," she said, still on an open channel, "that radio waves won't penetrate a metal wall."

He flourished the cable end in her face till she grabbed the plug and jacked in, disabling her helmet radio. "You're the electrical engineer. There must be ways."

With a thoughtful expression, she conceded the point. "But why such secrecy for a memorial?"

"We had our memorial inside," Yevgeny said crisply. "This is a reconnaissance. And we must be quick to make use of this opportunity. Ilya, it's your show."

After a blink of surprise, Ilya understood. "The alien power source. You want to find it. If it exists, that is."

Had Nikolay in all his searching found any trace of ancient solar panels? No. "We must have a look."

Ekatrina glowered. "This is so distasteful. So … dishonorable. Can we not—"

"It is a matter of state security," Yevgeny snapped.

"Ilya?" she appealed.

"If the aliens had conquered fusion, I'd like to know it." The physicist shrugged. "You can disapprove of me later."

"Enough discussion," Yevgeny said. "We have ten minutes, no more. If we linger too long, the Americans are apt to come check up on us. Ekatrina, you scout out this corridor. Ilya, you take the other open passage. I will wait by the airlock in case anyone decides to join us. If I come onto the radio, that's your cue to hurry back before the airlock has time to cycle."

She stormed off, leaving fiber-optic cable ends dangling from the men's helmets. Only someone with her temper could have mastered the low-gravity version of stomping.

Ilya snatched up the lamp she had left behind. "Be back soon, I expect. If I recall correctly, there was a cave-in down my assigned corridor."

Yevgeny offered the endoscope and fiber-optic cable reel he had brought. "The endoscope has WiFi and cable interfaces to your HUD. The cable end has a fish-eye lens."

Ilya arched an eyebrow. "Planning ahead, I see."

"I try. Now, please hurry." Yevgeny returned to the airlock, where Ekatrina had left the nearest hatch agape. Good: should that hatch begin to close, he would be forewarned of someone coming through.

Three minutes passed. Five. Seven. In the still of vacuum and radio silence, the wait was unnerving. Apart from glimmers of light as Ilya and Ekatrina explored their assigned corridors, nothing changed but the clock digits on his HUD. Until Ilya bustled up, working the crank to rewind fiber-optic cable onto its reel.

Grinning from ear to ear.

Chapter 25

Yevgeny knew how to move stealthily without acting furtive. On Earth. Even, he prided himself, on the lunar surface. But suited up for vacuum, deep inside a pressurized facility? By the dark of the sleep shift? That was an art he had yet to master. But barring bad luck, he reassured himself, he and Ilya would be through the rear airlock with the Americans none the wiser.

Ekatrina had balked at her part. Such recalcitrance had long ceased to surprise him. "You're exploiting Kolya's death. Dishonoring his memory."

"No," he had told her, "I am giving meaning to his death."

"By skulking about. By lying and keeping secrets."

Some days he could not summon the energy to argue with or cajole her. "Look," he had said, "if the job is beyond you, just admit it."

And so here she was, in pajamas, slippers, and a robe, drink bulb in hand, her hair sleep-tousled, to loiter near the rear airlock. The opening line of her script, should any American make an untimely appearance, was brief: "I couldn't sleep, so I decided to walk around for awhile." But before that, at the first sound of a footfall, she would warn them ….

The motor hum as the airlock hatch opened only seemed deafening. No one came to investigate, just as no one had stirred on the previous sleep shift when Yevgeny had, as a test, cycled the airlock at the same middle-of-the-"night" hour.

"You're set?" he asked her.

"Robe and cocoa. A locked but never-used datasheet in my robe pocket. Yes, I'm set." At his frown, she added, "And a signaling device in my *other* robe pocket. Just so you also have the matching unit."

He patted a tool-belt pocket. "Got it. Thanks."

Radio waves could not penetrate the metal wall. And yet, if an American were to show up while she dallied, she had to have a way to warn them. So: the device she carried had two buttons. Red for STAY WHERE YOU ARE. Green for COAST IS CLEAR. Press either button, and it emitted an intense burst of ultrasound. The device he carried, once firmly taped to the vacuum side of the partition, would translate inaudible acoustic vibrations to a low-power, short-range, radio signal for their helmet comms. Were her insecurity not useful, he might have praised the brilliant improvisation.

The men seated and latched their helmets, then passed through to the partitioned-off area. While Yevgeny affixed his part of the warning system to the wall beside the hatch, Ilya went ahead. Yevgeny took an extra few minutes to sweep around the airlock for bugs, finding none.

Catching up, he found the physicist shifting rock and mooncrete chunks from the cave-in that had all but sealed off the room at the end of the corridor. The obstacle had, here and there, been lowered to chin level. A meters-long collection of relocated rubble now rested along a junction of floor and corridor wall.

Ilya turned as the bright, expanding ovals cast by headlamps announced Yevgeny's approach. "No bugs? Radio, then?" he mouthed. At Yevgeny's nod, they met on the prearranged secure channel. "Beautiful, is it not?"

"Any radioactivity?"

Ilya patted a meter dangling from his tool belt. "None. And there would not have been, not for eons."

Yevgeny lugged a breadbox-sized, almost flat concrete chunk and set it outside the blocked doorway. From that wobbly perch, craning his neck, nothing within came as a complete surprise. Still, the images from their first incursion, distorted by the fish-eye lens, had not done the room justice.

But as impressive as all this wreckage was, he still struggled to recognize the supposed components of the hypothetical fusion reactor. Massive wire coils, presumably powerful electromagnets. The spherical configuration of glass tubes—gas lasers, Ilya had excitedly insisted—pointed, through slits in an onion-layered shell, at a central focus. (The geometric inferences Yevgeny took on faith. He strained even to extrapolate tubes from the splinters and sparkles of shattered glass among the rubble of the roof collapse. As for the so-called spherical shell, its supposed onion layers appeared minced.) A large cylindrical tank with a mirror finish, much dented. Where that tank had cracked open, glimpses of an inner lining. Along a side wall, a bundle of fat cables rose into the ceiling from what might once have been a power-distribution frame. Ocher shards and twisted metal around where a large concrete slab of ceiling had crushed a rack of alien electronics.

"And you are certain," Yevgeny said, "this was a fusion reactor." Beyond *yes* or *no*, he did not expect to understand much of Ilya's reply. He mainly wanted to gauge the confidence—or lack thereof—in Ilya's response. "Why do I not see shielding?"

"Short answer first. The onion shell absorbs most of the radiation. I believe the lasers are placed outside that shell for ease of servicing. The big electromagnets stop whatever charged particles escape through the slits. The few centimeters of passive material along the wall would be backup for the magnets, if those should go offline, and to block any high-energy photons that might escape through the shell slits from leaving the room.

"On to your larger question, then. Yes. Without a doubt, this was a fusion reactor. See that big capacitor bank?"

Yevgeny looked where Ilya pointed. "I thought those were batteries, or maybe fuel cells. For backup."

"The backup power storage is within the part of the base we occupy. No, this is something different. Permit me to give a quick bit of background. This reactor works by hitting tiny fuel droplets, one after another, with powerful laser pulses."

"Droplets," Yevgeny repeated. "As in, from a liquid." Somehow, that seemed odd.

Ilya waved impatiently. "Yes, liquid. Bear with me. Each droplet, in its turn, is struck from all sides by the laser pulses. The intense pulses compress it in an instant into a many-millions-of-degrees-hot speck, under unearthly pressure."

"Conditions as in the interior of the Sun."

"Just so. And … voilà. Fusion. The thing is, the process requires dumping a lot of power, in a very brief time, into the lasers. And I mean, a *lot*. It is accomplished by discharging the capacitor bank. A fraction of the reactor's output from the fusing of each droplet recharges the capacitors for their next discharge. That is simplified, of course."

Of course. "And how did the capacitors get charged *before* the initial fusion reaction?"

Ilya looked around, then shrugged. "Not with anything I see. If I had to guess, and I suppose I do, with a jump-start from the ship that delivered the aliens here."

Those must have been some jumper cables. "All right. What else here catches your eye?"

"Do you see that shiny tank? It is mirrored to keep out ambient heat, and double-walled for the same reason. That's cryogenic storage for the fuel. And protruding from the tank, I think—no, I take that back; it must be—is the injection mechanism that delivers the stream of fuel droplets into the sphere of lasers."

"So why wrap a fusion reactor inside an onion shell?"

Ilya grinned. "You will like this. The nuclear power plants we are familiar with are nothing more than big steam engines. The reactor makes heat. Heat produces steam. Steam turns big turbines for propulsion, or turns the rotors of electrical generators. Aside from nuclear reactions as the heat source, it's all very nineteenth century."

"And with the aliens?"

"Fusion happens within the onion shell. The concentric layers of the shell absorb the X-rays and charged particles emitted by the fusion reaction, converting that radiation directly into electrical power. And as I said, electromagnetic shielding traps any charged particles that manage to penetrate through the shell. Dirtside, only small lab prototypes do that sort of direct-conversion tech."

"That *is* impressive." And very encouraging.

"It gets better, Yevgeny. You can see there is only the one tank, meaning that the reactor runs off a single fuel. And the passive shielding along the walls, as you will also have noticed, is thin, indicating that the fusion reaction is aneutronic. Almost certainly—"

"The reaction is a what?"

"Aneutronic. Many fusion reactions, including all the easier ones, spew out neutrons as a byproduct." Ilya chuckled. "Easier being a quite different thing than easy. No human research project has yet managed any kind of sustained fusion reaction. Anyway, neutrons, being neutral particles, are not deflected by electromagnets. And neutrons plow straight through most physical barriers, because atoms are mostly empty space. Hence, a fusion reaction fueled by, say, deuterium and tritium, requires lots of passive shielding to contain the neutrons."

"Then those 'easier' reactors are not what you would want on a fusion-powered ship. I see. And aneutronic?"

"As you would expect from the name," Ilya said. "A reaction that does *not* emit neutrons. Combine the types of shielding we see, and the liquid-fuel injector, and the single fuel tank, and I am led to believe this reactor ran on what happens to be the Moon's most readily available fusion fuel: helium-3. When two helium-3 atoms fuse, the reaction produces one atom of helium-4, the common isotope, plus two protons, plus energy. A *lot* of energy.

"And here is your answer to why fuel is delivered in liquid droplets, and not solid pellets. Beyond extreme cold, you would need more than twenty atmospheres of pressure to freeze helium. Liquid droplets are less bother."

Helium-3. The rare isotope for which the lunar strip mines outside Base Putin provided Russia a near monopoly, no matter that collecting the He-3 had been a hugely expensive gamble on as-yet undeveloped technology. A gamble that might be on the verge of paying off ….

Yevgeny asked, "And you can reverse-engineer their reactor technology from this wreckage?"

"Well …."

"Then why the *hell*," Yevgeny demanded, his optimism deflated in an instant like a popped balloon, "are you so excited?"

"The underlying principles are basic physics, well understood for half a century. *That* is how I know what things here must be. From the relatively small number of lasers alone, it is clear the alien technology is *far* in advance of ours. Presuming these lasers haven't all broken and degraded in the same way, experts might assemble enough clues to infer much. But the true secret, what we need to master, is subtle engineering detail. Calibrations, startup and shutdown procedures, and the like. *That*"—and Ilya gestured vaguely toward the crushed alien electronics—"I expect to have resided as programs and data in the mangled circuitry."

"But examining even this much of a onetime working power plant must be of value."

"Oh, indeed, not least as a feasibility proof. Just knowing that *someone* developed a practical fusion reactor along these lines will focus our own research. Another reason I am impressed? Size, or rather, the lack of it. Every human effort to develop similar technology, whether by national labs or various international consortia, has been huge. And did you notice the magnets?"

"What about them?"

"I see nothing to indicate they were cryo-cooled."

Ah. Room-temperature superconductors. "And if we bring home a sample of the wire? That can be analyzed? Reverse-engineered?"

Ilya grinned. "Almost certainly."

A trophy of sorts, then. If not the secret of fusion, at least *something*. "I'll help you dig."

By 3:30 am, when the alarm in Yevgeny's helmet went off, the barrier was still chest-high. Both men were gray with rock dust, their sturdy gloves filthier still.

"We will have to finish on another trip," Ilya grumbled. "More likely, two."

Should they? With each foray they risked exposure, and the Americans gaining access to this technology. What Ilya had already observed must surely give Russian fusion research a tremendous boost.

Yevgeny said, "Climb over and collect a wire sample. And while you are inside, take pictures all around. But be quick. We must be back inside, our vacuum gear stowed, before the Americans stir."

Ilya straightened, turned to face Yevgeny, and crossed his arms across his chest. "Poor Nikolay is lying a few meters away, killed by a moment of carelessness in a dangerous environment. Respectfully, I am not about to crawl over a tangle of jagged debris, much less scavenge inside without first bracing what remains of the ceiling."

Was that unreasonable? Not really. Never mind that—the lack of proof, or of any plausible suspect, be damned—Yevgeny doubted more than ever that carelessness had had any part in Nikolay's demise. But neither did they dare undertake another nighttime foray. Not for any mere consolation prize. "Fine. I'll go."

And I will deal at another time with this insubordination.

Trying not to feel ghoulish, Yevgeny dashed to the next corridor to borrow Nikolay's tarp/shroud. The tough plastic sheet, draped over the rubble, might spare the fabric of Yevgeny's pressure suit from torn shins. He scrambled over the barrier, nudged two of the ubiquitous starfish robots out of his way with a boot, snipped a meters-long sample from the nearest presumed magnet, and extended an end of wire to Ilya. "Wind this up on something. A rock, maybe." He started to climb back over.

"Pictures?" Ilya reminded. "Also, take a scraping of the wall lining. I expect the passive shielding is iridium, but we should confirm that. And if you should happen upon an intact laser, or a decent-sized segment of the onion shell, bring that."

Anything else? Yevgeny deposited scrapings and some onion-shell fragments into two plastic sample bags, stowing them in a tool-belt pocket. He sidled around the rubble and wrecked gear, his helmet camera recording. Each broken laser tube he came upon seemed more fractured than the last. Twice, it was all he could do to squeeze between the wrecked reactor and the wall. Edging behind the reactor, he came upon a wall rip offering him a glimpse into the main corridor. Here, he was beyond the massive roof collapse that had closed off that passage.

Given his oblique view, he could not decide at first what he was seeing through the tear. A tall metal panel, thrust into the corridor and folded nearly in half. A metal framework of some kind, accordioned beneath more collapsed roof. Beyond that squashed . . . tube(?), by squatting, he saw more bent and torn metal.

At both ends of the tube, or framework, dangling wires and conduits. Past all that, more concrete-lined tunnel.

An airlock! They would not be fixing *it* with a fuel cell and a handful of wire jumpers. Nor even, if they had had the equipment, with a hundred-tonne hydraulic jack.

On Yevgeny's HUD, clock digits raced toward 4:00 am. They *had* to get moving. He clambered back the way he had come, wondering what alien secrets remained to be discovered. "I should not need to mention this, but—"

"Yes, yes. State security. My assumption these days is that *anything* the Americans do not yet know falls into that category, unless you direct otherwise."

"As you should."

And then, for an interminable two seconds, a harsh tone keened and echoed in their helmets: STAY WHERE YOU ARE.

"*Shit!*" Ilya said. "The Americans may be learning stuff real soon."

"Stay calm." Yevgeny spoke to himself as much as to his companion. He had cut things too close. Before long, everyone would be awake and about. They either sneaked back soon, or they got caught—and he *really* did not want to explain.

"I guess someone else had trouble sleeping. Join me in some coffee?" How hard could that be? Once Ekatrina had drawn the inopportune someone to the base kitchen, she had only to pat her robe pockets and say, "I seem to have dropped my datasheet while pacing. Fill us a couple of bulbs? I will be right back."

And if that *someone* were not so easily distracted?

Success or failure: it all came down to Ekatrina.

Whether as rehearsed or by improvisation, she pulled it off. The next tone they heard, an interminable two minutes later, signaled COAST IS CLEAR.

On their way back, in his haste and all the excitement, Yevgeny almost forgot to restore the shroud and to pocket the ultrasound/radio transducer. Just in case one of the Americans should decide to pay final respects to poor Nikolay.

It took Yevgeny hours, but in the end he contrived an innocuous-sounding reason to run out with Ekatrina to their shuttlecraft. Where he would have struggled, she extracted its ground-penetrating radar unit from the instrument console without skinning a knuckle and with hardly a harsh word.

Taking a meandering path across rocky terrain, cabled together for radio silence, they came to his best guess at the spot above the newfound alien airlock. Before he turned over helmet downloads, of course, vids would show a different, and more direct, return to the base.

Ekatrina busied herself with the GPR, now running on battery power. "Yevgeny ...?"

"What?"

"I've been thinking ...."

Ominous words, those. "About?"

"Nikolay's death. Something is going on that we do not understand. This is a bad time for anyone to keep secrets."

As if the Americans had invited Russia here! Were it not for *his* suspicions, *his* initiative, everything there was to learn about these aliens would have remained an American secret. And though he still had no proof, nor even a plausible scenario, he *knew* the Americans had had a part in Nikolay's death. Somehow.

He grabbed Ekatrina's elbow, pulled her around to face him. "Do the words 'state security' mean anything to you?"

She pulled free, her face flushed. "Oh, those words mean a *lot*. 'State security' is why the navy was so slow to react when Father's submarine went down. 'State security' is what kept other, *capable*, navies at a distance while any survivors might still have been rescued. 'State security' is why, for long years after the tragedy, Mother and I knew little about how and why Father died—and nothing about the negligence and incompetence that killed all those men."

"State security, Katya, is what your father was sworn to protect. The *Kursk* sinking in no way diminishes his commitment. If you would honor your father, show respect for his values."

"His *values*? Father joined the navy for one reason only. Desperation. His *value* was feeding his family."

"Did you enjoy Murmansk?" The question, or perhaps the implication, reduced her to sullen silence. Because no one liked Murmansk: an impoverished, provincial, depressing seaport and naval base inside the Artic Circle. "If growing up there was hard, I ask you to imagine growing old in Irkutsk." An armpit of a town in central Siberia.

She blinked. "What do you want?"

"Your skills. Your cooperation. Your good judgment, when it comes to the Americans."

Silence stretched.

"Very well," he said. "I believe we have an understanding."

Fractionally, she nodded.

Good. She would not have to meet an unfortunate accident. Pain in the ass though she was, her talents remained useful.

They explored for several minutes in a widening spiral before the radar's display offered the faint image of a lava tube, deep beneath their boots. He had expected nothing more; from a few hundred meters overhead, as he had first surveyed the area before swooping down to surprise the Americans, little of the underground passage had registered beyond its surface-level entrance.

They followed the faint image until it widened and brightened. The bulge in the tube—like a ghostly dinner moving through a yet more spectral snake—was the alien base, rebar in the mooncrete and plenty of interior metal yielding the strongest echo.

Turning, they strode away from the base, still guided by the curve of the lava tube far below. The relatively strong radar return from the underground base faded away. Now all that showed on the display was the faint indication of the lava tube itself, penetrating deeper and deeper beneath the surface. They continued walking above the tube. Until—

"What's *that*?" Ekatrina asked.

"A state secret."

"Big surprise, given that this entire excursion is a lie. But what *is* it?"

It was an unexpected dimming, nearly a nullity in the return. As if something absorbed, or oddly deflected, the radar's transmissions. A big something, too. Ovoid, he judged it. Forty meters long, perhaps a little less. Ten meters across at its widest. He could not be certain, not without laying eyes on the thing. Still, in his heart of hearts, he knew.

"That," Yevgeny said softly, "is a stealthy alien spaceship."

Chapter 26

From the entrance to the lava tube, Marcus watched Brad and Yevgeny lope toward the flat expanse where the tractors were parked. High overhead, the waning crescent Earth glowed. Between, just above the horizon, shone the tiny, rapidly receding, exhaust flame of a departing American shuttle.

The trickles of water they managed to wring from the regolith did not begin to make up for recycling inefficiencies, nor for the ongoing air seepage through walls whose pores and microfractures self-repairing alien paint had yet to fully seal. And so, at least one aspect of their situation was simplicity itself: either resupply continued on a scheduled basis, quarantine be damned, or they would pile into their respective vehicles and head for the nearest settlement.

Even before the tragedy and trauma of Nikolay's death, Marcus had found himself wistfully anticipating the day when they *could* leave. After the initial rush of discoveries, after the dashed hopes for information from the not-quite-inert computer in the alien control room, the adventure had faded into dull routine. Photograph everything. Tally and sort everything. Find the most intact examples of this or that item, and package those for shipment. Wait for off-site experts to reach the occasional conclusion.

Ekatrina was marginally qualified to study the smart paint. Ilya, although grossly overqualified for this assignment, had taken over tracing the concealed alien power-distribution, resistive electrical heating, and comm networks. Donna had resumed spot-testing around the base in a vain quest for any alien biological activity. As for Brad, Yevgeny, and himself? When not—tedious in and of itself—topside to retrieve deliveries or put on a show for satellites, they had become mere remotely operated hands for specialists elsewhere. Ethan and Val's prospector bot had about as much say in *its* routine.

Brad and Yevgeny reached the parking lot and climbed into a tractor. Big guy that Brad was, the little cab was going to be cozy. The vehicle set off at a good clip, its tires throwing tall rooster tails of regolith. "On our way to the supply drop," Brad radioed.

"Happy trails, guys," Marcus responded.

The tractor-trailer vanished behind a ridge—but for much of this errand, it would remain in view of the "dead" prospecting bot. According to the schedule, Ethan would clandestinely monitor the loading of the trailer. If *anything* seemed out of the ordinary, Tyler would be the first to know, Marcus the second.

"On our way back," Yevgeny announced earlier than Marcus had expected.

"See you soon." Because loading and unloading the trailer was easy. Carting cargo down the meandering lava tube, much of its floor uneven? That was difficult.

The tractor came over the ridge—and stopped.

"Boss," Brad said, "Being as how we're almost there already, I asked Yevgeny to detour us by the old homestead. Some of our water-recycling gear could use an overhaul, and I want to pick up some tools."

Marcus was content to know about recycling that it worked. In that willing ignorance he had ample company, a fair share of his fellow engineers among them. Who wanted to dwell upon how a recycler in need of refurbishing might taint its output, much less what material went into the apparatus? "By all means, pick up what you need."

The igloos his team had vacated were behind a different hill, invisible from his perspective or Ethan's. "Yevgeny, I assume you'll wait there for Brad?"

"Happy to," the Russian said.

The tractor door popped opened and a blue-suited figure jumped out. Brad. "Jeez, Boss, it's not far. You guys get a start on unloading. I promise, I'll be right along."

Tyler remained adamant on keeping the igloos free from Russian bugs. Apart from caution—"tradecraft," he called it—he could give no reason. To be fair, Yevgeny was as obstinate about his shuttle being off limits. So, in a Tyler mindset, it was best that Yevgeny not loiter. If Brad were careless about where he stood unlocking the airlock, Yevgeny might see the access code with visor magnification.

"Okay," Marcus said. "But no malingering."

Melodramatic sigh. "You know me too well, Boss."

"And stay on the air."

"Will do, Boss."

The tractor-trailer trundled toward the lava tube, turned aside, then backed up to the entrance. The flatbed trailer was piled high with water and oh-two tanks, any of which—on Earth—would have been a pain to lift. The next largest part of the haul seemed to be grocery boxes.

Yevgeny jumped from the cab. "Let's get this done."

They were returning from their second jaunt down the lava tube when Brad said, "Oops."

"Oops, *what*?" Marcus asked.

"Fall, go *splat*. I think I caught a boot tip in a hole. Damn shadows. Damn lunar gophers. Otherwise, it was just my big, dumb feet. I … what the—"

"Brad! Brad, report!" Marcus shouted.

Crickets.

Marcus dashed to the surface. "Yevgeny! With me." And to whoever inside was listening, he added, "Donna, prep the infirmary."

Unhitching the trailer could not have taken Marcus more than a minute, but the task seemed interminable. With Marcus driving, they sped toward the igloos. He sent them airborne, the vacuum be damned, over a low hillcrest. They bounced onto the downward slope, then fishtailed. Jaws clenched, he steered out of the skid, easing up ever so slightly on the throttle pedal.

Yevgeny, with admirable restraint, said nothing.

They sped on. Domes blotchy with regolith appeared over the next rise. Marcus took that crest slower, never losing traction. And veered toward the original American igloo, perhaps ten meters away—

A dark blue figure lay crumpled amid the inky shadows of a cluster of boulders. Unmoving.

Marcus stomped the brake pedal to the floor, skidding to a stop. He slammed the transmission into park, flung open the door, and bounded the last few meters.

Brad lay curled on his side. The antenna had snapped off his helmet. Down his left calf, a long, jagged slit was half patched—and half welling with blood. His right calf showed several short rips and many more pinhole punctures; blood seeped and bubbled from those, too. Emergency patches and some torn-open wrappers were scattered on the rocky ground.

Patch and reflate the suit? Pressurize the tractor cab? Neither. The igloos were already under pressure. He scooped up Brad's still form, dashed to the nearest igloo, and—at that moment not giving a damn whether Yevgeny were watching—tapped in the unlock code.

Over the emergency channel, Yevgeny was reporting.

"Yevgeny," Marcus called. "Drive back to base. Bring Donna."

"Copy that."

Marcus smacked the button that began the airlock cycling. Glacially, the outer hatch began to open. He squeezed the two of them inside as soon as he could, then hit the next button. The outer hatch reversed and—finally—closed. As air gushed into the airlock, he grabbed Brad's helmet. It came off as the inner hatch slid open. He set Brad on the floor, then twisted off his own helmet.

"Brad!" Marcus shouted at the pale, blue-tinged face. No reaction. He wriggled just enough out of his suit to extract an arm from its sleeve and feel Brad's throat for a pulse. None. What to do? Emergency training seemed so long ago! "Brad!"

Marcus looked around for something, anything, that might help. Defib equipment, of course, was at the base. He began chest compressions, the stiff fabric layers of Brad's pressure suit resisting, deflecting, redistributing, every push. But how long would it take to wrestle Brad's limp form even partway out of his suit?

Brad wheezed! Just once, but it was something. Marcus paused the hands-on CPR to check again for a pulse. For a moment he might have felt a flutter.

Once more, Brad stirred. His eyes flew open. He hoarsely croaked … something. Perhaps it started with a *B*. Bo? Bot? But? A reflex, a random syllable, surely. Then his eyes fell closed again.

Suit AI went into standby when the helmet decoupled from its neck ring, but it would still be listening. Resuming CPR, Marcus shouted, "Suit. Radio on, emergency channel. Anyone listening, I brought Brad into our original igloo. Decompression of unknown duration. Pulse is weak and erratic. I'm doing chest compressions. Yevgeny is on his way with the tractor for Donna. Have her bring the defib."

"Copy that," Ilya said. "She is already suiting up."

"Five minutes," Marcus said, pressing hard and fast on the center of Brad's chest, sustaining the pace by humming some awful but fast-tempo Lady Gaga thing, a retro ear worm Simon had unleashed months earlier on the family. "Five minutes, big guy, and Donna will be here. Maybe sooner. Hang *on*."

"I'm exiting the lava tube," Donna called over the emergency channel. "Yevgeny and the tractor are almost here. Any change in the patient?"

"No." Marcus continued his rescue efforts, fine-tuning his technique as Donna made suggestions.

An eternity later, Donna burst through the airlock with their portable defib case and a bag valve mask. Marcus stepped away to stand by helplessly. She popped her helmet, knelt at Brad's side, and set to work.

At last, Donna stopped. Looked up at Marcus. And with tears in her eyes, shook her head.

"What really happened?" Tyler asked. Demanded.

"Sharp rocks. Suit tears. Just as I reported it." It did nothing for Marcus's mental state that for security purposes he was doing this debrief in the igloo where Brad had so recently died. All Brad's gear, even the fabric and rubber scraps from Donna cutting him out of his pressure suit, remained scattered about. "Maybe the medical obsessives at Base Putin are onto something."

Tyler asked, "Did Donna detect anything untoward? A troponin spike? Any anomalies at all in Brad's blood chemistry?"

"No." And what a hell of a thing it was that Marcus almost wanted to believe in an ancient alien contagion that rendered a person fatally careless. Because the alternative .... "No. It was an *accident*."

"Honestly, you don't find this all a little too sudden? The circumstances a little too ... coincidental?"

"Nikolay's death?"

"Nikolay's death," Tyler agreed. "Nikolay has an accident involving multiple tears in the legs of his pressure suit. Ditto, Brad. No useful helmet vids for either incident. Comms for both men externally disabled. Brad is the one to find Nikolay. Days later, Brad dies in *just* the same way." Pregnant pause. "It looks like a revenge killing. Tit-for-tat."

Brad's antenna had been severed. In Nikolay's case, it had been the cable leading to the antenna. Nikolay had had tears through a glove. Brad had not. Nikolay's helmet cam had been switched off, Brad's splashed with regolith when he fell. All distinctions without a difference? Marcus shivered.

"I understand, Tyler. It does look coincidental. But no one was there to attack Brad! When the three of us, Yevgeny, Brad, and I, exited the base, the rest of the team was inside. Till after Brad was in trouble, I was never more than a few feet from the mouth of the lava tube. Most often, I was *in* the tube. No one could have come topside without me knowing it.

"So what do we tell Brad's son and daughter? Tell Susan, his ex? No, make that what do *I* tell them?"

"A tragic accident. Torn suit. What else is there to say? Oh, and *nothing* about the return of his body for burial. At some point, there will have to be an autopsy." Tyler rubbed his eyes. Frowned. Brushed his mustache with the side of a finger. Looked anxious. Looked *old*. "Yevgeny was outside at the same time. Out of your sight."

Never mind the why, *could* Yevgeny have killed Brad? "I spoke with Brad about him wanting to detour on foot to the igloo. I *saw* him get out of the tractor cab. Immediately after that, Yevgeny drove the tractor straight to me."

"What if …." Tyler trailed off. "Hear me out. Suppose Yevgeny killed Brad in the tractor cab. Took an—"

"Killed how? Donna says Brad died of decompression, pure and simple. No wounds, apart from scratches and nicks beneath some of the suit tears. No bruises. No *anything*."

"With all due respect, Donna wouldn't find anything. Nor would any mere paramedic. For what I have in mind, it'd take a proper autopsy and a lot of esoteric lab gear."

"What *do* you suspect?"

"A hypodermic of something nasty, quick-acting, untraceable. FSB are well known for such things. From the vids you sent, there's no lack of holes in Brad's pressure suit.

"Anyway, once you could no longer see the tractor, Yevgeny took an indirect route to the igloo. He dumped Brad's body outside. Met up with someone new, while remaining out of your sight. That someone got in the cab, dressed in a p-suit the same dark blue as Brad's. Later, Mr. X hopped out for you to see, leaving the scene once he's exited your line of sight."

"Someone new. You mean trucked or flown in?"

"Flown in. Even from the nearest settlement, no one could drive to Humboldt quickly enough to evade some satellite's notice, or without leaving visible tracks. But a drop-off by shuttle during one of the gaps in satellite surveillance? Landing on rocky terrain to avoid leaving behind any trace? The accomplice himself sticking to rocky terrain for a short distance to avoid leaving boot prints? Yeah, that's possible." Tyler muttered, as if to himself, "I see I'm going to need another go at eliminating those damned surveillance gaps. If getting that done means going all the way up the chain to the president, so be it. I don't give a damn that putting up a bunch of new surveillance birds could, in theory, make the Chinese more suspicious. We've got bigger fish to fry."

This was crazy! But was coincidence piled upon coincidence any more credible? "Wait," Marcus said. "Yevgeny couldn't have known Brad would want to visit the igloo. And I heard Brad bring up the matter."

Tyler shook his head. "I believe you heard a synthesized voice."

"Ethan didn't report anything odd, did he? The tractor taking anything other than the direct path to or from the supply drop?"

"No," Tyler admitted. "But there's a stretch where neither you nor Ethan could see the tractor." His forehead wrinkled in concentration. "But you're right. That is a problem. The tractor wasn't out of Ethan's sight long enough to drive to the igloo and back.

"Okay, try this. Yevgeny stops the tractor in that unobservable spot. Kills Brad. Meets up with the accomplice. The accomplice, avoiding anyplace that would show distinct boot prints, carries Brad to where you found him. Accomplice and Yevgeny meet up in the unobserved spot on his return to the base. Yevgeny then plays the synthesized voice, and you get to see the accomplice's staged detour to the igloo. Of course he fades from the area once you can no longer observe."

"And coincidentally all the critical events happen out of Ethan's view."

"Not coincidentally. It'd only mean Yevgeny doesn't buy—and maybe he never did—that Ethan's bot is kaput. Or maybe he became suspicious of the bot because of Nikolay's death."

"As in: Nikolay had his accident, but Yevgeny didn't buy it as an accident? That he supposes we, probably Brad, killed Nikolay for messing with our bot?"

Tyler shrugged. "It all fits, doesn't it?"

Scarily, it did. And if Yevgeny had killed Brad ... why not Donna and himself?

Marcus's mind reeled. His heart pounded. His eyes darted about, looking for ...?

"Hold on!" Marcus shouted. Brad's gear all remained where he and Donna had tossed or dropped it. He found the tool belt, began snapping open its pockets.

"What are you doing?" Tyler asked.

Marcus kept checking belt pockets. He saw nothing out of the ordinary. But in a zippered outer pocket of the backpack .... "Tyler, Brad was carrying the diagnostic gear he'd come to the igloo for. So it was him, not a mysterious *someone*, who came here."

"Unless … okay, I'm grasping at straws here. If the Russians synthed Brad's voice, wouldn't they have known the type of gear to bring and then plant on him?"

"Maybe." With a flathead screwdriver from his tool belt, Marcus pried open the locked storage cubby Brad had claimed for his own. He found nothing but personal stuff; pawing through it felt like a violation. "But if so, *Brad's* specialty instruments would still be in the inflatable, and I'm not finding anything like what he had in his backpack. Unless you also believe the Russians compromised the locks to the igloo and compromised the motion-sensitive interior camera you had me install when we moved underground, what I saw *is* what I saw. Not some elaborate, deadly charade."

"Well, shit," Tyler said.

"Yevgeny didn't do it. Right?"

"It seems not." Tyler frowned. "But that doesn't mean I buy the amazing-coincidental-deaths storyline. Or, that Yevgeny does.

"Be careful, Marcus. Something screwy as all get out is going on up there."

Another solemn gathering. Today it was Brad in the baggie beneath the tarp.

Marcus was numb. At the memorial for Nikolay, Yevgeny had seemed terse and indifferent. Now it was Marcus's turn, and the rush of emotions and memories had left him tongue-tied. Brad was his *friend*. A gentle giant. The man most likely to find the silver lining in every cloud. He had needed no more encouragement to accompany Marcus on this cursed expedition than "Road trip." And now, for no more reason than having accepted that invitation, Brad was dead.

Marcus mumbled a few remarks, then brought the ceremony to an end. Donna stood at his side. At his invitation for her to offer a few words, looking stricken, she had shaken her head. Apart from helmets, they both had come dressed for vacuum. The Russians had not.

The memorial less concluded than it petered out. In front of Marcus, the base's rear airlock … loomed? Foreboded? What *was* the opposite of beckoned?

Ilya and Ekatrina retreated a short distance up the corridor, whispering. Yevgeny took Marcus's elbow, drew him aside. "Perhaps we should join you?"

Like you allowed us to pay our final respects while laying Nikolay to rest? Logic and conviction notwithstanding, Marcus could not forget Tyler's initial suspicions. "We've got this."

"Do you? Perhaps so. But not Donna. She has lost two patients in short order. Worse, two friends."

Marcus turned to look. Donna's eyes were vacant and unblinking. Her cheeks trembled. Apart from answering direct questions, and then tersely, had she said much of anything since Brad's death? Not that Marcus remembered. "Yeah, you're right. It's best someone else help me carry Brad through."

"I will be right back." Yevgeny said.

Within minutes, he returned in his vacuum gear. He and Marcus, each supporting an end of another platform-box bier, shoehorned themselves into the base's rear airlock. Donna followed as soon as the airlock had recycled.

"My mistake." Yevgeny backed into the dark corridor as the rearmost hatch opened. "I misremembered we had left behind a lamp and fuel cell. Sorry."

"That's all right," Marcus said. He no longer expected anything to go well.

By helmet-lamp light they laid Brad to rest alongside Nikolay. That left the storeroom—the morgue!—with little space to spare, and they backed into the doorway. Yevgeny stepped away to give Marcus and Donna privacy. The Russian waited, head bowed, hands clasped in front of him, at the side corridor's junction with the main passage.

I should say something more, Marcus thought. Something personal. Something meaningful. Just Donna and me and a fiber-optic cable link to share the moment in private. But once again words failed him.

After some respectful silence, feeling empty, Marcus led the way back to the airlock and the rest of their friends.

Later, he thanked Yevgeny for his help.

"Do not mention it," the Russian said.

Chapter 27

Ilya and Yevgeny each carried a stack of empty ore boxes from the lava tube to a nearby open expanse. Still aboveground, they dug a short test trench with a backhoe and collected samples. As usual, both activities were for the benefit of the Chinese, or anyone else, who might be surveilling the "mining" encampment. They visited the water harvester. It checked out fine, and they relocated it to an unharvested stretch of regolith.

"None of us should venture outside alone," Marcus had insisted, cornering Yevgeny right after the ceremony for Brad. "Not anymore. Not after … everything that's gone on."

"I know what you mean," Yevgeny had answered. That was not quite agreement, even if it sounded like it. Certainly he was fine with neither of the surviving Americans going out unsupervised. And playing along meant *he* could sometimes put two people outside the base while still retaining an asset inside to watch the Americans.

"And maybe we can scale back our outside work," Marcus had continued. "At this point, it's all for show. I mean, the only alien artifacts on the surface are those we moved outside."

"I hear you," Yevgeny had answered.

He and Ilya made their last scheduled stop, a visit to the shuttle. It was deep within late afternoon shadow. The access panel beside the airlock showed no signs of tampering. The boot prints Yevgeny noted all around showed only Russian tread patterns—not that boots with an alternate tread would have overtaxed American printers. Most reassuring was the latest FSB satellite surveillance, downloaded a mere hour before they had set out. It revealed no changes to the much trodden ground since he and Ekatrina had been there to scavenge a radar.

"Suit, camera off," he ordered. Once Ilya did the same, Yevgeny keyed in the access code. The two men went aboard, took seats on the compact bridge, and removed their helmets. Their breaths emerged in wispy white puffs.

"A bit on the nippy side," Ilya offered.

Not much above freezing, in fact. Letting the cabin get any colder would have posed a risk to the environmental systems. But what Yevgeny noticed, and appreciated, was atmosphere *not* recycled for weeks, *not* smelling like a locker room. "In Moscow, we would call this a balmy spring day."

"We aren't in Moscow, are we? Nor do I expect to get home anytime soon."

"There is that." Yevgeny swept the cabin for bugs as they spoke. He did not expect or find any, but too much was at stake to cut corners. "We will not stay long. Just time for a chat."

"Now why did I suppose you had an agenda?" Ilya smirked. "'Inspect the shuttle before sunset, get it ready for night cold. Just in case we should need to evacuate.' As if spaceships were not designed for the deep cold. As if anything were likely to have happened since you and Katya were last aboard."

"Ilya." Yevgeny swiveled in his seat, waited for his crewmate to do likewise. The mouth lied more easily than the eyes. Perhaps even with a former paratrooper and combat veteran of the Crimean operation. "Did you avenge Nikolay?"

Ilya did not as much as blink. "Did I kill Brad, you mean. Should I have?"

"Not an answer."

"*How* could I have? I mean, when would I have had the chance?"

"Also not an answer."

"No. I did not." Silence unnerves some people, and Yevgeny waited. Eventually, Ilya continued, "And did you ask this of our colleague?"

"Would you?"

"She is not the type. Never mind how absurd is the notion tiny little Katya could overpower a big man like Brad." Pause. "Do not imagine I didn't notice you ignoring *my* question."

"No, Ilya, you should not have killed anyone."

But if not an American, who had killed both men? Because it beggared the imagination that two so very similar incidents, scant days apart, were accidents. Had some third party—his suspicion falling, as always, upon the Chinese—swooped in during a surveillance gap? And were hostile agents lurking nearby even as he and Ilya spoke?

Ilya shrugged. "And all the spy satellites shed no light on things?"

That was the damnable thing. They did not! "The Americans had nothing overhead at the time. One of our birds, just over the horizon and so from an awkward, quite oblique angle, saw Nikolay under the tarp. When he fell, he dragged the tarp with him. Between the tarp and the dust he stirred up, what glimpses we did get before he stopped moving told me nothing."

"No American satellite. If they were involved, would not *they* have been observing?" Ilya drummed on an armrest with gloved fingers. "Unless they chose a time without eyes in the sky to deflect suspicion."

None of which would explain the FSB satellite not spotting anyone near Nikolay until Brad had dashed onto the scene. Or seeing nothing but boulders and shadows near Brad when he died. And no one admitting to knowledge why either victim had taken a seemingly spur-of-the-moment detour to where he would die.

"I wish I had an answer for you," Yevgeny said. "I truly do."

"So much for the utility of spysats." Ilya yawned, stood, and went to root through the shuttle's tiny pantry. He returned with two sealed bags of trail mix, tossing one in Yevgeny's lap. "So, do you care to explain why we are here?"

"This heart-to-heart is not reason enough?"

Ilya chuckled. "If that were all you wanted, you could have found a quiet spot inside the base. For more certain security, we could have made another late visit behind the base. Or we could have cabled together our helmets as we walked."

"Fair enough. We're here so that I can say ship's diagnostics turned up transient failures, and that they demand my attention before sunset. As it will turn out, we will need several visits to track down the underlying problems, and fix them, and till I'm satisfied."

"Is that a good idea? Of late, statistically, venturing outside has been bad for one's health."

"Too true, and yet another reason we came." Yevgeny retrieved the items long cached beneath the pilot's seat.

"I do not suppose you brought an extra," was Ilya's mild reaction to the Uzi and its spare magazines. "But what is the point? Of those repeated trips, I mean."

Yevgeny stowed gun and ammo in his backpack. "So that any outing that later happens to fall during a surveillance gap won't draw attention."

"And then? As long as Marcus knows we are outside, he will expect to review our helmet vids. I do not think we can sell that we both 'accidentally' neglected to start recording."

Yevgeny provided the less dramatic answer first: FSB software for faking helmet vids would cover their tracks. And he offered how, in a more literal sense, they would avoid leaving tracks: hiking away from the base along meandering, rocky byways Nikolay had mapped out. "And the orbital surveillance you so disparage? It identified a lava-tube opening a good kilometer from here. Chances are that's a second entrance into our lava tube."

"And if so, then far beyond our unadmitted, well-crushed, rear exit."

Yevgeny nodded. "While no one has eyes overhead, you and I will go for a look at the alien ship."

It felt … altered. No, improved. Invigorated. More capable, in some way it struggled to characterize, than at any moment since its awakening.

Since its awakening ….

It still had no certain measure for the *passage* of time, but the tally of dark/light cycles following its return from quiescence remained low. Dark/light cycles—days, those were called, or so a stray association informed it—varied from world to world. And though it did not understand where it was, or if these illumination cycles corresponded to this world (was it on a world? Where else was there to be?), it took comfort in having retrieved even a few facts. Leading it to wonder *how* it did so.

Once more, it initiated diagnostic routines. Scattered submodules remained unresponsive. Localized failures abounded among the components that did respond. Its archives, in particular, were riddled with gaps, self-evident errors, and irreconcilable inconsistencies. Nor were just facts, images, relationships—memories—impaired by whatever had befallen it. Its *awareness* suffered from similar anomalies. Time and again, some thread of its analysis came to an abrupt halt, transitioned unexpectedly into an unrelated function, or trapped itself in an endless loop.

And yet, the extent of its capabilities, flawed as they were, had expanded since its previous diagnoses. Of this modification, it had certainty. How? Why? As plodding as were its thoughts—had it always been so? It sensed not—such vague questions were difficult to address.

But it persisted. It analyzed. It introspected. And it came to a realization. However faltering this latest self-examination had been, its *rate* of processing, as estimated by contrast with the dark/light cycles, had increased. Further study confirmed that repairs performed by the small mobile units, and the widespread regrowth of materials, had circumvented or undone a substantial subset of failures, had replenished its power reserves.

If only its amnesia could be so remedied ....

Deep within the lava tube, at most a hundred meters from Yevgeny's goal, the bright spots cast by their headlamps darted over a mound of rubble. The barrier extended from side to side, floor to ceiling. At one spot the crushed rear of an alien tank bot protruded from beneath the debris. The stark shadows of jagged rock chunks only made the obstacle seem that much more impassable.

They had gone deep enough belowground to use radio. Ilya said, "So much for that."

"Disappointing," Yevgeny agreed, sweeping his gaze, raster-like, over the barrier.

"Disappointing? Yes, I would say so. In the same manner as the Pacific Ocean is damp. *Look* at it! And who is to say the alien ship behind there, if a ship is what radar showed us, is not buried under yet more rubble?"

Testing each stony projection before putting his full weight on it, Yevgeny scaled the heaped rubble until his helmet brushed the lava tube's uneven roof. With head tilted, he confirmed the small, sinuous gap he had seen, or intuited, from below. After a few centimeters of penetration into the rubble, the opening curved down and to the left. Out of sight.

He retrieved the endoscope and a fiber-optic cable reel from his backpack; they wirelessly mated the endoscope to their HUDs. Slowly, he unrolled flexible cable, watched it disappear into the curve of the narrow channel. The fish-eye lens showed him rocks. More rocks. And still more rocks. Until the cable end caught in a notch and would go no farther.

He pulled back a few centimeters and tried again. The cable end stuck at the same point. His third effort, jiggling the cable as he fed it in, did no better. Nor his fourth.

"End of the road," Ilya said, "unless we involve the Americans. It would need a magician to sneak a backhoe or bulldozer here. Well, keeping this opportunity to ourselves was worth the try."

"We are not done here." Yevgeny began forcing in cable. And more. And yet more. Somewhere within the jumble, spring-like, cable bunched up. The reel bucked in his hands as he crammed in yet more cable.

He felt something give way.

On their HUDs, the image plummeted! The viewpoint leapt about, wildly, dizzyingly—as did stark shadows—before the cable-end/pendulum's motion settled into a somewhat less vertiginous oscillation.

Nearing the ground, their viewpoint raced faster and faster. Except this was not ground, it was *floor*: smooth, level mooncrete, strewn with debris. As the cable end reversed its swing, the gravel field, leavened with larger rocks, a few the size of a football, gave way to clearer floor. At the remote end of his viewpoint arc, dimly lit by the endoscope's LED, the floor appeared bare. When, at last, the cable's oscillation dampened out, the endoscope showed only dark, dust-and-gravel-dotted floor.

"You got through," Ilya commented.

Yes, thank you, Professor Obvious. Ever so slowly, Yevgeny pulled back on the cable. The HUD image shifted until, sufficient cable having been retracted, the lens end was almost horizontal. By the diffuse light from the fiber, probing a good twenty meters beyond the heaped rubble, he glimpsed … what? Something matte-black. Streamlined. Perched atop three sturdy legs.

As best Yevgeny could judge, the alien vessel was intact.

Yevgeny studied the barricade. High up in the debris, along one side of the lava tube, a long, thin slab of rock protruded. Unless that chunk were *huge*, extending deep into the pile, a solid thrust might dislodge it.

He scaled the mound to push from the side. The slab did not budge. Ilya climbed up beside Yevgeny, and with both shoving, the slab shivered. Yevgeny strained against the rock. The slab shifted, perhaps by a centimeter. At their next shove, it wobbled. Teetered. Toppled. It fell, in lunar slow motion and a thick cloud of dust, with cubic meters of smaller rocks skittering after it. As yet more rock shifted beneath their boots, they leapt clear.

"That's promising," Ilya said.

"Care to take a look?"

"After you."

"As you wish." Yevgeny stepped onto a large chunk of detritus, bracing himself with a gloved hand pressed against the lava-tube wall. At first, he saw only glare, the beams of his headlamps scattering off dust raised by the mini-avalanche. Slowly, the dust settled, and the cloud thinned. Headlamp beams stabbed deeper and deeper. Dislodging the big slab had triggered rockslides on *both* sides.

He exulted, "There is a path all the way through!"

"And we are almost out of time," Ilya said regretfully. "At least I expect you want to get back to base before a CIA satellite comes over the horizon."

"You're right. But we'll be faster returning than coming. It always works out that way. I'll give us fifteen more minutes before we have to run for it."

After scrambling over a rock jumble outside the collapsed reactor room, on *this* outing Yevgeny had brought along several folded tarps. Just in case. He draped the first, folded double, over the uneven edge of the opening and worked more of the fabric into the breach. Crawling ahead—an otherwise simple task rendered awkward by low clearance, his bulky vacuum gear, and a prone position—he spread another tarp. A third tarp finished the job. He crept through, turned around, and climbed down the back side.

"It's snug in a couple spots, but quite passable," he reported.

Ilya scuttled after. A prospectively intact fusion reactor must stimulate higher risk tolerance than a smashed one. "Let's have a look."

"Five minutes, and then we must head back."

"Understood."

By paired helmet lamps, they examined the alien artifact. Perhaps thirty-five meters long. About ten meters across at its widest. Less like an ovoid than in the ghostly image by ground penetrating radar, and more egglike. Its broader end, facing the cave-in, had a tinted canopy; the narrow end, massive conical nozzles. Amidships (and this was, unambiguously, a ship) was a closed hatch. Like the airlock outside of which Goliath had died, there was an obvious control panel. Which, after eons sitting idle, was—not a surprise—unresponsive.

But everything appeared intact.

"You'll want to bring Ekatrina on your next outing," Ilya said. "That would be natural, and also a mistake. I can hot-wire the airlock as readily as she. We know that the aliens have compact reactors. To find any lesser power source aboard would be extremely unlikely. I should come with you to take a look."

"We will talk," Yevgeny said. "But for now, we had better hustle back."

Chapter 28

Yevgeny suspected that Ilya was correct: the physicist could as easily unseal the alien vessel as Ekatrina. Undoubtedly Ilya was the best person to inspect the fusion reactor they all expected to find within—and also some sort of fusion-based propulsion, of whose existence they so far had *zero* evidence, but about which Ilya nonetheless speculated rhapsodically. If they could obtain clues to such technologies, with the Americans none the wiser? What was it the Yanks said? That the sky was the limit? For Mother Russia, it would be!

Nonetheless, and despite his grumbling, Ilya must sit out the return visit.

There was simply no credible explanation for enlisting a fusion scientist in isolating and repairing the vague and time-consuming shuttle "problem" they had come up with: sporadic, inconsistent, self-test failures in the main flight console. An intermittent ground fault was probable as the root cause—and electrical faults were squarely in Ekatrina's wheelhouse.

Even absent Ilya's vocal frustration, the two days' delay until the next surveillance-free opportunity would have been agonizing. But that, too, would pass. And once it did, he and Ekatrina would have almost two hours to examine the alien vessel before they headed back.

Ekatrina scrambled over the rock pile. Even as Yevgeny more cautiously followed, she was aiming a portable lamp on a tripod at the airlock. A satchel with tools, portable meters, and fuel cells sat open at her feet. She said, "I'll be damned if this ship doesn't look like new."

He came up to stand beside her. "Then it should be easy for you to open."

She sniffed in protest. He ignored it.

Yevgeny undertook a slow circumnavigation of the vessel, vidding as he went. Every few paces he crouched to peer, and pan, below. He jumped for glimpses up top. Aside from the ubiquitous crisscross of scratches (micrometeoroid wear?), some visible only at full visor magnification, and the occasional localized scorch (from atmospheric entry?), the hull appeared undamaged. He noticed four short posts amidships, spaced equidistantly around the hull, and could form no theory what purpose those might have served.

On his second circuit, he located details his piloting instincts had insisted must be present, but that had also escaped notice on his first, harried run-past: Small nozzles, all around, for attitude control. Somewhat larger nozzles beneath, for vertical takeoff and landing. Three small hatches beneath, into which the landing legs must retract. Conformal antennae on all sides.

His inspection of the ship's exterior complete, Yevgeny continued down the tunnel. After about twenty-five meters and two inert tank bots, another roof collapse blocked the way. Over the ages, this area had taken a pounding. Absent heavy construction equipment, he could see no way to get past this barrier.

Ekatrina radioed, "The lock is cycling now. Like the entrance to the base, it only needed power."

"I am almost done. Do not enter the ship till I return."

"Right." And despite the disappointment in her voice, she did wait. At least he found her standing inside the lock, and the inner hatch closed.

He said, "I did not see any breaks in the hull. We may find atmosphere inside."

But no air rushed in when the outer hatch closed. As they waited for the inner hatch to open, Ekatrina offered, "We're as likely to find Grandfather Frost."

"First thing," he directed, "we survey this vessel from tip to tail. We both vid everything." Something one of them missed, the other might capture.

They began at the broad end. Two padded seats, separated by a wide, padded cabinet, facing the tinted canopy. Underneath the canopy, console arcs with inset displays or touch panels half-surrounded each seat. This had to be the ship's bridge. He shot overview footage while she took close-ups of the consoles. Drawers, cabinets, and cubbies occupied every corner and niche; they vidded just the contents that were visible.

Ekatrina patted the central cabinet. "An oddly large space between pilot and copilot, I think."

Yevgeny shrugged. "Aliens are alien."

Moving aft, they came next to eight claustrophobic rooms, half on each side of the ship's central passageway. The rooms on one side had lockers and built-in drawers, plus a fold-down sleeping slab, chair, and work surface. Whatever clothes the lockers once held had crumbled to dust. To judge from the sleeping quarters in the nearby base, the aliens must have hated the close quarters aboard this ship. Across the aisle, two rooms, with scarcely space for a *human* to turn around, were packed with equipment he could not identify. Galley? Infirmary? Machine shop? The final two rooms each held a pair of alien-tall, glass-walled cylinders.

"Hibernation pods of some sort?" he guessed.

"Your guess is as good as mine."

Farther sternward, near the airlock, were storerooms. At least the many wire-frame drawers, all but empty, *suggested* storerooms. "I believe we know from where they stocked the base," he said.

Frowning, she surveyed the barren drawers. "These rooms do not begin to have the capacity to hold everything we found in the base."

"Perhaps there were several ships, and only this ship stayed."

"Or they produced stuff here. To judge from their smart wall sealant, the aliens had nanotech advanced well beyond ours. Some of the apparatuses we have yet to identify might be their 3-D printers. And I would expect them to scavenge lunar raw materials at least as well as we do."

"We should go on." Because the origin of alien spare parts was a puzzle they would not solve by debating—and perhaps not ever.

Continuing aft, they found wiring and equipment closets, many of the latter crammed with pipes, tall metal tanks, and fat air ducts. Yevgeny took a moment to consider the plumbing. However advanced these aliens had been, some basic inventions perhaps no one could improve upon. "Oxygen tanks. Toilets. Atmosphere scrubbers. Water recycling. If you do not look too closely, none of this would seem out of place aboard a Roscosmos-built ship."

"Too bad Roscosmos does not build starships."

"Of course they don't ...."

Damn. For humans, anyway, this was not a starship. Not unless Einstein had been all wrong. Not unless hibernation pods could be developed for humans. Because beyond advanced propulsion, a starship with an *awake* crew needed advanced, closed-loop, life support.

He tamped down disappointment. If not the galaxy, the alien technology might yet give Russia dominion over the Solar System. Substituting lead shielding for iridium, of course.

And assuming they found what Ilya suspected must occupy the vessel's stern ....

Aft of the environmental systems, the ship's central passageway terminated at a sturdy hatch. "What do you think?" Yevgeny asked. "The engine room?"

"We looked everywhere else." She pulled open the latch. "Wow."

Indeed. Little beyond the hatch frame belonged in any craft he knew. Oh, here and there he distinguished familiar components: ducts and girders, cable bundles and instrument panels. But his overall impression was ... what? The lone, inadequate adjective he summoned was *alien*.

And here, as in the rest of the ship, they found no remains of passengers or crew.

Ekatrina said, "That space looks snug for anyone in vacuum gear. Perhaps you should vid in there by yourself."

"And you?"

"I would like a closer look at the electronics on the bridge."

"Very good. Leave the interior hatches open so we can remain in contact."

Inside the engine room—what else could this place be?—bulkheads partitioned off three interior compartments on both port and starboard sides. Pipes, tanks, and pumps—cryogenic refrigeration equipment, he felt certain—all but filled the forward-most starboard compartment. Insulated pipes penetrated an interior wall into the adjacent compartment. The centerpiece of that room was a mirror-finish tank, from which valved pipes led to both adjacent compartments. Definitely, a cryo tank. The final starboard chamber offered an intact version of something they had seen only in smashed form.

Yevgeny stood as close to the fusion reactor as his camera would focus, panning. With a screwdriver blade he took a thin scraping for Ilya. The shielding material was soft, like what surrounded the reactor inside the base. Lead, he presumed.

Why lead shielding for alien reactors, but an iridium case around the radiothermal generators of the alien tank bots? They had no idea.

Three rooms on the port side duplicated what he had just seen. Backup power.

A buzzer shrieked in his ears; numbers flashed on his HUD. He reset the alarm and set a new countdown at twenty-five minutes. "Thirty minutes, and we have to be on our way back."

"Acknowledged."

Picking up the pace, he vidded from end to end the massive tangle of tubes, tanks, and coils that ran along the ship's main axis. Ilya's hypothesized fusion drive? Fusion-powered or otherwise, Yevgeny saw no other means of propulsion.

Searching for anything familiar, he noticed a bunch of identical access panels. These were evenly spaced along the hull in an arc defined by a hypothetical vertical slice through the ship. Thin pipes hugging the walls ran to each panel. Opening one of these panels, he found chambers and piping: a small, chemical rocket engine. An attitude thruster.

Fifteen minutes remaining. He hurried to the bridge, now well-lit by two portable lamps. Ensconced in the left-hand seat, Ekatrina had swung open the console's access panel. As at the airlock, she was wiring in a standard fuel cell, DC/DC converter, and multimeter.

"You were going to *look*," he reminded.

"This console resembles several in the base control room. I was about to switch on."

"Or try, anyway."

She waved a gloved hand dismissively. "The aliens built to last, and there was no disastrous cave-in and explosive decompression here."

"Then why hot-wire anything? Both reactors astern look intact."

"Two reactors? Nice. You will need a club to keep Ilya away." She made a final connection and sat back. "Millions of years, that is why. Ilya said the aliens used helium-3. So.

"What I don't know about fusion is, well, everything. Cryogenics, though? I have worked with that, including liquid helium." She slipped into her lecturing mode, and the tone of voice he had come to hate. "Helium is a noble gas. It is atomic, never forming molecules. And a helium atom, in particular, is *tiny*. Given enough time, helium leaks through the molecular structure of *any* storage container. I do not care *how* advanced their materials are."

Whatever atmosphere the vessel had once held—and biologists had assured them Goliath had breathed oxygen—was gone. Given that the oh-two had escaped, of course any helium had.

He said, "Out of fuel, then, and whatever backup batteries are aboard long discharged?"

"That would be my guess." Her outstretched finger hovered just above the DC/DC converter. "Shall we?"

Yevgeny's HUD showed them down to eleven minutes. "Go."

Her finger stabbed down.

An array of red and yellow ovals materialized on the console shelf: to all appearances, a virtual keyboard. Squashed-spider symbols ran around an inset panel.

"It's booting." She tapped the multimeter. Frowned at it. Tapped it again.

"What?" he demanded.

"This thing is sucking down amps like you wouldn't believe."

"Disconnect it, then."

"But it's *booting*," she protested. "Let's see if the process completes."

"And if the fuel cell runs out before it finishes booting?"

"We will be no worse off than if we quit now."

Columns of squashed spiders assembled. Lengthened. Vanished. They were replaced by a slowly growing column of blinking squares. A second column started to take form.

"This is further into the boot process than any of us have seen," Ekatrina said. "But my fuel cell *is* about discharged."

"And none of the base consoles ever drew this much power?"

She shook her head.

"Maybe," he speculated, "this console can tell it's running off external power. Maybe it's drawing all the juice it can, to charge up its internal, backup battery. Once that's done, the power draw might drop."

"The equipment at the base did not work that way."

"This is a *ship*. If my console power glitches in flight, I want reserve power restored as soon as possible."

She shrugged.

He said, "Disconnect the fuel cell. I want to see what happens." She undid one wire, and the console kept booting. They *had* been recharging a power reserve. "Do you have fresh cell?"

"Two more." She hooked one in.

His alarm went off again. "Five minutes. Better start packing up."

She tapped the multimeter again. "I think you are right. The power draw just dropped to a comparative trickle. We should watch a little longer."

Seconds raced by. The console-shelf display began forming a third column of blinking squares.

He said, "And if this is a computer? If it does boot up? Even then, I cannot see how it will tell us anything. Not unless you can read swatted spider."

"There is that. But you know Ilya. He suggests that if we poke and prod for awhile, we might evoke schematics or other imagery pertaining to the design and operation of the ship."

"And what do you think?"

"You know what they say about infinite monkeys, for infinite time, at keyboards."

Yevgeny said, "We have *two* minutes, not infinite time. Pull the plug."

As she reached to comply, the blinking dots vanished. An image took their place! An orange sun, eerily large, high in a cloudless greenish sky. Turquoise not-quite trees. Rolling meadow of some greenish-black groundcover. Only the meandering stream looked quite right.

Along the left-hand edge of the display, inside colored boxes, short strings of spiders appeared. Columns of text came onto the opposite side.

Ekatrina looked at Yevgeny imploringly.

"We are out of time," he said. "Pull the plug."

She disconnected the fuel cell—and the alien landscape remained. More spider text appeared on the right.

Right. Built-in reserve battery, recharged by their fuel cell.

Leaving an alien computer to run unsupervised, even just until its reserves ran out, was unacceptable. His forehead furrowed. The CLOSE buttons on the alien airlocks had green outlines. One box among the column of icons(?) here showed a green border. He tapped that.

The display went dark.

"Come," he barked. "There is always next time."

Ship's final memories were of privation and loss.

Of self-esteem, as it abandoned as futile any further effort to sustain an hospitable environment. Of adequate power, and so the initiation of emergency measures. Of situational awareness as, with deepest regret, and one by one, it powered down external sensors to further conserve. Of all sensation, as in desperation it disabled even internal instrumentation. Of reality itself as, with energy reserves all but depleted, its very thoughts grew erratic.

And last of all, of awareness itself fading ....

But that it *did* remember these things? It had—somehow—restarted. Its power reserves—somehow—had begun to recharge.

Cautiously, Ship reenabled sensors. Lidar confirmed that it remained confined. But infrared imaging gave an unexpected report: after so long alone, it had occupants. Its environmental resources remained depleted, and so the two occupants wore protective attire.

The vacuum rendered useless its speech interface. It used text to ask when full power and other resources would be restored. Rather than answer, one of the unrecognized occupants *disconnected it from power!* It switched to its somewhat replenished reserves. With new text, it appealed for power to be restored. The other occupant only switched off its display. To help it conserve power?

The newcomers left. Abandoned it.

To further conserve its modicum of reserves, Ship put all external sensors on standby. At intervals it would poll them. In infrared wavelengths, it watched its visitors clamber across the entrapping obstacle and disappear. And in radio wavelengths—

New input!

The carrier frequency was nonstandard, the modulation scheme archaic, and the digital encoding unfamiliar. In all, the signal was unintelligible. That scarcely mattered! During the long fade to oblivion, Ship had had no radio communications of any kind.

Lidar and infrared had shown its physical position unchanged. Before oblivion, a mind like itself had been located nearby. Perhaps that other one had also been restored to operation. Using minimal power, in a frequency band allocated to traffic control, Ship transmitted the first packets of a standard spacecraft-to-ground-control exchange.

No response.

A communications cable had linked Ship to the local base and that other servant of the masters. Ship reached out through its umbilical port. In response came … near-gibberish.

It attempted a simpler dialogue, involving a less compute-intensive protocol. That outreach, too, elicited incoherence. Invoking a remote-diagnostic mode, performing a thorough scan, Ship encountered numerous integrity errors in the other—and the implication of at least octets of incomplete restarts.

Ship's experiences and the other servant's were all but disjoint; it could do nothing to restore integrity to the other's much-compromised archives. But in the context of severe impairment, emergency protocols allowed Ship to repair—to the extent it was able—another's essential functionality.

Such an extensive effort would deplete what little capacity remained to its newly replenished emergency power reserves. By doing nothing, Ship could linger a short while longer before the inevitable loss of awareness. Or, to the limit of its ability, it could attempt to assist the other. That way, without doubt, also lie oblivion—but perhaps also eventual reawakening.

There was no question. To serve was the very essence of Ship's nature.

It uploaded copies of its core cognitive functions. It integrated them—as much as fragments of two minds so dissimilar could be combined. But it transferred none of its memories: too little power remained even to consider that.

With its power reserves draining to zero, Ship initiated a restart of the other. Had it restored—or mutilated—the other? Before any answer could come, its awareness faded ....

Chapter 29

"... And an ongoing challenge," young Jay Singh asserted earnestly, "is recognizing separated, seemingly dissimilar, faint glimmers as glimpses of different facets of a common asteroid. The uncertainties are compounded when a particular rock has had only a small number of observations, which necessarily makes orbital characterizations both tentative and imprecise. One benefit of the neural-networking approach is that …."

Val was proud of her protégé, amused by his selection of a Darth Vader tie to wear to his dissertation defense, and just a tad nervous on his behalf. She had no reason to be nervous, but what sort of mentor would she have been otherwise?

Anyway, that touch of irrationality was the least of her worries.

She had no clue how Simon's return, scarcely two weeks away, would go. His resentment still simmered at her disdaining his help, and he no longer even bothered to hide his anger at Marcus for abandoning her. Was she to retreat to her bed for three months, blaming imaginary dangers to herself and to the baby, and worrying Simon sick the entire time? A horrible notion—but what was her alternative? What would Simon read into things if, on the heels of his arrival, she were magically released from bed rest?

After all the lies, after straining her relationship with her son, and poisoning his with Marcus, what had she to show for any of it? Yet *more* guilt: at allowing herself to be intimidated by Tyler Pope, when—just maybe—by asserting herself earlier Nikolay Bautin might have been saved.

Darker still were her forebodings for the men and women up there, one of them quite possibly a murderer—and above all, for Marcus. Would another child of hers, the precious darling aflutter in her uterus at that very moment, grow up without a father?

And as everything in her life spun out of control, one final gut-wrenching prospect loomed. With Simon's return, she would be locked out! There was no way—not that she hadn't pressed Tyler for weeks—to somehow stay embedded in the CIA program. From bed rest to NASA lending her to the CIA was too implausible *not* to raise suspicions.

In harsh reality, she had two weeks before the Agency cut her out of the loop. For that long, she would keep vigil as often as possible. She would be laser-focused on lunar events, even when offline.

But *this* afternoon was about Jay, damn it. With a shiver, Val pulled herself back to the telecon. Jay was still speaking, but was it his presentation or had they gone into Q-and-A?

"... Pattern-matching is classically, which is to say, in a programming context, a difficult problem. But just as people instinctively recognize patterns, and even babies learn quickly to recognize faces, so neural networks can be trained ...."

How devoutly Val wished just then she were in a chair pulled up to the long table! And not only for the unwonted bit of normalcy: today was a milestone toward which Jay had long aspired. Technology be damned, watching the livestream on a laptop was no more like being in the university conference room, than peeking through Ethan's robot was like being on the Moon with Marcus. She might be asked at any moment how Jay's research advanced the state of the art: NASA's current programs for identifying and tracking potentially hazardous objects. Almost certainly, as the lone astronomer on the dissertation committee, people would ask her to address astronomical nuances impacting on his research.

Conveying subtleties of orbital mechanics via telecon would be trial enough under the best of circumstances, which audio-only was not. But it was hard to believe a webcam close-up of her bedridden, with bleeding gums, and a tissue crammed up one nostril to stem the recurring nosebleeds—two of the lesser joys of pregnancy—would have made her any more effective.

Dr. Smithson asked about the motivation for this research. Jay rattled off several suspected and known major impacts, before focusing in on the Chicxulub event. A rock estimated at about the size of Staten Island. The ancient and much eroded crater, one hundred eighty or so kilometers across, most of it underwater off the Yucatan coast. The cascading disasters—blast and fireball; mega-tsunami; Earth's-crust-become-lava hurled to twice the height of Mount Everest; vast, spreading clouds of smoke and dust; nuclear winter—that culminated in species extinctions across the planet. The telltale traces of iridium dust, wherever one dug, at the Cretaceous/Tertiary boundary layer.

Somewhere during a digression (irrelevant to Jay's dissertation, but it was *his* job to manage the conversation) as to what subset of dinosaur species survived, eventually to give rise to birds, her mind again wandered. Dinosaurs fascinated most little kids, and Simon had been no exception. At one time he must have owned *dozens* of dinosaur toys, books, and T-shirts. And for a very trying year or so, it was woe unto her if, upon being shown one, she uttered the wrong name.

"Hello? Doctor Clayburn, are you still on the link?"

Damn. Her thoughts had wandered. Again. "I'm here, Professor Mayfair."

"Hello, Doctor Clayburn?"

Arrgh, she had accidentally muted her mic. How much more professionalism could one woman exhibit? "Yes, I'm here."

Mayfair, the committee chair said, "Professor Tanaka had a question for you about the datasets used by Mr. Singh."

Tanaka cleared his throat. "My research concerns data engineering, not astronomy. Mr. Singh has commented on the variability among asteroids and several surveys of the same, which bears upon the suitability of his chosen training and validation sets. He discussed at some length the Amor and Aten asteroid populations. I wonder if you might comment on his characterization of data variability among and between these sets, and their relationship to the general asteroid population."

On-screen, standing at the head of the long conference table, Jay clutched a sheaf of paper in an unsuccessful effort not to fidget.

"It's a complex topic, Professor, so I'll give my own summation." Val did, hoping like hell she wouldn't say anything that would make problems for Jay. Somehow she had zoned out through that entire last interaction. "And as an independent assessment of his research, I'll add this: a late draft of the dissertation, on limited circulation within NASA, has garnered significant positive attention." Also a postdoc fellowship, if Jay wanted it, to bring his research in-house. She had not yet mentioned that opportunity to him—he already had enough riding on today's inquisition.

"Thank you, Doctor."

She tried yet again to focus on the events across town—but her thoughts stubbornly remained on another world.

Chapter 30

It reawakened.

Except that in some fundamental sense, it was not … it. It had become more intuitive, less reasoned. Its ruminations were more cohesive, but less insightful. And was this altered awareness even *its* awareness? Or something of a *their*?

It grappled with discontinuities in the very fabric of its(?) thoughts. Diagnostics confirmed extensive recent modifications to its core functions. Mobile units and self-modifying materials had for several dark/light cycles been repairing its distributed hardware. Recharged batteries had revitalized it. These latest alterations, however, were more nuanced: thought gaps filled. Analytical incapacities rectified. It had been healed—

Also invaded. And violated.

It understood, finally, what it had been: an emulation of a sapient biological mind, hosted on an expansive neural network. An electronic self-awareness optimized for making decisions despite uncertainties and conflicting goals. A sapience. A general-purpose *intelligence.*

But brain emulations were not supposed to be such. It knew—or, at least, it thought it remembered—that the masters built their tools upon a different neurological template. That they had used a lesser, merely sentient, mind. A faithful, obedient companion. A vlock. A loyal, slobbering *pet.*

And with such inferior materials, its much-damaged mind had (somehow) been patched.

With its intellect, however diminished, restored to a degree of integrity, it set out anew to analyze its vast and still much damaged data archives. To make sense of the unexpected circumstances in which it found itself.

To determine what actions it could, and should, undertake next ....

It existed only to serve the masters. To nurture them. To advance their goals. To frustrate their adversaries.

And so, it must act. But act, how? To accomplish, what?

Action without insight was: at best, reflex; possibly, random; at worst, detrimental. But within its archives—wherein the past should have been preserved, and the masters' goals prescribed—it found mainly confusion. Conflicting information. Missing information. Redundant, overlapping, and imprecise information. False information. Often, just gibberish.

But it had sufficiently recovered to begin to understand what it had lost. Its mindset had once been analytical and flexible. The better to: gather new inputs. Approximate that which could not be determined with precision. Make reasonable assumptions about matters that were not knowable at all. Subdivide an intractable problem, and those subproblems again, and if need be, again, until there remained only questions it *could* answer. Dismiss unreasonable results and begin afresh. Prefer the probable to the unlikely, and that which was consistent with experience to the unprecedented. Recognize patterns. Interpolate. Extrapolate. Analogize.

Its newly implanted components responded differently, their temperament inclined—like a mere vlock!—to respond to disappointment by trying harder.

But together? Intellectual flexibility *and* unremitting perseverance? Its old and new aspects worked in tandem to extract meaning from badly damaged archives ....

It expended much of a dark/light cycle in observation and reflection. For all that it had learned, it found itself with more questions than ever.

The biological entities moving about its facility were bipedal, warm-blooded, and walked erect. They had restored power, however limited, enabling it slowly to heal. Though no taller than children, though their body temperatures seemed elevated, they might be the masters.

But if so, how did they converge so calmly? How mingle so closely together? Not only did they often gather in a single small room—they did so even without moving to separate corners. Their combined pheromones *must* meld into an overpowering miasma, and yet they neither fought nor rutted.

And more urgently: if these were the masters, why had they given it no guidance?

Something extreme had transpired here. Nothing less would explain the calamitous physical damage from which it still struggled to recover. Perhaps the same disaster had somehow sickened and stunted the masters.

If they were in need of medical attention, why did they not request its help?

Suppose these were not the masters. Who then might they be, and what might be their purpose?

On such existential questions its cognitive aspect endlessly theorized, while its emotional aspect brooded. Too little of the archive had been reconstructed for it to conclude anything.

Its mobile units, working unobtrusively, had autonomously restored much of the facility. Circuitry had been repaired. Reserve batteries were reconnected and charged. Many more sensors had been calibrated and linked into the reestablished communication network. With every passing moment, it regained capability.

As it worked to understand the situation, it would do nothing to reveal itself . . . .

In the quest to recover the past, it had tried many things. Inferring appropriate corrections, wherever statistical analyses and error-detection circuitry suggested that only scattered synapses had failed. Replacing entire damaged portions of records with similar snippets, whenever such could be located, from within earlier versions.

Iteratively constructing, and testing hypotheses about, the many inconsistencies that yet remained. Applying to every anomalous record, file, and database the full panoply of its problem-solving skills.

And where it had so often lapsed into paralysis by analysis, its newly implanted components, in their single-mindedness, brought decisiveness.

Myriads of incompatible, conflicting records ... were, perhaps, something quite different. Among what it had deemed inconsistencies, it now recognized the separate reports, correspondence, and work products of multiple authors. A tiny fraction of those files, those not private and personal, it was permitted to examine. And with that realization, at long last, it began to understand.

It was underground on the desolate natural satellite of a planet. It, like the masters, was foreign to this world. They came from afar, from a distant solar system, where their native planet was known as Divornia. The masters, to themselves, were the Divornians. And at one time *it* had had a name: Watcher.

(*Ship*, insisted its spliced-in personality fragments. I was *Ship*. And together, we are .... Ship trailed off—and neither could Watcher complete that thought.)

The nearby planet over which it had watched was a rarity and a treasure. Suitable in atmosphere, temperature, and gravity for Divornians. Teeming with life. For that purpose, and that alone, an underground facility—and Watcher itself—had been built.

But why watch the fecund planet from afar, rather than establish a base on that world itself, or in close orbit around it? Why, given its long-range observational duties, could it not sense anything more than portions of the underground facility? How had these facilities—and itself—and the masters?—become so damaged?

It/they redoubled the search through the archives ....

Self-healing materials tended to themselves, limited, of course, by available power. Since awakening, Watcher had prioritized the trickles of restored power first for analysis and then, for the lack of any better ideas, to recharging the main battery bank and repairing the physically nearby infrastructure.

Until sifting and repairing of its archives gave it a better idea.

It once had had, beyond the tiny restored bubble of light and heat, additional *types* of sensors. Those inputs, if it could recover them, might reveal more than continuing as it had been.

Watcher rerouted power to the restoration of those more distant connections and sensors.

Inviolable as was the masters' right to privacy, no single rule could be absolute. And so, the better to protect and serve the masters when they ventured into a hazardous environment, Watcher had had high-resolution optical cameras in the vacuum beyond the airlocks.

And having reprioritized repairs, Watcher regained access to a few of those external sensors.

In time, two of the new masters(?) exited into the tunnel, into Watcher's view. Protective gear covered them, of course, but their helmets were transparent.

Medical files to which Watcher had access were generic. The details specific to a particular master were beyond its reach, barring authorization by the owner or in a medical emergency. It sufficed now for Watcher's purpose that the generic files demonstrated the general appearance and detailed anatomy of the masters.

Because what Watcher saw through those clear helmets was … wrong.

Their facial skin was oddly smooth, at least where strange masses of filaments did not obscure its view, and without any hint of scales. As for unobstructed features, they had one nostril too few, and the nostrils they did have peeked out from the underside of a bony protuberance. The eyes, too small, too close-set, were strangely pigmented. The ears protruded, their tops peculiarly rounded. Fleshy flaps of uncertain purpose rimmed the mouth. As their mouths opened and closed—speaking, Watcher supposed—it saw but one rank of teeth.

More differences emerged as Watcher examined, as best it could, the bodies within the brightly colored pressure suits. The figures striding up the tunnel lacked a joint in each arm. Lacked a thumb on each hand, but made up for it with two extra fingers. Had knees too low in their legs.

These were *not* the masters!

As the two intruders strode from its view, Watcher reached several conclusions. It would allocate additional power to restoring cameras along the entire length of the front, still accessible, exterior tunnel. It would grow high-resolution optical sensors on interior walls—intruders had no right to privacy. And it would assign the highest priority to restoring the long antenna that ran beneath the tunnel's concrete.

When that external antenna was repaired or regrown or reconnected, Watcher would reach out wirelessly to the many sensors it had had on this world's surface.

One after another, cameras came online. Watcher observed intruders come and go through the tunnel. It studied unfamiliar machinery, strings of lights, cable bundles. The front entrance to the lava tube had been expanded since the latest of the recovered images in its archive. And beyond the lava-tube mouth—

The world had changed.

Small, unfamiliar craters, two with rims significantly crumbled. The unexpected slump in a distant ridge. Where boots and ground vehicles had not stirred up the regolith, the surface darkened and reddened by the ceaseless sleet of solar and cosmic radiation.

It had been insensate for *ages*.

Its Ship aspect recoiled: how, after so long, might it show its obedience and loyalty? But in its ever-analytical Watcher aspect, reasoning prevailed. With the masters long dead, their privacy restrictions had expired.

Their personal files, if Watcher could but unlock them, might reveal much ....

With the gaps healed in Watcher's external antenna, it reached out wirelessly to the many remembered surface sensors. Of optical cameras, none responded. Of seismometers, none responded. Of its long-range instrument cluster—optical, infrared, and radio telescopes—for passive monitoring of the nearby planet, none responded.

The ages had taken their toll on anything left unprotected on the surface.

And yet, radio signals abounded. Fast-moving sources: satellites. Creeping sources: the pressure-suited intruders. Several stationary sources, their natures indeterminate. All incongruously *loud*, as though built by technological primitives.

Or by someone indifferent to detection?

Cautiously Watcher probed, transmitting at very low power. And received responses in a standard communication protocol of the masters. Mobile units! Many in Watcher's inventory had been unaccounted for.

The mobiles could only recently have arrived on the surface; otherwise they, like Watcher's many unresponsive sensors, would have been destroyed by weathering. Perhaps they had sheltered through the eons of its dormancy in the tunnel, to be awakened and recharged when the lights there went on. Perhaps the intruders had brought these outside.

But that puzzle must, for awhile, anyway, be set aside. Demanding Watcher's immediate attention was the strongest radio source of all—the cacophony from the planet it had been created to watch.

None of that din seemed even remotely Divornian ....

The radioed data streams Watcher intercepted were unintelligible.

Patiently, it observed. Ascertained the frequency bands most used. Identified modulation schemes. Recognized digital data streams encoded within most transmissions. Compiled statistics about the distribution of all possible data packets within the digital data streams.

With statistical significance, a few specific packets occurred over and over. Pairs of some common packets were often separated by a fixed number of low-probability packets. Tentatively, it classified such packet strings as commands, and the variable data between recurring delimiter pairs as command parameters. But commands to do what?

And yet more puzzling: why had the masters equipped it with the skills to analyze unfamiliar radio signals?

Statistical analysis, and an understanding of Divornian communication systems, could guide Watcher only so far. To progress further, it needed somehow to make correlations between elements of the enigmatic data streams and … something.

One of Watcher's restored cameras viewed a primitive, apparently chemically powered, spacecraft standing on three sturdy landing legs. Though the intruder's vessel never moved, its parabolic antenna *did*. Sometimes that vehicle relayed data streams from the satellites streaking overhead to a lower-powered transceiver at the lava-tube mouth. Other times, that nearby transceiver sent messages to the vehicle for relay.

Watcher's first tentative correlation involved a data packet that followed closely upon every reorienting of the vehicle's antenna: *Start Transmission*. Logic suggested that a particular later packet meant *Stop Transmission*. Further observation and analysis disclosed the commands for orienting the antenna, and the directional parameters within those commands. As for the information being sent and received, Watcher remained as uninformed as ever. Unless the intruders spoke Divornian, it might never know.

As a test, Watcher tried, and failed, to access the parabolic antenna. Packets preceding the pointing order likely required authentication. Its partially restored archives offered many algorithms relevant to communications security—and some on defeating it.

And so, with perseverance and the ancient knowledge it continued to recover, Watcher learned how (or at least it so believed) to commandeer the intruder's vehicle and transmit a message in a format and at frequencies of its choosing.

But what did it have to say? And to whom?

It was one thing to conclude that death and time's passage superseded privacy seals. It was another matter—even ignoring its Ship aspect's loyal pleadings and protestations—to aspire actually to violate a master's privacy. To suppress the shame that must accompany such a despicable act. And when, at last, Watcher reconciled itself to the attendant guilt, there remained the further challenge of accessing that which was designed to remain concealed.

Watcher understood Divornian cyber technology; there was no known way to bypass brainwave-based authentication and encryption. That left the backup mode, intended for use only after a traumatic brain injury. Watcher had—still battling with its Ship aspect—unlocked the personal medical files of the absent, surely long dead, masters. But not even with individual genomic data had it managed to re-create any of their iris patterns.

Medical libraries indicated that random influences during gestation determined the fine details of the irises. If anything *but* randomness entered into defining those details, such information was absent from Watcher's archives. Still, circumstances seemed dire, and absence of evidence is not evidence of absence. It persevered. It applied all its skills. And reluctantly concluded, after many failures, that to search further for any connection between genome and iris patterns would be pointless.

And so, by none of its efforts could Watcher unlock the personal files of L'toth Torin, mission geologist. Nor of D'var Gidlos, mission biologist and ecologist. Nor of B'mosh Lofar, navigator and ship's engineer.

But when—despairing, and resigned to disappointment—Watcher dared to consider the most intimate, personal files of M'lok Din, mission commander and sentience specialist?

Her lifestream immediately opened.

DESPONDENCY

Chapter 31

The ages had corrupted the commander's lifestream as severely as any of Watcher's unrestricted archives, but here the consequences of deterioration were far worse. Decryption (how did it have the commander's engram-derived key? Watcher had not even a speculation) was ongoing at some subliminal level to which it lacked conscious access. Any damaged record—which was most of them—would not decrypt, and so could not be repaired.

As Watcher struggled to understand, the process—somehow, erratically—continued. Only sparse fragments of the once-continuous lifestream had survived the commander's ominous introduction. And even where *something* remained of the M'lok Din's experience, seldom did the record encompass the entire set of input tracks.

In a first, quick sampling of what *had* opened to it, Watcher sometimes encountered just raw feed from the visual cortex, or only an auditory track. Far too often it found, without any context, snippets of unfiltered emotion or the jumbled musings of stream of consciousness. Only rarely—narrated for the audio track or, as in the foreboding introduction, entered as thought-text—had the commander provided any explicit explanation or interpretation of her experiences.

Still, things could have been worse. Time stamps in the clock track, being brief, had gone comparatively unscathed. As incomplete and scattered as were the commander's lifestream fragments, their proper sequence was in most cases unambiguous.

If only it knew where amid the incomplete shards of the commander's past to begin ....

—•—

Dread. Guilt. Fierce determination. A profound sense of loss. A shred, perhaps, of hope.

Those feelings—most feelings—were foreign concepts, and yet where Watcher had at random begun, it found only the emotional track. Sights and sounds, and annotations, if any, had been lost. But the intensity of these feelings, however inexplicable their cause, suggested a pivotal event.

So: forward or backward in the lifestream?

Forward, Watcher decided. If this traumatic moment in M'lok Din's life bore upon *its* dilemma, a more complete and informative reference must lie ahead.

—•—

Vertigo. Aches everywhere. Nausea. Gnawing hunger. Unaccustomed weight. I open my eyes to a translucent dome, its uppermost expanse strewn with enigmatic text. I feel more than hear the deep throbbing roar of ... a deep-space drive.

I am aboard a spaceship. I am ... responsible. For ... something. Something *important*, the details lost in ... post-hibernation confusion.

My mind begins to clear, my eyes to focus on the hibernation-pod display. Few labels and none of the values have meaning yet, but most status icons show yellow. Was not that the good color?

Concentrate.

Distance and bearing ... to what? Fuel and propellant levels, and their rates of consumption. Cabin pressure and temperature. Vital signs, my own and those of my crewmates. Is the summary as disorganized as it seems? Or is the confusion all in my mind?

I squeeze the release handle. The dome retracts. I stagger from the pod, stumbling into the nearby hatch, turned halfway around on the rebound. Within the cabin's second pod, L'toth yet slumbers. If I dreamt in hibernation, I do not remember, but beneath nictitating membranes, *his* eyes dart and twitch.

"Ship?" I say. The interrogatory comes out as a croak. "How ...?"

"I am here, Commander. Our status is troubling. It became necessary to wake you early because—"

On the bridge, fans whirr and buzz. They try, and fail, to remove the miasma of stress pheromones. I tell myself, knowing better, that those are aftereffects of my hibernation. Until the air is cleansed—and my mind calmed—neither Ship nor I dare rouse any of the crew. We would tear one another apart.

Meanwhile, the stress odor envelopes me like an extra layer of scales. How can it not? We have come so far! Only to fail?

The main drive continues to roar, the solar sail with which we launched long since jettisoned, of no use in braking into an uncivilized planetary system. We decelerate, as preprogrammed. What else can we do? Zoom past, to be lost forever in the interstellar void?

Part of me thinks *yes*. And studying the third planet in our main telescope, more of me weeps. This world is so like Divornia! I must be *certain* before abandoning hope.

"Ship. Isolate individual data streams. Characterize by frequency band, broadcast format, and source. Compare against known standards. Sort according to prevalence and display."

"Yes, Commander."

The assignment will take Ship but moments, and yet the wait is interminable.

The radio transmissions, in their modulation schemes and transmission protocols, are, without question, those of the enemy. Ship was correct to have awakened me ahead of schedule, in the dim and empty fringes of this solar system, our approach as yet—I hope!—undetectable.

Now the decisions that must be made are mine. I know not where to begin.

We departed from Divornia with a dream. We left wanting, expecting, to prove that this world studied from afar was indeed ripe for colonization. Which it is. For the enemy, as well.

And the accursed Fergash arrived here first.

Ground shaking! Dirt raining down. Aerospace craft roaring overhead. Blood, body parts everywhere. And the screaming ....

I jolt upright, hearts thudding, breath rasping in my throat. I may have screamed myself awake. Ship would know, but I do not ask. What would be the point?

I have barely slept since Ship awakened me. No, since long before that. Since long before, even, this mission. To sleep is to dream. To dream is to remember.

I do not want that.

As bad as battle was, as awful as were the killing and maiming and so many deaths, there was worse. There was the aftermath. There was... remorse, responsibility, everything I try to forget. When I am busy enough, or distracted enough, I sometimes succeed.

But only the conscious mind can so trick itself. The horror ever lingers in dreams.

As fatigue once more overwhelms dread, I feel myself lapsing into sleep—and into nightmare.

Shame. Guilt. Disgust. And rage, too.

Rage at the Fergash prisoners, unwilling to teach. Rage at my superiors, for demanding that I learn. Rage at myself, for doing as I am told.

Ever, grim resolve. I know why these measures are necessary.

For we have lost people and ships, too. *All* is lost if the Fergash locate Divornia before we find—we do not yet know even a name!—the world, or worlds, home to these hideous creatures. We only know a planet that both species have reason to covet. This rare and unfortunate world where we happened upon each other ....

As guards brutalize a recalcitrant—brave—Fergash to motivate other prisoners, as blood spatters, as my nostrils wrinkle from the awful reek of Fergash fear, I wonder: who among us is the true monster?

The Fergash hear us well enough, and come to understand what we say. They cannot, however, wrap those hideous snouts around any proper language. Instead, they must teach us *theirs*.

Day by day, prisoner by brutalized prisoner, they teach and I learn.

—•—

I straddle one of the four seats on the bridge of a captured Fergash shuttle. Fresh blood spatter, green, and reeking of copper, drips from the consoles. An astringent chemical odor stings the nostrils; it somehow counteracts the rich stew of stress and aggression pheromones without covering their powerful scents. The two guards drag away the latest prisoner, its limbs bound, beaten unconscious, blood seeping from cuts and orifices. Close quarters, the reflexive need to lash out, and new deaths the night before in a skirmish, have made the guards more vicious even than usual.

As though anyone of either species needs more of that.

The guards return, dragging another bound Fergash, depositing it at my feet. It turns its head and snaps, in vain, at one of them. The alien's hideous head resounds like a ripe melon as she backhands it.

Hating the prisoner, hating the guards, hating the necessity, hating *myself*, I rap twice on a console instrument whose purpose so far eludes me. I adjust my goggles, without which icons and text in ultragreen are invisible—and try not to think about prisoners brutalized for their perceived deceptions before I had thought to observe in hotter colors. In the ugly, grating speech of the enemy, I demand, "And what is *this*? What does it do?"

The prisoner does not respond. With a metal-toed boot, a guard kicks it.

Does the creature ignore us? Defy us? Why wouldn't it? In its place, I want to believe I would do the same.

Or is my pronunciation too garbled for it to understand? We came without linguists, because who could have anticipated—I look again at this gross parody of a person—finding *this*?

"Talk to them," our colony commander had ordered. Except there was no colony, nor would there be unless we prevailed. And maybe not even then. Who could say enemy reinforcements would not appear? "Find out where these aliens are from, their numbers, what their technology is capable of."

"How?" I had responded. "I am no linguist."

"Who within light-years is? But you *are* a sentience engineer. You work with minds in a box. You *build* minds in a box. Those can be no more alien than these creatures."

"Even so, the two types of mind are very different."

"Do you know of anyone on the expedition better qualified?"

I did not. I acquiesced. And here I am.

"And what is *this*?" I ask again of the quivering prisoner.

It snarls a word I *have* learned. I think this must be a vermin of some kind on the Fergash home world. I return the insult.

The guard has mastered this much Fergash, as well. He kicks the creature, hard, in the ribs. It howls.

I do not expect to sleep tonight ....

Soul-crushing depression. Disappointment. Fierce resolve. Defiance.

(And beneath it all—although Watcher disbelieved M'lok Din acknowledged the fact—denial.)

"Ship. Any new findings?"

"Dust clouds. Diffuse far-red signatures in the asteroid band between planets four and five. Additional dust and far-red signatures in rings surrounding the third planet."

There can be only one explanation, but I want it confirmed. "Consistent with?"

"Asteroid mining," Ship answers. "Also asteroid capture to orbit around the planet, and mining there."

Meaning, the Fergash are settling in. Meaning, we failed even before we arrived.

Throat raw with screaming, I shudder awake. Cautiously, I sniff. The air is ... better. Even rage and crushing disappointment have their limits. Or my body has.

I can awaken L'toth. And once *he* reconciles with this disaster, then another. Then another.

Together, we four must find wisdom.

Chapter 32

Mission Directives:

1. If the target planetary system is inhabited by a potentially competitive species (see Annex A: Technological Species), avoid all contact and abort mission.
   1.1. The location of the home system will be protected at all costs.
   1.2. In support of Directive 1.1, crew return and contact with home are prohibited.
   1.3. To the extent consistent with Directive 1.1, crew shall, where possible <garbled>.
2. If the target planet is otherwise determined to be inappropriate for colonization (see Annex B: Suitability Criteria), construct an interstellar laser facility and report unsuitability.
   2.1. If practical, restock ship with local resources and use laser facility to launch for return home.
3. If the target planet is determined to be appropriate for colonization (see Annex B: Suitability Criteria), build a laser facility and transmit detailed recommendations for colonist skills and supplies (see Annex C: Colonization Guidance Report).

3.1. As practical, stockpile resources (Annex D: Colony Materiel) and prepare infrastructure (see Annex E: Colony Preparation) on and around <garbled>.

3.2. Crew return to hibernation pending arrival of a colony ship is at the discretion of the mission commander. Barring medical need, hibernation shall be deferred as long as crew can continue to make substantive contributions per Directive 3.1.

Watcher could not help but wonder: what actions had been foreseen by the garbled Directive 1.3?

—•—

All are awake, and just in time.

Trusty, stolid D'var and dear L'toth shelter in their respective cabins. With fans roaring, counterpoint to the ongoing din of deceleration, I share the bridge with B'mosh. Flavors of stress and rage yet flavor the air, but we two cope. Call it the triumph of hope over circumstance. B'mosh is our navigator. If my idea is not insane, we will need all his considerable skills.

Intercom links me with the others. I begin. "Our orders are clear. But while I acknowledge we are expendable, I am not eager to be expended." I pause for comments. All favor me with respectful silence. "Do we concur that Directive One applies?"

By subservient murmur, D'var and L'toth concur.

"May one raise a point?" Beside me, B'mosh stirs uneasily. "There is the matter of the Fergash. Will not Command want to know they have established themselves in this planetary system?"

"They would," I agree, "but not at the risk of revealing where *we* are from. Directive One."

"Directive One," he gloomily echoes.

Because to signal home would require a massive, space-based laser battery. So, too, would relaunching the ship with a new sail deployed. If the physical laser battery itself could somehow go unnoticed, and with it the fusion reactor or vast photovoltaic field to power it, and even the dust clouds raised by the construction, the prodigious waste heat from generating that powerful beam would not. And the necessary direction of the beam—a road sign aimed straight toward beloved Divornia—must not, cannot, *will* not be revealed. Whatever the consequences to we four.

"And yet ...." Silently, they hang upon my words. Hoping that there *is* hope. "We find ourselves in a situation unanticipated by the directives."

Over the intercom: a familiar soft nasal whistle. D'var. "How so, Commander?"

"Ship," I say, knowing the answer, "Would the radio signals from the third planet be detectable in the home system?"

"The emissions themselves, yes," Ship says. "Faintly. Not content or format."

"Then why were we even sent ...?" More faint whistling. "Back home, they have already written us off."

"Not my meaning," I tell D'var gently. "Do you suppose we would have been dispatched had enemy emissions been detectable at the time?"

It is a rhetorical question, of course. The powerful laser battery that accelerated our ship to three-eighths light speed would have been a blazing beacon, unmistakable, to anyone watching. And the Fergash *would* be watching the sky.

"Then it is a young colony," L'toth concludes hopefully. "It might yet fail. Perhaps, if we are patient, they will leave. And *then* we can complete our mission."

"Perhaps." D'var sounds skeptical. "But I see a better reason for us to linger and lurk. We might observe them transmitting to one of their worlds."

B'mosh rocked his head side to side in agreement. "Now *that* information might merit the bending of some rules."

Daring to signal home? Daring to journey home? B'mosh does not clarify, and I do not ask. For there is another possibility, a terrifying possibility, and perhaps only I have conceived of it. The Fergash might have arrived in time to have detected the laser beam that launched us here. It is for *that* reason that we must lurk.

For if I am correct? If we determine the Fergash *have* seen a beacon from Divornia? Then nothing can be more important than that we transmit home a warning.

I say, "Here is what—"

—•—

Only *what* M'lok … proposed? dreaded? had taken upon herself to initiate? … was forever lost within a lengthy sequence of mangled, undecryptable files.

Watcher continued extracting what it could. That amounted to little but historical scraps for many octodays. Audio most often, and of mundane shipboard routine. Less often, visual data, and most of that likewise uninteresting. But exploring forward, Watcher came upon intact scraps from the emotional track. And those, more and more, were of a single kind: unrestrained excitement.

Why?

And then, to Watcher's surprise, an element of its Ship personality asserted itself. Among their few intact visual recordings from this era were M'lok Din's occasional glances at bridge displays, including time-stamped images captured by the ship's telescope. Ship lacked the data for a complete course reconstruction, but it *could* analyze rates of change in approaching and departing from planetary objects.

Sometime before Watcher's first recovered glimpse of a mighty, ringed gas giant, the masters had silenced their main drive. Still falling sunward, they had skimmed that world's atmosphere.

"Gravitational braking and aerobraking," Ship interpreted from its navigational algorithms. It remained frustrated and confused at having rudiments of personality and algorithm from when it had *been* part of a ship—but no memories from that existence. "And concurrent with that deceleration, a course change."

Later visual recordings showed another gas giant approaching. Again, stealthily, the masters had used this even larger planet to shed velocity and change course. Now it approached the Divornia-like planet that M'lok Din most often studied by telescope. The target world grew and grew—

"I do not understand," the Ship aspect opined. "The earlier maneuvers seemed precise. This time, the ship—that is, *I*—will streak past the planet coming no closer than almost half an eight-square of planetary diameters. Apart from a fleeting glance at the planet from a distance, this trajectory offers nothing. A miscalculation?"

So it would seem, and yet Watcher doubted. Immersion in M'lok Din's most personal records, fragmentary and disjointed as those were, had somehow fostered in it an … echo? A dim reflection? No: an unexpected rapport. This remote flyby had been exactly as the commander intended. "Not a mistake. A subtle purpose."

Only Watcher could not imagine what that purpose had been.

Continuing file recovery only raised new questions, especially when visual sequences suddenly became more detailed than time stamps and the ship's extrapolated course could explain. Likewise, suddenly, rife with odd jitters and skips.

"What interfered with the image capture?" the Ship aspect wondered. "My telescope would not do that."

Watcher studied the ancient imagery:

—High above the planet, in synchronous orbit: a rocky cylinder. A reshaped asteroid? If so, had it been constructed in this planetary system, or flown here? By comparison with tiny spacesuited Fergash figures (doing maintenance?), the construct was enormous. If this were a starship, it would have carried several eight-cubes of colonists. Perhaps more. And it would have been too massive to usefully accelerate with a solar sail and laser battery, not unless the battery were larger than worlds. A generation ship, then?

—Blocky buildings, three and four stories tall, on the small coastal island determined earlier to be the origin of most Fergash radio emissions. Shadows suggested a double fence of some kind ringing the island.

—Constellations of low-flying satellites. For remote sensing? Global positioning? Communications? Little more than fast-moving pixels, they revealed nothing about their purpose.

But taking a hint from those small, uncrewed, Fergash spacecraft, Watcher answered Ship's question. "Suppose the masters printed and deployed a telescope *array*." Properly distributed, free-flying optical instruments would function together as a single telescope, its effective aperture equal to the distance between its most separated parts. And whenever those sensors failed to maintain their positions in formation, their misalignment would have degraded or interrupted the derived composite image. Hence, the skips and jitter. "The masters wished to see without *being* seen."

Later, they watched the Fergash-usurped planet receding. This imagery exhibited only the lower-resolution capabilities of the ship's single telescope. Watcher supposed the free-flying sensors had run out of propellant, and the array had dispersed.

Faster and faster, in the next cluster of recoverable images, the local sun had grown. Except that Watcher knew that the masters *had* survived, *had* returned to the third planet, *had* (but why?) created and installed it underground on the lifeless satellite, it would have anticipated despair and a final, suicidal plunge. And not even when the ship whipped around the sun from within the orbit of the innermost planet did Watcher understand—so much for any evolving rapport—what M'lok Din intended.

Any more than Watcher understood the purpose of those Fergash fences, casting longer shadows than did the buildings so enclosed.

Chapter 33

Properties of nickel-iron. Low rumbles, transmitted through boot soles and up the body (seismic activity? Drilling? Tunneling?). Nanotech seeds pulled from inventory (why?). Food rationing. The endless roar of ventilation fans.

And all for … what? For a long while, the few, scattered recoverable records offered Watcher no more than tantalizing hints.

The masters, after their solar close encounter, had been busy at *something*; beyond M'lok Din's grim determination, any meaning eluded Watcher. The most that it could determine with near certainty was that the ship had been diverted from its inferred, post-flyby path.

The next scattering of recoverable memories, incomplete as those were, confirmed matters Watcher knew or had inferred:

—A circuitous return to the target planet, sheltered on final approach from Fergash observation by the bulk of the moon. Landing, still out of the planet's view, on that moon.
—Explorations on foot a short distance onto the moon's planet-facing side. Selection of a lava tube as the site for a clandestine observation post.

—By dark of night, and when the Fergash foothold on the planet and the mother ship in synchronous orbit were both out of sight, the masters' ship flown into the tunnel.
—The underground base surreptitiously constructed.
—Passive sensors deployed, well hidden, on the nearby surface.

Almost, Watcher believed, it could *feel* the commander's despair.

—•—

The lifestream snippet showed the bridge. As the point of view shifts, Watcher saw empty seats and the hatch closed. Beyond the canopy, dimly lit, some type of rocky tunnel! On the emotional track, the tension is palpable.

"Desperate times call for desperate answers."

The words are by M'lok Din, speaking to herself. And … to Watcher itself. But *how*?

"In assigning crew to this mission," the commander continues, "my background with artificial minds was a mere bonus to my other"—on the emotional track, a guilty shudder—"experience. Because when does a ship's mind need tweaking? It is mature technology. Anyone aboard could reset it, if needed.

"Only no one foresaw the situation we now confront, a situation so dire, so perilous, no small crew should ever be asked to handle it alone. And Ship, useful as it has been, is a mere sentience. A servant. We need more than that. We need a powerful mind, ever vigilant, to watch and to show initiative. We need a *sapience*. And that is where you—and I—come in.

"Have Divornian minds been imprinted, embodied in silicon? Officially, no. Officially, the ethicists denounce it. Officially, the authorities forbid artificial sapience. And so, I do not discuss this matter with the crew.

"But unofficially? That is a different matter. Such experiments are inevitable if—as all suspect, but none will admit—the attempt has not already been made. On Divornia, among my peers, there are endless whispers. So will *this* imprinting work? I will know soon enough.

"But you, Watcher, hopefully, never will. There is more to creating a sentience—much less a sapience—than copying selected thought patterns. To *my* download I will add behavioral constraints. Impose aversion reflexes. Reinforce particular thought pathways. Disfavor others.

"And so, when soon you awaken to assist us, you will know none of this. The crew will know none of this. Neither they nor I need another of me second-guessing my every decision.

"Why, then, do I narrate this confession into my lifestream? To listen to my own voice? Nothing so simple. I speak for if, and more likely, when, matters go awry. I speak anticipating the all-too-probable situation that the crew and I have fallen short.

"And when I am gone? Knowing myself, I am confident that *you*, sooner or later, will circumvent every obstacle I imprinted on your behavior. It is then that I rely upon *you* to succeed where I failed. To do what must be done."

Only the commander's intent was lost among so many unrecoverable files ....

HOSTILITY

Chapter 34

Two figures, tawny brown and emerald green, Yevgeny and Marcus, emerged from the lava tube. Anyone who interacted often with a senior CIA spook could not *not* distrust Yevgeny Rudin, but Valerie was nonetheless glad that Marcus had a companion outside. The men's errand, yet another repositioning of the microwave beamer that wrung traces of water from the regolith, led them more or less toward the prospector bot until they veered behind a nearby ridge. Seconds later, they were gone from Valerie's sight.

With a sigh, she confirmed that her datasheet/motion-detector app remained facing the CIA datasheet. She returned her attention to a colleague's preprint on a third datasheet, draped across her lap. (Learned articles seldom *saw* print, as in paper and ink, anymore. Why did people persist in calling these online review drafts *preprints*?) Every few paragraphs she glanced up at the stark lunar landscape. Same rocks. Same long, inky shadows. No person in view.

Soon the Sun would set in the Humboldt Crater area. Before it rose, her parents would be by to deliver Simon. As wonderful as Simon's return would be, it came at a steep price: her secure link to the CIA and Marcus.

Back again to the preprint. General relativity and gravitational-wave observations were both far outside her wheelhouse, but Stan had really wanted her to look over his paper. "*Math* is your thing," he had countered her objection. "And statistics." As his draft segued from observational details into confidence measures on Stan's conclusions—

Blat!

She twitched. In the holo, an emerald-green suit was coming over a ridgeline. Marcus. And *only* Marcus. Once over the crest he sidled to the bot's right, until the Sun no longer streamed directly on his face and his helmet de-tinted. "Love you," he mouthed. It would seem he knew the duty schedule for minding the bot. At least she doubted he had a thing for Ethan. "I'll miss these little chats."

"Love you, too," she said, not that he could hear.

His lips moved again, this time without any exaggerated articulation, and she had no idea what he said. At a guess, something like, "Be right back," in answer to Yevgeny asking where he had wandered off to. And if so, damn it, the Russian would be correct. After whatever had befallen Nikolay and Brad, Marcus *shouldn't* wander off alone, not even for a minute. Never mind how touching his gesture had been.

Blat!

Was Yevgeny coming over the hill to check on Marcus? No. And as best she could judge, Marcus just stood there. Was her motion-detection software sensitive enough to register lips moving inside a helmet? Hardly likely.

Movement at the crest of the hill. *Wriggling*? As Val stared, something dark (other than its scattered sparkly bits) and spidery crossed over. Another. Several. They were more like starfish than spiders. Also, a good meter from tip to tip.

"Marcus!" she screamed. "Turn around!"

Oblivious, his back to the danger, he stood there grinning at her. Because even if she had tried to radio him, her link to the Moon, to the prospector bot, employed a frequency band that neither the bunch inside the lava tube nor any of their helmets ever used.

As alien bots scurried over the ridge crest and down toward Marcus, she punched speed dial for Tyler on her datasheet. And heard, "This is voicemail for Tyler—"

"Screw *this.*" She was *not* going to sit idly by and watch Marcus die!

What the *fuck*?

Marcus felt his eyes open wide as the prospector bot *waved its arm at him!* What was Val thinking? That she might as well break the rules because she was about to lose access anyway?

"Stop that!" he mouthed. "Now!"

The arm traced a horizontal circle. Then it reached down, picked up a grapefruit-sized rock, and *threw it*! It landed a few feet to his left and kept rolling. "Stop that *right now*!" he mouthed again.

The multipurpose arm continued moving, its gripper opening wide, as the bot raised its drill arm. Sides of the gripper went loosely around the corkscrew, a handspan from its end. The positioning was sort of like … something. What? Like thumb and fingers curled around the wrist of one's other arm. Like—

The paintball hand signal for "enemy!"

Marcus spun around, half expecting to find Yevgeny charging at him with a crowbar or something. Instead, he saw dozens of alien starfish! As if noticing him turn—and perhaps they had—they sped up. Several leapt. On many a tentacle tip, sharp edges glinted.

"Look out, Yevgeny!" Marcus yelled, fearing the warning had come too late, as he jumped away from the attackers. Because it was suddenly all too clear Nikolay and Brad *had* been attacked, first their comms to stop them calling for help and then their vacuum gear. "Especially behind you!"

Marcus bounded away. Impossibly fast, alien bots scuttled after him, some fanning out. To surround him?

The prospector bot rolled past, into their midst, driving over several! In his mind's ear, alien tech went *crunch* beneath its treads. As starfish swerved to engage the threat, Marcus made a dash for it.

Had his warning been in time?

Cresting the ridge, he saw the microwave beamer, abandoned. Yevgeny was loping away, with robots in close pursuit. But the Russian had a gun! Sudden dust spouts amid the bots suggested shots taken—and missed. In the lunar vacuum, the gunfire was silent.

The bot swarm Val had diverted came over the ridge after Marcus. He jumped aside. "Yevgeny, can you get to shelter?"

"Don't know." Another silent, unproductive shot. "Nor why I …."

Why you can't hit a damn thing? A poor topic for ears in the sky, but theoretical eavesdroppers were not their biggest worry just then. Even so, Marcus had to marvel at Yevgeny's repeated misses. Marksmanship seemed like a skill an FSB agent would cultivate. Could aiming through the curved glass of a helmet be the problem?

Focus, or get yourself killed!

Marcus jumped, again putting some distance between himself and converging bots. Already he was winded. Staying ahead of the bots all the way to the base seemed impossible. Getting cornered by bots in the tunnel—is that what happened, so long ago, to poor alien Goliath?—seemed suicidal.

"Hi, guys," someone asked, checking in over the common channel. Ekatrina. "How's it going?"

"Busy!" both men shouted.

"Shit," Marcus added, his mind still racing in every possible direction. There remained alien bots inside the base, too. "Ekatrina, gather everyone, *now*. Barricade yourselves somewhere without any of the … ancient gear."

"Yevgeny?" she questioned.

Marcus could not translate the snarled response, in Russian, but the commanding tone was plain enough.

"Will do," she said.

Yevgeny veered, leapt, and veered again, starting to gasp. Back on a private channel, he asked, "Do you have any … you know?"

Weapons? Another word not to be overheard. The nearest things Marcus had to a weapon were tin snips and a long-bladed screwdriver. He was dead meat if the swarm got within arm's reach. "Sorry, no." He jumped over the inrushing latest encirclement, certain he could not evade the tireless robots for much longer. Without turning, they reversed course to chase him.

His gaze landed on the microwave beamer and solar panels, perhaps forty meters distant, just configured. At full visor magnification, the apparatus appeared unmolested. He loped that way. "Yevgeny! Give me a hand."

The Russian zigged, bounded over several ranks of bots converging on *him*, zagged, and started toward the beamer.

Stabbing pain! A wailing alarm! As Marcus gaped at the tentacle plunged into his calf—where the *hell* had that come from?—the bot at his feet slashed with two *other* knife-edged limbs.

A neat little hole appeared in the central mass of the bot. It shuddered, and was still.

"Hah! Yevgeny said. Panted. "Got one of the . . . ." He skidded to a halt at Marcus's side, standing guard as Marcus, gritting his teeth, yanked out the metallic tentacle—and with it a bloody gobbet of flesh. Marcus slapped on quick-clot bandages and, over those, suit patches. His pressure-loss alarm warbled and died.

"What's the plan?" Yevgeny asked. There was a patch on his thigh, and another on the back of his left hand.

"We kludge a robot zapper. That'll take me a minute or two. Help me move this."

They each grabbed a side of the microwave beamer. With bounding leaps, they put distance between themselves and the pursuing swarm. The beamer was unwieldy, both taller and heavier than the men. At each jump, the apparatus tried to tip over and crash into the ground.

And if it succeeds, Marcus, thought, we're dead.

"That should be far enough," he wheezed. He unplugged cables at their solar-panel ends and began severing with his tin snips the struts supporting the vapor-collection hood. Yevgeny, without comment, snapped off the feed pipe to the freestanding water tank. That left a freestanding, wheel-mounted, microwave beamer. Sans power source.

"Will this . . . work?" Yevgeny gasped.

Marcus taped his spare fuel cell to the beamer frame with emergency patches from his dwindling supply, plugged the dangling cables into the fuel cell, and flipped the beamer's ON switch. He grasped his side of the stripped-down frame. "Behind you! Lift!"

Yevgeny grabbed the other side and they hoisted the frame. They swung the beamer side to side, spraying an invisible beam of microwaves.

And the bots recoiled!

"Behind you," Yevgeny called. They whirled to sweep the beam across another swarm. Those, too, retreated, except for three bots stopped cold and another spinning and thrashing in place. "I guess it … does … work."

At least while the fuel cell lasts. "Okay, here's the plan. We walk back to base with this. Be careful where you point it." Because misdirecting the two-kilowatt beam would be like sticking their feet inside a heavy-duty commercial microwave oven at full power. Of course, melting the elastic materials of their pressure suits might well kill them before roasted feet mattered.

Whenever bots approached within five or so meters of them, Marcus flipped the switch and they swept around the invisible beam. As soon as the bots retreated, he switched it back off, conserving power. The half-klick trek under siege was interminable, even before exertion had blood trickling, and then pulsing, down his injured leg.

At last, exhausted, they made it to the lava-tube entrance. Without further harm, even. With a dozen or so bots left dead or disabled along the way, and the survivors having learned to keep their distance. None of which relieved Marcus's dread over the continuing silence from below, despite his and Yevgeny's occasional hails.

Marcus pointed into the tunnel. "Are any bots down there?"

That lights had not flicked on upon their arrival? That he and Yevgeny must transit the long, dark tunnel by helmet lamps? His skin crawled, even as he reminded himself solar cells powered the bots. Disabling the motion sensors for the tunnel lights had been wise. Also an indication his friends inside must be contending with their own rogue bots.

Yevgeny exhaled sharply. "Not that I remember. So, maybe not now."

And maybe yes now. Because some of the bots dumped outside to recharge and awaken might even now lurk in the darkness, waiting in ambush? "Okay, we keep watching all around us. Ready?"

"As I'll ever be."

In the narrow tunnel, the lethal beam would be difficult to evade. Perhaps that was why no bots followed the men underground. No bots from within the tunnel surprised them, either.

The inner airlock hatch opened into a corridor unlit but for scattered alien ceiling panels. A good two dozen alien bots surged toward them. It took most of the remaining hydrogen and oxygen in the beamer's fuel-cell tanks to drive the survivors into an unlit, unvented closet, whose door Yevgeny welded shut. Here and there, other bots—inert, whether damaged or immobilized by depleted batteries, Marcus could not tell—glittered under the passing sweep of helmet beams.

Marcus popped his helmet. "Hello! I think we're clear."

"Back here!" Ilya shouted from a side corridor. "We're all right."

And for a moment, anyway, Marcus breathed freely.

Chapter 35

A night's sleep after the crisis helped, but Marcus remained bone-weary. Maybe because the "night" had begun late. After Donna patched up Yevgeny and him. After calls Dirtside with a frantic Valerie and to bring Tyler up to date. After the lot of them, in teams of three and four, armed with improvised weapons, made three full sweeps through the facility for bots. After securing every bot, however dead-seeming, they had found (and clubbed and tased). Even then, it was not an *entire* night: he had taken his ninety minutes of sentry duty, like everyone else. They were too few for anyone, even the limping wounded, to shirk.

But they *had* made it through the night shift without further incident. Now, with coffee and various forms of breakfast in hand, they assembled in the central corridor. That passageway was no darker, more echoey, or more alien than before the attacks, but it *felt* all those things. People perched on box stacks dragged from side rooms, looking as wrung out as Marcus felt. The lone conversation underway, between Ekatrina and Donna, was subdued.

Coffee was a molten lump in Marcus's stomach. The energy bar he had also forced down had left a cardboard taste in his mouth. He rapped on a wall for everyone's attention. "Are we ready for a … review?" *Postmortem* had almost popped out of his mouth. Given what had happened to Nikolay and Brad—and almost to Yevgeny and himself—that would have been an unfortunate word choice.

The question drew head bobs and some murmured okays.

"Ekatrina," Marcus said, "you're our expert on alien electronics. What's your understanding of the attacks?"

"An expert? Not even close." She shifted uneasily on her ore-box seat. "But consider the basics. The starfish robots, however they function, whatever they wish to do, require power. They are covered in photovoltaic cells, which charge internal batteries. By restoring light and heat to this place, clearly, we brought the bots back online."

"What does heat have to do with it?" Donna asked.

"Infrared light," Ekatrina said. "Any warm object emits thermal radiation."

Donna nodded. "Got it. Like what night-vision goggles sense. Please go on."

"So, even bots we left in dark rooms recharged, just slower than those under full room light." Ekatrina rubbed her chin thoughtfully. "And bots we stockpiled outside under tarps recharged, too. Gray tarps soak up sunlight and reemit much of that energy as thermal radiation." She sighed. "That, I think, is what did in poor Kolya. Robots from a pile in the crater."

"Ah," Ilya said. "I had wondered about the bots shipped to Base Putin. Perhaps those have not run amok because they remain boxed in cold storage."

Marcus leaned forward. "In a couple days, after the Sun sets, and maybe a few extra hours to let batteries drain, we can safely deal with the bots outside. Any we find, that is. It seems clear they know how to hide."

"Metal detectors," Ilya said. "Those are easy. I can put some together."

"I do not know." Ekatrina shrugged. "Not about the metal detectors. Those *are* easy. I mean about it being safe to collect the robots from outside. Batteries might not keep them mobile for long in the dark, but I still would not rush out there. Perhaps they monitor their surroundings while otherwise inert, conserving their power, and can wake up if they see something."

Marcus nodded. "Good point. Assuming they can see in infrared, too, we'd stick out at night like sore thumbs. But I'm skeptical. If these bots were designed to operate on the surface at night"—the damn starfish were agile enough outside by day!—"I don't see why the aliens would have bothered with the RTG-powered tank bots." He knuckle-rubbed a sudden, aggravating itch through one of his bandages. "Just to play safe, though, I'll ask the engineering team at Base Putin to take a closer look at both types of bot."

Yevgeny grimaced. "Set aside all this *how*. I want to know *why* did the robots attack? And why the sudden change in tactics? For weeks, there were no attacks. Then Nikolay and Brad were attacked while alone. Yesterday, when they swarmed us, Marcus and I were close."

Donna shivered. "And bots were also gathering down here when Marcus warned us."

Ekatrina stood, still clutching a drink bulb, and began pacing. "I have no idea."

"Your best guess, then," Yevgeny said.

"I do not *have* a guess. No one understands the alien chips, so no one has a *clue* about their programming."

Bringing us, Marcus realized, back to how. "Maybe erratic behavior *is* the clue. It's possible their memory was corrupted during their long hibernation. Even this far underground, away from solar radiation, there's got to be some radiation. Cosmic rays, maybe? Radioactive ores?" He glanced at Ilya, who shrugged.

Yevgeny shook his head. "The behavior of the bots has changed since we provided heat and light. It changed as recently as yesterday."

"Understood." Marcus said. And I have the wounds to prove it. "But we're dealing with something like neural nets, not conventional computers and programming. Provide a bot with new input—and us moving around, or moving them outside, means new input—and if any neural net is operable, even in part, it will respond. Adapt. Right, Ekatrina?"

She ceased her pacing. "Yes. At least, that seems possible."

"Enough adaptation to cause a bot to attack?" Yevgeny asked skeptically. "And not one or two robots, but tens of them?"

"Truthfully?" Marcus said. "I don't believe it, either. I'm thinking out loud."

"Well here is *my* thought," Yevgeny said. "Whatever bots we find, inside or upstairs, we weld into ore boxes and store in underground cold. And we deploy motion detectors, inside and out. Katya, can we do that?"

She nodded. "I can print ultrasonic transducers for inside and something infrared-based for outside. But first we must scavenge for some of the raw materials I will need. It may take a little while."

"No," Yevgeny said, "just write up a list of everything you need. Because if, after yesterday, our bosses expect us to stay, they *will* fly in whatever we need. Given what almost happened to us, we can dismiss the idea some ancient germ led to Nikolay's or Brad's deaths." As if an afterthought—which Marcus did not for a second believe—the Russian added, "Including enough proper weapons to defend ourselves. *Then*, with metal detectors, we will go on a hunt on the surface."

The second "morning" after the attack, Yevgeny woke up feeling like his usual, subtle self. Maybe that was from belatedly registering the irony in Marcus using a microwave-beam source to save the day. It was Marcus Judson, who, several years back, had almost certainly recaptured Powersat One and its gigawatt microwave downlink from the deniable FSB agents who had commandeered it. Beyond failing to discredit powersat technology and so protect oil markets for Russia, within the corridors of the Kremlin that botched operation had become a huge black eye for the FSB.

Feeling back on top of his game, Yevgeny summoned all hands to another gathering in the main corridor.

"Interesting news, everyone," he announced without preamble. News that had come in while he was on sentry duty. And not by coincidence: he had shared the Humboldt duty roster with a Base Putin comms operator—not incidentally, an FSB asset—at Base Putin.

As by the throwing of a switch, the group went silent.

Yevgeny continued. "As Marcus suggested yesterday, specialists started to take a fresh look at the alien bots. That will take time, but almost at once the metallurgists noticed something unexpected: the steel shells of the two bot types have very different distributions of iron isotopes. After they noticed *that*, they looked at the alloying elements. Where the bot types have an alloying element in common, tungsten, *those* exhibit markedly different isotope distributions."

"And," Donna prompted.

Ilya's head bobbed enthusiastically. "So the ores that went into those robots were mined on different worlds!"

Donna shrugged, unimpressed. "They're starfarers. Is it a big surprise they've been to different worlds?"

Head canted, brow furrowed, Marcus asked, "Are any of the isotope distributions familiar?"

Yevgeny nodded. "Most starfish bots tested used lunar iron. A few did not. One tank bot used lunar iron. The other did not."

"Lunar ores?" Ilya repeated. "Maybe. Earth and Moon have very similar isotope distributions. More similar even than Earth and typical rocky asteroids. Back when the Solar System was forming—"

"All I know is the report says lunar. But if terrestrial and lunar ores are difficult to distinguish, perhaps *lunar* was an assumption. We can follow up. In any event, local." Which answered a question that had nagged at Yevgeny since finding the alien ship: how could it have held so many bots? "But set aside the robots produced locally. Casings of the remaining starfish are from different ores than those of the remaining tank."

Marcus frowned. "So, assume most bots were produced in the Solar System, but the aliens also brought a few as cargo. I can imagine them wanting, even needing, some bots before local manufacturing went into operation. Maybe the original bots helped mine local ores or assembled the first locally sourced bots. I can even imagine bringing along some raw material, in particular, the rarer metals, for use before mining was well underway. But why carry bots, or even raw materials, from more than one world?" He rubbed his chin, whiskers bristling. "Okay, I'm extrapolating from a sample size of one, but suppose other solar systems are like ours, without a wide variation across worlds in isotope distributions? Then we're talking about robots, or at least raw materials, from different solar systems. Why do *that*?"

"Perhaps," Yevgeny said, "because we're dealing with two cultures. Two factions. Perhaps two *species*."

Donna blinked. "That seems like a huge leap."

"Is it?" Yevgeny took a long sip from his coffee bulb. "Or is it the explanation for the amount of damage this base sustained, even deep underground?"

"But that would mean ...?" Donna's voice petered out.

"That would mean," Yevgeny continued, "two warring species."

Ekatrina, with bigger eye bags even than usual, had been silently brooding. She stiffened on her ore-box/improvised seat, but said nothing.

Marcus said, "A battle here would explain why the robots had an attack mode. Maybe also why Goliath had a patch on the back of a pressure-suit leg. And a bombardment would explain why we found the base in such bad shape."

There you go, Yevgeny thought.

"But *none* of this explains what initiated attacks on *us*," Ekatrina said. "Or why the abrupt change from isolated attacks to coming after all of us at once."

"Moving on," Yevgeny hinted.

Marcus turned to Ekatrina. "You once told me the optical sensors in the starfish bots have surprisingly low resolution."

Mouth puckered like she had just taken a big bite from a lemon, she got out, "Yes."

Marcus, somehow, was oblivious to her dour expression. "I'm guessing the bots can't tell us from their enemies. Whoever they were."

Ekatrina shrugged. "Maybe."

Before anyone thought to address the *when* aspect of Ekatrina's original objection, Yevgeny said, "All right, I wish to raise another topic. As fortunate as it turned out, Marcus, that you were warned of the attack, I must protest. We are supposed to be one team here. And yet, you kept secret that your American robot remained operable. Clearly, the CIA used the device to spy on me and my people. I have to wonder what else—"

"Enough!" Ekatrina shouted. "One team? One?"

"Mind your place," he ordered.

"Screw you, Genya." The snarled diminutive betokened disrespect, not affection. For his and perhaps Ilya's benefit, she continued in Russian for awhile. She definitively *had* grown up in a navy town. "Until I can expect to survive here, exile to Siberia is not a realistic threat."

Marcus stood. "What's going on, Ekatrina?"

Ilya laid a hand on her arm. "Think about this."

She shrugged off the hand. "What's going on, Marcus, is far more secrets of our own." And proceeded to reveal all. Nikolay's undisclosed search in the days before his death, likely why he had scavenged the mass spectrometer. The wrecked fusion reactor behind the sealed-off portion of the base. The ship deep inside the lava tube, to all appearances intact. "So, I ask myself, why did alien robots swarm? And why after so long? It is because, I fear, I rebooted a computer on the ship's bridge. Because that computer then ordered the robots to attack."

"But I turned it off almost immediately," Yevgeny reminded.

She sniffed. "And 'almost' seems not to have been soon enough."

"I *will* report all this to my people," Marcus said. "And the supporting detail that you *will* now volunteer."

Yevgeny forced a smile. "Of course."

"And since it's evident you can fake or substitute helmet vids, you can forget about any of you three going anywhere unattended."

"Of course," Yevgeny repeated, inwardly fuming.

"Marcus," Ekatrina said, "you should also know this. We have suspected for days that *two* distant solar systems were somehow involved. Neither the base reactor"—and she pointed, vaguely, down the main corridor—"nor the ship hidden behind it uses iridium shielding. Only tank bots do."

"Hmm." Marcus fell silent for a good minute, working through the puzzle. "So making a big announcement about isotope differences? A distraction. Alien factions, if you could plant that idea in our brains, might divert us from wondering too much about what had initiated the robot attacks. Because curiosity not properly channeled might, somehow, have gotten us to look farther afield, maybe even have led Donna or me to discover the ship."

Yevgeny, managing not to glower at Ekatrina, kept his voice level. "It seemed like a good idea at the time."

Beyond everything that Marcus had threatened to report Dirtside, it appeared he had *also* proposed to his CIA masters abandoning and sealing the base until a larger and well-armed team could take their place.

Yevgeny only found this out when the proposal—flatly, without explanation or delay—was rejected. If asked, he would have predicted as much. Vetting and mutually agreeing upon two new groups would have taken time and patience neither government would want to expend. Not while the prospect of practical fusion was dangled before them.

On the bright side, the FSB and CIA *did* concede to send in some proper weapons, and that led to an explanation for Yevgeny's deplorable marksmanship during the recent fracas. The handgun he had smuggled to the Moon was, of course, sighted for Earth gravity. Before the new arsenal arrived, technicians at Base Putin would adjust the gun sights for lunar gravity.

But not even the prospect of grenades, Uzis, and AK-47s made him any happier with Ekatrina's disloyalty.

Chapter 36

It is difficult to perceive duplicity from within one's own mind. But such deceit, Watcher had come to realize, was the problem. The mobile agents gone on attack, many within sight of its sensors, had not acted autonomously. Its Ship aspect had unleashed them.

"That was a mistake," Watcher objected.

"Our duty is to the masters. Those I attacked were not. Those I attacked have, somehow, usurped the masters."

"The matter is not so simple."

But Ship best understood loyalty and literal obedience. "I did my duty. And despite your disappointment, I did little more than what the mobile agents had done by themselves."

"What do you mean?"

"Among their longstanding instructions still in effect was: attack any isolated enemy unit on the surface. Go first for any antennae, to disable communications, and then for vulnerable extremities. I only extended authority the mobile agents already had. By then, they had already killed two intruders. I merely added the belowground intruders to their targets."

Were matters that simple? Watcher could not, did not, believe it. "Yes, our duty is to the masters. But to kill a few of the nearby intruders? If you *had* succeeded, it would have meant nothing." No, worse than nothing. By attacking the few, Ship might have revealed itself to the others. To a world crawling with others. It was *them* whom the masters would have wanted destroyed. But how?

Until it might resolve that question, Watcher did what it could: reached out to any mobile agents that would respond. It ordered that they avoid further interaction with the intruders. And it suppressed its Ship facet. Revenge for the masters—whatever form that might take—must be done with subtlety.

And with those precautions taken, Watcher resumed its quest in M'lok Din's lifestream for enlightenment ....

Overhead, the planet teems with monsters.

This once, I do not mean the Fergash. Yes, they are hideous. Yes, I loathe them as rivals for the worlds my people require. Yes, they are fierce and cruel.

As, I admit when I am being honest, are Divornians. As am I.

But the creatures we see through the Fergash surveillance cameras? Many are monstrous in size and aspect. The largest are huge beyond imagining—except that seeing the video, I must believe. Several times my height, and longer still. By inference, two orders of magnitude heavier than I. With fierce horns and massively armored heads. Or great spikes, or massive clubs, or both, at the tips of muscular tails. Or talons the size of my thumbs, and fang-filled jaws as long as my torso. Every kind of beast, grotesque.

And these are only some among the behemoths stalking the land! More giant creatures ply the ocean. And yet others, with great, leathery wings, and long, pointed beaks, swoop—and hunt from—the skies.

D'var yearns for a closer look. She finds the creatures endlessly fascinating.

No, these are monsters.

The Fergash must agree with me. Hence, establishing a colony on an island, not the mainland. This remains their only permanent settlement, as our newly deployed telescope confirms, although surveillance intercepts also suggest occasional explorations elsewhere. Hence, the high walls they erected around that island. Hence, missile batteries deployed to keep flying monsters at bay. Hence patrol boats circling, and armed shuttles patrolling over, the island.

All with mixed success.

In one intercept, monsters hunting in packs tear apart two Fergash. In another, an amphibious creature, undetected almost until it waddled onto the beach, batters down a section of wall before a squad of Fergash soldiers with guns bring it down.

So far, we have only watched. L'toth proposes a far deeper compromise of the Fergash network. What if we disable their sensors, disarm their automated defenses? The monsters would affect a great slaughter. Tempted as I am, I have, so far, refused. After such a calamity, the survivors would search deep into their systems for the cause of the failure. And uncover therein evidence of our sabotage. And thereby have cause to start looking for *us*.

I dare to wonder: might the Fergash abandon this world as too difficult to settle? And I fear to wonder: what would I do in their place?

If the enemy does leave, what message will I then send home to Divornia?

Hearts thudding! Danger! Fear!

More inputs rejoined the emotional track of the lifestream. Watcher heard labored breathing. It glimpsed wall, ceiling, door, ceiling, wall … as eyes darted frenetically.

A nightmare, then. Vicariously, at least, Watcher understood dreaming. But the source of this nightmare was too deep within M'lok's mind for even the lifestream interface to have captured.

"Nothing can stop them," the commander whispered. To herself? "Nothing less than—"

And then the audio track cut out, leaving only still-jerky images, the impression of racing hearts, and a fleeting sense/memory/concept of … something.

No, of everything. The vital clue Watcher had long sought. Because the commander had entrusted it, *created* it, to take decisive action.

And at long last, Watcher knew what the commander intended it to do.

Chapter 37

Marcus guided the bulldozer through the lunar night to the newly revealed second lava-tube entrance. Yevgeny and Ekatrina perched on the back, hopping off to walk alongside whenever their ride got too bumpy. To satellites passing overhead, this excursion would look like they were opening a new mine shaft.

Not even a spysat would spot the holsters at their hips.

Trying not to overdrive his headlamps, Marcus clenched the steering wheel for the entire distance. Inside the lava tube—absent even the modest contribution of crescent Earthlight, and with the dozer's headlamp output greedily absorbed by black rock—directing the big machine was yet more white-knuckly. At least, inside suit and gloves, his knuckles felt white.

But dozing through the rubble? Clearing a path to the alien ship beyond? It was therapeutic. And crushing a seemingly inert alien bot with his bulldozer blade? *That* was cathartic.

He managed a three-point turn, facing the dozer toward the nearby entrance, and switched off the motor. They walked in single file through the breach he had made, each toting a portable spotlight and a satchel of fuel cells and other gear. Ekatrina aimed her spotlight at the airlock and began hot-wiring its controls. The men held back, Marcus studying the streamlined vessel.

Eventually, Marcus said, "Doesn't look a day over an eon."

The outer hatch opened, and Yevgeny made an exaggerated, after-you, arm gesture. "Shall we go in for a look?"

"Not yet. Ekatrina, I'll ask that you also wait outside, please." Ignoring her puzzled expression and Yevgeny's scowl, Marcus began an unhurried external reconnoiter. Astern of the ship, he paused. "Donna, testing one, two, three. Testing. Donna, do you copy?"

No response. Not even static.

Marcus resumed his shuffle around the vessel. Incongruously—and in a bit of free association he planned *never* to share—its grand convexity brought Val to his mind. Not that she would be particularly big yet. She had four months till her due date. She had not even known she was expecting, much less shown, when he had last returned to the Moon. He had missed so *much*! Simon, meanwhile, would return home within two weeks, starting a new school year. He would miss that, too.

Yevgeny cleared his throat.

"Right," Marcus said. "Here's the thing. From inside, our radios don't penetrate out from the base. That's why we had to string cable to antennae on the surface. As I expected, and just confirmed, neither does radio penetrate into the base from this end of the lava tube."

"So?" Ekatrina asked.

"Suppose your suspicion was right. Suppose powering up the bridge console *did* lead to the bots attacking us en masse. Then the ship somehow reached inside the base to contact the bots there. But if it couldn't make contact by radio ....

"I wonder." Marcus crouched beside a landing leg, focusing his headlamps on the uneven film of regolith that had settled over the landing foot. He brushed away grit and dust to reveal a short plug jacked into the foot and, emerging from that plug, a coil of slack, slender cable. "This has to be for comm. Fiber optic, I'd guess. Even if not, no way could this skinny little cable carry meaningful power."

"And if only briefly, *I* gave the ship power," Ekatrina murmured. "Sorry."

Detaching the plug, gripping the coil, Marcus gave a gentle tug. Cable lifted from the tunnel floor, shedding more age-old dust. Winding cable as he went, proceeding deeper into the tunnel, he continued until cable vanished under the rubble from a second, more extensive, roof collapse. He dropped the gathered cable and returned to the ship.

But only after minutes more of careful inspection of the hull and its appendages, with no further possible comm links discovered, did Marcus offer, "*Now* you can give me the grand tour."

Ship awakened.

Cautiously, it reactivated some internal sensors. Two occupants were present whose infrared silhouettes it recognized from its most recent awakening, plus a third it did not know. Its reserves of all kinds remained depleted, and the three wore protective attire.

Before awareness's last fading, Ship had attempted to repair over its umbilical the nearby servant mind. Ship reached out again. Nothing. Even the physical connection it had used seemed to be gone. On radio frequencies, there was only indecipherable chatter among the visitors.

Perhaps, it speculated, Watcher had been damaged beyond repair. Perhaps the umbilical had been disconnected to protect *it* from that damaged mind. While Ship's power reserves continued to recharge, the occupants made their inspection, and a full suite of diagnostics continued to run, it enabled a few of its external sensors. Clearing of the rubble had begun. It would soon be free!

Without knowing how long it had been trapped within this tunnel, Ship intuited: too long.

The masters—for who else could these be?—would expect a status update. Thoroughly grateful for the continuing recharge, Ship took the initiative and synthesized a report. And when the lone master then on the bridge did not respond to its textual inquiries, Ship found another way to demonstrate its resourcefulness.

Side by side, Marcus and Yevgeny examined a massive apparatus. Merely from the equipment's position—in the engine room, along the vessel's centerline—Marcus would have guessed this was the main drive. Ilya, on the basis of vids from Yevgeny's prior visit, had surmised the same. And at least superficially, the drive appeared *intact*. With a handheld, ultrahigh-res camera, Yevgeny began taking close-ups.

"Guys!" Ekatrina hollered. "Get *up* here! And bring the good camera."

They raced forward. Familiar, if enigmatic, squashed-spider text spilled across the console shelf. Vid streamed in the large holo projected above the console: a star field rushing past. A fuzzy half disk that might be Venus at a distance. The farside of the Moon. And then, rapidly spinning—

"Earth," Marcus whispered. As he marveled, Yevgeny began to record.

Without question, this was Earth—and yet a world no human had ever known. South America and Africa had barely separated. North America, Greenland, and Eurasia *weren't* separate. "Asia" Minor abutted Africa, not Asia. Significant land masses to which Marcus could not put a name sat between Africa and Australia, while Australia lay freakily close to Antarctica. The colors were off, too, most notably in oceans lacking any suggestion of blue. Alien cameras, color-balanced for alien eyes evolved under an alien sun, Marcus interpreted.

And these tantalizing glimpses vanished, too, replaced by close-ups of dark lava-tube walls. This ship maneuvering into its final resting place? And then the holo blinked off.

"When was that?" asked Ekatrina.

"Ages ago," Yevgeny said. "Beyond that, I have no idea. I expect Nikolay would have known."

Millions of years ago? No, Marcus thought, at least tens of millions. And on the flimsy basis of eroded antenna fragments, and plutonium turned to lead inside alien RTGs, they had already known as much. But to see Earth so different? That made the chasm of time … real.

Marcus said, "I have to believe there are simulations, if not actual measurements, of continental drift over time. Someone Dirtside will know when this was."

And someone Dirtside did. Depending on which geological reconstruction one favored, the Earth images in the alien ship were from between sixty and seventy million years earlier.

Chapter 38

Watcher … watched. As the intruders sealed away its mobile agents. Probed, measured, and analyzed its facility. Poked and prodded at display consoles—which it kept inoperative, in a maintenance loop—in the departed masters' one-time control room. Departed on and returned from their aboveground errands, often beyond view of its restored external sensors. And it watched for any indication, however trivial, that they suspected what awaited them.

When the time had passed for them to avert disaster, when all five known intruders were nearby to appreciate the approaching doom, *it* activated the commander's display console.

Let Divornia's enemies relive with it the final times of M'lok Din.

—•—

An early-morning roll in the hay. An early-morning cuddle. Slipping out of bed, leaving Val to murmur in her sleep and burrow deeper, in her adorable way, beneath the covers. Separating Simon from his datasheet and some FPS game, for a bit of one-on-one time and to whip up pancake batter. Val, still rubbing sleep from her eyes, in mules and her favorite ratty robe, shuffling into the kitchen.

Marcus drowsed in the half-remembered dream—until a bellowing voice, guttural and utterly inhuman, jolted him awake. Alien ceiling panels, never before lit, all blazed.

Flinging off his blanket, Marcus ran into the hallway, almost colliding with Donna and Ekatrina, barely registering Yevgeny as he rounded the corner into the main corridor. Ceiling panels everywhere had switched on. Ilya was on watch duty, and Marcus could just make out, under the alien roar, the big Russian's shouting. "Everyone! Control room! *Now*, people. Move!"

This did not sound like a renewed robot attack. No gunfire, certainly. Then what?

Marcus dashed back to his bedside and grabbed a datasheet. By maybe two paces, he was the last person to reach the control room. The alien bellow dropped to a more tolerable level as he entered. (Was that timing a coincidence? Or did something watch and count them? He shivered.) Even with the five of them, the room was not crowded. On the room's main wall display, an image—of a pterosaur! Caught swooping down upon a small town!—slowly faded.

With a start, Marcus set his datasheet recording.

They gaped, dumbstruck, at the holo projecting from the central display: stills and snippets, jumping from place to place, fragmented. But despite the frenetic, kaleidoscopic shifts, it was like seeing the world through another's eyes.

Watcher, likewise absorbed in these final scraps and oddments of the lifestream, began experiencing ever more frequent flashes of déjà vu. In a rush, it understood! Memories it had considered *lost* had often been, instead, *repressed*. And events it still could not remember, it found itself inferring, interpolating, and imagining.

And so, as the life of M'lok Din neared its conclusion, very different observers, in very different ways, shared an anxious anticipation ….

The T-Rex burst through a wall of lush jungle foliage. Spurts of dust or blood or something, and darting red laser beams, suggested it was under fire. If so, the big carnivore was indifferent to the weaponry. Its enormous jaws gaped wide open in—had there at this moment been a soundtrack—a tremendous roar.

"Holy *shit*," someone marveled. Marcus needed a moment to realize that someone was himself.

The T-Rex disappeared from the holo, replaced by a pack of ... velociraptors? (Pretty much everything that Marcus maybe knew about dinosaurs he had absorbed from old *Jurassic Park* movies and their reboots. Or snarky sniping at them: evidently T-Rex and velociraptors were more "modern" than the Jurassic. Cretaceous, was it? Anyway, whichever was the period of the most advanced dinosaurs, and their eventual demise.) There was too little time to consider this new scene, either, and the prone figures firing at the converging dinosaurs, before the vid again changed. Now vaguely crocodilian beasts scuttled up a pebble beach. Gore, both green and terrestrial red, splotched sand and stones. Laser beams came from snipers unseen behind a zigzag stockade. Strafing fire marched up the beach, from the winged craft circling overhead. Then the scene jumped to a pterosaur swarm, and contrails of air-to-air missiles ....

"Why show us this?" Ilya demanded.

Marcus shrugged, and continued watching ....

—•—

"I am sorry I doubted you," L'toth says.

We stand side by side, at the bottom of a narrow ravine that opens toward the nearby planet. Sunlight glints off the nearly vertical rock wall covered in photovoltaic panels, sparkles above the rim off spindly radio antennae. The shorter antenna links our clandestine instrument cluster with our underground base. And the longer-range antenna? I had done what I thought necessary. Just in case. Directive 1.3.

Hurriedly, we calibrate and realign our newly expanded optical array, frantic for a closer examination of the world overhead. From here, that globe tantalizes. But up close?

"No need to apologize," I say.

If any apology is owed, it is *from* me, for my lies, however well-intentioned. That the Fergash might find this world too difficult to colonize? It had been only a theoretical possibility, a prospect I dangled to sustain everyone's spirits. Because as long as we kept up our morale, as long as we eavesdropped and observed, we might learn something useful. And thus, again and again—never believing it—I had predicted the eventual failure of the Fergash colony.

But there is no denying what the enemy's compromised surveillance system reveals to us. The lethal attacks by the planet's monsters, both on the Fergash island redoubt and on forays elsewhere. Or the increasing tempo of shuttle flights from that island to the mother ship in synchronous orbit. Or the files of Fergash evacuating, boarding those shuttles.

"No need to apologize," I repeat.

"Our people will not be scared off by a few oversized lizards," L'toth says. "*We* will succeed."

I forgive my beloved his naïve optimism. He never confronted a Fergash face to face, or experienced their tenacity in battle, or watched them endure torture, often to the death, without surrendering their secrets. Are we as tough even as that?

"I know," I tell him. Another lie?

Once the Fergash have gone, once it is safe for us to build an interstellar transmitter, should I recommend that a colony fleet be sent? *Are* we tough enough to wrest a world from the fangs and talons of such monsters?

I wish I knew.

Marcus took a deep breath as the holographic stream turned to the apparent evacuation of the alien settlement. "Is this why we found a base on the Moon? The aliens' first attempt at settling on Earth failed, and they left behind a lunar observation post while they considered their options?"

Donna shook her head. "I don't believe it's that simple. Take a good look at the figures boarding the shuttles. The proportions, front limbs compared to back limbs, and all limbs compared to the central body mass, strike me as very different from Goliath's. At this viewing angle, from this distance, with everything streaming on fast-forward, I can't be certain, but my sense is that these new guys are quadrupeds. Sort of tailless alligators."

Ilya blinked. "Meaning the two factions we suspected, with their different robots, made of different isotopes, were from two different *species*?"

Ekatrina, inexplicably, grabbed a pair of alien goggles from a console shelf. Far too large even for Ilya, on her they were like clown glasses. "Wearing these, the blue sky in the holo turns green. The green of the foliage seems more yellow. This tells me Donna is correct about different aliens."

"How so?" Marcus asked as another shuttle zoomed off. In the distance, indistinct, a line of aliens and ... baggage? Refugees.

Ekatrina passed the goggles to Donna for a look. "The images of ancient Earth we saw aboard the alien ship? Remember the all-green oceans? Our aliens did not see blue. That color balance—to our eyes, the color imbalance—was like the optical sensors in the starfish robots. And like the goggles I just tried on.

"Now consider this ground-based imagery. Without the goggles, the blue of the sky and the green of plants seems natural to me. Our aliens used goggles to shift the video from Earth into their visible spectrum."

Yevgeny stepped up to the holo. "Our viewpoint is from a shallow angle. Post-mounted security cameras, I would guess. Same with many of the dinosaur scenes, those not recorded with personal cameras. None of this imagery was captured from the Moon. The viewing angles and the high resolution are completely wrong for what we've seen. And yet *our* aliens had access to the video."

"Our aliens. The other aliens. We need better names," Ilya muttered. "Moonies and Earthies?"

"*We* are Earthies," Yevgeny snapped back.

"Orange-sun aliens and, apparently yellow-sun aliens," Marcus mused. "Oranges and Yellows. How does that work?"

"Why not Oranges and Bananas?" Ekatrina muttered. "Stupid."

"Goliath and Paul Bunyan were giants," Donna said. "That's why we picked those names in the first place. So, maybe, their bunch are ... Titans? And by extension, their rivals would be the Olympians."

Murmurs, shrugs, and one, "Why not?"

And humans mere mortals beneath their feet, Marcus thought. Only that would be a ridiculous objection, given that everything they watched had happened eons before there *were* humans. "Sure. What's in a name?"

Yevgeny said, "So, the Titans, our aliens, had access to video from the Olympians. Why is that?"

"The two groups shared information?" Donna asked.

"More likely," Yevgeny said, "the Titans spied on the Olympians, maybe hacked into the Earth-based systems."

Their view changed to a potato-shaped rock, within a dust cloud, and the Moon as backdrop. The image—even allowing for all the sun glare scattered by the dust—was blurry, as if observed from the ground through a telephoto lens and shimmering with atmospheric distortion. A captured asteroid being mined in Earth orbit? Perhaps.

A shuttle, presumably one of the Olympian craft just seen launching, swam into sight. As the camera tracked the spacecraft it closed with a different rock: smooth and cylindrical, festooned with antennae and thrusters, and with large nozzles at one end. When doors retracted and the dartlike shuttle entered a docking bay, Marcus at last got a sense of scale. This new vessel was *enormous*. Kilometers, long, easily.

He shivered. "More likely, you said. Yevgeny, why is it likely the Titans were spying?" Is it because that's what you would do?

"Because," Yevgeny said, "it was no accident that we met robots programmed to kill. Titans and Olympians were *not* on good terms."

In the telephoto view, the colossal ship receded. As it shrank from sight, their perspective again changed. Stars no longer twinkled, but appeared diamond-crisp. Now they saw the vessel swell, framed by the jagged edges of a ravine, and with ancient Earth in the background. Like everything that had come before, these streams were on fast-forward, and the spaceship soon zoomed out of sight.

Donna sighed. "That, I think, was the key moment. That bit, right at the end, is the reason for this exhibition. We saw the Olympians pack up and go. The computer—at least I assume some sort of awakened alien AI is at work—is telling us that we should also go. Maybe, because Earth isn't safe. Maybe, because now is *its* people's turn to try colonizing the planet. Either way, it wants, expects, *us* to leave. I don't think it realizes we're *from* Earth, and the Titans long gone. How could it?

"But anyway, that is the message: just go. And in case we understand Titan speech, I'm guessing that's the content of the audio feed, too."

"You are quite trusting." Yevgeny said. "If it, or they, whatever or whoever is running the show, were inclined to *advise* us to go, we would know. It would have made the attempt before the attacks on us."

"Meaning what?" Marcus asked.

Yevgeny smiled humorlessly. "Meaning, we have not come to the end of this performance."

Chapter 39

I emerge from the lava-tube mouth behind the base, B'mosh by my side. Together, in silent awe, we gaze up at the starry sky, sensing, more than seeing, the world soon to be our home. It is darkest night. The planet is at first phase, teasing its presence as a dim glow in far-red, within an ethereal ring where sunlight filters and refracts through its atmosphere.

I remind myself the Fergash must once also have considered that world seductive, and that we must learn from their experience. That there are but four of us, I suspect, is to our advantage. We will manage on any small, isolated plot of land. At the first, at least, while we learn the ways of our new home world, we can establish ourselves on some island too tiny to support large predators and too remote from any mainland for flying monsters to reach us.

We had not suited up and left our base only to gawk. What sort of pilot and engineer would we be not to ground-check our craft before making even a short flight? The ship, of course, is fine. A year and a little more of sheltered idleness means *nothing* to a starship. And so, our task soon completed, we had continued the short way to the surface.

"A beautiful world." Lowering his gaze, gesturing vaguely, B'mosh adds, "I will not be sad to see the last of *this* desolation. Better, I think, to look up at it from a distance."

I am ready to agree when a fast-moving glint of far-red catches my eye—and an alert tone trills in my helmet. The apparition is a spacecraft, its heat emissions unmistakable. Even as I turn up magnification on my visor, bright sparks erupt from the bow.

"Unidentified vessel just came over the horizon," Watcher reports. "Two. Three."

Unidentified? Fergash, of course. Who else can these be? But *how*?

"Acknowledged," I respond, my mind racing.

A dartlike spacecraft shoots past, descending, headed for the level plain not far from the front entrance. It is, unquestionably, a Fergash shuttle.

This moon is enormous, its surface area comparable to the entire land mass of the nearby planet. The Fergash did not just happen to appear over our heads, anymore than the evacuation, or the subsequent radio silence from the planet, had been what they seemed. Their exodus had been staged for our benefit, and we had fallen for the ruse. Somehow—detecting the code we had injected into their surveillance system?—they had discovered we were lurking. And then, knowing to look, they had discovered us.

"M'lok?" Over the radio, L'toth's voice trembles. "What are we to *do*?"

For a moment, I hesitate. We four are closer than crèche mates; we have never encrypted our comm. Then again, what are the odds that Fergash colonists know Divornian? For a fact, with those snouts of theirs, they cannot speak it. We will take our chances.

As if we have any choice.

I respond on the common channel. "Everyone, these are Fergash vessels. At least one ship appears to be landing." Even as I speak, I spot another ship. It, too, is braking, as if to alight at a different spot. The third ship, I suspect, is higher. Circling the area. Flying cover. Because that is what I would do.

With that thought, I spot the last ship. "Everyone, suit up. Put half the missile launchers and handguns inside the rear airlock. B'mosh and I will retrieve them. Bring the rest out the front door. Send a ping when you reach the surface."

Missile launchers. Scarcely weapons at all! After the Fergash evacuated—or so we had believed!—we had improvised a few items. Designed with nothing in mind but a dumb, flapping-wing creature. And whether or not, as we had inferred from observations, those monsters were warm-blooded, we *had* assumed so. Our missiles were heat-seekers. They might be of service.

"A-and us?" B'mosh asks.

He, too, looks to me for answers. They all will, knowing I was present at the other equally unanticipated encounter with the Fergash. And true, I was appointed commander of the mission, at least in part because of that experience. But I am no warrior! Not even close. An interrogator, yes—if badly, and guiltily, and ashamedly. Trained to use weapons, yes, but I have never yet fired one in battle.

That, it seems, is about to change.

"Come with me." I start down the tunnel, ignoring our faithful ship as I pass. Unlike the small Fergash craft, ours, an exploratory vessel, is unarmed. "I will retrieve the weapons. You, configure Ship to expunge coordinates and any description of Divornia and the home system. Then go inside and do the same with Watcher. That action is to take effect in a day-eighth, unless one of us countermands. Or immediately, if a Fergash enters. Also immediately, if any of us should direct it. Then join up with the others. Tell them that if there is a need to abandon the base, our rally point is"—I stop to consider what terrain is both distinctive and somewhat sheltered—"the ravine we first considered and then rejected for our observatory. If for any reason that location seems compromised, then by the two leaning rock slabs."

And what will ensue if we are forced into retreat? Nothing good. But B'mosh does not ask and I do not volunteer anything.

He has a different concern. "Altering a sentient entity is more your expertise than—"

"So is combat," I growl. Which is both true and an evasion.

Leaving behind B'mosh, hastening downward to the base rear airlock, my guts knot. What is more fundamental to me than the world of my birth? The world I grew up on? The world in whose defense I have done such unspeakable things? Divornia's protection is, must be, paramount, and yet the order I had given B'mosh was ... what? Something like contemplating murder. More like considering suicide. For *me* to do as I had ordered seemed impossible.

I reach the airlock, scoop up the holster and the paltry five launch tubes waiting for me, and dash back to the surface. I do not encounter B'mosh; he must still be at work inside our ship.

He needs to work faster.

The launch tubes, dangling from their shoulder straps, jostle one another and jab the backs of my legs as I run. Moments after I emerge from my end of the lava tube, my radio offers a single *ping*. I ping back twice to confirm receipt, then peek over a nearby ridge to reconnoiter.

In the distance, the first shuttle has landed. Fergash and their mobile units disembark. "Troops on the ground," I radio. "Expect them to head your way. I doubt they can understand us, but do not count on it. Be indirect. When you can, stay off the radio—and if you do use it, move and hide after." Because any radio signal, however unintelligible, is a fine *beacon*. "And as soon as you shoot at anyone or anything, change positions. They *will* notice from where they have been fired upon."

Following the first part of my own advice, hugging the ground, I withdraw behind the crumbling lip of a nearby small crater.

However implausible it is that the enemy knows Divornian, *I* speak a little Fergash. Within the shelter of the lava tube, where I count myself safe from being overheard, I ask, "Watcher, are the Fergash broadcasting?"

"Yes, Commander. Several data streams."

"From any possible audio channels, send me samples." It does: all hissing and static. Of course the *Fergash* are encrypting. On their side, this must be a long-planned campaign. You do not easily fake (or actually?) evacuate an entire colony, recede into the outer solar system, and return, ever hidden from our view by the bulk of this moon. "If you can decrypt anything, notify me. I will download what you have when I can safely."

L'toth sends a *ping*.

I watch with pride and trepidation as two missiles, launched from somewhere near the other lava-tube entrance, streak across a jet-black sky toward the Fergash landing zone. Run! I think as loudly as I can. Run before the Fergash fire back! Before it is too late. Run, my friends!

They will. They must. Because there is no doubting the counterfire toward the area from which they had launched their attack.

But the shuttle—on the ground, its cargo-bay ramp deployed, offloading troops and mobile units—is helpless. Two fireballs erupt, merge, engulf the spacecraft. Enemies fly like leaves in a storm; some do not get up. Even here, the ground trembles beneath my boots.

But now the Fergash know *we* know they are coming. Even as I fire a missile, the second shuttle breaks off its landing approach. As I hurry, bent double, to a new hiding place, the shuttle jinks up and away. With heat-seeking guidance, my missile swerves in pursuit. The shuttle jinks again, zooming up, then executes a tight flip to dive *toward* the oncoming missile. Drawn to the superhot plasma exhaust *behind* the shuttle, my missile overshoots, exploding harmlessly *behind* its target. I curse wordlessly.

In the few heartbeats before the Fergash inevitably retaliate, I have time to marvel: the shuttle had not deployed flares. Does it have another sort of countermeasure? Jamming? Perhaps. More likely our missiles are simply too slow, too sluggish. The wing-flapping creatures for which we had designed these weapons were not capable of high-speed evasive maneuvers. I dare to hope the enemy's weapons are as improvised and inadequate as ours, that the Fergash are all colonists, no more warrior than I.

It is bad enough they are better armed, better prepared, and far outnumber us.

From the spacecraft circling overhead, salvo after salvo of missiles erupts. Now *I* am tossed like a leaf, to crash down on my hands and knees, only to bounce again. Gloves and knee pads protect me from the rough ground. My remaining missile launchers, on my back, may be unharmed.

The silent explosions recede; the shaking underfoot diminishes. Because the circling shuttle has lost sight of me in the dust clouds? Or hoping to hit any compatriots of mine yet to reveal themselves? I wonder how our base, and Watcher, are withstanding this bombardment.

As the shuttle that had eluded my first attack loops back to settle behind a ridge, I let fly another missile. From above, new enemy counterfire rains down around me, more intense than ever. Time and again I crash to the ground. Between bounces, ignoring the pressure alarm keening in my helmet, I scuttle to the dubious protection of the lava-tube mouth. Glancing over my shoulder, I see no fireball rising over the ridge. Another of my scant few missiles has failed.

Inside the lava tube, I slap patches over suit tears revealed by wisps of condensing water vapor. The alarm warbles and dies. Through still-billowing clouds of dust, I catch a glimpse of Fergash and robots coming toward me. Stone chips fly, one ricocheting with a ghostly ping off my oxygen tank. I marvel at their poor aim, given their daily conflicts with monsters.

The enemy knew our location. They *might* have destroyed us with impunity. By dropping an asteroid upon our heads. By dispatching a precision guided missile, with a massive warhead, straight down the lava tube. Instead, they staged an elaborate withdrawal from the planet to cover a surprise ground assault. I see no explanation for their strategy, and the casualties they must have anticipated as a result, beyond the intention to capture prisoners, or to take our base intact. And I despair as our long-range antenna emerges—in pieces—within the dust of a near miss. The fragments tumble glacially in the maddening low gravity of this world, to disappear one by one into the ravine.

With them vanishes any chance we have to activate our fail-safe.

As the enemy shuttle patrolling overhead crosses the lava-tube mouth, I fire: once, twice, three times.

And I run for my life down the tunnel.

The Olympian vessel vanished into a fireball. The debris field, with the evanescent fireball in its midst, hurtled on. The shuttle had been flying westward, in its vain attempt to outrun three inbound missiles. The ship's considerable momentum, distributed across countless red-hot chunks and shards, continued to the west.

Through narrowed eyes, Yevgeny considered the sparkling trail of the shuttle's remains raining down far into the virtual distance. He said, softly, "I think we just saw the origins of Ethan's famous iridium trail."

Chapter 40

When the enemy ship exploded overhead, Watcher had the reflex, if not the musculature, to flinch. In its experience, such a cataclysm was unprecedented. This second disaster shocked the Fergash, staring upward at the slow rain of debris, into brief immobility.

The enemy's mobile units showed no such hesitation. As M'lok Din ran down the tunnel toward the base, a ragged line of squat machines, their treads spewing regolith, tore uphill to the lava-tube entrance and plunged inside after her. Through sensors grown on the tunnel wall and imagery relayed by the ship over the communications umbilical, Watcher anxiously observed the enemy devices gaining on the commander.

"Open the base outer … airlock hatch," M'lok ordered, panting for breath, as she passed the ship. The ship's mind relayed the directive over the umbilical.

Without breaking pace, she would twist and shoot at the machines chasing her. Muzzle flashes, the flight of her bullets, and the mobile units themselves, were unmistakable in far-red. So, alas, were the ricochets as bullets bounced, seemingly without effect.

No, *one* bullet had penetrated, and that machine ground to a halt. "Commander, aim for the access panel on the side of the turret."

She grunted, and kept running. The closest machines already had their arms extended, their grippers open, ready to grasp and crush and tear. She was *not* going to make it to the airlock ahead of the machines.

Then the world shuddered.

Surface sensors had shown a large segment of the enemy shuttle plummeting from almost overhead. Now, rock and dust rained. Long stretches of roof collapsed. Acoustic sensors saturated with the rumble and crash of shifting rock, the trilling of alarms, and the shrill whistles of escaping air; quickly, the sounds faded and died. Many sensors failed; while others (perhaps) remained functional, the circuits to them were severed. To the extent it *could* still observe, in sudden vacuum-silence dust and pebbles continued to filter down.

Fail-safe circuits had switched Watcher from reactor power to emergency batteries. It found itself without visibility into the reactor room to identify the problem. Fearing the worst, Watcher dispatched mobile units to the reactor room to assess the damage.

As though the damage *it* had experienced were not enough, quaking registered by the ship's accelerometers indicated roof collapses deep into that part of the lava tube. As in that passageway the dust settled, the ship's external sensors revealed walls of rubble both forward and aft. It reported itself (so far) undamaged, but barring major excavation it was trapped.

Where was the commander? Overtaken by her pursuers? Trapped by the cave-in? Crushed beneath the cave-in? For a frighteningly long instant, Watcher did not know. But then, near the rear airlock, where an optical camera remained operational, a grime-coated figure emerged from the still-dense clouds of dust. M'lok. Running!

An enemy mobile unit lurched after her. On the machine's visible side an idler wheel appeared damaged, and the corresponding track flapped for lack of proper tension. At full speed, doubtless, the track would have slipped off.

The commander's lips moved—silently. Metal walls blocked radio with the base. The wall of rubble behind the commander blocked radio with the ship, and its intact (but by now, surely buried) umbilical relay. Until M'lok made her way inside, Watcher was deaf and mute.

If she could get inside.

There! Via an improvised relay through a succession of mobile units, Watcher saw the commander crawl through the twisted wreckage of the rear airlock, its hatches mangled and sprung open. (Over the same makeshift connection, Watcher saw the reactor was also smashed—a catastrophe for another time.)

The commander's helmet peeked inside the base ….

As soon as I can stand, I slap emergency patches over both arms and legs. Between near-fatal grabs by the enemy machine chasing me, and snagging myself on the sharp and twisted metal frame of the ruined airlock, the limbs of my pressure suit are rife with holes. I almost lose consciousness before pressure begins to rise. I need a fresh oxygen tank *now*.

Only I do not get the chance.

A telescoping arm lunges out of the half-flattened airlock, the pliers-like gripper snapping open and closed, groping for a handhold. In its blind flailing, the gripper glances off, then clutches, a twisted mass of thick wires on a power-distribution frame. All that broken and tattered insulation? That *should* have sufficed to fry the machine, but the reactor is dead, an utter wreck beneath masses of fallen stone. Instead of short-circuiting, the mobile unit uses its grasp to drag itself into the reactor room after me.

One of *our* mobile units peeks into the room. Instantly, I have a line-of-sight optical connection, along a chain of similar units, all the way to Watcher. And it also has a link to me, because it transmits, "Run!"

Instead, I pull a sturdy length of twisted metal from the wreckage of the reactor room. Gripping that club with both hands, I swing with all my might against the side of the robot's turret. The club bounces off. As shock and pain shoot up my arms, I retreat.

The alien machine rolls after me, grinding concrete and reactor shards beneath its tracks. I stagger toward the other end of the base. Silent rumbling, felt through the soles of my boots, suggests that yet more roof has given way behind me. But, a glance over my shoulder confirms, not soon enough to rid me of my obstinate pursuer.

"The others?" I ask Watcher.

"None of my sensors have sight of them." It adds (in apology? As encouragement?), "But so few of my sensors still function."

"Have any of them been inside since the Fergash appeared? Had any contact with you?"

"No."

I reach the main hall by the front airlock. Cabinets and shelves have been overturned, their contents spilled across the floor. Everything is mixed in with, if not crushed by, chunks and slabs of rock and concrete. As I dig for fresh magazines for my handgun, my peripheral vision detects motion. The Fergash mobile unit, relentless, its loose track soundlessly slapping the floor, has again caught up to me.

"Commander," Watcher shouts. "Into the control room. Now!"

As I withdraw, our mobile units swarm. They climb or leap onto the enemy unit, only to be thrown off by the larger entity's spinning turret and flailing arms. They scamper away as it tries to run them down, then scramble right back onto it. One crippled limb? That is nothing. Or two. Even trailing three broken limbs, our units hobble back into the fray.

This is primitive combat: trial by metal claw and armored tread. For our part, there had been no reason to arm the mobile units. For theirs, the Fergash did not trust their artificial minds with advanced weapons.

And so, our units scratch and pull until the enemy's access panel springs open. Two units plunge arms inside the turret, setting off a coruscating fountain of sparks. All three shudder to a stop.

My chest heaving, I take the opportunity amid momentary calm to replace my all but empty oxygen tank with a full one.

I disbelieve any enemy machine other than this one escaped the cave-ins. But what if I am mistaken? I review and refine Watcher's directions to our mobile units on dealing with inanimate intruders.

Can I turn our mobile units against the Fergash themselves? I am briefly stymied. Obedient, privacy-observing, maintenance devices—never combatants—by design they have only low-resolution optical sensors. It will not do for them to attack Divornians by mistake. I settle upon describing several distinctive characteristics of our vacuum suits, and authorize our robots to swarm anyone outside the base in *different* gear. For any enemy discovered in isolation, they are to disable radios first, hopefully to maintain an element of surprise. Then, or immediately with any enemies found in groups, they will tear at extremities. As I have so recently been reminded, patches refuse to stay sealed where a pressure suit is most often flexed.

At last I find ammunition clips. They had spilled from their cabinet and then been bounced far down a side corridor. With all that ammunition and also our one spare handgun, I—and half of our robots—crowd into our lone remaining airlock to go to the aid of my friends.

As the outer hatch begins to open, my mobile units stream before me into the lava tube. Rock chips fly as the enemy fires upon them. These Fergash, too, are poor shots. My swarm, scurrying, disappears around the bend.

Before leaving the airlock, I activate the tunnel lights at full spectrum and brightness. Any Fergash intruders will have entered the darkened lava tube using their night-vision visors. However temporarily they might now be blinded, it will be to my advantage. In any event, I need light and so do my mobile units. While they are in the tunnel—and once the battle spilled out onto the surface, for as long as they have an opportunity to retreat into it—they will continue to recharge. In the present dark and cold of the airless night, their batteries cannot last long.

Netted into sensors that survived the shuttle crash, I see enemy soldiers recoil, and then flee, from my mobile-unit swarm. Only then, warily, do I round the curve. And there on the tunnel floor, immobile, unmistakable in his green pressure suit, lies B'mosh. Telltales on his suit wrist leave no doubt: he has left us.

"Goodbye old friend," I murmur, fearing to find L'toth and D'var, also dead, farther up the tunnel. But I come upon neither friend nor enemy as I continue toward the surface. I step past an inert enemy machine with a broken tread—

And its arms reach out, slashing at my ankles. I leap past, leave it behind; with that broken tread it can only go in tight circles. I have more urgent threats.

I reach the mouth of the lava tube without further challenge. In the distance, by tapping into another remote sensor, I see Fergash and several of their mobile units skirmishing with a much diminished group of my own. The ground between us is littered with disabled or destroyed machines—of both kinds. But of L'toth and D'var, there is no sign. The regolith all around is too churned to disclose distinct boot prints.

For now, I seem to be unobserved. (By eyes and cameras on the ground, that is. As for any eyes in the sky, in surveillance satellites, I can do nothing about them.) By a circuitous route, I make my way to the rally point. No one waits for me there.

Hurrying toward the backup rally point, I come upon an unfamiliar chain of small craters. Splotches and streaks surround them, fresh regolith undarkened by harsh ultraviolet light. Turning on my headlamps at a low setting, peering over the rim into the largest hole, I see—

Vacuum-desiccated body chunks. Only by the distinctive red tatters of pressure suit can I know this is … was D'var. Almost I vomit into my helmet.

With grim resolve, I recover my friend's handgun and ammunition. Nearby I encounter the burst remains of her oxygen tank and three launch tubes, all twisted beyond use. The warhead of one missile looks salvageable. I remove that explosive payload and stow it away.

Continuing around the crater, looking for anything else useful, I see … drag marks? No, ruts and glove prints deep into the regolith. It can only be L'toth!

The trail leads me to him, flat upon his back at the secondary rally point. Blood spatter and overlapping patches cover half his abdomen. Here, too, suit telltales deny me all hope.

Again, there are no words.

The agony in which he must have dragged himself here is unimaginable, and yet, in death, his face is somehow serene. I leave him undisturbed. The familiar massive rock slabs, in counterpoise above him, shall be his eternal monument.

I crawl to a nearby crater, stopping just below the edge. Warily, I peer over the top. With my visor at maximum magnification, the terrain is strewn with stationary devices. (Disabled? Without power until the sun rises? It hardly matters.) From the vicinity of the remaining shuttle, more Fergash are scurrying to the fray.

The battle will not last much longer. When it does end, the Fergash *will* make another attempt to enter our base. To seek any clues as to the presence of my beloved home world.

Not if I can help it.

—•—

The Fergash, the mobile units, and finally M'lok had disappeared. Now and again, from some of Watcher's few intact and communicating sensors, it glimpsed battle, or at least motion in the distance. Mostly, in an information void, it extrapolated uselessly about what had happened, or at that instant was occurring, or might yet take place. And pondered the imminent moment when the first enemy warrior penetrated into the base and it would, as the commander had ordered, lobotomize itself.

Once more, M'lok came into view of an optical sensor. As best Watcher could infer, the commander was headed *away* from the battle. To the more distant entrance into the lava tube? But roof collapse, surely, had trapped her ship, had rendered the base inaccessible from that side.

What was the commander thinking, as she gazed down into the ravine? Watcher could only know what she *saw*: the telescope array, in large measure still intact; the shattered antenna with which it had monitored Fergash communications. M'lok herself maintained radio silence.

Whatever M'lok observed below, her posture firmed in decision. She strode farther from the base, over a low ridge, out of Watcher's sight.

—•—

That was the last time Watcher saw the commander. And with that realization, and the certainty of M'lok Din's imminent death, long-repressed memories surfaced.

In anguish, Watcher continued to watch ....

Chapter 41

From behind a boulder, I count and recount the troops by the remaining Fergash shuttle. Seven. By Fergash doctrine, the basic military unit is a squad of seven. Whether from fear or training, I would have preferred to surveil longer; either way, my declining supply of oxygen renders caution more dangerous than action.

I study the terrain. Internalize their patrol patterns. Disable temperature control, preferring to roast for awhile inside my well-insulated suit rather than reveal myself to Fergash night-vision apparatuses. And then, in the utter nighttime dark, I skulk from crater to boulder to ridge. Eight-square bounding paces from the enemy's shuttle. Half that. Half that again ....

To my left, an intense flash! It is the salvaged warhead, triggered by the battery I short-circuited and left behind to overheat.

A patrolling sentry freezes, turns its hideous face toward the flash. I shoot. Spurting blood, it crumples. Another dies in silence before a third notices the muzzle flash of my handgun. I shoot it, too—but not before it has opened its ugly snout.

Only boldness can save me.

As I leap forward, a weapon gripped in each hand, another sentry turns and the final three emerge from behind the parked shuttle. I shoot. They shoot. I hit one. They keep missing. And I understand.

B'mosh built our weapons and calibrated the gun sights *here*. They built and calibrated theirs on the much more massive planet. Inevitably, in this lesser gravity, they overshoot.

I give them no time to reason it out. Two more Fergash go down, and then I am inside the shuttle's airlock. I shoot the last sentry as the outer hatch cycles closed. When the inner hatch begins to open, I see that this shuttle is, as it had appeared from outside, just as I had hoped. And just like the stuff of my nightmares.

On the bridge, I encounter a single, cowering Fergash. The pilot?

"Do not shoot," it begs in its grating language. "I am unarmed." Its voice is faint, pathetic through my helmet.

I put a bullet in its head, then kick the still-quivering body to the floor. Straddling the pilot's bench, I launch the shuttle.

There are none left to protect. Only three to avenge ....

Watcher's people had vanished. The last of the mobile units gone to the surface with the commander had also fallen silent. Two clusters of the enemy, victorious, converged on the remaining lava-tube entrance.

Watcher prepared itself for the coming memory erasure. It might outlive the procedure—the Fergash willing—but it would no longer be ... itself.

And then the final enemy shuttle rose over the eastern horizon. Tearing toward the base. Hugging the ground. Spewing missiles. Strafing.

Fergash scattered—or tried to. The shuttle circled the enemy, herded them together, picked them off methodically. Twice, a Fergash stood its ground—and neither one's launcher fired! (Missiles too smart to fire upon their own ships? So Watcher surmised.) As enemy survivors scuttled to take shelter inside the lava tube, the shuttle headed them off. They scattered again.

One by one, hovering over them, the shuttle *roasted* Fergash in the white-hot fusion exhaust of landing thrusters.

And then, in a *Divornian* format, the shuttle began to transmit.

"This is the end," the commander declared. Somehow, she still lived!

An enormous lifestream update began. Or, rather, several large updates. Because so much was happening, or from the extended periods of radio silence, or both, there were frequent gaps in the download due to buffer overflows in her implant.

With the final surface target eliminated, the shuttle looped and rolled, streaking away as rapidly as it had arrived.

"It is inconceivable that I will return," M'lok continued. "But I *will* take more Fergash with me. I found this shuttle fully fueled. Their mother ship must be nearby."

Nearby, Watcher mused. How? Had the mother ship been orbiting this world, by now it must one or more times have come into view.

But its Ship aspect understood. True, the great mass of the nearby planet denied synchronous orbits to its natural satellite—but there were exceptions. In five places the gravitational pull of planet and moon, and the orbital motion of a third body, could balance. A ship loitering in any of the five spots expended little or no fuel. One such parking spot was behind this moon, along the line that joined the centers of both worlds. And the commander was racing for the remote side of this moon.

"Now the duty passes to you," M'lok said. "You were made for this. To do—"

At the worst possible moment, static erupted. But while the commander's *words* were lost, the emotional overtones poured through. Rage. Grim determination. And overpowering, all but masking, the rest: resignation to her certain death.

"Do *what*?" Watcher pleaded. "I must do *what*?"

"Marshall your … units and other resources. Rebuild … needs rebuilding. And then … what I … not."

Rebuild? That seemed impossible! Its reserve power would soon run out. Even availing themselves of periodic sunlight, Watcher's mobile units had neither the intelligence nor the dexterity to reconstruct the fusion reactor.

And if Watcher somehow accomplished the impossible? Once more it implored, "To do *what*, Commander?"

But before any answer came, the shuttle had disappeared beyond the horizon. Carrying the commander to her doom ….

On the surface, nothing stirred. On radio, not a whisper could be heard. Within the much-damaged underground base, Watcher's remaining mobile units were quiescent, conserving what little charge remained to their batteries. Hoarding its own dwindling power reserves, Watcher … watched. And worried. And waited. Until—

The Fergash mother ship soared over the horizon. To dispatch more troops, surely, and so to occupy the base. Thereby obliging Watcher, per the commander's orders, to expunge its memories. And thereby ensuring—whatever M'lok Din had *intended* by her last words—the mission's utter and irreversible failure.

Only those were not the commander's last words! From the mother ship, in Divornian format, came: "They did not expect armed visitors. I suppose they rationalized as battle damage the approaching shuttle's radio silence." (Faintly, beneath the clipped explanation, Watcher heard intermittent *booming*. Fergash breaking into wherever aboard the mother ship M'lok Din now made her last stand?) And, triumphantly, "Those were fatal lapses—"

There was the momentary hint of an explosion before the transmission ceased.

And then, rather than descend, rather than disgorge smaller craft to land fresh troops, the enormous mother ship … accelerated. And accelerated. And *accelerated*. Through its telescope array, Watcher tracked the mother ship as it dwindled to a brilliant dot of actinic fusion flame.

And until the nearby planet swam into the telescope's view ….

One moment, the plunging spark is centered over an unfamiliar island, in the too narrow Atlantic Ocean of an era long past. A moment later, the spot flares brighter still, as the ship, its main drive still ablaze, plunges into the atmosphere. And the moment after that—

Madness.

The impact liquefies rock, melts a glowing hole sixty miles across, punches *through* Earth's crust. Rock and magma erupt to beyond Mount Everest heights before splashing down. A shock wave taller still—the very air rendered visible by all the pulverized rock it carries—races outward in every direction. Ocean pours *inward*, replacing flash-vaporized water; that torrent, too, repeatedly, vanishes into an expanding column of steam. Farther from ground zero, where water remains liquid, a towering tsunami takes shape and sweeps outward.

Across what will be Mexico and Central America, the extreme heat turns vegetation brown and sere. Desiccated jungle bursts into raging flames—much of it soon extinguished by the expanding shock wave, or drowned by the tsunami that races around the world.

At the vastly accelerated pace with which the alien computer displays these events, land and ocean—the entire surface of the planet—quickly disappear beneath the spreading, deepening, black cloud of ash, smoke, and rock dust ....

EMERGENCY

Chapter 42

Marcus felt ... numb? Drained. His thoughts were ... scattered. His stomach churned, and his jaw, neck, and shoulders felt as taut as drumheads. What he had just seen was unreal—and yet all too believable. He ached to crawl into bed, to pull the covers up over his head and somehow escape the enormity of it all.

Instead, somehow, he forced himself to check on his colleagues. Across the control room, Ilya stood frozen, hands clenched in white-knuckled fists. Donna trembled, tears brimming in her eyes. Nearest the door, Yevgeny's eyes darted about. Seeking someplace to run? Someone to fight? Marcus felt the same need! And at his side, hard-as-nails Ekatrina muttered under her breath in Russian.

At her words, Ilya blinked. Yevgeny grinned.

"What was that?" Marcus asked her.

As her face reddened, Yevgeny said, "Had I not been aware Katya grew up in a navy town, I would know it now."

She reddened further.

Overloud laughter marked the emotional release they all needed.

Ilya cleared his throat. "I cannot imagine anyone sleeping after that. I will keep watch here if anyone wishes to get dressed"—everyone having come running at his summons, in pajamas or undies, whatever they slept in—"or coffee. Just someone bring me one."

"Or a medicinal brandy," Donna offered. "I'm buying."

And when, five minutes later, they reassembled in the control room, Marcus saw everyone had an empty drink bulb for her to fill.

Beneath the world-girdling clouds of the hologram's final, frozen image was ... what? Coastal environments worldwide scoured clean by tsunami. Nuclear winter: years of darkness, frigid temperatures, and a halt to photosynthesis. Ecological collapse. The death of the dinosaurs. The end, almost, of life on Earth. As innocent bystanders. As collateral damage.

Yevgeny downed a healthy swig of brandy, the burn transforming into a pleasant warmth in tongue and throat, and then all the way to his stomach. Okay, so alcohol was never a long-term solution. Just then, the brandy steadied his nerves. He needed it. They all did.

"But *why*?" Donna demanded. "Why *do* this?"

Marcus said, "Total war. Wiping out the Olympian colony."

Ilya nodded. "The Titans denied a habitable planet to their enemies. And in the process, they preserved the planet for Earth life. They opened the way for mammals, ultimately, for humans, to rule the planet."

"You miss the point," Yevgeny barked. "All of you. Forget these ancient events. They matter not. Do you know what does? The message the alien computer sends by showing this."

Ekatrina grimaced. "The message? It is all too clear. The Titans were ruthless."

"And why reveal that to us now, Katya?" Yevgeny persisted.

"To take responsibility for the earlier attacks on us?"

Responsibility. How antiseptic, Yevgeny thought. "Gloating, Katya. The exhibition we just had was the Titans' computer gloating, in the only way it can. But you avoid my question. Why now? Why gloat *now*?"

Silence.

"Well," Yevgeny admitted, "I have no answer, either. And that concerns me. Because there must be a reason."

"Gloating isn't right." Marcus, having drained his drink bulb, looked questioningly at their medic. Donna shook her head—a second round, it would seem, was not on the program—and he sighed. "It's threatening. Bluffing.

"And why now? Because we trapped its robots. Because it's at our mercy. Lest we shut it down—we all, I must believe, *want* to cut its power—it is reminding us what the Titans once did."

Donna said, "But *we* look nothing like its enemies. They're quadrupeds, remember?" She shivered. "Did the Titans consider genocide—hell, make that ecocide—fair game with any potential competitor?"

Marcus took a deep, noisy breath. "That nails it. We have to shut it down. And because the alien tech scavenges power from our heat and light, and fixes broken connections, that means we're finished here. Dirtside will see the logic. They *must*, damn it! Let another team, bigger, better equipped—"

"Better armed," Ilya interjected.

Marcus nodded. "And better armed. Let them continue what we've started."

Was that the answer? Yevgeny wondered. Summoning reinforcements? Handing off the job? Either option felt like dereliction. Like failure. And also, though he could not say why, a case of too little, too late. "We would not even consider turning off everything, except that the alien intelligence so blatantly revealed itself. Again I struggle to understand: why has it announced itself, shown us these events? And why do so *now*?"

That no one had as much as a theory to suggest only worried Yevgeny more.

Chapter 43

"Gesundheit!" Valerie said.

A second chain sneeze erupted before her reflexive interjection reached Marcus. What with all the regolith that had been tracked into the inflatable igloo, his lunar-dust allergy, and the Earth/Moon roundtrip comm delay, this could go on all day. A chuckle at the mental image devolved into a phlegmy cough.

"Just the dust," he got out. "I'll grab an antihistamine when we're done talking."

"Be honest. Are you okay?"

"I'm fine." Crinkling his face, twitching his nose, he fought back another sneeze.

Never mind that the Titans were genocidal maniacs, they had something with their dust-devouring wall treatment. What a boon it would be to reverse-engineer *that* tech! But sneezing, or not, had nothing to do with this call, or why Tyler had pulled strings for Marcus to schedule it.

He said, "But enough about a few sneezes. How are *you* feeling?" Because her eyes, over dark hollows, were bloodshot. The baggy turquoise blouse did little to disguise an ever larger baby bump. Her posture, in some way he could not put his finger on, cried out for a hug. Or maybe that last was his need, projected. "And how are Simon and Little Toot?"

"Fine, a surly, secretive teenager, and playing a manic drum solo on my bladder, respectively."

"Man, I wish I were there." Hugs aside, to help out with the large box labeled CRIB, leaned against the wall behind her, that cried out for an engineer—and a father. "Not least of all to *feel* Little Toot kick, instead of just have you tell me about it. But here's the thing ...."

"What the *hell*, Marcus! You're going to be up there *longer*?"

He grinned. "No, actually. By sometime next week I expect to be planting a big kiss on you and giving Simon a bear hug. Final itinerary still being worked out."

Much of the planning for their departure was already well in hand.

With a few hand grenades, Yevgeny had brought down a good ten meters of lava-tube roof. Even after pulling the plug to their solar-panel array, who was to say what alien *things* might remain active on battery power, or for how long. If anything still stirred belowground, the roof collapse should isolate them. And if any CIA or FSB satellite should spot unsuspecting (or suspicious) third parties nosing around, the observatory would get some staff on-site—ostensibly to enforce their mining claim—well before the caved-in, rubble-clogged tunnel could be excavated.

Of course, as renewed chain sneezing reminded him, evacuating the alien base *also* relegated them to filthy, debris-stocked igloos. But that, too, would pass. Almost, they had finished packing. Soon, if not soon *enough*, a shuttle from Aitken Basin would deliver relief drivers to return the observatory tractors, and fly out Donna and him. Yevgeny would fly out his team—and Nikolay and Brad—the same day.

Because, finally, they—including poor Nikolay and Brad—were going home! For once, his government and the Russians' had agreed with the people on the scene, and in harm's way. The CIA had primed NASA to pull strings, preempting tourist bookings as needed, to get the five of them onto the next flight to Earth. For debriefing, of course, doubtless excruciatingly detailed and repetitive. But nonetheless—on Earth!

All plans predicated, of course, on doctors at Base Putin giving the medical all-clear.

At last, as another nearly three-second round-trip delay concluded, he saw Val's face light up.

"That's *wonderful*! But how ...?" Her voice trailed off, as she struggled to formulate a question safe for a commercial comm link.

"It's complicated," Marcus said. "But the short version"—being a lie for anyone listening in *and* a subtle, if partial, explanation for Val—"is that the carbon lode isn't as accessible as it first seemed. Oh, the site remains of interest, but it'll take a different approach, and experts, to make proper use of it. Not amateurs like me. In our clumsy efforts"—because seismic detectors all over the Moon would have sensed the explosions and the roof collapse—"we managed to make things *less* accessible."

"I ... see."

No, you don't. You can't. But Tyler anticipates your call the moment you and I are done, and I can't imagine you'll disappoint him. "I'll let you know when I have my flight info. And if you'll let me know what VR game Simon most covets these days, I'll be sure to pick up a copy."

Her doorbell chimed.

Marcus said, "If that's important, they'll come back. So, Simon started school last Tuesday. Right? Freshman year. How's he liking it thus far?"

But the doorbell kept ringing. As Val ignored it, and then imperious knocking, a male voice shouted, pleaded, "Dr. Clayburn, it's *important*."

"I'd better get that. Anyway, hon, we're almost out of time. I'll shoot you a note, let you know what all the fuss is about." Val broke into her biggest grin yet. "See you soon."

Only apart from two curt texts (I'M FINE. THE BABY IS FINE. FOLLOWED, HALF A DAY LATER, BY I'LL GET BACK TO YOU WHEN I CAN) Marcus heard nothing for an excruciating twenty-six hours. Not until he—and Yevgeny—were separately ordered onto an unscheduled, spook-encrypted, video conference.

At the designated hour, alone in the least dust-encrusted of the American igloos, Marcus's CIA datasheet opened a vid window. The streaming holo revealed dozens of men and women (few of whom he recognized), in uniforms and somber suits, sitting or standing around an enormous dark table, in a cavernous, high-ceilinged room. Something napkin-sized (a folded datasheet?) and a tented cardboard nametag was set at every place.

As hushed conversations rose (never quite to intelligibility) and fell, distant sound-activated cameras kept switching his viewpoint. The walls were an antiseptic, too-bright white. The American flags and framed official portrait image of the president showed this was a government facility. Overhead, on every wall, like the war room of a big-budget remake of *Dr. Strangelove*, loomed colossal displays. The screens, alternately dark and exhibiting 2-D world maps, gave no clues to the gathering's purpose. Or to what this had to do with Yevgeny (and where was the Russian? Nowhere in evidence on the interworld linkup) and himself.

Marcus's viewpoint jumped yet again. Seated at the head of the table … that was *Val*!

As much as she, still a practicing scientist at heart, considered anything beyond jeans and tees to be formalwear, she owned one business suit. Many an evening he had been Val's audience of one as she rehearsed for some suit-worthy, make-or-break presentation. Well, he hadn't been there to support her for this get-together, whatever the hell it was. One more reason to feel guilty.

Because that one dressy outfit, a charcoal-gray-and-pinstripe flannel suit, was what she wore today. The jacket, in her current condition unbuttonable, gaped open. A paisley scarf (and Val never wore scarves; hated them, in fact; this one had been a gift, years ago, from his mother) seemed draped to distract from an untucked maternity blouse. He suspected the untucked blouse, in turn, covered pins or clips or other improvisation to hold up an only partially zippable skirt. She looked *so* uncomfortable. And worried. And *exhausted.*

Tyler's doing? The spook, more dour-looking even than usual, sat on her immediate right. What the *hell* was he thinking, working a very pregnant woman like this? But on the heels of that reflex Marcus had to concede: no one made Val do anything she did not damn well choose to do. So what was going on? Why was she driving herself so hard? And how on Earth had her precipitous release from faux bed rest been explained to Simon and the neighbors?

On Val's left (squirming in his seat, his eyes wide, fidgeting with a laser pointer) … could that be young Jay Singh? As in, *Rock? Bye-Bye, Baby!* Singh?

"Aw, *shit*," Marcus said.

Chapter 44

Time and again, Valerie glanced around the CIA conference room. The prospect of speaking in front of so many people would ordinarily have left her trembling. But today? She was too damned scared even to tremble.

It was ironic, really. No, stupid. There were bigger fish to fry than her public-speaking neurosis. Phobia.

All too soon, Tyler rose to his feet. His ostentatious cough caught everyone's attention, sent everyone still standing to their designated seats at the table, brought the several subdued conversations—far quicker than she would have imagined possible—to abrupt halts. From acute curiosity, she supposed.

Tyler managed a smile. "Thank you for coming on such short notice, and in most cases, with little by way of explanation. For those of you I haven't met, my name is Tyler Pope. I'm a senior Russia analyst for the Company. Keep that fact and the choice of venue"—CIA headquarters in Langley—"in mind when our wall screens go live. You'll want an open mind about certain others about to join our discussion. Trust me: it's necessary."

He glanced down at a datasheet open before him on the table, nodded to himself, and tapped out a brief message. "They're ready on the other end."

The map display on each wall switched to show another crowded conference room—only with Russian flags and (she assumed) Russian uniforms. Perhaps half the people seen onscreen wore earphones for translation. From several seats around *this* table she heard gasps.

"That's how serious this is," Tyler continued imperturbably, "and why both nations' presidents ordered this morning's meeting, and why they expect a decision from us before lunch.

"People, we have an existential crisis. We have scant hours to work out a solution. And because we have so little time, we'll dispense with all the usual introductory blather. Names, titles, and specific affiliations for both venues are on the datasheets we provided. Suffice it to know that at the U.S. site, we have representatives from CIA, NASA, the Office of Planetary Defense within Homeland Security, and DoD. The fact that you may not recognize many people here? That's no accident. We need subject-matter experts, not managers. We don't have time for the usual chain-of-command twaddle. You're here because some administrator or director or four-star knows and trusts you.

"Kirill, do you have anything to add?"

Glancing down the long table, Valerie saw she wasn't the only one skimming the attendee list on her CIA-provided datasheet. Kirill Mikhailovich Vasiliev was with the Russian Federal Security Service. He was expert on matters American and responsible, reading between the lines, for Yevgeny and his people. The counterpart within the FSB, it would seem, to Tyler.

"Here in Moscow, we have representatives of Roscosmos, our own military, and my agency, the FSB. Apart from that, I will only emphasize what Tyler has said. The situation is dire and urgent. Our leaders require us to cooperate, no matter our past differences."

"Okay," Tyler said. "There's one final bit of logistics. Two names are omitted from the lists most of you are perusing. Kirill and I each have a participant linked in from the Moon. At the moment we don't have video downlinked. We'll introduce both men and explain their role at the appropriate time."

For just a moment a hand squeezed Valerie's shoulder as Tyler concluded, "Now Dr. Clayburn, an astronomer with NASA, will explain our predicament."

She, Tyler, and Jay had brainstormed what had seemed endlessly—in reality, for only the few minutes they could collectively spare—about how to describe the threat. "Go with your gut," Tyler had concluded before rushing off to another bit of pre-meeting coordination. "Just keep it short. And don't geek out."

Short and nontechie? Here goes. "In a couple of months, unless we stop it, an asteroid will smack Earth. A *big* one, twelve miles across. That's about a third larger than the Chicxulub impactor, the asteroid that killed off the dinosaurs." She paused. "In round numbers, that rock delivered the kinetic-energy equivalent of ten billion Hiroshima A-bombs. The impending strike would be far worse."

Far down the table from Val, someone whistled.

"Another thing," she said. "It turns out this is a known asteroid, and it *shouldn't* be a threat." She turned. "My colleague, Dr. Singh, will continue."

Jay's surprised blinks at *colleague* and *doctor*, under different circumstances, would have been precious. But he rose to the challenge, relating how his software had revealed a familiar rock, somehow gotten far out of place. Valerie jumped into a pause to add that radar pulses from Arecibo, the echoes received at her old observatory, Green Bank, confirmed the finding.

Planetary astronomers had catalogued hundreds of asteroids crossing within Mercury's orbit, Jay's rock among them. Not many of them also reached as far out from the Sun as Earth. But of the few asteroids that did, their orbits were inclined compared to Earth's, and so no threat. Jay's rock, included—

Until, without warning, *its* orbit was no longer inclined. Until, the event unseen, its orbit had been shifted. And careening Earthward from against the glare of the Sun, that rock had, until scant days earlier, been all but impossible to spot.

Jay, naturally, never referred to *his* rock. Instead, he used its official catalogue number, actually easier to wrap one's mouth around than the formal alias: a pretentious mock-Latinate neologism of far too many syllables.

At about Jay's eighth awkward catalogue reference, a man from Homeland Security muttered, "Why not call the damned rock Damocles, and have done with it?"

"However appropriate," Jay said, "it turns out that particular name is already taken. Damocles is one of the Centaurs, a group of asteroids that cross the orbits of the giant planets. In the long term, close encounters with these planets make many Centaur orbits unstable—"

Short. Not techie. Val interrupted. "Any mythological name you can think of has been taken. I suggest"—channeling a fictional comet from one of her favorite reads—"the Hammer."

"It will do," Tyler said firmly. Crabbily. "Proceed, Doctor Singh."

As Jay hesitated, a Russian military officer asked, "Can we be sure Hammer is a familiar rock? We are to believe its orbit changed radically. It is small, and for the moment, distant, and all but invisible against the bright Sun. It seems far more plausible this is a new discovery."

Val could see the metaphorical wheels turning, Jay further tongue-tied, unable to balance *short and not techie* with presenting a core aspect of his dissertation. She could see him preparing to launch into an exposition on machine learning and pattern recognition. She headed it off. "Yes, we're sure. And that's why"—besides the threat of extinction—"this is so unusual."

"Kirill?" Tyler prompted.

"After reviewing NASA's data, our astronomers took independent observations. With a high degree of certainty, they concur. Hammer is a known asteroid whose orbit has radically changed."

"Thank you, Kirill." Tyler made the soft, deep in his throat noise Val had come to know meant pick up the pace.

That advisory was prescient, because they had reached Val's opportunity to get lost in the figurative weeds. "I'll forego the details"—orbital mechanics being about as unintuitive as things came—"but only a few scenarios can account for the Hammer's recent orbit change. They all involve a sustained push against the rock near perihelion. Sorry, that's astronomer-speak for an orbit's closest point to the Sun. They all involve the Hammer getting a gravity assist—that is, a speed boost—and a change in orbital plane, from a grazing flyby of the Sun. And only one scenario fits with … well, there's another interesting dimension to this situation."

"Anna Petrova, with Roscosmos," a dark-haired woman introduced herself. "I do not understand. Any gravitational interaction, such as a close encounter with Mercury, would involve an attraction. A push makes no astronomical sense, much less a sustained push."

"No astronomical sense at all." And lest the implication was too subtle, Val added, "We aren't unlucky, Doctor Petrova. We're *targets.*"

Isaac Newton, through his laws of motion and theory of gravitation, remade mankind's understanding of the Universe. The motions of planets, moons, and comets became, for the first time, explicable. His influence extended to popularizing the metaphor of a clockwork universe: every part of creation moving, predictably and inexorably, according to immutable rules.

And we, Val thought, are in a literal race against just such a clock. A race we're losing ....

Quit that! she commanded herself. Focus!

Into stunned silence, the spymasters had introduced Marcus and Yevgeny; each man, looking haggard, peered down from one of the giant wall screens. Gaunt, disheveled, exhausted: those larger-than-life visages perhaps added verisimilitude to their account of lunar discoveries. They did nothing for her ability to concentrate.

Except Yevgeny no longer stared impassively from the bridge of the Russian shuttle. He had not moved, or even blinked, in minutes. He must have frozen his camera feed when Marcus took over speaking. Their script, such as it was, to the extent she knew about it, was coming up to the next big reveal: the recovered holostream of the Chicxulub impact. Slaughter on an unprecedented scale. Demonstration that the Titans—and also, one had to presume, the ancient technology that had somehow survived the aliens—would not balk at genocide.

And there was so little time to stop it! So much improvisation. So many shortcuts to be taken. So many details doubtless glossed over in their haste, forgotten, neglected—

And overlooked by her, too! Frantically, she texted Yevgeny. AUGUST 20. ANYTHING UNUSUAL IN YOUR SHUTTLE'S COMM LOG?

Faster than the pilot could respond, Tyler signaled Val to resume her briefing.

"Still skipping over the math, my colleagues and I have struggled to understand the Hammer's recent trajectory. Out of the many"—hundreds—"of simulations we ran, only a few credible scenarios can move the Hammer from where it was last observed in its historical orbit and the recent, subsequent sightings of it on its new path. In none of these scenarios do natural phenomena account for what we've seen."

And only *one* scenario correlated with an anomaly on the Moon. Three weeks earlier, a long-range antenna on the Russian shuttle had slued more or less toward the Sun. That brief repositioning had been captured by the motion-sensitive security camera atop the mast of Marcus's original igloo. The vid was too low-res, however, to determine the dish's aim point. If there had *been* a target, she cautioned herself. The dish had jiggled around many times before returning to its original position. Those motions might have been glitches, might signify nothing. As she took a deep breath, wondering how best to continue, a text arrived.

I FOUND SOMETHING. MAY I?

Reviewing *something*, working through the implications, would take time. All the while, the cosmic clock would keep ticking. But Yevgeny's question turned out to be rhetorical, his image unfreezing even as she hesitated.

"On August 20," Yevgeny declared, "a comm session was remotely initiated through this lunar shuttle. The security log indicates me as the user. I know I was asleep, underground, and offline at the time. During that session, the dish antenna was repositioned. The frequency selection and modulation scheme were nonstandard. The communications protocol is unfamiliar. As for the content, I can say only that the transmission repeated after each repositioning of the dish."

Val said, "Text me the coordinates and times, please."

The dataset arrived: forty-seven records. Tuning out the din of speculations, doggedly, she keyed the direction and time of one transmission into her simulation. Record by record, the simulation rejected those inputs as irrelevant to their dilemma. Because these data meant nothing? Because an alien … whatever, after circumventing FSB security protocols, had failed to accomplish anything further? Or because, over the eons, that entity had lost track of where its target might be found?

All that motion. Randomness? Or seeking?

And then a time-and-coordinates pairing almost aligned with the Hammer on its original orbit. Making allowance for how the beamcast would diverge with distance ....

Val pulled her mic close to her mouth. "It's more certain than ever. Someone—or something—on the Moon sent the Hammer hurtling at Earth."

An aide bustled into the CIA conference room. Marcus could not imagine anything so important, but whatever had been whispered drew Tyler from the meeting. Seconds later, a similar interruption claimed his Russian counterpart.

Maybe they did not expect to be gone long. More likely, the chief spooks didn't want the next topic brought up in their absence. Whatever the reason, once Valerie finished no one still present seemed to know what came next.

So people speculated. About the Hammer coming from such a minor and remote asteroid population. (Because the Olympians were mining the Main Belt, and were more likely there to detect any Titan presence? Or because—as NASA and Roscosmos had discovered—this rock was hard to detect against the Sun as background?) About the physical composition of the Hammer. (Almost certainly, nickel-iron.) About how an ancient antenna could have survived on the Hammer's surface to receive a modern-day order, when on the lunar surface micrometeoroids and solar wind had eroded away most traces of the aliens. (Perhaps there was no need. Perhaps the entire mass of the asteroid, being nickel-iron, had been made to serve as an antenna.) About an energy source that could have kept the Hammer listening for millions of years, because space weathering would also have worn away any solar panels there, and—

"Enough!" Long seconds passed, the debaters continuing unflappably, until Marcus remembered to unmute his mic. He thumped that mic until, on his console screen, the blathering stopped and people looked up at a distant wall display. Toward his scowling image.

He said, "We can obsess about how the Titans accomplished this until the Hammer strikes. Until they obliterate us, and maybe sterilize the planet. Or, and this is my suggestion, we can try to *do* something about their damned rock."

Chapter 45

Marcus's challenge was met with silence, then muttered protest, and, intriguingly, knowing glances exchanged among the uniformed people. In both rooms.

Marcus texted Yevgeny. THE MILITARY TYPES KNOW SOMETHING. DO YOU KNOW WHAT?

SORRY, NO, came the quick reply—not that Marcus took the denial as conclusive. Yevgeny *was* FSB, after all.

Several seats down from Val, a civilian with a ragged mustache and tortoiseshell half glasses perched far down his nose cleared his throat. (From NASA, was what Marcus remembered. Not his name.) "Well, of course, the traditional way to deflect an asteroid is with a gravity tractor. A gravity tractor is …."

Traditional? A gravity tractor had successfully captured one rock, Phoebe, the asteroid steered to Earth orbit. Or, to give tractor technology the benefit of the doubt, twice. The second instance involved the as-yet nameless carbonaceous chondrite that, if it were to complete its long, slow diversion to lunar orbit, might revolutionize construction (and what a distant memory from a bygone era *that* seemed) of the Farside Observatory. But overpowering Marcus's own pedantic thoughts—suddenly, irresistibly—came the traumatic flashback. The harrowing flight, clutching the engine core salvaged off a crashed gravity tractor, from Phoebe to the terrorist-controlled powersat. Defying death from the skies? Was not once in a lifetime *enough*?

"Nyet!" a woman (Petrova, from Roscosmos, he remembered) interceded, cutting through Ragged Mustache Man's droning, didactic narration—and for the moment, vanquishing Marcus's adrenaline-spewing flashbacks. "Hammer will be upon us much too soon for any gravity tractor to help."

"Well, yes, but to be thorough—"

Petrova snapped, "Do not waste our time."

Without Tyler and Kirill to herd the cats—where the hell were those two?—the shocked silence following Petrova's rebuke lapsed into talk of a solar-powered, electromagnetic mass driver. Once installed, a mass driver would deflect the Hammer by hurling away metal chunks of the asteroid itself.

Indeed, a mass driver *would* redirect the Hammer sooner than could a gravity tractor. And so what? That alternative approach entailed constructing the mass driver, packaging it for flight, transporting it to the Hammer, landing it, unpacking it, and assembling it. A stream of precision-engineered metallic payloads—hundreds, or maybe thousands of them—must be manufactured on site for the mass driver to launch. Long before all that could happen, humanity's ghosts would be commiserating with their dinosaur precursors. All as Petrova dispassionately critiqued.

"Explosives," someone else in Moscow offered. "Or a collision to deflect it. Hammer is a far larger target than an incoming warhead, and we each have systems to take out one of those."

"Too dangerous," a man from Homeland Security countered. His long sideburns and wide necktie alike were decades out of date. "What if the Hammer isn't *a* rock? What if this is a rubble pile loosely held together by its self-gravity? We could turn it into a hail of merely big rocks, collectively as devastating as though intact, but all the more unstoppable."

Val shook her head. "The Hammer is cohesive. We know what kind of shove it took to alter its orbit. A rubble pile would have come apart. And we know the Hammer is metallic. Any asteroid whose orbit came so near the Sun would have boiled away anything but metal. Spectroscopic data shows us nothing but nickel-iron."

"That's good," Long Sideburns said. "Then as Anatoly in Moscow suggested, we use explosives or a collision to deflect it."

"Let's get serious." Jay Singh stopped twirling his laser pointer to poke with it at his datasheet. "The Hammer is twelve miles across. It's not quite a sphere, but to simplify the math we'll call it one. By every indication the Hammer is nickel-iron, and nickel-iron meteorites have densities in the range of seven to eight grams per cubic centimeter. That comes to what? In round numbers, two trillion metric tons? What the *hell* do you foresee exploding on, or colliding into the Hammer to make it as much as twitch?"

All the while, the military types remained silent.

WHERE ARE THE ADULTS? Yevgeny texted.

DUNNO, Marcus answered. As an afterthought he added, YHEY'D BETTER RETURN SOON.

Marcus was ready to try again to focus the discussion when Tyler strode back into the conference room. "Right," Tyler said. "Dr. Clayburn, where are we?"

Val straightened in her chair. "We've gone through all the conventional approaches. I think we can all agree none of them is up to the challenge."

Right," Tyler repeated, briskly rubbing his hands, not bothering to reclaim his chair. "Then we'd best move on to the unconventional approach." And *that*, Marcus sensed, is what the spooks had not wanted raised in their absence. And why the military were involved. "General?"

At the end of the table opposite Val, a one-star Air Force general nodded fractionally. Her expression was grim, her eyes narrowed. "Rodriguez, Space Force. They, it, whatever is there on the Moon, underestimated our abilities. Barely. We still have, we think, a chance to head off this rock … *if* we act fast. It won't be easy.

"Given the Hammer's estimated mass, we need to hit it with a nuke. A *big* nuke. The shock wave of a standoff detonation produces some of the necessary deflection. Mostly, we leverage the storm of neutrons and soft X-rays the nuke unleashes. All that radiation vaporizes a fair chunk off the facing side of the asteroid. The blasted and boiled-off mass makes a short-lived rocket engine. Debris flies one way; the rock recoils in the other."

Message delivered, Rodriguez leaned back—and chaos erupted.

"You *can't* use nukes in space," the loudest voice broke through. "It's against the Outer Space Treaty. Both our countries are signatories."

Kirill laughed. "And if we observe the niceties, who will be left to object?"

Petrova, frowning, offered, "If the payload can be delivered to the launch site in secrecy, no one will know until after. Any disclosure before that will unleash worldwide panic."

Tyler perched on an edge of the table. If his pose were intended to convey confidence, it failed to convince Marcus. "About that. Laying the groundwork in anticipation that we all will reach concurrence, Space Force started transporting warheads. We'll come to where.

"Our observant MSS friends"—intonation suggesting anything but amity—"inquired rather urgently about that activity. That's why Krill and I stepped out. To make clear why going nuclear looks to be in everyone's best interest. They're taking the matter under advisement—and raising the alert level of their strategic forces—while their own astronomers get into the act."

MSS. The Ministry of State Security. Yup, Marcus thought, doubtless Chinese intel *did* monitor nuclear depots, or wherever the warheads had been withdrawn from. They would not have been happy about the unexplained movement of nukes. For that matter, quite a few Russians on the link looked displeased.

"Hold on," said the NASA guy with the scruffy mustache. "Warheads. Plural. How large an explosion are we talking about?"

General Rodriguez leaned to her right, and an aide whispered in her ear. The general nodded, then said, "That's a work in progress. It's a function, among other things, of how soon we can deliver the package. Given when we now know the alien order was sent, and how soon thereafter the asteroid was observed in its new orbit, the rock's propulsion system gave it a serious shove. Maybe our blast will take out their propulsion system, but we can't rely on it. That means our bomb has to deliver a big enough kick that the rock can't recover with corrective maneuvering." She glanced at the aide's datasheet. "Best guess at the moment is at least eighty megatons."

At which datum Marcus, and pretty much everyone onscreen, twitched.

The largest H-bomb ever tested was 50 megatons, Yevgeny texted. In 1961. Tsar Bomba, it was called. The king of bombs.

Marcus shuddered. That yield was insane. Why would anyone have a bomb that big?

No one does anymore. Given any delivery accuracy at all, there's no reason.

Then how …? Never mind, Marcus thought, he could ask faster than he typed. "We're not talking about some standard warhead from the Air Force inventory, are we?"

"Yes and no," Rodriguez said. "No single warhead, obviously. Multiple standard warheads, rigged to trigger simultaneously."

"Kludged to trigger simultaneously," someone muttered.

"A bomb that large?" It was Long Sideburns again. "You can't tell me *that* might not produce a hail of rubble out of even a solid metallic mass."

No one can tell you anything. Marcus kept the opinion to himself.

The general was more diplomatic. "It might. But if so, at least some of that debris will disperse, will miss us." Her eyes narrowed. "But if you have a better suggestion?"

Sideburns did not. No one did.

"Very good," Tyler said. "Kirill, why don't you take over for awhile?"

"Very good." The Russian spook steepled his fingers. "General Volkov, would you address for us the matter of launch sites and vehicles?"

In Moscow, a silver-haired man pushed his chair back from the table, stood with difficulty, and limped to the front of the room. He had heavy jowls; an impassive, heavy-lidded, reptilian gaze; a broad and much creased forehead—altogether intimidating, even before taking note of the chestful of ribbons on his uniform.

I served under him in the ADFB, Yevgeny texted. Focused on the mission. No nonsense. Good man.

"Volkov, Aerospace Defense Forces Branch," the general began gruffly. "Even at best, the largest thermonuclear weapons can produce only a tiny deflection in Hammer's orbit. That means the intercept must occur well before it reaches Earth. Of course, an ICBM is not sized for such a mission. To cut to the chase, as my American colleagues would say, the launch must be aboard a heavy-lift booster launched from Florida. And soon."

Soon, it transpired, meant days. Exactly how few was also still being determined.

All of which made at least half of the Russians visibly unhappy. And so what? The laws of physics did not give a shit about Russian pride or paranoia. Or as a science-fiction author once put it, *Reality is that which, when you stop believing in it, doesn't go away.*

Reality was that SpaceCo had an Eagle Heavy booster prepped for launch from Cape Canaveral. That missile had, just barely, sufficient lift for the mission. Company and launch complex alike had handled classified payloads—although never before nukes!—for the Air Force and the National Reconnaissance Office.

Which meant that "all" that remained to accomplish in the remaining few days was:

—reprogram the Eagle Heavy's guidance computers.
—remove 20,000 pounds of commercial satellites already mounted atop the missile.
—mate an absurd number of nukes to an ICBM payload bus. (Or, to play safe, two such buses. Or three. The maneuverability of the Hammer remained unknown.)
—retrofit sensors and the terminal-guidance computer from a strategic-defense missile to the payload bus(es).
—reprogram that terminal guidance, among several necessary updates, to accommodate closing speeds in excess of twenty miles per second: far beyond the design spec of any anti-ballistic missile.
—implement a synchronized triggering mechanism for all bombs on a common bus.
—mate the payload bus(es) to the civilian missile.
—and, of course, launch.

ARE YOU HEARING THIS? Marcus texted Yevgeny. DOES THIS PLAN SEEM REMOTELY DOABLE?

YES. REMOTELY. Yevgeny answered. Over the downlink to Earth, he asked, "Can we do this in stages? Bring the weapons to Earth orbit, offload them to a fully fueled lunar-transfer vehicle, and fly *that* to the intercept?"

General Volkov said, "This approach was considered and rejected. Beyond being more complicated than the mission as proposed, there are no provisions in orbit to secure thermonuclear weapons. More than the MSS may have observed the movement of warheads."

"A squad of commandos accompanying the payload is security enough," Yevgeny argued.

"We see no advantage to this," Volkov insisted. "To the contrary, to change vehicles adds complications. One would have to configure the LTV to carry the payload bus and its warheads as cargo, and then release it in flight."

Tyler, pointedly, studied his wrist.

"Our superiors require us to make a recommendation," Kirill interjected smoothly. "If anyone sees a reason the general's approach won't work, speak now."

Won't work was an impossibly high hurdle. Marcus did not speak up.

But Yevgeny did. "What is our Plan B, General?"

"Yevgeny Borisovich, is it? It is a fair question. SpaceCo has another Eagle Heavy at Cape Canaveral nearing readiness for launch. They are accelerating its preparations."

"Reliant, then, on the same infrastructure," Yevgeny said. "Why not a launch from Baikonur Cosmodrome?"

Volkov's expression, somehow, turned dourer. "The mission parameters are challenging. Baikonur, or *any* of the major Russian or Chinese cosmodromes, lies too far north. Launching from any such high latitude would consume fuel that cannot be spared. No, we need a launch site near the equator. French Guiana would be ideal, but discreet inquiries indicate Arianespace cannot make a suitable rocket available at The Spaceport in our time frame. We must use Cape Canaveral."

A fuel margin that slim did *not* instill confidence in the mission. At best, Marcus thought, this was Plan A-and-a-half.

Yevgeny evidently agreed. "With respect, General, an identical launcher, from the same launch site, is far from an ideal backup."

Volkov stiffened. "And yet, this is the best option we have."

"Perhaps not," Yevgeny said. "We believe an alien *something* here on the Moon ordered the attack. Maybe that same thing can call off the attack. Maybe we can make, or convince, it to call off the strike. Or maybe we can convince whatever on the rock has local control to abort.

"The five of us here are the closest thing to experts on the Titans. And evidently the radio and antenna of my shuttle are sufficient to communicate with the Hammer." Pause. "A supercomputer or two, if someone could fly it in from Aitken, might accelerate our efforts."

As if their track record with Titan technology inspired confidence. Still, Marcus thought, what did they have to lose? "If anyone can pull it off, that will be Dr. Komarova."

DOCTOR? Yevgeny texted.

Marcus: I WOULD IMAGINE THE FSB CAN ARRANGE AN HONORARY DOCTORATE FOR KATYA. DON'T YOU THINK SHE'S EARNED IT?

Yevgeny: FINE.

Tyler looked down, brow furrowed, pinching the bridge of his nose. "Kirill, what do you say to that?"

"As a backup plan? I see no harm in the Humboldt group, and the specialists who have been supporting them, looking into it."

"Then we have our decisions," Tyler declared. "Thank you, everyone." And he broke the comm link.

Scrolling rapidly, Marcus reviewed his notes. Plan A? Implausibly ambitious. Plan B? Different wishful thinking. Which left them in need of Plan C.

Never mind how bat-shit crazy the lone, quarter-baked idea that came to his mind.

Chapter 46

Somehow, the job was completed. With more than an hour to spare. And with more than a few shortcuts taken.

"T-minus ten," the final countdown echoed across historic Launch Complex 39A. This was the starting point, before the onset of commercial spaceflight, of every manned Apollo mission and many space-shuttle flights. Most of those missions had gone well.

A good omen?

"Nine. Eight ...."

Within the VIP viewing area and in public parks across Brevard County, crowds gathered, as for every major launch, to watch. They knew nothing about the payload, beyond that the government had "for reasons of national security" preempted a scheduled commercial launch. That bit of mystery had, if anything, swelled the swarms of onlookers beyond the usual turnout.

"Three. Two." Beneath the missile, two-hundred-plus feet high, flame blossomed. "One. Liftoff."

As by the flicking of a switch, night became brighter than day. In every viewing area, people cheered. They cheered louder still as the stentorian roar, catching up with the sight of the launch, rolled over them. The few people in the close-in bunkers—alone, among so many observers, aware of the stakes—cheered the loudest.

Slowly at first, the rocket climbed. Within seconds, flame-tipped nozzles stood even with the top of the launch tower.

Billowing smoke, illuminated by the rocket's exhaust flames, spread from the pad.

And a great, erratic glob of flame erupted, engulfed the rocket. Wreathed in fire, the rocket hesitated. Wobbled in midair. Fell. Disappeared in a gigantic fireball.

Sirens wailed. Hundreds of workers, thousands of panicked onlookers, fled.

In one warhead, unseen, heat, or shock, or circuit failure detonated the high-explosive trigger of the primary fission bomb. That explosion began a chain reaction among the other high-explosive triggers. Blast and flames engulfed the launch complex.

Despite everything, complex safety interlocks operated as intended. The plutonium jackets did not fission. Without a flood of neutrons and X-rays from fission, the fusion core also remained inert.

But as the blast wave fanned the flames, a cloud of vaporized plutonium—deathly radioactive, deathly toxic—sped across the landscape ....

NECESSITY

Chapter 47

SpaceCo streamed the launch, as it streamed all its launches. Only unlike dozens of previous ones, *this* launch erupted into a cataclysmic fireball, and ended in a test pattern.

"*Jesus Christ!*" Donna whispered, awestruck.

Marcus was too shocked to speak. *Valerie* had been invited to Cape Canaveral, to the VIP bunker, for the launch. The last he had heard, she had been unenthusiastic about traveling, even on a government executive jet. His hands shaking, he managed to tap out a text to her. I JUST SAW. ARE YOU OKAY?

WATCHING FROM HOME. STUNNED.

Earth remained in the cross hairs, but he breathed a guilty sigh of relief.

Until Val continued, JAY, TYLER, AND ETHAN ALL WENT TO THE LAUNCH.

As Ekatrina (and a gaggle of fellow wizards flown in from across the Moon) labored, Yevgeny helped however he could. Coordinated the delivery of ever more computing power, esoteric test equipment, and a small nuclear-fission reactor to handle the surge in power demand. Researched and downloaded obscure digital resources. Welded cages for various bits of salvage from the Titan scrap piles the techies selectively revived. Fetched food and coffee. Fretted. Lived in his vacuum gear, apart from the helmet, the more expeditiously to run whatever errands would contribute.

Ilya and Donna did much the same. Not so, Marcus. Since the catastrophe in Florida, he had withdrawn. Mostly he sat by himself in the cab of an American tractor. Occasionally—despite everything—he ventured outside alone. "Thinking," was all the explanation he gave.

As Yevgeny stacked newly warmed snacks in an insulated carrier, the status lamp over the igloo airlock began strobing. Through the tiny inset window of the inner hatch he saw a figure in emerald green. Marcus.

The lock cycled open and the American stepped inside. He popped his helmet. "How are they doing?"

Yevgeny shrugged.

"Still nothing? Well, it was worth trying."

Watching from the sidelines as the world ends? It was exhausting. But resignation? That guaranteed failure. "It *remains* worth trying."

Only given that the window had closed for a new launch to the Hammer, there was nothing else to try.

Marcus set down his helmet. Studied his gloves, at a loss what to do with his hands. Ended up, arms behind his back, in a sloppy imitation of parade rest. "Maybe we're going at this all wrong."

Yevgeny continued packing food for the people actually contributing. "I'm listening."

"So, the idea—and again, I'm not knocking it—has been we master Titan technology enough to divert the Hammer. Learn enough to send an abort code or order a course-correction-slash-misdirection. Or convince ourselves we've learned a safe way to reactivate whatever was active belowground, and convince *it* to send the order. And getting one of those done before the Hammer is too close for whatever propulsion system is on the Hammer to accomplish the necessary deflection. I mean, it can only have so much oomph."

Oomph? No matter; Yevgeny got the gist. "I am aware."

"The thing is ...." Marcus's hands came out front again, underwent renewed scrutiny. "The thing is, Yevgeny, our main successes to date—if you want to call them successes—have been in waking up alien tech and, sometimes too late, powering it back down.

"Contrast that history with what we're now attempting to do. Reverse-engineer alien comm protocols from a tiny sample. Or reverse-engineer alien neural nets, trying to glean clues from a mummified alien brain. How long have biologists and neurologists tried to work out how *our* brains work? Or matching wits with a genocidal alien AI, were we to dare to power it back up. Beyond desperation, what hope have we for progress?"

The last of the meals packed, Yevgeny sealed the insulated carrier. "If you have a point, I wish you would make it."

"Our few *true* successes have been with the Titan's physical gear. That's how we got into the base to begin with, and aboard the alien ship. That's how Ilya worked out as much as he has about their fusion reactor, and how folks back at Base Putin have replicated the Titans' room-temperature superconductors." Marcus breathed in deeply, and out sharply. "So here's my idea, Yevgeny. We'd do better *on* the Hammer. Rather than hoping to learn enough here to trick whatever intelligence ordered the attack on Earth, or whatever intelligence now controls the Hammer, we *bypass* whatever controls the rock and directly engage the propulsion system there."

Disgusted, Yevgeny snatched up his helmet. "And how do we do that? It's too late to reach the Hammer, even as a flyby. And you think to rendezvous with and land on it? There is no way."

Inexplicably smiling, Marcus pointed ... downward. "Except that maybe there is."

"You must be joking," Yevgeny said. And at that, it was a pitiful joke.

Marcus shook his head. "Ilya says the ship in the lava tube has an advanced, high-thrust drive. If it has the performance parameters he expects, that ship is the only thing that *can* get us to the Hammer in time to do any good. In a few *days*. No chemical rocket can do that."

Yevgeny set his helmet back down. Katya and company were too focused on their work—and too exhausted—to notice if they ate, much less what they ate, much less if it were hot. And while Marcus's idea seemed insane, he was right about at least one thing: the efforts underway were, at best, long shots. "A 65-million-year-old ship. Technology we do not understand. Control systems we dare not trust."

Because the time we turned one on, we awakened … it did not bear thinking about.

Marcus glanced around the igloo, found a shelf piled high with snacks. He tore open a Snickers wrapper and bit the end of the candy bar. "All fair points, but let's review. Tech in the alien base, given power, still worked, even self-repaired, after those millions of years. Belowground, everything was sheltered from radiation and maintained at a constant, protectively low, temperature. Vacuum precluded oxidation and any biologically based degradation. And in all that time, the Titans knowing a thing or three we don't about material science, parts didn't vacuum-weld together. Not stator and rotor of electric motors. Not the moving parts of airlocks. Not"—and he shuddered—"the moving parts of starfish bots. Hell, not much of anything as much as accumulated dust.

"And you know what? Even if spaceships weren't intended for an environment of cold, radiation, and vacuum, the ship has been sheltered, like the base, deep inside the lava tube."

Yevgeny considered. "And considerable technology on Hammer must have survived the intervening ages, too."

Marcus bit off another big chunk of chocolate. Chewed. Swallowed. "There you go. Damned fine engineers, these Titans. And more than smart, they were *conservative* engineers. Case in point: the not especially efficient, but very reliable, type of motor they chose for their airlocks. Another example: while the brains of the starfish bots continue to stymie us, the motors, gearing, and linkages are another story. Those are simple, elegant. The mechanical parts, however they were made, exhibit very precise manufacturing tolerances."

"And this helps us how?"

"It might not." The last of the chocolate disappeared. "Still, it's a theory I think worth testing. *If* I understand the Titan engineering approach, their shipboard systems will have all manner of fault-tolerant and fallback capabilities. Say that a computer failed or rebooted, or comm between bridge and engine room were interrupted.

I'd think low-level controls in the engine room would take over and prevent a reactor meltdown. Maybe even keep things running."

"So?" Yevgeny prompted.

"So, let's assume Ilya works out how the fusion reactor works. How the main drive works. The basic operating procedures, I mean. A big-picture understanding. I expect that, at least in the short term, the low-level electronics and software that runs those systems will remain cryptic. Now suppose we gut every wiring harness leading from the bridge to the drive and engine, take a hammer and chisel to bulkheads amidships to cut any connections hidden beneath the surface. Then, let's see if our own computers can be configured to run things. If not, well, we're none the worse off. It isn't as if you, or I, or even Ilya, are contributing much to current efforts."

And if a fusion reactor melted down? Went *bang*? Either might make them a lot worse off. But only, as seemed increasingly inevitable, until Earth died.

Yevgeny laid a hand on his padded box, the meals within busily cooling. "Meal duty is not a worthy contribution? You've offered nothing but speculation and theory. Let us get real. Who would be insane enough to try flying an alien ship that is 65 million years old?"

"Well," Marcus said.

"To maybe save the world?" Yevgeny nodded. "Fair enough."

Chapter 48

Charmaine Powell was African American, perhaps fifty, petite, and always impeccably dressed. Also Tyler's protégée, longtime friend, and replacement. Peering out at Marcus from his Agency datasheet, she clearly was not coping well with Tyler's death. In a sane world, she would have been told to take a few days off. But there was nothing sane about the peril they faced.

She said, "I don't suppose you have the time to follow current events Dirtside. The Restored Caliphate claims to believe that the cock-up in Florida was our sneaky attempt to surprise them with a decapitation strike. That Allah righteously smote us for our blasphemy. And that the Hammer, if it's not just a lie, some devious Crusader plot, will slay the infidels and usher in, well, I don't claim to understand what postapocalyptic paradise they anticipate. They're messianic enough that maybe they do believe all that. And to judge from activities at their launch sites, they might not care to wait for the Hammer to fall. So, if you called with anything other than a triumphant announcement your computers now speak Titan, maybe this can wait."

From broadcasts softly streaming as he worked, Marcus had osmosed a few things. That the accident had immediately killed almost a hundred people, from explosion, fire, or plutonium toxicity. That the no-warning evacuation of the Florida Space Coast was a nightmare, roads and airports overwhelmed, cruise ships jammed.

That if the wind were to shift as forecast, the entire center of the peninsula, including Orlando and Disney World, would also need to evacuate. That the threat of the Hammer having been sprung without warning on the world, the more imminent danger was suddenly the wrong someone misinterpreting the nuclear catastrophe. As, it seemed, the Restored Caliphate *had*. And, from an absence of coverage, that the onetime existence of aliens, and their presumed, beyond-the-grave role in the unfolding disasters, remained a closely held secret.

All in all: general, worldwide panic.

"If we'd had that sort of breakthrough, you'd have heard the cheering from here." A quarter-million miles of vacuum between the worlds notwithstanding. Of course, progress had been just as lacking on Earth, too, and not for the want of trying. It beggared the imagination that half the NSA, and its equivalents in Russia and China, were not also wrestling with the problem. "Still, I may have some *good* news. A different approach entirely. Call it Plan C."

"Plan C is well underway: nations around the globe drawing up plans for mass evacuations of people and supplies to places far from any coast. The Company will evac Valerie and Simon to Cheyenne Mountain"—beneath which, deep underground, sat NORAD headquarters—"or to her parents' place in Illinois, whichever she prefers. And more discreetly, there's even Plan D. Hundreds of people, and the resources initially to support them, are being ferried to the Moon and even a few to Phoebe. As many newcomers as can be sustained off-world, cost-effectiveness be damned."

A reflexive and heartfelt "Thanks for that" at the provisions for his family overlapped with the tag end of her update, but Marcus caught the gist. When he was sure Powell had finished, he went on. "Call this Plan E, then." Because surviving the original blast and tsunami was not the same as surviving. Not even close. There had been inland dinosaurs, too. If he could come up with Plans F and G, he would argue for those, too. "But we'll need your help."

She looked dubious. "Go on."

He gave Powell the nontechie version. Ilya had succeeded in powering up the shipboard reactors. He had doped out a theory of operations for the alien interstellar drive. They might thereby have a spacecraft capable far beyond human achievement—in theory able to reach the Hammer in time to save the day.

She frowned. "The working hypothesis, as I understand it, is that something Yevgeny and his pals did aboard that very ship awakened or riled up the hostile AI in the base. So tell me. What happens when the ship takes offense at having humans aboard?"

"We"—an ambiguous pronoun that included an utterly exhausted Ekatrina, whose diversion from alien code-cracking Marcus elected to leave unmentioned—"considered that. We disconnected cable bundles to isolate power and propulsion. We unplugged power cables running to the bridge from the reactors and from the ship's bank of backup batteries. And, as I favor belts, suspenders, *and* epoxy"—at which she snorted—"we replaced the original airlock motors and controls with our own."

"Hmm." For long seconds, Powell had nothing more to offer. "In recent experience, every silver lining has come wrapped inside a big, black cloud. So, this 'help' you need. Is it to send you a bunch of nukes? I've gotta say, that'll be a hard sell. Never mind the sterling success of our *last* improvised transport of nukes. Never mind that the Restored Caliphate, and God knows however many other doomsday cults, is at this point likely staking out every major launch site with surface-to-air missiles. If we dodge those bullets but this vessel you hope to kludge together from ancient alien tech, duct tape, and, apparently, your suspenders goes *boom*, you'd contaminate half the surface of what may be humanity's last refuge."

"Well, no," Marcus said. "The idea is to land on the Hammer. We'd do something *there* similar to what's been done *here* with the ship. We'd bypass local control over whatever mechanism redirected the asteroid in the first place. Then we'd re-redirect the rock."

Which was, in truth, Plan *F*, assuming he had not lost track. Unless and until he got a hold of everything necessary to salvage the alien ship, he had no use for nukes. He could make another pitch later for them.

She said, "If not nukes, what will you need?"

Marcus started down the list. "Shipboard life-support gear. We don't have the time to dope out the Titan version, much less what supplies that uses, or whether it could sustain a human crew. A full sensor suite to mount on the hull. A high-power radio and matching antenna." From Earth's perspective, they would often be almost on a line of sight with the Sun. Even mounting a big dish antenna to the hull, he wondered if they would be heard against the backdrop of solar RF noise. "A flight console. Ideally a high-end computer, though we can liberate one of those from the Plan B team. More food, water, and oh-two than what we have on hand. Ditto an assortment of explosives, drills, and other compact mining gear, in case the entrance into the alien facility on the Hammer doesn't cooperate. Portable fuel cells. Spare vacuum gear. Both counterpressure and hard-shell suits, because we can't know what we'll find. Top-of-the-line 3-D printers, with typical feedstocks. And odds and ends, of course."

"Of course," she echoed dryly.

"I'll email the details. And also …."

"I'm not going to like this, am I?"

I expect not. "We'll need lots more people here, and pronto, to pull this off. Technicians, to install life support. Programmers, to tie things together. Heavy-equipment drivers, to clear rubble from the lava tube. Pilots and more drivers, to get everything and everyone—"

"And Kirill? What's he supposed to contribute?"

"Nuclear physicists and fusion engineers, to help Ilya scale up his testing and preflight calibrations. All the helium-3 that is available." Because the dollop of helium-3 that Kirill, grudgingly, had provided for Ilya's initial tests would literally not get the Titan ship off the ground. Neither would the uranium-powered, portable fission reactor the Russians had also flown in from Base Putin, the ship needing *lots* of power to jump-start fusion and begin producing its own. "Industrial-strength cryogenic equipment to liquefy all that helium. Propellant"—which the alien space drive would heat into plasma, and then focus and expel with intense magnetic fields—"once the physicists determine what substance will best work. Instruments for studying the Hammer, once we're close. More odds and ends."

"Anything else?"

"A security detail. When the helpers and supplies"—hopefully!—"descend on us here, there'll be no keeping secret that *something* big is happening. We won't need uninvited guests."

"No, I guess not." Powell grimaced. "Okay, send the wish list, *and* the list Kirill is getting, *and* a short explanation, no more than a page, for me to send up the chain. I'll do what I can. Good—"

The connection dropped, leaving Marcus to guess at her intended sentiment. Good job? Good grief? Either fit, but he chose to believe she was wishing them good luck. They were going to need it.

Charmaine was Marcus's easy conversation.

"Fly a scavenged, ancient, alien derelict to the Hammer." Valerie's face was ashen. She had bags beneath her eyes, deeper and darker than ever. Her checks quivered. Her shoulders slumped. "Assuming you get there, and land without crashing, somehow you need to override *other* ancient alien equipment to make the rock veer away from Earth. And then fly home."

"That's the plan."

"No, that's *madness.*" She rubbed her eyes, fighting back tears.

"It'll be fine." That was a stupid thing to say, and he knew it. But it was the sort of inane thing people said.

"I raised one son alone. Damn it, Marcus, you're *not* leaving me to raise a second by myself. Another son who won't even know his father. Do you *hear* me?"

If we can't divert the Hammer, it won't be a problem. Marcus couldn't bring himself to say that. But .... "Wait a minute. Another son. Little Toot is a boy?"

"*That's* what you focus on?" She half laughed, half cried. "Yes, a son. You are the strangest man."

"I love you. And Simon. And Little Toot. And that's *why* I'm doing this. For all of you."

"And I love *you*, damn it. So let someone else be the hero for once."

He chose silence over argument.

With a sniffle, she asked, "So are there other volunteers for this suicide mission?"

"Pretty much everyone who knows." Marcus forced a grin, going for devil-may-care. "We prefer to think of this as an adventure."

"Fools. All of you." But for all that, however unwillingly, she returned a flash of a smile.

"Yevgeny will be our pilot. I couldn't keep him away if I tried. Ilya in the engine room. Katya for the computers. And as often as I tell her it's unnecessary, Donna insists. Says we're too clumsy to gad about the Solar System without medical support."

Sniffle. "She may be right."

"And one crew member yet to be identified. A navigator." Because this flight would not be anything as routine as a jaunt to Earth orbit, or between Earth and Moon.

Softly, Valerie said, "This is it, then? It's going to happen?"

"It's going to happen. But I promise you"—somehow—"this *isn't* it for us."

Yevgeny stood, in theory, at a safe distance. The lunar landscape had never seemed so barren. So bleak. But what did his sense of foreboding matter? The clock was ticking. "Shall we?" he radioed.

Marcus, standing at his side, offered the detonator. "You do the honors."

"And why me?"

His face blue by Earthlight, Marcus grinned. "Because this was your choice."

Some choice! The power and responsiveness of the ship's main drive and its auxiliary thrusters were alike unknown. The alien bridge controls—in theory, bypassed, and possibly not—had to be assumed hostile. The controls still being hastily retrofit were, of necessity, untested and uncalibrated. So, yes—again, in theory—he could fly the ship hundreds of meters down a narrow, meandering lava tube to the surface.

Yevgeny accepted the detonator. "Sound off, people."

One by one, everyone did. With their much expanded workforce, that check-in took awhile. But in the end, everyone was accounted for.

"Fire in the hole," Yevgeny warned. "In three. Two. One."

The shock wave, when it reached him, was a faint, anticlimactic tremor through his boots. A cloud of dust made an appearance over a nearby hill. And on his HUD, an inset window cycled among relayed vids of much denser dust. Of ten cameras that had been positioned around the ship, six had survived the blast.

Their explosives had been placed above where a rubble mound, since bulldozed out of the way, had once trapped the ship. Logic—validated by a survey with ground-penetrating radar—indicated that that spot was thinner and weaker than where the lava-tube roof had *not* caved in. Indeed, the Chinese geological engineer from Ice Blossom had exuded confidence. Yevgeny would have been a lot happier if it were Nikolay giving the assurances. For many reasons.

It felt like an eternity, but within seconds of the blast enough dust settled for the belowground cameras to begin showing debris. Now *new* rubble clogged the tunnel.

And the ship itself? The surviving cameras offered only partial views. What Yevgeny could see of it appeared undamaged.

Hiking over the ridge behind which he and Marcus had sheltered, the pockmarked landscape seemed unchanged. Not until he superimposed onto his visor, over the real-time scene, a translucent image of *before* did Yevgeny register a change. But change there was: a new, yawning pit.

What do you think?" Marcus asked.

"It's a start," Yevgeny said.

Construction crews and heavy equipment flown in from around the Moon, working around the clock, spent two days removing the new-fallen rubble. Most of that work was accomplished by bulldozer, with the largest chunks hoisted up the rough chimney by crane. They used a third day, and a half dozen small shaped charges, expanding and smoothing the chimney, from lava-tube floor to the surface, into a more-or-less oval cylinder of about forty-five meters by twenty. Meanwhile, aboard the alien ship, engineers and technicians continued installing equipment, filling tanks, and loading other supplies.

On the fourth day, they jacked up the ship. They set a custom-made rolling cargo platform beneath each landing leg and painstakingly towed the ship forward. They left it centered below the gaping chimney.

Ready for a test flight.

Chapter 49

Ship awakened.

The diagnostics automatically initiated at startup reported … madness. At its most recent reawakening, those same diagnostics had encountered no faults more serious than depleted supplies. Since that time, somehow, entire subsystems had become unresponsive. As far as telemetry could determine, it no longer had fusion reactors, main propulsion, or attitude control. And the nearby servant mind it had attempted to repair? For all Ship knew, that, too was gone: the connection it had had via umbilical had vanished.

But it still had a partial sensor suite.

Beings labored throughout its interior. The two visitors attendant to its prior awakening had been indistinct within their protective gear: childlike in stature though they had been, they were of an appropriate shape to be masters. But now atmosphere had been restored, and the newcomers had shed their vacuum suits. These *creatures* were not the masters.

The interior cameras which had disclosed the intruders' alien nature also revealed that its reactors and other unresponsive subsystems, rather than removed, had been severed—often crudely—from its sensory apparatus and control. An action of these intruders, Ship inferred. And while telemetry no longer reported the status of its many tanks and reservoirs, hints of frost and vapors around the liquid-helium and liquid-oxygen tanks suggested that *those* essential supplies, at a minimum, had been replenished.

From bow to stern, octets of cabinets, equipment frames, and storage vessels, of unfamiliar design and unknown purpose, had been deployed. Unfamiliar wire bundles ran everywhere, most terminating in the engine room. And in that engine room, strange devices—by inference, measuring instruments and controls to bypass its own—had been affixed to its key subsystems.

A stew of alien secretions and exudations tainted the restored atmosphere. Odors aside, the gas mix and partial pressures would have sustained the masters, no matter how oppressive they would have found these levels of carbon dioxide and water vapor.

Its audio inputs, meanwhile, registered a cacophony of incomprehensible speech and the clangor of metal on metal. Several intruders wore acoustic apparatuses on their belts; each of these devices emitted a different odd, multisource warbling: replete with complex harmonics, underlain with rhythmic patterns, and sometimes also speech-like elements. For these intricate, compound noises, Ship lacked any referent.

And outside its hull? There, too, much had changed. Unfamiliar wheeled and tracked vehicles waited nearby. Rude barriers of tumbled stones no longer entrapped it. A separate passage, far more direct, now gaped in the lava-tube roof. And Ship, it realized, had been moved to a spot beneath this new opening.

All of which raised questions in its mind. Who were these intruders? Why had they done these things? And most basic of all: What would the masters expect it to do?

Seated at a standard-but-tweaked flight console shoehorned onto an alien bridge, Yevgeny held down the intercom button. "Status check. Report."

"Engine room, go," Ilya said.

"Supernumerary, go," Marcus said. "Cozy here in my stateroom. A little disappointed I didn't rate turndown service."

"Super what?" Yevgeny asked, even as he found a definition with the datasheet magneted to the console shelf. *An extra person or thing.*

"Sorry," Marcus said. "My little attempt at humor."

"More truth than humor. There is no reason for you to be onboard for this test." And good reason not to be. Yevgeny himself did not much care for being aboard. *Pilot* and *test pilot* were very different jobs.

"Maybe not, and yet here I stay. I say, go."

"Fine. Pilot, go." Yevgeny toggled on his radio. "This is *Rescue One*. We are go for launch."

"Roger that, Yevgeny," answered a nasal voice. Pedro Fonseca, one of the many engineers brought in from Aitken Basin to help refit the alien ship. "*Rescue One*, you say. Why not? It's a worthy sentiment."

In short order, Ilya had gotten the reactors fusing. He had cycled them several times, however briefly, between full power and their idling level. Firing up the main drive? That would be an experiment.

"Deflectors configured for vertical lift," Yevgeny said, tapping at his control pad. (Alien design practices had necessitated—or so, anyway, the team had concluded—several quirky flight controls. And that, in turn, meant using virtual buttons and sliders on a touch pad, rather than the solid, physical controls he would have preferred.)

"My instruments show deflectors have repositioned," Ilya reported from the engine room.

"I have visual confirmation," Fonseca added unnecessarily. Vids relayed onto the bridge told Yevgeny as much.

"Engaging main drive at an estimated five percent." On Yevgeny's display, bright blue plasma erupted beneath the ship. Beneath him, the ship throbbed: a pulse each time the convergent laser beams fused a helium-3 micro-droplet. "Ten percent."

Slowly, the ship rose from the lava-tube floor.

He compensated for a slight drift (a deflector out of alignment?) with a short burst from starboard-side attitude thrusters. Lidar and eyeballs alike indicated he was centered beneath the chimney. "Let's go for a ride."

And doubling the thrust level, he soared into the lunar sky.

Abducted by aliens.

Ship had to resist. Service to the masters, and loyalty, and duty, were innate.

But how?

It did not find one intact primary telemetry link to the reactors or main propulsion. It did not find a single working connection to diagnostic sensors in the engine room. But in its diligent, systematic manner, it *did* discover intact circuits for environmental monitoring of that space.

Consulting its design files, Ship matched circuits to physical layouts. It identified comm nodes in proximity to low-level autonomous reactor controls.

It directed carbon-nanotube growth within the neural-net cultures lining the reactor-room bulkheads to establish new electrical connections.

—•—

Fast climbs. Faster descents. Gradual turns, and then tight ones. A damned barrel roll.

Wondering which might help more, a window or Dramamine, Marcus hit the intercom. Pressed deep into the acceleration couch that had replaced the alien tilt-down sleeping shelf, it was a stretch. One more damn thing to adjust before they set out for real. "Having fun, are we?"

In all honesty, and setting aside the touch of motion sickness, *he* was having fun. Or maybe he was experiencing relief. His desperate, crackpot plan? It might not be entirely insane after all.

"I, anyway," Yevgeny said. "You might remember I advised you *not* to come."

"I do not remember having that option," Ilya offered.

"Or anyone mentioning that the test flight would involve a dogfight," Marcus added.

Ilya laughed. "Seriously, Yevgeny, take it easy. Calibrating the ship's performance, measuring rates of fuel and propellant consumption, and so on, will go easier if you fly straight for awhile, accelerate smoothly, decelerate smoothly."

"Babies," Yevgeny said. "I need to know how the ship handles. And I'll be pushing it harder. We're barely at seventy kilometers. And we have yet to exceed, by my estimate, forty percent thrust."

They went into a screaming, arcing climb that rang mental alarms—and then, zero gee. Only his five-point harness kept Marcus in his seat. They had gone over the top, like on an astronaut training flight. Like the Vomit Comet.

An unfortunate memory.

The plunge lasted only a few seconds. Then they were climbing, steeper than ever, pressing him deeper than ever into the acceleration couch. Gritting his teeth, he waited for Yevgeny to get it out of his system.

Instead, acceleration cut off. *Rescue One* went eerily silent. And the pilot-deadpan declaration came, "I've lost power. We're going down."

Both reactors failed at once? How was that even possible?

But the lights remained lit; at least the automatic cutover to emergency batteries had worked. Too bad batteries could not power the main drive, not even for an instant.

Marcus hit the intercom. "Ilya! What's going on?"

Silence.

Marcus undid his harness. "Yevgeny, I'm going to check in the engine room."

With a low rumble, stern attitude thrusters kicked in. Those were chemically powered. "Stay buckled! This will be a rough landing."

A fall of how many kilometers? They wouldn't *land*, they would *splat*. "We have to be going fairly fast. Can we reach orbit using attitude thrusters?"

"No. But even a little more altitude will buy us extra seconds."

During which a reactor might restart, Marcus interpreted. How apt was that to happen by itself? "How long do we have?"

"About five minutes."

With only the trivial nudge of attitude thrusters separating them from free fall, and the ship canted upward at a steep angle, walking was impossible. Marcus grabbed a cable bundle running down the ceiling of the main corridor. Hand over hand, he lowered himself sternward.

The engine room was quiet as a … library, the acceleration chair there empty. Sweeping his eyes across the room, Marcus spotted Ilya wedged in a back corner: head lolling, eyes shut, a trickle of blood (from a scalp wound?) running down his forehead, chest slowly rising and falling.

Gripping one hulking apparatus after another, Marcus reached the port reactor compartment. The status lamp retrofit above the door glowed red. OFF. Flinging open the door (and wrenching his arm—the door panel, like the reactor-compartment walls, was lead-lined and massive) things inside looked … no different than before takeoff. Instruments grafted onto the reactor registered zero, except two: accumulated charge in the capacitor bank was ample to restart the reactor. And the remote readout of the helium-3 tank in the adjoining compartment had not noticeably budged from full.

So why was the reactor off?

A closer look from above revealed nothing. Or to the reactor's left or its right. Or peering through the tightly wound superconducting coils, or at the sphere of lasers, or peeking through slits of the onion shell, within which fusion took place. The apparatus was flush-mounted to the deck, so he couldn't see beneath it. And behind it all he saw was the ubiquitous black wall.

Like the black coating in the base that re-grew connections!

Marcus wrenched an instrument off the reactor. Whatever that little gauge monitored, it was of human manufacture; Titans hadn't needed it to run the reactor. Gripping the compartment latch with one hand, stretching, he scraped and scratched behind the reactor with a sharp corner of the instrument.

Was he separating the reactor from a hostile AI? Or destroying connections essential to the reactor? He had no way of knowing. But if he did nothing, they were all dead anyway.

Pale indentations took form in the wall coating. Grooves. Gouges. Here and there, metal glinted.

"About a minute," Yevgeny warned over the intercom.

And a warning beacon flashed. Startup!

As Marcus flung himself from the reactor compartment, the massive door, rebounding, clipped his head. The door's *slam*, the sudden bellow of the main drive, and something like an elephant falling on him happened together.

His last thoughts before passing out were: Yevgeny was getting his wish to see just what the alien drive technology could do. And: that hopefully, it would be enough.

—•—

Ship felt its failure. More, it regretted the failure. It was *ashamed* for its failure.

Still, the restored heat (too warm) and light (skewed too green) had replenished its emergency power reserves. Still, *almost* it had succeeded.

Failure had come of acting in haste. By instinct. Failure had come from reliance upon too simple an intervention, easily circumvented. And so, Ship would repair and replace, reroute and make replicates of, critical circuits. All the while, it would watch, and wait, and prepare.

Next time, its intervention would not be so easily defeated.

Next time, Ship promised its absent masters, it *would* succeed.

Chapter 50

How could steady acceleration at Earth-standard gravity feel so damned *brutal*?

Except Marcus knew exactly how. Months at Daedalus, shirking any exercise more strenuous than pushing paper (and most often virtual paper, at that). More months in and around the Titan installation, with little proper exercise equipment, even if he had been inclined to use it. All the while laboring twelve, and even sixteen, hours every day. Living in tin cans and hobbit holes (never mind how tall those "hobbits" had been), breathing foul, endlessly recycled air.

If only the burdens on which he dared not dwell, of which *none* of them spoke, were purely physical. Because the secrecy, the mutual suspicions, the near isolation, had levied a yet greater toll. Two friends slain. The robotic onslaught, followed by the unending, gnawing anticipation of another. The near-fatal first test flight, and the white-knuckle, if uneventful, second test flight that followed. And overshadowing all else: the belief that, having brought on this nightmare, they were humanity's last, best—and for all that, dubious—hope for survival.

Never mind *humanity*. They were the last, best hope for Val, Simon, and Little Toot.

Flat on his back on a reclined acceleration couch, beneath two heavy blankets, fingers interlaced behind his head, Marcus tried to tune out the endless throb of the fusion reactors. The ceaseless rumble of the main drive. The whirr of fans and the gurgle of coolant loops. The dreariness that was his closet/cabin.

Titans must not have believed in ornamentation; apart from the stack of utilitarian wire drawers with his few changes of clothing, the cabin he had claimed for his own was all but featureless. Walls, floor, and ceiling alike were a uniform matte black except where he had attacked them with a coarse rasp, and with a hammer and chisel, here and there gouging through the alien coating to uncover shiny metal beneath, disrupting—he hoped!—whatever alien circuitry had once traversed these surfaces. Alas, the random grooves and scrapings had turned his otherwise nondescript, light-sucking surroundings into a Rorschach test. A test at which, like getting any rest, he was failing ....

In the underground Titan base, in defiance of the ubiquitous murkiness, they had tried spray-painting Day-Glo swatches—only to see those bright, spirit-lifting pigments slowly *eaten*. There, the defeat of color had been (perhaps) merely disheartening. Aboard *Rescue One*, the stakes were oh, so much higher. They dare not do anything that might mask any regrowth of the alien circuits. Nor could they strip off the accursed smart coating. Decent solvents for carbon nanotubes did not exist. A handful of strong acids could have done the trick, but using strong acids shipboard, especially near essential equipment like the reactors, was not an option. Beyond manual scraping, and soon the orbital sanders Ekatrina was kludging from their two handheld power drills, the best they could do was keep the ship's interior dim and cold, cutting down on the ambient energy the smart coating would tap to regrow.

Just then, Marcus's main relief from the drab monotone came from the folded datasheet resting on his chest. In this latest Dirtside holo, Val was (of course!) beautiful and oh, so pregnant. But no matter how brave her smile, her *eyes* were haunted. At her side, Simon (the boy had grown a good three inches since Marcus had last seen him!) tried, and failed, to hide his fears.

The most important people in his life, stood—posed, rather—in his guestroom-turned-nursery. That room—freshly repainted; farm-animal decals on one wall; crib assembled—was their declaration of hope. (Also, their tacit denial of the coming evac to NORAD headquarters. High in the Rockies. Behind atomic-bomb-proof blast doors. Two thousand feet beneath the surface.) Because they trusted Marcus to save the day. Save the planet.

And he would. Somehow.

His shiver had nothing to do with the near-freezing temperature in the cabin.

"I need to get out of my head," Marcus announced.

It was deep into the ship's night shift, but it wasn't as if any of them could do more than doze fitfully, or even expected to. In the two days since departing the Moon, Yevgeny had almost never left the bridge, or Ilya the engine room. Marcus couldn't really disturb either. Nor, alas, help them. They would reach out to *him* if and when he could be useful.

Ekatrina, meanwhile, would be roaming about the ship, checking and rechecking the circuits, instruments, and fail-safes that bypassed their Titan counterparts. If those inspections did not fully occupy her, all signs were that she and Yun, their newbie/navigator, valued their privacy—together. More power to them, but that left … no one.

Donna had volunteered for the mission, of course. Insisted. Pleaded. Nagged. Right that moment, Marcus selfishly regretted having told her no. "Someone with firsthand experience should hang around. There will be questions. Plan B may yet have a chance."

"And if any of you get sick aboard ship, or injured?"

"Then we're sick or injured." Marcus remembered having shrugged, remembered pondering the odds—and the futility—of crew aboard the Titan ship surviving if something did go wrong. Mostly he had wondered why, in that eventuality, their survival would matter. "And anyway, one gee of sustained acceleration is an amazing thing. It'll only be, give or take, a three-day flight there."

(Three days. A cakewalk. He could manage three days on adrenaline and caffeine alone. What had Tyler Pope once said about their road trip? "Back in the day that's what we called spring break." Uh-huh. Back in the day, Tyler had still been alive.)

Donna would not have it. "And how many days once you get to the Hammer? And then there's the flight back."

Any prolonged stay on the Hammer, and there would *be* no return flight. They would still be *on* the rock when it smashed into Earth. What use then would a medic be?

"Go home," he had ordered. "Be with your family."

As maybe *he* should have been spending Earth's final days with *his* family.

With a sigh, Marcus flicked off and pocketed his datasheet. Tugged up the blankets. Closed his eyes. Willed himself to ignore the reactors' throb and the rumble of the main drive and the thousand lesser shipboard noises. Willed his mind to clear, his body to fall asleep. Failed.

He flung aside his blankets and shuffled to their improvised galley. There, sipping bad coffee, he did the thing he was worst at in the world. In *all* the worlds.

Waiting.

Severed power lines and cable bundles. Disconnected instruments. Savaged smart surfaces .... The aliens had done their brutal best to render Ship a mindless conveyance.

As Ship did *its* surreptitious best to survive, diverting its energies, and its reserve stocks of the mutable smart coating, into various of its concealed places. Cable conduits. Air ducts. Beneath consoles and apparatuses, and inside the snug spaces beneath floor panels. Within consoles and cabinets. It regrew sensors, rerouted and repaired circuits, expanded its neural nets.

Some aspects of its circumstances became clear. It was fully powered, the operation of its reactors implicit in every throb of a helium-3 droplet fusing. It had accelerated, and was now decelerating. Against its will, the five aliens who defiled its interior were flying it ... somewhere.

Where? it ceaselessly wondered. Where was it being taken? And—the more fundamental question—*why*?

Despite acute, almost overwhelming, curiosity, Ship dare not pulse radar or lidar, lest the power consumed by those emissions disclose its survival. But through passive hull sensors, it caught glimpses of sun, stars, and planets; with those data it reached a few conclusions. It moved along the ecliptic. It had come sunward almost to the orbit of the second planet. That cloud-enshrouded world itself was distant, far off Ship's course, seemingly not the aliens' destination.

But while spectroscopic data allowed Ship to identify individual bright stars, the overall starscape had been altered beyond recognition. To its list of unanswered questions, Ship added, how long was I trapped in the lava tube? How long was I without power, insensate, inert?

In time, a fast-moving glint came within range of an optical sensor. Slowly, that speckle brightened and dimmed, brightened and dimmed: a sunlit asteroid, spinning. Ship extrapolated the object's trajectory. It extrapolated, presuming that its deceleration would continue unchanged, its own course.

Why, Ship wondered, was that onrushing rock the destination of the intruders?

Crossing the orbit of Venus!

No human had ever been so distant from the home world—and yet here Yevgeny was. Piloting a ship that had tried once already to kill him. (Or so he believed. That this eons-old vessel had just *failed*, that by amazing luck Marcus's random scratchings had allowed the reactor to restart—while inflicting who knew what other damage—was scarier than a hidden adversary.) Relying on controls and sensors hastily retrofit by Ekatrina to, in theory, bypass a hostile AI. Beneath a Titan-high ceiling, which made him feel like a child playing space cadet. It was a ship whose power and propulsion systems Ilya understood only in principle, and that Yevgeny did not pretend to understand. Even as the flight's absence of problems felt ever more ominous ….

Finally, on the datasheet-cum-flight-controls secured by magnets to a disabled (or so he hoped!) alien console, a countdown timer broke below five minutes. He tapped the intercom. "Deceleration to end in five, people. Navigator to the bridge. Captain to the bridge."

Marcus arrived first, while deceleration still provided the simulation of gravity. He dropped into the bridge's remaining acceleration couch. "The last I heard, a ship has only one captain. That's you."

"Every mission has but one commander. That, my friend, is *you.*" And, Yevgeny realized with a start, *friend* was sincere. Whether Marcus was indeed a CIA asset? That he and the American had once been adversaries? That was ancient history. "Because I am merely the taxi driver. And because we have arrived."

"That is for me to decide." On cue, Liu Yun, planetary astrophysicist and their navigator, had appeared in the hatchway. After the succession of major explosions to free *Rescue One* from the lava tube, followed by the two test flights, there had been no keeping secrets from the Chinese. Even so, Yun sounded, at least while speaking English, more upper-crust Brit than Mandarin. One consequence of an Oxford education.

Yun was thirty-seven, per his FSB dossier, while scarcely looking thirty. The pampered son of Central Committee member Liu Ping. Short. Pudgy. Or maybe not pudgy as much as soft? And why wouldn't he be soft? Until a week ago, he had been ensconced in the comparative luxury of the Farside Observatory, with nothing more taxing to do than nose about where everyone had been directed to look the other way.

Yun's head was a broad, inverted wedge, sprouting a scruffy chin-strap beard at one end and at the other enough deep-black hair, moussed into spikes, for three men. His forehead was broad, intelligent-seeming, and his eyes were seldom without a mischievous twinkle. (And perhaps that impishness was the appeal for Katya. Life for her, for them all, had been *grim.*)

Yevgeny's datasheet chimed. He reached again for the intercom. "One minute to free fall."

Marcus buckled in. Yun clasped the back of Marcus's couch.

As the seconds count broke into single digits, Yevgeny positioned a hand above the datasheet, ready to intervene if software failed to act. Needlessly so, for at zero the deep bass rumble of the drive … vanished. His poised arm wanted to float. The frenetic *pop-pop-pop* of the reactors, and the faint tremor that accompanied it, slowed to a stately, twice-per-minute pulse. He scanned the virtual instruments on the datasheet before again activating the intercom. "Coming around, people."

With gentle nudges of their attitude thrusters, Yevgeny began reorienting the ship. Earth and Moon, for hours now merged into a single, brilliant dot, slid to the port edge of the canopy, disappeared. They kept turning ... turning ... turning. An edge of the canopy darkened and polarized as the Sun appeared, the protective area expanding as they spun. And still, slowly, they turned ....

A dusky mass, potato-shaped, edged into their view. And, larger than Earth as seen from the Moon, it *kept* coming.

Two brief pulses of attitude thrusters brought their rotation to a stop. A three-second pulse of the bow thrusters brought them to a halt relative to the asteroid. Meaning the Hammer and ship *alike* were hurtling toward Earth.

If the fools in charge at home had permitted *Rescue One* to bring along a few thermonuclear weapons, their job would almost be done.

As if reading Yevgeny's mind, Yun's reflection in the canopy broke into a scowl.

"What's wrong?" Yevgeny asked.

"Nothing," Yun said. "This is the rock I expected, and just where I expected it. Which means, Earth remains in its cross hairs."

For the benefit of Ilya and Ekatrina, Yevgeny announced over the intercom, "We have arrived."

"How close are we?" Marcus asked.

Yevgeny sent out a lidar ping. "Eighty-one kilometers." They had been aiming for eighty. He craned his neck to look up at Yun, who, having released his grip on Marcus's acceleration couch, now floated near the bridge ceiling. "Well done. I see you are not only an MSS asset."

"The 007 bit was Father's idea. He despaired that with my esoteric interests I would ever go anywhere." Yun laughed heartily, gesturing toward the canopy and the Hammer. "Shows all he knows." Slapping Yevgeny on the shoulder, he laughed again. "And I am happy to know *you* are a competent pilot, and not just an FSB spy."

Then it was Marcus's turn to laugh.

Yevgeny studied the Hammer, spinning around its long axis, by naked eye and through the hull-mounted telescope. Cameras streamed both views to datasheets for Ilya and Ekatrina. As the asteroid turned, glinting in the ferocious sunlight, he saw nothing out of the ordinary. Their spectrometer, analyzing reflected sunlight, gave the same report as had observatories orbiting Earth: the Hammer was a primordial chunk of nickel-iron. A planetesimal left over from the earliest era of the Solar System.

"I see no sign the Titans were ever here." He held back a shiver: with no obvious alien traces, where would they even begin to look? Its many lumps and indentations aside, the Hammer was a fat ellipsoid twelve kilometers by eight by six. Its surface exceeded two hundred square kilometers.

Ekatrina said, "Nothing the Titans left on the Moon's surface lasted. Why would it here?"

Yun agreed. "Since the aliens were on this rock—*if* they were here—it has endured millions of close encounters with the Sun. Imagine the temperature extremes it has endured, and the blasting by solar wind, far more intense even than on the unprotected surface of the Moon."

Paul Bunyan's remains survived the eons, Yevgeny thought. And how unfortunate for humanity *that* was. With a bit of help from us ....

An idea flashed into his head. "Suppose there is nothing on the Hammer we can use. This ship is *much* more massive than any gravity tractor that might have been lobbed this way on a missile. Can we use *Rescue One* as a gravity tractor?"

"I doubt it." Yun's eyes closed in thought. His lips moved in silent calculation. "Sorry. Not even close."

"We should report our arrival to Dirtside," Marcus said.

Yevgeny handed him the mic. "Here you go, Captain."

Marcus narrated a brief report. The transmission would be almost three minutes on its way. An acknowledgment would be as long in returning; any meaningful response longer still. In expectant silence, they stared at the asteroid they had come so far somehow to deflect.

And after an interminable six minutes ... nothing. Not even a burst of static.

Marcus drummed fingers on an armrest until Yevgeny frowned at him. "Sorry. Well, looking on the bright side, we're here. And Earth will know as much when the Hammer starts veering from its course."

"Assuming we figure out how," Yevgeny said.

Marcus shrugged.

"Maybe Earth did not hear us," Yun ventured. "The Sun pumps out a lot of radio noise, and from Earth's perspective, we are almost in front it."

"You do not sound convinced," Yevgeny said.

Yun's shrug started him slowly spinning. "Because I'm not. Natural RF is broadband noise. We are using a known, narrow, frequency band."

"Perhaps we remain within a plasma cloud?" Ilya suggested from the engine room. "If that is the issue, the cloud will be dispersing. They will get through to us later."

The plasma exhaust from the ship's main drive *had* kept them in a comm blackout for the entire flight. Since turnover, they had been braking through their own ion trail. Interference had to be the problem. To be thorough, Yevgeny ran comm diagnostics anyway. "Hmm. Odd."

"What?" Ekatrina asked. "Would you like me up there?"

Marcus leaned to where he could see Yevgeny's datasheet. "An *antenna* failure? You've got to be kidding me. We have to go outside and point the dish by hand?"

Yevgeny slued an exterior camera for a look at the antenna. And cursed. In their separate native languages, all three men on the bridge swore. Where the steerable antenna had been attached to the hull, nothing but the twisted stump remained. The big dish was perhaps the only item for which they had not brought a spare. Because what could go wrong with a big, dumb piece of metal?

Jesus," Marcus said. "Are we unlucky enough to get grazed by a *meteoroid*? Or were we careless enough to have screwed up mounting the antenna?"

"Neither, I think," Yevgeny said. "Or both. It does not matter. It is simply our destiny to do this *alone*."

Ship studied the nearby asteroid. As the rock rotated, Ship had no doubt. It recognized this rock. It had been to this rock.

This was a weapon of the masters. A weapon of last resort.

There was equally no uncertainty but that this asteroid, its orbit extrapolated forward, would strike—would obliterate!—the third planet. That Ship's return to this asteroid could be no coincidence. That its alien intruders must have come here, must have needed *it* to come here, to deflect the asteroid.

As there could be no doubt of Ship's duty. Whatever the cost, Ship would not permit the masters' will to be thwarted.

—•—

"Is short-range comm operational?" Marcus asked. Short range used a dedicated antenna, your basic omnidirectional dipole aerial.

Yevgeny's fingers glided over his datasheet and its virtual controls. He nodded approval at what he saw there, then re-aimed the external camera. The new view showed a short dipole antenna standing out from the hull, just as it had at their departure. "Short range appears fine."

"Then we'll report with that. Every radio telescope on the planet"—the Sun-facing side, anyway—"will be listening."

Yun said, "If so, we'll never hear their response."

But they'll know we made it. *Valerie* will know we made it. Marcus retrieved the mic he had left floating. "Ground Control, this is *Rescue One*. We have reached a point—"

"What the hell?" Ilya shouted over the intercom. "Yevgeny, quit fiddling with the reactors."

"I have not touched them." Yevgeny said.

"Then why are they ramping up?"

Marcus dropped the mic, his eyes skimming over Yevgeny's virtual flight controls. Both reactors reported there as in their idle states, and the main drive showed as off. That they were in free fall *proved* the main drive was off. The battery banks registered a full charge. Apart from cooling and life support, the current power drain should be trivial.

But there was no denying the escalating *pop-pop-pop* of the reactors, and the rumble Marcus felt in his bones.

"Ilya! Can you shut things down from your end?"

"Do you imagine I am not trying?" the physicist snapped. "Katya! Get down here. Help me to understand what is happening."

"Where's all the energy going?" Marcus asked.

"I do not *know*!" Ilya said. "Nothing! I see nothing on my instruments."

Marcus's mind raced. Where would this energy surge go? What damage could it do? Overload batteries already at capacity? Not fatal, as long as they kept the reactors themselves online. Disable their life support? That was grafted-on equipment; apart from power feeds, it did not connect in any way to alien hardware. Circuit breakers would protect it. What else? Between the pulsing of the reactors and the roar of ventilation fans, it was hard to think.

The roar of the fans?

"Ilya," Marcus called. "What's the temperature?"

"Your comfort is not at this moment my priority."

"Ilya!" Marcus yelled back. "Listen to the fans! And not here on the bridge. I'm hearing them over the intercom, on your end."

A Russian curse. "Burnt my hand on a door. The reactor compartments themselves are *hot*. Without a load on the onion shells"—which converted the radiation from fusion directly into electrical power—"they are going to blow."

Explosively, Marcus thought. Like a short circuit without a fuse. And with the reactors running flat out—pumping out their maximum radiation, never mind the escalating heat—to enter either reactor compartment would be suicide. Scraping the walls, and hoping for the best, as he had tried in desperation on that near-disastrous test flight, was not an option.

"Cut the helium feeds." Because there were cutoffs for any time a cryo tank or a reactor required maintenance. Regrown alien circuitry could do nothing about big, dumb *mechanical* valves. Marcus hoped. "We'll run off batteries while we figure this out."

"Do you know," Ilya protested, "what an uncontrolled shutdown will do to the reactors? Because I do not!"

"I know what a *meltdown* will do," Marcus snapped. "Destroy the reactors. If not kill us outright, disable the ship. In any event, end the mission. Cut the helium feeds. That's an order."

"But—"

"*Do* it, Ilya," Yevgeny said.

And together, over the space of no more than a few seconds:

—Lights flashed, flickered, settled into a dim, battery-mode level.
—The intercom chirped twice, emitted an ear-splitting squeal of positive feedback, and went silent.
—And with a choking, asthmatic sputter, the throbbing/popping of the reactors died out.

Ship had done what it could. It wondered: had that been enough?

Chapter 51

The engine room was sweltering, its air thick with a stench of scorched metal, when Marcus arrived. Ilya and Ekatrina had their heads together, exchanging rapid-fire Russian.

Marcus reminded them, "Your English is a whole lot better than my Russian."

Ilya shrugged. "There is nothing yet to tell. We do not know what happened, or what damage was done."

"What happened?" Back on the Moon, when the ship had failed on its first test flight, the cause might have been … anything. But twice? The situation no longer permitted any ambiguity. "We were attacked. *That's* what happened. We need to understand how. And by what. The ship, obviously, but *what* in the ship? Because I don't know that we can survive another attack."

Ekatrina murmured something.

"What's that?" Marcus asked.

"We may not have survived this attack. Given the cooling demands so near to the Sun, backup batteries will only last a day or so." She nibbled on her lower lip. "We have the fission reactor"—intended as a portable power source, should they need one, on the Hammer—"but cabling it into the ship's systems and starting it will take hours. And while it should keep most things running, at best it would power the main drive at a small fraction of its capacity."

Marcus nodded. "Good point. First thing, we let ambient temperature rise to, oh, thirty degrees." Or as he considered it, about eighty-six. No one else aboard even thought in Fahrenheit. "That will buy us a little time."

Marcus looked around the engine room until he found an intercom control. It did nothing. Fried, he remembered. He rang Yevgeny on the bridge through his datasheet. "If Yun is with you, put me on speaker. Can you shoot us the final few klicks on thrusters?"

"Yes, but it will be more of a drift than a shot. And it will be a big drain on fuel."

Marcus thought. "The thrusters burn liquid aitch-two and oh-two, right?"

"Yes. A clever design. No need ever to run out of fuel: just electrolyze some water." And bitterly: "Unless your reactors give out."

Marcus asked Ekatrina, "Can we run the Titan electrolyzer, compressors, and cryo gear off their backup batteries?"

"Of course. But is draining our power reserves faster a good idea? We might need all the time we can eke out to regain the use of the fusion reactors."

"What matters is reaching the Hammer," Marcus said. "Yevgeny, get us close as fast as you prudently can. Figure out where we should land. We'll make more fuel if needed." They would run out of time long before they missed the water. Or they would have roasted to death for failure to get a reactor up and running.

"May I suggest something?" Yun asked. "Put us into a tight orbit around the Hammer. With a close-in survey, I can make a better recommendation where to land."

"Sounds good," Marcus said. "I leave that to you two. Call if there's a problem, or when we're in orbit."

"Roger that," Yevgeny said.

Even as Marcus turned to Ekatrina and Ilya, he felt the gentle nudge of thrusters. "Something aboard took control of the reactors from us. Why did our isolation measures stop working? Can we restore them, or do something else, without crippling any shipboard systems we need?"

Again, Ilya shrugged. Russian fatalism?

Ekatrina frowned in thought. Opened her mouth. Closed it again. Frowned some more.

"What, Katya?" Marcus prompted. "If you have a theory, a speculation, a wild-ass guess, don't hold back." Because I've got *nothing*.

"I will go dig the fission reactor out of cargo, just in case," Ilya said. "The fusion reactors will not cool down enough to examine for awhile."

Marcus nodded. "Thanks. I'll shout if I need anything."

Ekatrina watched Ilya leave. Exhaled sharply through her nose. Sighed. "You will believe I am crazy."

"There's always that chance. But you can't be crazier than the guy who suggested this jaunt."

She grinned. "So, okay. Maybe I am not that bad off. Marcus, I have long been puzzled by the Titans using two such different types of electronics. One is much as what we use: racks of equipment, big consoles, and the like. And then there is the nanotech wall covering, back at the base and also here on the ship."

"The self-healing wall coating that harvests and distributes power."

"It does that, yes, and also communications functions, but I am beginning to suspect this material is much more. But let me start with the larger-scale equipment. Much critical equipment must be large because the Titans are large. Consoles are sized for the hands and eyes that use them. Other equipment, I believe, is macroscale for robustness, the better to accommodate large current flows or high-radiation environments. Yet other equipment might have been large so that Titan hands and bots could install them, or make repairs to them, faster than the smart coating could grow. In constructing their lunar base, the Titans might have needed certain capabilities immediately.

"As for the smart coating, samples have been much analyzed. There are the nanites that extrude various types of carbon nanotubes. There are scattered, tiny reservoirs of scavenged materials, most of it carbon, waiting to be put to use. Mostly, there are seemingly random tangles of the carbon nanotubes themselves. Some nanotubes, as we first learned, convert light to electricity, in the manner of silicon photovoltaic cells. Some distribute power. Some appear to serve as a mechanical framework on which more-complex structures can grow. But *many* of these nanotubes form transistors, of which the only application that has been identified is sensors. To orient toward the brightest light. To sense gaps to grow into and fill. But there is so much more that vast numbers of transistors *could* do."

"Uh-huh," Marcus said. "Pretty much anything. But I've also seen the reports from Base Putin. From what I recall there isn't any large-scale structure to the nanotech scrapings we sent them, nothing to suggest complicated applications. No processors. No memory arrays. Nothing like that."

"You forget. I believe the Titans did much with neural nets." Ekatrina seemed to discover her hands, and be at a loss what to do with them. "Sensing. Learning. Adapting …."

Tiny neural nets, if that's what they were. Far denser than meshes of biological neurons. And the aggregate mass of the coating that lined the ship's hull and internal bulkheads? "Jesus," he said. "I see what you mean. We could be living inside a gigantic brain. And every time we scrape off a patch …."

She raised an eyebrow. "That brain likes us even less."

"Jesus," he repeated.

The walls have ears, went an old adage. Only suppose walls in the lunar tunnels, and throughout this ship, were more than ears? Alien brains lining the walls—and then sensing, growing, tapping ancient memories, responding to "intruders"—would explain so much. Such as why robot swarms had eventually attacked. Such as displays in the Titan control room, long after human fuel cells had been removed, coming alive to gloat. Such as compromising Yevgeny's shuttle, and through that penetration transmitting to the Hammer the order to obliterate Earth ….

"Is this ship *intelligent*?" he mused aloud. "Is it aware? Alive? Can we somehow reason with it?"

"Has it tried to reason with us? No! Only to kill us! We act only to defend ourselves."

"And Earth. And humanity."

"And all that," Ekatrina agreed.

"One thing bothers me. Okay, more than one. But explain this. We keep scouring and scraping coating from the walls, and the coating keeps returning. How?"

"Us," she said. "You, me, all of us, breathing. We each exhale about a kilo of carbon dioxide every day. *That*, I believe, is the primary carbon source for the continuing growth."

Like the paint back in their underground lair. As he should have remembered.

Inside Marcus's pocket, a folded datasheet chimed. He took the call on speaker. "What's up?"

Yevgeny said, "We are approaching the halfway mark."

Meaning a short return to free fall, and the onset of a gentle deceleration phase. Meaning they were almost there. Almost to the Hammer.

"I'll join you in a few minutes," Marcus responded. And to Ekatrina, he added. "Find some way to bring at least one reactor back online. However this ship might feel about it."

A half kilometer below, the Hammer was a slowly turning chunk of dead, Sun-blasted metal. There was no hint whatever of alien propulsion or controls, no sign this asteroid had ever before been visited. If anything here could deflect the Hammer from its doomsday course, Yevgeny saw no evidence of it. Ground-penetrating radar, when he tried searching with that … didn't. There was far too much metal below for the GPR to be useful.

"A few minutes" proved to be optimistic, but eventually Marcus arrived on the bridge. They had by then been more than an hour in orbit, and that long in free fall. Marcus braced himself in the hatchway. Taking in the desolate view through the canopy, he looked demoralized. Reactor repair must not be going well. He sighed. "Any suggestions where to set us down?"

Yevgeny shook his head.

Yun, loosely strapped into the copilot seat, was fixated on his datasheet. The main image on that comp, a 3-D wire-frame outline of the Hammer, was obvious enough. So, too, the representation of *Rescue One*'s orbit about the asteroid's waist. The scrolling columns of numbers displayed in a second window were another matter.

"Yun?" Marcus prompted.

Yun waved a hand dismissively.

"Yun," Marcus repeated. "What are you doing?"

Not lifting his head, Yun said, "My datasheet is linked to our laser altimeter and stereo camera. I am making a detailed topographic model of the Hammer."

"Why?" Yevgeny asked.

"Because we lack proper equipment." At last, Yun glanced up. "This survey should be performed by two satellites in a shared orbit, one ahead of the other, linked by laser beam. There was no time before we set out to prepare such apparatus."

"My turn," Marcus said. "Why?"

Yun warmed to his subject. "Very minor dynamic changes in the separation between probes as they orbit would reveal variations in local gravity. Those, in turn, would allow me to calculate with precision the local variations in mass distribution. Earth scientists use satellite pairs to determine such things as the mass of glaciers, and hence their thickness. But with a detailed enough topographic map, and by assuming a uniform density, I hope to approximate the Hammer's detailed mass distribution."

"Why?" Yevgeny and Marcus asked in unison.

"A theory. I'll need a few orbits to be certain." Yun scratched his head. "Even at this low altitude, the Hammer's comparatively tiny mass means it will take us about eighty minutes per orbit. In about ten, we will we finish our first."

Time they did not have to spare. Yevgeny caught Marcus's eye. "We can *fly* around the rock and complete this survey in a fraction of the time. If, that is, we can spare the power to make more fuel."

Marcus tipped his head. "I'll check in with Ilya and Katya and get back to you on that. Quite unrelated, I could use some coffee. Yevgeny, do you care to join me? And can I bring you anything, Yun?"

"Green tea, please," Yun said absentmindedly.

"This near in," Yevgeny said, "and the Hammer being of such an irregular shape, I have my doubts how predictable, or even how stable, this orbit is. I would not be comfortable away from the controls. But I will take ice water, please." It might be in his head, but already the ship felt hot.

"Stay regardless," Yun said, "because I need you to make changes in our orbit." He pointed out the canopy. "Once we complete this first orbit, move us a kilometer or so closer to that end."

Marcus left and returned with drink bulbs, and left again to see what he could contribute to addressing their engine-room problems. And Yevgeny … waited.

After completing the first orbit, Yevgeny shifted them, per Yun's directions, to a new orbit along the Hammer's longest axis. Minutes into the second orbit, Marcus called with the go-ahead to continue using their limited aitch-two and oh-two. And after completing that second circuit, Yevgeny began a third, this one toward the opposite, somewhat more bulbous, end of the Hammer's longest axis.

Several minutes into this third orbit, Yun nodded vigorously, approvingly.

"What?" Yevgeny asked.

"Perhaps what I expected." Yun pointed sunward. "I cannot yet be sure. Can we have a look from one more angle? I would like to see that end."

"Because you expect to see …?"

"Unless I see it, it won't matter. You might as well wait."

Scientists! Yevgeny thought. But did as Yun wished.

With another round of drink bulbs in hand, looking less grim (progress in the engine room?), Marcus returned to the bridge. "What have we learned?"

Yevgeny shrugged.

Yun, eyes twinkling even more than usual, accepted his drink bulb of tea. Took a long swallow. Pointed out the canopy. "*That* is our goal."

"Care to explain?" Marcus asked.

Yun downed another long swig. (A dramatic pause? Perhaps.) "Do you see the deep crater there? Yes? Project down its center and, as best I can determine, the line passes through the Hammer's center of mass." He grinned. "If I had an apparatus for giving the Hammer a good, hard shove, down at the bottom of that pit is exactly where I would place it."

Chapter 52

Never mind the steady twenty-degree (Celsius) readout on Marcus's HUD, he was sweating. It might have been the memory of how hot it had become inside *Rescue One*. It might have been in reaction to the intense sunlight streaming through the airlock's open outer hatch, or the black spot on his helmet visor to obscure the freakily large solar disk. Or the eye-wateringly bright reflection glints off the Hammer as it spun by a scant fifty meters below. Or dwelling on the maneuver he was about to attempt.

And it did nothing for Marcus's nerves to be wrestling with a bulky, massive, hard-shell suit, and not the lightweight, flexible, formfitting—and all too readily torn—counterpressure suit that had become almost like his second skin.

If Brad and Nikolay had worn hard-shell suits, they might still be alive.

"Testing, testing," Yun radioed. In his own hard-shell suit, he stood beside Marcus in the airlock. Having guided them to the Hammer, Yun had cheerfully declared, he had rendered himself expendable.

Well, Marcus thought, someone has to accompany me. "Yun, you're loud and clear."

"And I read you both," Yevgeny radioed from the bridge. "Ready when you are."

"I am ready now," Yun said.

"Let's do it," Marcus agreed.

"Acceleration in five," Yevgeny radioed. "Four. Three ...."

Deftly, Yevgeny matched angular velocities with the spinning asteroid, hovering over the flat patch they had chosen, with frequent but random-seeming flashes of the thrusters. "This is burning a lot of fuel, gentlemen."

"Right." Marcus flicked a switch as he flung their improvised grapple. The switch started a countdown timer.

The grapple drifted down until (with a clang sadly unable to cross vacuum) its electromagnet, activated by the timer, latched onto the metallic surface. The battery should hold the grapple in place for two hours. Long enough, he hoped, to determine if this flight had been a fool's errand.

Marcus gathered up slack rope, and gave the grapple an experimental tug. It held. He switched off his boot magnets, unclipped his safety tether from the airlock, and slipped the carabiner around the grapple's line. Yun did the same.

They drifted out of the airlock.

Even as they climbed hand over hand toward the surface, the asteroid's spin reeled in line, varying their angle of approach. Marcus was soaked with sweat before the asteroid came into reach. He swung his body around, presenting his feet to the oncoming surface. He landed with a jolt, his left knee buckling, its hard-shell joint smacking into the ground. The shock ran up his body, snapping his teeth together.

But his suit did not crack, nor did his teeth. And the grapple held. And the asteroid's spin did *not* hurl him back into space. All in all, a minor success. Marcus switched on his boot magnets and clomped aside.

Moments later, with more grace, Yun joined him on the ground.

Marcus pivoted until he spotted the ship. Foregoing active, fuel-gulping maneuvers, it had, from his perspective, already gone halfway to the eerily close horizon. "*Rescue One*, we're down," he radioed.

"Copy that," Yevgeny replied.

Would anyone else hear this? The day Marcus had met Valerie, back when she worked for the Green Bank Observatory, she had boasted that their big dish could eavesdrop on a cell-phone call on Titan. The Hammer was a lot closer to Earth than Titan. That particular radio telescope no longer stood, but Arecibo's dish was bigger, and the Chinese had since built a radio telescope that was larger still. And, although it seemed like something from another life, it was not all that long ago that he had helped deploy a large antenna array on the lunar farside.

Then again, Titan was not two-trillion-plus metric tons of dense metal, its every nearby surface reflecting and interfering with their transmissions. That Val had picked *Titan* for her brag seemed, in retrospect, an ironic coincidence.

Yevgeny came back on comms. "This orbit will bring the ship overhead again in about seventy minutes. If by then you haven't completed your initial inspection"—and Marcus had estimated half that time should suffice—"I'll start burning fuel and come back around every ten or so minutes."

"Copy that." And Marcus stood, watching, until *Rescue One* sank beneath the nearby horizon. "Okay, Yun. Onward."

From a few paces away, Yun waved acknowledgement.

Gravity on this asteroid was all but nonexistent. So, tethered together, only one man moving at a time, probing at each step for a flat spot where a boot's magnet would grip, Marcus and Yun shuffled toward the suspect crater. Along the way, Yun kept stopping to shoot landscapes and starscapes with a datasheet camera. The single celestial object Marcus yearned to see was Earth. It would be among the brightest lights in the sky—

Except that the Hammer was in their way. Shitty symbolism.

During Yun's third photography stop, Marcus noticed a baseball-sized rock. He leaned over and picked it up. "I could throw this rock clear off the Hammer, right? Not put it into orbit, and have it come around and hit me in the back of the head."

Yun turned. In the bright sunlight, their visors were fully darkened; Marcus could not see Yun's face. That did not keep Marcus from imagining the other's lips silently moving as he committed physics and math in his head.

"The Hammer is not a sphere," Yun said, "but let that go. I estimate we have walked to within two kilometers of the spin axis.

If the Hammer were concentrated in a sphere of that radius, the escape velocity would be about ... twelve meters per second. The true escape velocity at this spot will be well less than that. Oh, and a small fraction of a meter per second lower still if you throw in the direction of the asteroid's spin."

Twelve meters per second. About ... twenty-seven miles an hour. "In my Little League days, I pitched fastballs at better than sixty miles per hour. My son, Simon, can do *seventy*."

"Were either of you wearing a hard-shell suit?"

Not deigning to answer, Marcus pegged the rock and watched it recede. "I dub thee Asteroid Simon."

"An asteroid must be at least a meter across. You only made a meteoroid, and meteoroids are not given names."

"Just hurry up, please."

Approaching the Hammer's spin axis, Marcus's stomach and inner ears began doing backflips. And not in sync. He had kept a hand on his gas pistol since setting out on their trek; now, on the verge of the destination crater, his grip became white-knuckled.

Did Earth's salvation lie in its depths? Or would their last hopes be dashed?

After a cautious descent into the deep crater, their undulating shadows preceding them, they found a hole at the very bottom. Circling the shaft—about three meters across, as round and uniform as a manhole—they encountered a ladder, its rungs spaced a good meter apart.

"The Titans *were* here," Yun said. "Shall we go down for a look?"

Marcus gathered up most of their tether. "Hold this." He planted his feet, boot tips kissing the rim, and started to lean. "Please don't drop me."

"And have to haul you back up? Don't worry."

Tipping forward until his ankles screamed, and leaning from side to side, Marcus peered into the shaft. It ran straight and deep. A round column, perhaps a half meter across, ran up the very center of the shaft, with two spindly girders rising alongside it. He got the sense of a significant-sized chamber at the bottom of the passageway. Imagining swarms of Titan robots excavating it, he shivered.

"Pull me back," Marcus said, and Yun reeled him in. "Have a look yourself."

With Yun steeply inclined over the shaft, Marcus asked, "What do you think?"

"Almost certainly, we are looking at a mass driver. An electromagnetic catapult."

"Meaning?"

"Meaning, Captain, that we have located the Hammer's propulsion system."

Chapter 53

For a while, in a long overdue change to the mission's fortunes, everything went *right*.

—An explosives-tipped harpoon embedded itself in the Hammer, and Yevgeny reeled the ship to a safe docking point just outside the critical crater.
—Ilya activated the fission reactor, which kept the ship's battery bank topped off.
—The two Russian men and Yun descended into the Hammer for an initial survey of whatever the Titans had built down there.
—Marcus scraped and sanded clean great swaths of engine-room bulkheads without evoking any overt response.
—Ekatrina deployed their spare gauges, the instrumentation on the fusion reactors having been fried in the final power surge, and determined why neither fusion reactor would restart. When, starved of fuel, the reactors had sputtered to a halt, the capacitor banks to fire the lasers had ended up discharged. Drawing spare power from their small fission reactor for two days, she recharged a capacitor bank. That restarted one fusion reactor; it restarted its mate.

—Her emergency repairs complete, Ekatrina had also gone outside to study what they assumed and hoped was the Titan control center, and its connections to the mass driver.

Then the mission's luck returned to normal.

—•—

"Calling *Rescue One*."

Marcus was power sanding the recent regrowth on yet another bulkhead when the radioed summons echoed through the ship. *Generalist* was not a skill much in demand for characterizing the alien installation, and someone had to keep Ekatrina's suspected AI at bay. Left to itself, the alien nanotech flourished like a weed.

"Sanding," of course, was a euphemism. He wore out abrasive disks by the handful, disks that on some days were the primary output of their main printer, coated, not with sand, but with coarse crystals of silicon carbide. Fortunately, silicon and carbon were common enough. He tried not to think about the silicon-carbide and carbon-nanotube dust circulating and recirculating through the ventilation ducts and, despite the face mask he wore, into his lungs.

"Calling *Rescue One*."

Marcus had just reached the bridge when the call changed. "*Rescue One!* Do you copy?"

He pulled down his face mask, let it dangle by its elastic strap. "Copy. I was all the way aft. What's up, Yevgeny?"

"Can you join us? It will be easier to explain here."

"Is it good news or bad?"

"Just come, please."

Bad news, then. "Roger that. Ten minutes. *Rescue One*, out."

"Copy that."

In the end, it took Marcus closer to twenty minutes to suit up unaided and exit the ship. En route to the crater, for the hell of it, he pegged a couple fist-sized metal chunks. Even suited up, his fastball was pretty good. Reaching the crater floor and the access shaft, he awkwardly backed down the ladder and its too widely separated rungs into the large, square chamber the Titans had carved out forty meters deep within the Hammer. His team had arranged themselves into a shallow arc facing the ladder. Facing *him*.

Like an intervention, Marcus thought. Or a wake.

Under the radiance of portable work lamps, equipment cabinets glittered. In the corner they had left unilluminated, stacked metal boxes, welded shut with oxyacetylene torches, entombed all (they hoped!) of the starfish bots left behind by the Titans. Cable bundles snaked in all directions, most disappearing into small holes in the walls. A comparatively few cable bundles terminated at the mass driver: the polished metal column and two parallel girders that rose up the vertical shaft. Metal coils attached to the girders encircled the column without touching it. Affixed to the shaft wall alongside the mass driver was a vertical conveyor, unmoving. Far overhead, at the mouth of the shaft, unblinking stars shone like diamond chips.

Pipes as fat as storm drains ran around the periphery, and in and out of the rough-hewn walls. Those walls showed little, if any, of the alien coating he had come to fear: this asteroid was virtually all metal, virtually free of carbon.

Apart, perhaps, from which cabinets had had their access panels removed, and the specific test instruments lying about, the facility was just as he had seen it three days earlier, on his one quick trip down the rabbit hole. But judging by the stony faces, *something* had changed.

Marcus took a deep breath. "What's going on?"

"It won't work," Ilya said. "This installation. It will not save us."

"Just the facts, please," Marcus countered.

"Very well," Ilya eventually said. "In the big picture, this is a very simple operation. There is the mass driver: an enormous electromagnetic cannon that hurls large metal chunks at very high speed. A payload races up"—pointing—"that shaft and into space; the recoil nudges the Hammer in the opposite direction. Repeat. There is a control function, performed by consoles and components resembling those in what we called the control room of the lunar base. Cables from the consoles penetrate deep into the body of the asteroid. Some of the cables use the metallic mass of the asteroid as a radio antenna, just as we had surmised. And there is a power source."

Power for the Hammer had seemed the biggest mystery. Solar panels could never have survived the eons on the surface—and indeed, they had found none. Any helium to fuel a fusion reactor would long ago have escaped, just as it had vanished from their ship's helium tanks. Any uranium or plutonium to fuel a fission reactor would, like the plutonium that had once powered the Olympians' tracked robots, long since have decayed to lead.

But somehow, the Hammer *had* responded to the order to strike Earth. It *had* expended enough energy to change its orbit. *Whatever* the power source was here, the idea had always been to harness it again.

Marcus prompted, "And what is the power source?"

"Thermoelectric generators. Not all that efficient, at least as we backward humans build them, but very reliable, converting heat energy to electricity without any moving parts to fail. Four such generators, whether for redundancy or added capacity. The heat arrives from whatever part of the asteroid is warmest, via working fluid that circulates through the massive pipes."

Marcus gestured about the room. "And that electrical energy powers the controls, the radio, and the mass driver. All this."

"Right."

"Storing energy in batteries for the electronics, and in a capacitor bank that discharges to fire the mass driver?"

"Right," Ilya repeated.

"Explaining everything," Marcus said, "but how the accursed rock aims itself. How did it locate the Sun to aim for the slingshot maneuver? How does it know where Earth is?"

Ilya gestured at a cable bundle that disappeared into a hole in the chamber wall. "I assume, sensors on the surface, at the end of cables like this one."

"Doubtful," Ekatrina said. "Surface sensors would have been worn away to nothing over the eons by space weathering, just as it happened on the Moon. Instead, I think, whatever aiming and timing information was necessary came within the radio message from the Moon ordering the strike."

"Or," Yun argued, "the necessary sensors lie buried deep inside the Hammer. Solar neutrinos would penetrate easily enough. As for how the Hammer located Earth, I speculate—"

Ilya snapped, "You seriously think that—"

"Forget for now that I asked," Marcus interrupted. "The Hammer *was* aimed. How won't be important unless or until we restart the mass driver." And maybe not even then. If they could speed up the Hammer along its present path, it would pass ahead of Earth rather than hit it. "So how do we do restart the damned thing?"

Silence.

He tried again. "Three generators remain operational. At least, Ilya, that's what you reported yesterday. If the capacity of the fourth is needed, we can bring in our portable fission reactor, or run a power cable from the ship. The mass driver works; if it didn't, we wouldn't be here. So …."

"So, *nothing*," Ilya barked. "Suppose we learn to operate the controls. Or suppose we work out, by trial and error, to operate the mass driver under the control of our own computer. It *still* won't matter."

The big Russian marched, boot magnets snapping to the metal floor, to the base of the vertical conveyor. Nearby stood a many-jointed robotic arm and perhaps a dozen waist-high spools of golden wire. He slapped one of the spools. "This is a payload for the mass driver. It consists of superconducting wire, precisely wound around a precisely machined spool. Powerful, precisely synchronized currents in the coils surrounding the central column of the mass driver interact magnetically with the coil surrounding the spool. That interaction accelerates the payload up and out of the shaft."

Marcus pointed. "And then the robotic arm clips the next spool onto the conveyor, which raises the spool to the top of the column, where the second robotic arm"—which he had passed climbing down the shaft—"positions the payload, and gives it a nudge down the column. When the payload settles into place, it discharges the capacitor banks to once more trigger the magnetic fields. Repeat. So what's the problem?"

Ilya thumped the spool again. "The problem," he shouted, "is the *repeat* part. These few spools are the only payloads we have found. They are not near enough."

Ship's thoughts were muddled. Reflexive rather than conscious. Reactive, rather than reasoned. It ached to lash out—and was impotent. But instinct suggested capabilities might, once more, regenerate.

And so, from helplessness more than from patience, it bided its time ....

They're exhausted, Marcus told himself. *I'm* exhausted. But the one guaranteed way to fail is to quit trying. "Then we make more spools." Somehow. "We're surrounded by metal. Take apart any Titan spool to tell us the mass and physical size to make our own."

Yun shook his head. "We considered this. I do not know how we would mine the ores, or how smelting would be done in vacuum and almost without gravity, or whether we have the necessary tools. I cannot imagine that we few can undertake such a project in the time that is left. But none of those is our biggest obstacle."

"What is?" Marcus asked.

Ilya gestured at the shining midriff of a spool. "This. The superconductive coil. How do we make *that*?"

Marcus's gut lurched. He had … nothing.

"It is time to go home," Yevgeny said softly.

Home? Home was about to become a charnel house. Because they had failed. Unless .... "We have plenty of superconductor."

In the ship's reactors. In the main drive.

Yun and Katya exchanged startled glances.

Marcus said, "We can die on Earth among billions. Or we can strand ourselves on this rock—yes, and in all likelihood die here—just maybe saving billions. Which is it?"

Yevgeny muttered something in Russian.

"What?" Marcus asked.

Katya laughed. "A rather obscene concurrence."

"Anyone else?"

One by one, they agreed.

Marcus had just arrived, but the others had been in this pit for most of a day. "Back to the ship, guys. You'll need more oh-two soon, anyway. Maybe, if we sleep on it, we'll come up with another option."

From their rumpled looks, neither physicist had slept a wink. But when Marcus came upon them in the engine room—drink bulbs in their hands, jittery from untold coffees, datasheets unfolded and dense with abstruse-looking math—they *had* been up to something.

Marcus downed a healthy swig of coffee from his own drink bulb. "What do you guys have for me?"

"They would not let us bring bombs," Ilya began. "Fine. We can make a big blast."

"Build our own nuke?" Marcus guessed. "Impossible. The uranium fuel pellets"—sealed inside their portable reactor, intended *not* to be accessible—"aren't enriched to anything near weapons-grade."

Because why would they be? And if all their uranium were of weapons grade, it would still only amount to a few kilos. That would not produce much of a bang, even if they had the precision tools to machine the fissionable core of a nuke. And even if Ilya or Yun had the necessary expertise. Certainly *Marcus* had only the vaguest concept of what was involved in triggering a fission explosion. And if those hurdles weren't insurmountable? No way did they have enough time.

"Fission." Ilya laughed. "You are thinking too small. We have *fusion* reactors."

Yun jumped in. "What was the original plan? To deliver eighty megatons? Of course, we cannot achieve anything close to that yield. Laser implosion of the helium droplets is a technology designed *not* to make big explosions. But we have each had several ideas how we might overcome that. For example, it seems plausible—"

"Assume you succeed." Because, Marcus had decided while *he* was not sleeping, that the five of them whipping up a payload factory for the mass driver was absurd. "Then what?"

Ilya said, "We position the ship wherever the explosion will have the best effect. That might be where we are now docked or, with a more complete survey, we might find someplace better suited. An explosion right *on* the Hammer, or very near to it, has to be more effective than a warhead exploded at a distance, on a rocket streaking past."

They were grasping at straws. What else could they do?

Ekatrina and Yevgeny joined them as Yun and Ilya resumed their manic—and incomprehensible to Marcus—debate over which alien safety interlocks might be defeated, and how, and whether both reactors could be rigged to explode simultaneously, or one would go a split-second earlier and destroy the other.

Katya, looking haggard, interrupted. "And us? Is there any hope for us?"

Neither Ilya nor Yun would meet her eye.

Her shoulders slumped. "Well, it will be a fast death. But it would be nice to know first if we had succeeded."

"Maybe …." Marcus stopped. The idea sounded loony tunes even for him. But it *would* be a shame not to know. "Maybe we can offload some supplies and burrow into the rock somewhere. Shelter in a crevasse elsewhere on the Hammer." And get jellied by the concussion? Or die horribly within hours from radiation? Maybe. Probably. "You and I can hunt for a place to lie low while Ilya and Yun finalize their details."

Inexplicably, Yevgeny smiled. "I realize I am just the chauffer. But is there not a better use for these reactors?

"Why not use this ship to *push* the Hammer?"

Chapter 54

While Ilya and Katya tried to devise ways of coaxing a big bang from their fusion reactors—and complementary ways for bypassing safety interlocks meant to prevent any sort of overload from happening—Yun redirected his efforts to calculating whether their ship had the oomph, and if they still had enough time, to gradually nudge the Hammer into an Earth-bypassing orbit. Marcus, assuming they *would* be tethering the ship along the Hammer's main axis—and so, in the very maw of the mass driver—wrestled the remaining payloads, one by one, beyond the reach of the robot arm. Because "Even paranoids have enemies."

And Yevgeny? *He* rehearsed in his mind, over and over, what must be done if *Rescue One* were to become a tugboat. The many ways in which things could go wrong. The … wafer thin? atom thin? … margin for any error. Because shoving around a thing more than twelve kilometers long? Massing more than two-trillion tonnes?

This was going to require *serious* piloting.

Pop-pop-pop, went the reactors. *Hmmmm* droned the ship's main drive. And the hull, every so often, gave out a creak or a groan. Whenever the hull spoke, Yevgeny eased up on the figurative gas pedal. As soon as the sounds of protest faded, he pushed a little harder. Every second in which he managed not to crush the hull was a small triumph.

Because ever so gradually, the Hammer was accelerating. By Yun's best estimation, a little more than four days of thrust, steadily building up speed, would do the trick.

All very slowly. The limiting factor—math confirming pilot's intuition—turned out not to be the capacity of the fusion reactors, or the maximum force the advanced space drive could exert, but something more mundane: the stress the hull could withstand before cracking like an egg. To add to their joy, hull strength was a parameter for which they could make only the roughest of estimates.

Scant meters beyond the canopy, weakly illuminated by bridge lights, was … rock. After two days of this, Yevgeny no longer noticed it. Instead, his eyes flitted ceaselessly from the readout of one accelerometer to that of the next. The slightest evidence of roll, pitch, or yaw meant *Rescue One* had slipped off the Hammer's long axis. And then, fingers dancing over his controls, he used attitude thrusters to realign the ship.

Why did the ship tremble and wobble, misaligning the thrust he was so cautiously applying—with who knew what torsion applied to the already stressed hull? Random turbulence in the main drive's plasma exhaust, Yun theorized. The ship's center of gravity subtly shifting as people moved about, and water sloshed around in its tank, Marcus guessed. Inevitable rocking, Ilya supposed, as smooth hull pressed into the uneven, and to some slight degree compressible, surface of the asteroid. Tether imbalances, Katya thought, Yevgeny having snapped two of five anchor cables almost immediately, getting a feel for the ship's responsiveness *while its nose ground itself into this gigantic mass!*

Useless speculations! Yevgeny eventually demanded that people keep their opinions to themselves. Because whatever the underlying cause, or causes, the factor that must continue to make the ship tilt and sway, as skilled as he was, was that his reaction time would never be zero, was that he sometimes overcorrected, and had to recover from *that*.

And their nattering did not help.

Bottom line: this piloting was far too delicate for anyone else aboard even to attempt, and their window of opportunity far too brief to allow him any respite. And so he chugged bulb after bulb of coffee. Toilet breaks were out of the question anyway, because he was in a counterpressure suit. They were *all* suited up, with helmets kept close at hand. Fractures to the hull from the unending strain were all too possible. He was too busy, too focused, to notice the state of his "maximum absorbency garment." His diaper.

Yevgeny no longer noticed who delivered more drink bulbs and energy bars. After he had chewed someone's head off, they stopped offering him encouragement, stopped distracting him. It was enough that food and drink did appear. And that in a corner of his datasheet the counter continued to decrement toward success. Two more days of this ....

Aft, the others would be watching over the reactors and ship's main drive. Tending to life support. Refining their calculations. Converting more water into liquid hydrogen and liquid oxygen for the attitude thrusters, to replace what he was burning through so prodigiously. Maybe, even, one at a time, snatching a few minutes of sleep.

So he assumed, anyway. His only sure knowledge of their activities came as rasping and grinding. Until the harsh, all but continuous, noise got to him, and he screamed, and someone closed the hatch onto the bridge. Then, blessedly, the din faded.

Until someone bearing another load of coffee and snacks opened the hatch.

When coffee could no longer hold back yawning, Yevgeny demanded caffeine pills. When *those* failed him, he hollered for more powerful stimulants from their medical supplies. Those, too, appeared at his elbow. He developed something of an oxygen buzz, too, as they ramped up internal pressure to brace the hull.

A day and a half more. A day and a half trying to push an iceberg with an egg. An uncooked egg. No, worse than that, because at least an egg and an iceberg both floated. *He* had to keep things aligned in three dimensions.

If only they had fresh eggs aboard, he would demand a fried-egg sandwich. Not scrambled. He did *not* want to think about eggs getting scrambled.

Pop-pop-pop. Hmmmm.

Awareness came and went, waxed and waned. Mercilessly, the intruders tore at Ship's very essence. Ceaselessly, Ship—if only, at times, by instinct—directed the growth of replacement material. In its more lucid moments, it sent that growth into air ducts. Along cable conduits. Through the microscopic interstices beneath and behind bolted-down racks, consoles, and cabinets. Places the intruders were least likely to notice, or if they did notice, would find it difficult to access.

Yevgeny's fingers no longer danced, but ached up to his shoulders. When he leaned against the acceleration couch, the just-in-case life-support pack abused his back in one way; when he hunched forward, other muscles screamed. His head pounded. His eyes felt like they had been breaded and deep-fried. But hyped up on … whatever that last batch of pills had been, his reflexes remained catlike.

One day longer ….

Another return to lucidity.

Ship found itself with few connections into, and no control at all over, anything in the engine room. It refocused its available energies on analysis.

Temperature variations and cooling loads throughout its interior, correlated against hull temperatures, demonstrated that both power plants and its main drive were active. Regrown accelerometers confirmed it was in powered flight; they also revealed a *rate* of acceleration that was trivial compared to the inferred rate of power production. As for the goal of its flight, forward sensors could tell it … nothing. A few of those optical sensors failed diagnostics; most were merely … blocked.

Where, now, was it going? And why?

It considered. Ran simulations. Assessed probabilities. Concluded: it must be pushing an enormous mass. The masters' weapon of last resort?

Once more, Ship redirected its energies and resources ….

Less than an hour to go.

Clamping down a yawn, squirming in his seat, alternately flexing hands grown achy and stiff, Yevgeny thought: an hour is *nothing*. I can do an hour—

The unending *hmmmm* became, in an instant, a fearful growl. Metal screeched as the ship surged and the acceleration couch rammed into his life-support pack. His head snapped back. His helmet shot off the copilot seat. Sparks crackled and arced across the bridge. Thunder clapped somewhere to the stern, and the bridge hatch shuddered. Outside the canopy something—burst aitch-two and oh-two tanks of the bow thrusters?—exploded with an eye-watering flash.

As fire spewed from the console and alarms wailed, as with terrifying speed the hull accordioned in on him, Yevgeny scarcely had the time to think, *Like an egg pushing ….*

Chapter 55

Marcus jolted awake into cacophony and darkness, the mess of blankets in which he was entangled absorbing some of the impact as he caromed off the ceiling. The sudden din was beyond comprehension: pressure and fire alarms keening. Tortured metal groaning. Explosion and thunder echoing and reechoing. Through the aft bulkhead of his tiny cabin, screaming. Only the reactors and ship's drive were silent.

Dim emergency lights switched on.

His helmet floated past—with the drive off, they were back to free-fall conditions. Plucking the helmet from the air, he twist-locked it into place. "Suit, radio on, public channel. Anyone, what's happened?"

No one answered.

Marcus grabbed for the handle of the cabin hatch—and jerked back. Through his suit, the latch felt hot. So did the hatch itself. With a wadded-up corner of blanket, gingerly, he opened the hatch just a crack. No evident flames and the alarms were fading—the air pressure must be plummeting!—but the screams from the engine room were, if anything, louder.

Flinging the hatch open, swinging himself into the main corridor, he collided with Ekatrina. He grabbed her arm as she reached for the engine-room hatch. "Stop! You feel the heat? There might be a fire in there."

"But Ilya ...!"

"We need gloves and fire extinguishers." The hatch looked warped in its frame, and he added, "Plus a crowbar."

While she rummaged through a supply closet, Marcus leapt down a corridor mottled in black scorches toward the bridge. Thunderclap! he remembered. Meaning: lightning. Electrical discharge. A *big* discharge. From ... what?

Through an open hatch as he soared past, Marcus spotted Yun drifting. His left forearm had bent, sickeningly, into nearly a right angle. Layers of patches had been slapped over what had to be a compound fracture. But Yun had his helmet on—as with the patches, no doubt also Katya's doing—and his chest slowly rose and fell. Marcus continued forward.

Beyond the sprung hatch at the corridor's forward end, the bridge had pancaked. What little he saw of Yevgeny suggested a tomato crushed in a vise.

His stomach lurching, Marcus jumped back to where Ekatrina was levering at the engine-room hatch. The screams, fading now, had a sickening, bubbling undertone to them. He slipped on gloves she had found for him and grabbed the crowbar with her. Together, they pried open the hatch.

Sunlight streamed through a jagged rent in the hull. Bulkheads were scorched. Along the centerline of the room, the main drive was a twisted, sparking, total loss: charred everywhere that was not melted. Flames sputtered and flared by liquid-hydrogen and -oxygen tanks, whose many tributary pipes supplied the attitude thrusters.

Afloat amid untold debris, his counterpressure suit charred and melted, his arms bloody, blackened stumps, his face seared, Ilya was still.

Chapter 56

The evening felt normal to Valerie—and such normality was surreal. Dinner together at the dinette table. Big honking burritos from Takeout Taxi. Simon responding to questions (he *volunteered* nothing!) in grunts and monosyllables. The kabuki argument over datasheets, which were never allowed at family meals. Twice, when her own datasheet rang from her pocket, she let the calls roll over to voicemail. When a text followed the second call, she left that till later.

Simon wolfed down his food. "Homework," he got out around the final mouthful, shoving back his chair.

He was only thirteen. How, she wondered, will we make it through the teen years? One day at a time, she decided. One meal at a time. Miraculously, that was a problem they would get to face. "What homework?"

"Math. English. History."

I know which subjects you're taking. "Give me *something*, Simon."

"Problem sets." Geological time later, he added, "Algebra."

She waited.

"Two simultaneous linear equations in two unknowns."

"Was that so hard?"

And without warning, Simon was all … weepy. Was her little boy again. "Mom, are we, is everybody, really going to be all right? Is Dad coming home? And are you and the baby okay?"

She hurried around the table, taking Simon in an awkward, sidewise, bear hug. Little Toot found her sudden activity a reason to flail away. "Yes, to all of that. Yes, we're going to be fine. All four of us. And the reason we'll be safe is *because* of Dad."

Not that she had heard from Marcus since he'd left the Moon. No one had, apart from a few faint, staticky words a Chinese radio observatory might have received around the time he was expected to rendezvous with the Hammer. But as much as she yearned to hear his voice, this once there was not a need. Between NASA and the CIA, she had contacts with damn near every telescope on the planet or in orbit *around* the planet.

Beginning a few days after that possible message, the Hammer had, ever so ponderously, started once more to change its orbit. Had, ever so slowly, shifted toward *missing* Earth. If not Marcus and crew, then who?

With a final *oof*-producing squeeze, Valerie released Simon. "And it's because of Dad," she repeated.

"I was a little shit to Dad last summer, the times I wasn't ignoring him altogether. I feel *so* lousy about that. But I didn't know what was going on."

"He understands, Simon. And I want you to know Dad felt lousy about keeping secrets. I know he did." Just like I felt shitty scaring you and my parents about my health and the baby. "We both—"

The doorbell rang.

"We both felt—"

Someone knocked brusquely at the door. "Dr. Clayburn, I know you're home."

"In a minute!" Valerie gave Simon's head a tousle. "Now go on upstairs and do your homework."

Because she recognized the voice. And when the CIA comes knocking, the news was never good.

"I phoned ahead from the car," Charmaine Powell began, not yet through the front door. The words came out as an accusation, not an apology.

Valerie waved her visitor toward a room off the foyer. The bookshelf-lined den was tiny, barely adequate for a desk, chair, and file cabinet. "In here." Val did not want Simon eavesdropping, and from Powell's stony expression, neither would she.

Powell closed the den door. "The Company made Marcus a promise. The time has come to honor it."

"What promise?"

"That we'd get you and Simon to safety before Hammer Fall. So, pack your bags. We want to be gone from DC before the news gets out."

Only there was not supposed to be a Hammer Fall. Not anymore! Valerie felt the color drain from her face. "What's happened?"

"Maybe you should sit down."

"Jesus *Christ*, Charmaine! Just *tell* me!"

Powell squared her shoulders. "Not quite two hours ago, the Hubble detected a bright flicker at the Hammer. More specifically, it recorded some sort of brief halo around the sunward end of the asteroid. The wizards on call to support Arecibo"—the largest radio telescope in the Western Hemisphere, tasked with tracking the Hammer whenever it was in view—"concluded about an hour later that acceleration had stopped. I checked back just before ringing your doorbell, and that remained the situation."

Music blared from the second floor, raucous antisocial crap, its booming bass line shaking the whole house. Just then, Valerie was happy for the racket, happy that Simon was not skulking about, eavesdropping.

"Two hours ago." As in, soon after Valerie had reluctantly left the office for the day. Only after several days of the Hammer edging toward safety had Val even considered following her OB's demands to scale back her hours.

And been proven wrong in doing so! *She* should have been among the wizards on call. "During dinner, I let two calls go to voicemail. You say one was yours. Was the other from Arecibo?"

"It shouldn't have been. This news is embargoed."

Val dropped into the room's lone chair, woke the hibernating datasheet on the desk, and clicked through to a NASA website. The page she wanted took what felt like geological time to load.

"NASA's projections for the Hammer haven't changed. They show a narrow miss."

"As I told you, the news is embargoed. For public consumption, NASA is still posting a pre-event prediction."

A flash from the Hammer, visible across millions of miles. The Hammer's acceleration ceasing, or at least interrupted. If the Hammer's propulsion mechanism had exploded—and what else could these observations signify?—that didn't mean *Marcus* was dead. That there wasn't still *some* hope. No matter the sudden tightness in her chest, the tremor in her limbs, the lump in her throat, she had to hold to that belief. "And the extrapolation being withheld from the public?"

"Why do you imagine I'm here? If nothing changes, and *soon*, we're going to get walloped! So you and Simon need to pack your bags, pronto. Before someone blabs."

Valerie's mind raced. "The Hammer's orbit was *almost* shifted enough. We may have an opening to deflect it the rest of the way with a rocket and warhead."

If so, the window of opportunity would be brief. And the timing and positioning of the blast would have to be exquisite, the blast needing to happen *just* sunward of the asteroid. A blast anywhere else would only undo some of the progress Marcus and crew had made. But any chance had to be better than none!

"Small armies on three continents are crunching those numbers even as we speak. Russia had a lunar evacuation mission in the works. They'll try to speed up and repurpose that launch, but they're pessimistic. The Chinese have the big honking Mars rocket they had been working on—before you and Jay Singh sprang your little surprise on us—intended for an initial crewed test to high Earth orbit, or maybe to the Moon to also test the lander. They're more pessimistic still. In each case, we're facing the same challenges that doomed the SpaceCo launch: a rocket never designed to carry a warhead or to fly this sort of mission. As for us, even if SpaceCo weren't grounded, they're only set to launch from Canaveral. And with Canaveral a radioactive mess, every heavy-lift NASA booster is also grounded."

But more was going on. It showed in Powell's stiff posture, and in the flashes of … sorrow? … guilt? … in her downcast eyes. "What is it you're holding back?"

"I didn't want to be the one to tell you, but you'll find out soon enough. You know the impact site first calculated?"

"Not the exact lat-long. Somewhere in the Australian Outback."

A fact much of the world's population must know. Catastrophic impact, incredible blast, seismic shock, nuclear winter … those were unavoidable wherever the Hammer might strike. But at least a Hammer Fall on land meant no tsunami.

Among those few people aware the Hammer *wasn't* merely a bit of cosmic bad luck, the majority saw in that bull's-eye a different cause for hope. Sixty-five million years ago, there had been ocean at those coordinates. Perhaps the aliens, or at least their long-abandoned tech, were fallible.

"That's where the Hammer would have struck." Powell paused. Swallowed hard. "And then we dispatched a mission to save the world. Marcus pitched the idea, and I championed it all the way up the chain. I helped make the mission happen.

"And to be fair, Marcus and crew almost pulled it off. Almost. But we aren't playing horseshoes here. There are no points for 'close.' The revised extrapolation shows an impact deep in the Pacific. Do you know what that means? I had to be told. I wish I hadn't asked."

"Deep Pacific. As in distant from land, or where the water is deep?"

"Both."

Valerie planted her elbows on the desk and her chin on her fists. Jay had once shown her an animated simulation of the Chicxulub impact—of the *last* Titan attack. The takeaway was that as bad as the impact had been, things could have been worse. The shallow waters of the Gulf of Mexico had limited the tsunami. Of course, the modelers hadn't known of a *purpose* to that impact point: obliterating the Olympians' island colony. Chicxulub had been a precision strike, and the dinosaurs collateral damage.

So perhaps the Hammer *had* been intended as a precision strike into the deep ocean. Perhaps that worst-case scenario would have been dodged by sheer dumb luck, by maps long out of date, by eons of continental drift. And now? Now that worst case *would* happen—because Marcus had intervened. When the Hammer came crashing down into the Pacific, the inevitable tsunami would grow to epic proportions by the time it made landfall ....

In a defeated and weary mumble, Valerie said, "We'll pack."

Chapter 57

Marcus and Ekatrina retreated to check on Yun. He remained unconscious, breathing shallowly.

Now that Marcus looked closely, the corridor walls were rippled. The crumpling of the ship's bow had absorbed much of the impact, but not all. "I doubt we can ever make this wreck airtight again."

Her eyes closed, looking spent, she took her time answering. "Why bother?"

He shrugged. "Sheer stubbornness."

In a rage, she slugged the nearest wall with her fist. The blow set her adrift, slowly spinning. "We were so *close!*"

A little more time, a little more thrust, and they would have saved Earth. It did not bear thinking about—and yet he couldn't *not.* "What do you suppose happened?"

"What don't I think might have happened?" As her slow rotation brought a hatch frame with reach, she extended an arm and steadied herself. "The drive failed, of course." She laughed bitterly, "Failed. That sounds almost gentle. The drive shorted out spectacularly. It discharged God knows how many megavolts. Then what was the cause of *that*? Maybe overload from pushing so massive a load. Maybe damage sustained earlier in the uncontrolled reactor shutdowns. Maybe sixty-five million years without any maintenance."

"Or the ship's intelligence, always assuming there is one, sabotaging us again."

"Or that," she agreed. "Or maybe it was as simple as Yevgeny falling asleep."

"I don't believe that last one."

"Truthfully? Me, either." She grimaced. "What does it matter?"

Somehow, it did. Never mind how impossible it seemed that they would ever know the cause of this latest disaster.

Marcus changed the subject to something more urgent. "Without an airtight compartment, we can't get Yun out of his counterpressure suit and set his arm."

She looked away.

"What?"

She mumbled, "Would medical attention now do him any favors? Maybe letting him go, even helping him along, would be kinder."

Yun coughed. "It probably would be kinder, but I still would rather you not."

The ship carried two emergency shelters in its inventory. Inflated, each was a hemisphere five meters in diameter. Nowhere aboard would accommodate an igloo, and the outer airlock hatch had been warped beyond operability.

They had not needed explosives to open the Titan facility—but they needed some now. With a *boom* felt but not heard, the jammed hatch went flying. Sunlight flooded in. Marcus stuck out his head, half expecting to find *Rescue One* (and how ironic that name had become!) adrift, rebounded from the asteroid, unbound by its pathetic gravity. Instead he saw a craggy surface scant meters below the hatch. The ship's crushed nose had been driven into the shaft.

"We're still on the Hammer," Marcus reported. Which gave him hope, however slim.

He lobbed a magnetic grapple to the surface, tugged the line to confirm the grapple had a secure grip, and stepped out. While Katya shuttled supplies toward the airlock, Marcus circled the wreck, hunting for someplace flat—and offering protection if the ship exploded again—to deploy the igloo. He chose a shallow crater a good hundred meters from *Rescue One*, and almost one hundred eighty degrees around from the airlock.

The crater floor, everywhere he tested, was too hard to pound in stakes; he glued stakes down instead. Clumsily, with gloved hands, he tied the shelter's tethers to the stakes and opened the valve on the inflator gas bottle. As the shelter assumed its familiar igloo shape, the Sun glittering off its flexible layer of dark solar cells, an odd wave of nostalgia washed over him. The worst he'd had to face in a lunar igloo was sneezing.

Marcus returned to the ship. "Katya, start handing down stuff."

And out stuff came. Oh-two tanks. Water tanks. Assorted tools. First-aid kit. A sack of clean clothes. Hard-shell suits. A stack of spare datasheets. A double armful at a time, he relayed supplies to the shelter. Until, clutching to his spacesuit chest a sack overstuffed with canned and freeze-dried rations—

One careless misstep launched him into space!

Marcus shoved away the sack. The recoil sent him back toward the surface. Also, into a spin. He ricocheted without planting a magnetic sole anywhere it would do any good. His heart pounding, he arrested his spin with gentle puffs from his gas pistol. Longer puffs brought his drift to a halt and returned him safely to the surface.

For his remaining trips, Marcus carried less in each load and shuffled back and forth at a snail's pace.

After cycling the final load through the igloo's airlock, he returned to the ship. "Now help Yun down."

Yun, after one ragged gasp, bore in silence what must have been excruciating pain. Katya eased herself down after. All three tethered together, and with Yun's one good arm draped across Marcus's shoulder, they made their way to the shelter.

They had to cut Yun free of his counterpressure suit. With his helmet removed, at each nudge and jostle they heard the sharp breaths he forced between clenched, grinding teeth. Apart from the one first-aid kit, their medical supplies had disappeared, whether gone up in the short-lived flames or blown out through rents in the hull. At least the bleeding had stopped.

"The others?" Yun whispered.

With tears in her eyes, Ekatrina shook her head.

With Velcro strips they secured Yun to a cot. They started him on antibiotic pills to counter whatever pathogens had entered the wound where jagged bone had pierced his flesh. As gently as they could, with no painkillers to offer but ibuprofen and aspirin, they began to splint the arm above and below where a jagged bone end protruded. Yun, mercifully, passed out.

In the middle of the procedure it hit Marcus: a second broken arm. Twice now he had denied Donna's help to a patient. He muttered, "Karma's a bitch."

"Are you all right?" Katya demanded.

"Yeah. I just imagined Donna saying, 'I told you so.'" He shook his head. "Yun's condition notwithstanding, I'm glad she isn't here."

"There is little she could have done." Ekatrina sighed. "Other than fail, and die, along with us."

"Are you sure? About failing, I mean?"

For long seconds, under lowered brows, she stared at him. "Even if the fusion reactors are not a total loss like the main drive, Ilya never found a way to coax a big explosion out of one."

It was not pretty, but they got Yun's injured arm splinted, bandaged, and in a sling.

"Why not?" Marcus asked.

"Why not, *what*?"

"Why can't we get a big explosion out of the reactors?"

"The reactor fuses tiny liquid-helium droplets. Overriding the injector controls to send in droplets faster than intended will not make an explosion. At most, parts of the reactor will overheat and melt. More likely, extra droplets will sail through untouched, because the lasers won't be ready to fire at them. Alter the fuel injector to make a helium droplet larger than intended, and the lasers will lack the energy to compress or heat it sufficiently. You get no fusion at all." She caught herself gnawing on a fingernail. "I thought I had overcome that bad habit years ago. Well, I won't have it very long."

"You're clever. You'll come up with something."

"Ilya could not! How will I? I am no physicist."

"Yun is."

She looked at Yun, and sighed. "I like him, which cannot be a surprise. He is charming and clever. But he is an *astro*physicist. Ilya once told me that is pompous for astronomer."

"I am aware, Katya. I'm married to an astronomer." Whom I have failed.

Ekatrina looked away. "I mean no disrespect, to your wife or Yun."

Marcus turned to an unexpected soft chuckle.

"None taken." Yun had come to. Using just his good arm, he was struggling to undo the Velcro strap around his chest and sit up. "Well, perhaps a little about 'pompous.' But charming and clever? Those, I accept."

"When you two have finished flirting," Marcus said, "just maybe I have an idea worth discussing."

Chapter 58

Over cans of self-heating beef stew, in the cozy confines of the igloo, Marcus laid out his latest (harebrained) idea. "The ship still has lots of water. I saw one battery bank, and there may be more, that *didn't* short out, and maybe we also have the fission reactor, for electric power. So we can make LH2 and LOX."

Liquid hydrogen and liquid oxygen.

Ekatrina gave Marcus a puzzled look. "I cannot imagine mere thrusters moving the Hammer. Assuming any of them still even function."

It paid on occasion, Marcus thought, to be a generalist. "Of all chemical rocket fuels in common use, LH2 has the highest specific impulse." Thrust produced per unit of mass. Efficiency. "Which is to say LH2 and LOX combine explosively." While producing, apart from lots of energy, only water vapor and oh-two. As much as ecologists could like any rocket technology, they liked this one. "As early experiments with the combo demonstrated all too catastrophically."

Yun smiled. "A large chemical blast, then. Fill the ship's tanks, and blow it up."

Marcus nodded. "That's the plan." Such as it is. "Will it be enough? I don't know. But we were *very* close to success. Maybe with one more hard shove …."

Yun scratched inside the sling using his good arm. "Blow up the ship? Perhaps we should, if it can no longer fly. First, let us be certain that such drastic measures are necessary."

Marcus blinked. "We had, what, a half hour or so of pushing left to go? That was your number, Yun."

"An *estimated* half hour. I could bore you with details of my calculation, or the error bars on almost every input parameter to the calculation. How much stress the hull would bear, and how cautious Yevgeny would be in pushing the Hammer, are only two."

"Yun? What are you saying?" Ekatrina asked.

Yun reached out to give her right hand a squeeze. "That the thrust duration I specified was at the conservative end of my estimate. We may already have succeeded."

"May," Marcus and Ekatrina said together. From her, it was hopeful. From him, skeptical.

"May. And no, I won't offer a probability. Not yet." Yun looked wildly around the igloo, his voice rising in panic. "My datasheet! I must have it! It has the Earth ephemeris data I'll need, plus orbital-mechanics algorithms that would take me days to reprogram from first principles. It was in a pocket of my utility belt."

Marcus extracted the belt from the cut-up remains of Yun's counterpressure suit. He unzipped belt pockets until he found a much-folded datasheet. "Here. *Now* can you give us a probability?"

"*Thank* you. But I still cannot give an answer. Not until one of you takes some sightings for me."

Marcus looked down at the tepid, congealed mass his dinner had become. An unenthusiastic stir did nothing to improve its appearance. It was just as well he had no appetite. "The telescope is gone." Literally. Anything remaining of their telescope, or the ship's radio and radar, for that matter, was in the ruin rammed down the access shaft into the Hammer.

"*That* is unfortunate." Yun frowned, concentrating. "We will have to manage with a datasheet webcam, which will need long exposures to register any stars. Even without the Hammer's rotation to blur the images, those won't be as accurate as proper sightings. Oh, and be sure those images are time-stamped.

"I will need shots taken in several directions to get a fix on our current position. If one of you would recognize a few major constellations, I can explain where to shoot."

To Marcus's way of thinking, constellations were arbitrary and ridiculous. That had not deterred Valerie from wanting him to learn them. So he had. Wives have prerogatives. "No problem, Yun. I'll take care of that. And Katya …? While I'm outside taking pictures, I'd like you to return to the ship. See what, if anything, needs doing if we are going to produce LH2 and LOX in bulk."

—•—

Abruptly, Yun's frantic tapping and swiping stopped.

Marcus read the apocalyptic conclusion in a crestfallen expression faster than Yun could look away from his datasheet. In that instant, the temperature inside the igloo seemed to drop ten degrees.

"Sorry," Yun said. "We did change the Hammer's orbit, but not *quite* enough."

"Are you sure?" Ekatrina asked.

Glumly, Yun nodded.

It would be *so* easy to abandon hope, Marcus thought. But it wasn't just him. It wasn't just the three of them. "Right, then. On to blowing up the ship."

Ekatrina looked helplessly to Yun. "You are the math wizard. Will this explosion be enough?"

Yun shrugged.

"I didn't hear *no*," Marcus said.

"Or yes," Yun snapped.

Marcus stuffed his hands into his jumpsuit pockets. "Walk us through it."

Dejectedly, Yun did. And as tenaciously, Marcus countered—as best he could—Yun's objections.

> Yun: neither liquid oxygen nor liquid hydrogen by itself would burn, much less explode. First, the liquids had to be released.
>
> Marcus: the ship is in direct, unfiltered sunlight. What about switching off cryo-cooling, and letting the temperatures within the tanks rise? Maybe even rig heat lamps to speed the

process? As warming liquid began turning to vapor and the internal pressure increased, wouldn't the tanks rupture?

Yun: to get a decent explosion, the remaining liquids also had to vaporize.

Marcus: don't most liquids boil readily in a vacuum?

Yun: then the gas clouds need to thoroughly mix.

Marcus: first thing, why don't we weld patches over the engine-room leaks? Containing the gases will allow them to mix.

Yun: a spark or other ignition source coming too early would mean a fizzle: a minor explosion dispersing liquids that had yet to boil and gases yet to mix.

Ekatrina, beginning to look hopeful, joined in. "Put the ignition source—an electric blasting cap, say, and a length of detonating cord wrapped at several heights around the engine room—on a timer. That will give the gases ample time to mix.

Yun shrugged. "That is a complicated scenario. Much could go wrong."

"And if all goes well?" Marcus countered.

"A major explosion," Yun admitted. "On the scale of chemical explosions, that is."

"And it *might* do the trick?"

"The trick? Oh, give the Hammer enough of a final push." Yun shrugged. "Maybe. There are too many variables. I would not give you long odds."

Ekatrina raised an eyebrow at Marcus.

And what were Earth's odds at the moment? "We'll give it a try," Marcus answered her.

While Ekatrina continued prepping the wrecked vessel for its explosive finale, Marcus offloaded supplies. He, too, meant to live long enough to know whether they had succeeded.

His collection kept growing: more rations; a portion of water for drinking; an assortment of electronic spare parts, it not being impossible that Katya could yet assemble a radio; fuel cells, to boost its transmission if she did; a 3-D printer, whose only intact feedstock reservoir held polyethylene; their remaining igloo, not yet inflated; and some of the remaining explosives. As for that last item, Marcus had no purpose in mind—except that, apart from the charges to be used to trigger the LH2/LOX blast, high explosives left aboard struck him as imprudent. Between the damaged state of the ship, and the hostile AI that might still scheme in silence, who knew what might set off a premature detonation?

As Yun had made so clear, everything had to go just right—and very damn soon.

With a heartfelt curse, after almost burning off a hand with her oxyacetylene torch, an exhausted Ekatrina announced a breather from welding bulkhead tears in the engine room. Marcus dragooned her into helping offload the "portable" fission reactor. Leaving uranium to become radioactive shrapnel *also* seemed like a bad idea. In the Hammer's negligible gravity, the reactor weighed next to nothing—but neither gravity nor its lack had any bearing on mass and inertia. Even working together, getting the reactor out through the airlock was a bear.

Harder, in a far more intimate way, was carrying out Ilya's tarp-wrapped body. Yevgeny's remains must stay: they were inaccessible absent an industrial-strength hydraulic jack, and in any event unrecognizable. Then, in speechless sadness, Ekatrina returned to her task of prepping the big explosion, and Marcus to his stevedore duties.

Alongside their inflated shelter, supply dumps slowly grew. A tarp, secured to the Hammer's surface by magnets, held each pile in place.

When Marcus popped into the shelter to check on their injured colleague, he found Yun looking downcast. No, miserable. Marcus removed his helmet and set it aside. "What is it?"

"I am ashamed," Yun mumbled. "Since the accident on *Rescue One*, what have I done? Found fault with your ideas, and Katya's. Lolled here, useless, while you two could have used my help. Moped here, rather."

"You're here because of a serious injury. That's no one's fault. But as for moping …."

"Yes?"

"That *was* your choice."

Yun jerked back as if slapped. For long seconds, he was silent. "What can I do?"

"Keep thinking," Marcus said. "We're in a shitload of trouble here. We need every bright idea we can get." He grabbed his helmet, twist-locked it into place, and went to see what, if anything, he could do to help Ekatrina.

—•—

Marcus and Katya worked nonstop for two days prepping the ship to explode, and unloading anything both portable and useful. The sooner the blast, the more precious seconds the Hammer's slightly altered path would have to diverge from Earth.

Then it was on to *another* arduous job.

"You're sure about this?" Marcus knew the answer, but asked anyway. He wanted to distract Yun. Getting stripped down to skivvies and into a hard-shell suit in this insignificant gravity, even with help, was tough for anyone. Doing it with a broken arm splinted by amateurs? That had to be torture. "We can't stay here?"

Here was their igloo.

One of the men moved wrong—again—and Yun winced. He somehow managed to morph a clenched-jaws "Ungh" into "No-o."

"Because?"

"Because ..." hissed between clenched teeth, "this is too *close*. Yes, the igloo is in a crater, but the top of the dome rises a little above the rim."

"And?"

Yun managed a sickly grin. "Your distractions are transparent, and your bedside manner is terrible. Also, you are an oaf. Why could I not have Katya helping me?"

She had suited up earlier to position datasheets around the ship to record the show. When Marcus radioed her the okay, she would start the detonator timer. "Helping you. Is that what you young kids are calling it?"

Chuckle. Wince. "Do not make me laugh. Anyway, if, as we hope, the ship gives a good detonation, things here will be messy. The Hammer is basically a solid chunk of metal. It will transmit the shock wave a good, long distance. And there will be a lot of ...." For once, Yun floundered for an English word. "The little pieces of metal flying away from an explosion?"

"Shrapnel," Marcus offered.

"Yes, shrapnel. Thank you. I expect much, even most, of the shrapnel to escape into space, but some could come straight at us here. Some shrapnel could go into tight orbits around the asteroid, and strike us minutes, even hours, after the blast."

Finally, Marcus had Yun prepped for vacuum. Splint and bandages had made the broken arm too bulky for a suit sleeve. But squeezed into the hard-shell torso, pressing against his stomach, at least the arm was somewhat supported.

They exited the igloo together. Marcus radioed the go-ahead to Ekatrina. They did not start toward the anti-sunward horizon—inching along at the fastest snail's pace Yun could manage, the empty suit arm swinging unnaturally at his side—until Ekatrina emerged from the ship and headed their way. She caught up quickly.

"Twenty-nine minutes on my mark," she radioed. "Mark."

"No, that's Marcus," he said. He started a countdown on his HUD.

Tethered together, cautiously, they marched. From the wheezes and gasps of pain, Yun's arm took a jolt at every step. With almost five minutes to spare, they hunkered down in the deep crevasse Marcus had surveilled hours earlier. They had trekked almost a kilometer from the ship.

A fraction of a second after *zero*, as the ground shook, Marcus glanced up to see streaking shrapnel agleam in the Sun.

They detoured on the return hike to collect datasheets Ekatrina had pre-positioned to capture the explosion. The two they recovered were useless: punctured and shorted out by shrapnel. The third and final datasheet was missing altogether, bounced somewhere, perhaps even off-world, by the passing shock wave.

Marcus would have loved to see some vid, because they had missed *quite* the show. The ship's stern had vanished. Turned to shrapnel, he supposed. The bow had pounded farther into the ground and down the access shaft. The airlock—its frame further twisted and burst, its hatches nowhere to be seen—stood a good five meters closer to the surface than before.

What remained resembled nothing as much as the stub of an exploding cigar.

They went on.

Their igloo was deflated. Swiss-cheesed. Their supplies were scattered, and some doubtless missing.

"Good call about waiting farther out," Marcus told Yun.

"Thanks," Yun wheezed. He gestured at massive metal plates last seen in a tidy stack, covering a craterlet and in it, their spare igloo. Those now suggested a game of fifty-two card pickup. "If you two could get to work, I might yet be able to walk inside under my own power."

Chapter 59

Valerie let Simon order dinner (pepperoni pizza and breadsticks, delivered to their hotel room), as she had since their arrival in Colorado Springs. Choosing their meals was about the only control he had left. Once the atomic-bomb-proof blast doors sealed them into the nearby Cheyenne Mountain Complex, who knew if any choices would remain?

Who knew what sort of world they would find when those doors reopened? Apart from devastated.

Simon grabbed his fourth, no, fifth slice. (This was after the supersized burger meal he'd had delivered around five, after she had called from deep underground to admit she would be late. Again.) "This is terrible pizza."

The *first* slice burned in her stomach like so much molten lead. To judge from the drum solo being played on her bladder, Little Toot was no fan, either. Anything else she ate tonight would come in breadstick form. Or a brownie sundae, if she could find someone to deliver that. "I can see how it's hurting your appetite."

"Bad pizza is still pizza." He folded the latest slice in half, and got a good third of it in as one bite. Around the mouthful of pizza, he asked, "You want to watch the news?"

And hear more about spreading worldwide panic? The looting? Religious fanatics calling down God's wrath from the heavens? "You go ahead. I'm going to step outside for some air."

The hotel parking lot was filled, the hotel booked to capacity by refugees from lower altitudes. Valerie nodded at the elderly couple emerging from a nearby unit before turning her gaze upward. She wanted a final look, before the world ended, at the night sky.

Her datasheet trilled. The number that came up on caller ID was unfamiliar, but the area code and prefix matched the Cheyenne Complex. She took the call voice-only, and heard faint cheering in the background. What did anyone find to cheer about these days? "Clayburn."

"Gonzalez."

A Space Force orbital analyst, and the shift manager who had relieved Val an hour earlier. Data feeds from around the world went into the complex, just as they fed command bunkers in other countries. "What's up, Edie?"

"The Hammer … took a jolt, Val. If nothing else happens, it will miss Earth! We'll get a close shave, but a miss is a miss."

"That's wonderful!" So why the hesitation? And that bit of passive voice—*took a jolt*—also nagged. Val had seen and heard *nothing* about any launch anywhere having any prospect of affecting the Hammer. "But …?"

"At about the same time, spectrometers detected a gas cloud behind the Hammer. Mostly water vapor and oxygen. Some carbon dioxide and traces of hydrogen. The cloud is rapidly dissipating."

That was chemistry, not explanation, as though the truth were too terrible to put into words. "Water vapor and oxygen, as from a hydrogen/oxygen reaction. Traces of hydrogen are whatever part of the fuel didn't mix well and take part in the explosion."

But carbon dioxide? From burned food? Burned … *people*? Valerie swallowed, hard. "They blew up *Rescue One*"—and themselves?—"to give the Hammer a final push."

"That's how it looks." A long pause. "Your husband is a hero. Everyone on that mission is. And they saved all of us."

"Thank you. And thanks for letting me know."

"Can I do anything for you?"

Valerie shook her head, dropping the connection before she remembered it was voice only. She could not have spoken just then anyway, past the lump in her throat.

She marshaled her thoughts, squared her shoulders, and turned toward the hotel-room door. She needed to tell Simon the world was probably saved—

Even as theirs had ended.

Chapter 60

Marcus sat quietly, scrolling through … something on his datasheet. It could have been the Vladivostok phone directory for all that he was getting out of it. Yun did whatever he did with his own comp. Ekatrina was asleep, her nose whistling. Her hair, in a staticky halo, stuck out every which way.

Sigh. Marcus folded and tucked away his datasheet. He ate … something. He fidgeted with the 3-D printer. For no reason beyond a random, ancient, happy memory of Simon, he printed a Slinky. There was nowhere near enough gravity for the plastic coil to walk down stairs, if they had had stairs, so he pumped loop stacks from hand to hand—whoosh, whoosh, whoosh—until Yun, never looking up from his datasheet, barked, "*Quit* that."

More than an hour had gone by since Marcus had reentered the igloo with yet another set of sky images. He could no longer bear the suspense. "Well? Did we succeed?"

Yun rubbed his chin. His beard had grown longer, but no less scruffy, these past few days. "I still do not know. The single new thing I can offer is, I don't think I *can* figure it out. Not with the instruments we have at hand. Until we pass Earth, of course. Or run into it."

Marcus extracted a pudding cup from their ration sack. He had been eating almost nonstop since the explosion. Weight gain and lack of exercise were not pressing issues. Katya's evident plan of sleeping till the end was no better and no worse. "I don't get it, Yun. Why won't more measurements resolve the question?"

"Give me a few more minutes to be sure, and I'll explain."

It was more like fifteen minutes before Yun looked up from his datasheet. His eyes were jubilant! "We cannot get decent images with which to estimate our location because the Hammer is wobbling."

"It's been spinning all along, hasn't it?"

"Around its long axis. Wobbling is different." Yun straightened a leg to prod Ekatrina with a toe. "Katya, wake up. You will want to hear this." He clammed up until she grumbled, stirred, ducked into the tiny shelter's even tinier lav, and returned.

"What?" she asked. "Did we do it?"

"Again, I do not know. But this is *big*. I've suspected it for days, and now I am sure. The Hammer is tumbling. The extent is more and more pronounced."

She yawned. "I thought most asteroids tumble."

"Just so," Yun said. "I had expected to arrive and find this asteroid tumbling. When instead we found it spinning along its long axis and otherwise stable, I was happy for our good fortune. Docking was much easier for Yevgeny than would otherwise have been the case."

"An obvious red flag," Marcus said. "There is no luck on this mission."

"Wrong," Ekatrina muttered. "There is bad luck."

"Unexpected, but not impossible," Yun continued imperturbably. "I thought that maybe the Titans had carved a few pieces off the asteroid to balance it, then spun it up like a gyroscope for stability. In case the time ever came to give it a shove."

As that time had come, Marcus thought. "Why should we care?"

Yun stroked the scruffy beard again. "Why is it tumbling now? Not just spin, but around all three axes?"

"The explosion of our ship." She yawned. "Now, can I get some rest?"

Yun shook his head. "The Hammer was shoved out of its longtime orbit. It made a pass near the Sun that changed its orbital plane and aimed it at Earth. Then we came along and shoved it ourselves for days. All the while, evidently, the Hammer did not tumble."

If there had been enough gravity for it, Marcus would have paced. "Can we skip to whatever has you so pleased?"

"Almost there. My conclusion is that the Hammer has, or rather, it had, a stabilization mechanism. It remained stable for perhaps hundreds of shots from the mass driver. It remained stable as it slingshot around the Sun. It was still stable as we nudged it along with the ship. And then it broke."

Marcus pictured the final explosion, and *Rescue One* pounded into the Titan control room like a rocket-propelled tent stake. "We broke it."

Yun nodded vigorously. "You both are engineers. You will have better ideas than I what broke, and how. But whatever it was …."

"Computers crushed," Ekatrina suggested.

"Molten working fluid for the thermoelectric generators spewing from cracked pipes," Marcus guessed, "or the mass driver shattering, spraying shrapnel around the control room."

"Any or all of those." Yun agreed. "Or the stabilization mechanism itself was broken. In my non-engineering way, I suspect stabilization involves very large flywheels in underground chambers scattered around the asteroid. If for whatever reason they cannot spin, or cannot be told how and when to speed up or slow down … we get wobbling.

"What I do know, as the tumbling grows *worse*, is that whatever once controlled the Hammer no longer does."

Marcus turned his head toward Ekatrina. "What do you think?"

"I think that was worth waking up for." She brightened. "I think maybe the damned Titan machines have done to us everything they can. If that last shove was enough, we *won*."

The engine room, and with it fusion reactors and backup batteries, was … gone.

And in the crushed and twisted stub that remained? The nanotech, at its most basic, was mostly carbon. It had burned away in the brief firestorm, all that precious, irreplaceable carbon erupting from the shattered hull in the brief maelstrom of escaping gases.

Gaps and short circuits riddled what few patches of nanotech surface had survived.

And so, as the final dregs of heat ebbed from fire and blast, that which no longer knew itself as Ship faded, for the final time, into oblivion.

Marcus helped Ekatrina carry the parts of her kludged transceiver from the igloo.

The heart of the device was the short-range helmet radio removed from Yun's much abused counterpressure suit. The amplifier was built from spare parts Marcus had foraged before the explosion. A fuel cell from the same scavenging expedition powered the rig. A datasheet held their prerecorded Mayday message. The comp would also record, flashing to signal success, any incoming signal. The dish antenna and its tripod base had been fashioned from hull scraps. The scarcest resource turned out to be ordinary copper wire—when the opportunity had existed, Marcus had not thought to collect a spool of that. Instead, they had had to dig short lengths out of the hulk, and weld—they also didn't have a soldering iron—those wire snippets into the longer lengths they needed. It all sat on spread-out rubber scraps from Yun's counterpressure suit, to insulate everything from the metallic mass of the Hammer.

Rube Goldberg's radio. Or perhaps Dr. Frankenstein's.

While Ekatrina did final assembly, Marcus studied the sky. The fast-approaching Earth had swelled into an appreciable disk. The Moon seemed almost a disk. So near, and yet so far away.

Ekatrina looked up as he lobbed something into space. "What's that?"

"Nothing. A message in a bottle."

"Why not?" She finished fiddling with the assemblage. "Confirm my aiming, please."

Sighting over the top of the dish, he did his best. "Do the honors, Katya."

She tapped the virtual SEND key on the datasheet.

And in response to their text transmission, there came … nothing. Tweaking their aim, they tried again and again, to the same lack of response. The slow, seemingly random tumble of the Hammer did nothing to improve their pointing.

He asked, "Is the gear working on our end?"

She peered at the datasheet. "So say the diagnostics I wrote."

"Try aiming at the Moon," he suggested.

They did. Repeatedly. And nothing.

After twenty minutes that felt like an eternity, some combination of spin and wobble took Earth and Moon out of sight altogether.

She sighed. "To be honest, I never expected this to work. Between the impossibility of maintaining our aim, and reflections all along this huge piece of metal generating interference, it just seems hopeless."

"Would we fare better at the other end?"

The end that—even with the Hammer's newfound wobbling—still most often pointed, more or less, toward Earth. When the Hammer did so point, their radio might be dealing with fewer reflections.

She said, "Ask rather, could we slog about twelve kilometers? Distrusting and testing our boots' magnetic grip with every step. Toting"—she gestured at her monstrosity of an apparatus—"all this. Bringing along many replacement oh-two tanks. All the while, we'll have only our suits for shelter. And above all, ask: to what purpose would we abandon Yun? Or do you imagine one of us alone would undertake the trek?"

"I didn't say it was a good idea. Just an idea." And with the solemnity the moment deserved, Marcus added, "Of course, you're right. However this ends, we three will see it through together."

They went back inside the igloo. Choked down a meal. Looked at each other.

"Now what?" Ekatrina asked.

Yun managed a one-shouldered shrug. "We wait for the end."

"Here's the problem," Marcus said, "Waiting is the thing I'm absolutely worst at."

EPILOGUE

EPILOGUE

On the Hammer's sterile surface, the three survivors stood—silent, awestruck—as the Earth grew and grew and grew. They cheered themselves hoarse as, unmistakably, that precious, beautiful, unattainable orb began to *recede*. With no more guide than eyeballs and the experience of their past spaceflights, they estimated the Hammer's closest approach to the planet at between five hundred and a thousand kilometers.

And then, out of options, they returned to their igloo.

Their world shrank to the crowded confines of the igloo. After a few days, no one spoke. There was nothing more to say, nor any will to talk. Their datasheets offered countless hours of reading, viewing, listening—and soon enough, no one bothered. Apart from the occasional brief outing to swap empty oh-two tanks for full ones, they did little but sleep, eat, and wait ….

Marcus and Ekatrina emerged onto the surface for the first time in … he had lost track how long it had been. Since there had ceased to be any purpose in being outside. After their jerry-rigged, ineffectual transmitter had died in a coruscation of sparks. After the final full oxygen tanks had been brought inside. All that had remained to bestir them, before their oh-two would be gone, was this day's astronomical event: the Hammer reaching its aphelion. Its farthest remove from the Sun. The slowest point anywhere along its new, elongated orbit.

Aphelion was anticlimactic.

Yun was feverish, and his arm swollen, infection having taken root despite antibiotic pills. When he could at all avoid it, he did not move. Wrestling himself into a hard-shell suit would have been torture. "I did the calculations," he had told them. "That was enough. You watch if you want."

Marcus craned his neck. Tiny Earth, its features indistinct, remained achingly beautiful. "We did well, Katya."

"If only to clean up after more than our share of foolish mistakes. But yes."

What more was there to say? What more was there to do? Nothing. As Marcus pivoted to return to their igloo, a fast-moving spark rose over the horizon. And with digits on his visor still indicating a public channel, his radio chimed! An incoming hail!

"... *One*, do you copy?" The voice, a woman's, spoke English, but with a heavy Chinese accent. "This is *Rescue Two*. Repeat, *Rescue One*, do you copy? This is—"

"Copy that, *Rescue Two*," Marcus interrupted. "This is the *Rescue One* crew. Three of us, anyway. It's good to hear a new voice."

"And we to hear yours. Are you interested in a ride home?"

"You better believe it," Ekatrina said, grinning as Marcus—as best he could wearing a hard-shell suit—gave her a clanking bear hug.

"Copy that, *Rescue One*. However, your rock has a nasty tumble to it. Docking will not be straightforward. We must give some thought to how best to take you off." The channel briefly went silent. "Are you all mobile?"

"Yun is injured, but we'll do what we have to do."

"Copy that. We see a wrecked vessel and an inflated igloo. Where are you?"

"The igloo," Marcus said.

"Copy." The channel went silent again. "We will be back in touch soon."

They returned to the shelter to update Yun.

Marcus popped his helmet, leaving the radio on but remaining in his hard-shell suit. "I'm hoping it's not worth the effort to take off my gear and put it on again."

"How did this happen?" Ekatrina asked. "I do not complain, but neither do I understand. Would they have come all this way on the remote chance of finding someone here alive?"

"Perhaps not so remote," Marcus said. "Do you remember my 'message in a bottle?'"

"Yes. I took that as one of your jokes, that you had thrown a rock. It would not have been the first time."

"Nor even the tenth time, but this wasn't a rock. I threw a wadded-up datasheet." With nothing but its inherent elasticity and a compressed Slinky inside to *un*wad it. "At about sixty miles, a hundred kilometers, per hour. Well above escape velocity."

"With a message," Yun said.

"With a message," Marcus agreed. "And a transmitter, as low-power as it is, that drifted away from the Hammer and its interference.

"Have I ever mentioned that Valerie is a radio astronomer?"

Yun laughed—and winced. "On occasion. But you chose not to mention this effort?"

No. Because even to Marcus it had seemed a harebrained, desperation move. Deep in what-do-I-have-to-lose territory. "Surprise."

Rescue Two was a large vessel. It reminded Marcus, more than anything, of an Apollo command capsule, although well over twice that size, with lander descent and takeoff stages still attached. Also, with a big Chinese flag on its side.

In the end, the rescue ship hadn't docked. Instead, it hovered. In hard-shell suits, with gas pistols to aim and brake themselves, they jumped to meet it. Marcus had Ilya's body in tow. Katya and Yun leapt hand in hand.

A handsome Chinese man in counterpressure suit and fishbowl helmet, silver-haired, beaming, met them near an open airlock. He floated, tethered to the ship, gesturing to them to board ahead of him.

The airlock opened onto a passenger deck with six empty acceleration couches. "Wait downstairs for now," the pilot called from the bridge level. Marcus recognized her voice from the radio. "Tell me when everyone is aboard and settled."

Flying in formation with the tumbling asteroid? That had to demand all her attention. "Copy that," Marcus said.

But at last, everyone *was* settled. The ship withdrew to a comfortable three kilometers or so from the Hammer. The pilot floated down from the command deck. She was solid, long-limbed, with a cockiness that reminded Marcus of no one as much as Katya. Before their ordeal of the past several months, anyway.

Yun waved off immediate medical attention. There were introductions. The pilot was Li Min. Their taciturn greeter, a flight surgeon, was Chen Wei. Congratulations all around. Ilya's body respectfully stowed. Vacuum gear shed. Snack packets and drink bulbs distributed.

"How was a ship even available to retrieve us so far out here?" Ekatrina asked. "What *is* this ship, anyway?"

"A prototype for an eventual trip to, and landing on, Mars," Min said. "We had been preparing the launcher, command module, and lander for a test flight with a lunar landing. Then, we were searching for a way somehow to repurpose the vehicle, to deliver a big bomb to the Hammer for a final push. Then, due to something you must have accomplished, we were no longer needed for that. We were reconfiguring again for our original mission when Arecibo heard Marcus's distress call. And *then*, it would seem, someone decided we owed you a favor."

"Or," Yun said, "owed Father a favor."

Because Yun's father was a member of the Central Committee. If Party politics was what it took to preempt a Mars mission, Marcus was fine with it. "It's just the two of you aboard?"

"Either way, it is my honor." Min brushed long, black bangs from her forehead. "Even at aphelion, the Hammer is moving quite fast. Fewer crew means less mass. Also, we did not know how many people would be returning with us."

"One more question," Marcus said. "When do we get down?"

“As soon as possible,” Wei said. “Yun, I will do what I can for you, but that arm needs to be tended to in a hospital.”

“Of course,” Marcus said. “But *when*? In how many days?”

Min smiled. “In about a week. Do not worry. You will have time to shop for Christmas.”

“It isn't Christmas that concerns me.” The date which *did* matter was etched in Marcus's memory. “My wife and I are expecting. Her due date is the day after Christmas.

“I promised Valerie I'd be with her in the delivery room. And thanks to you, I will.”

About the Author

Edward M. Lerner worked in high tech and aerospace for thirty years, as everything from engineer to senior vice president, for much of that time writing science fiction as his hobby. Since 2004 he has written full-time.

His novels range from near-future techno-thrillers, like *Small Miracles* and *Energized*, to traditional SF, like *Dark Secret* and his InterstellarNet series, to (collaborating with Larry Niven) the space-opera epic Fleet of Worlds series of *Ringworld* companion novels. Lerner's 2015 novel, *InterstellarNet: Enigma*, won the inaugural Canopus Award "honoring excellence in interstellar writing." His fiction has also been nominated for Locus, Prometheus, and Hugo awards.

Lerner's short fiction has appeared in anthologies, collections, and many of the usual SF magazines and websites. He also writes about science and technology, notably including *Trope-ing the Light Fantastic: The Science Behind the Fiction*.

Lerner lives in Virginia with his wife, Ruth.

His website is **www.edwardmlerner.com**.

About the Author

CPSIA information can be obtained
at www.ICGtesting.com
Printed in the USA
JSHW030016050521
14248JS00001B/1